GW01162614

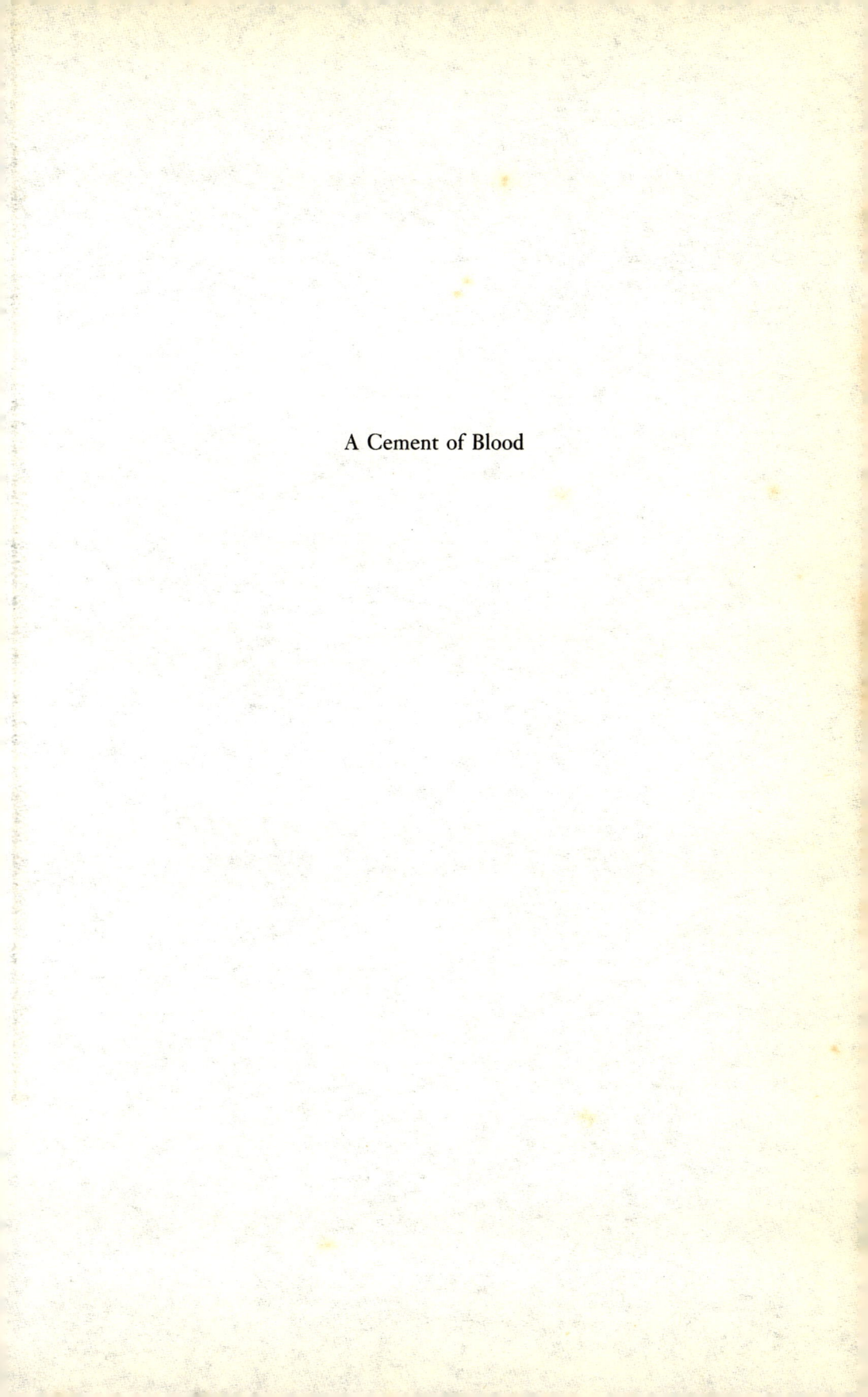

A Cement of Blood

Also by Gregory Hall
THE DARK BACKWARD

# A CEMENT OF BLOOD

Gregory Hall

MICHAEL JOSEPH
LONDON

MICHAEL JOSEPH
Published by the Penguin Group
27 Wrights Lane, London W8 5TZ, England
Viking Penguin Inc., 375 Hudson Street, New York, New York 10014, USA
Penguin Books Australia Ltd, Ringwood, Victoria, Australia
Penguin Books Canada Ltd, 10 Alcorn Avenue, Toronto, Ontario, Canada M4V 3B2
Penguin Books (NZ) Ltd, 182–190 Wairau Road, Auckland 10, New Zealand

Penguin Books Ltd, Registered Offices: Harmondsworth, Middlesex, England

First published 1997
1 3 5 7 9 10 8 6 4 2

Copyright © Gregory Hall 1997

All rights reserved.
Without limiting the rights under copyright
reserved above, no part of this publication may be
reproduced, stored in or introduced into a retrieval system,
or transmitted, in any form or by any means (electronic, mechanical,
photocopying, recording or otherwise) without the prior
written permission of both the copyright owner and
the above publisher of this book

Typeset in 11/14.5pt Monotype Janson by
Rowland Phototypesetting Ltd,
Bury St Edmunds, Suffolk
Printed in England by Clays Ltd, St Ives plc

A CIP catalogue record for this book is available from the British Library

ISBN 0 7181 3906 2

The moral right of the author has been asserted

For my son Philip ('Pip')
20 November 1987
*Ave atque vale*

For without a cement of blood (it must be human, it must be innocent) no secular wall will safely stand.

W. H. Auden: *Horae Canonicae*

# Contents

One
**THE MIDAS TOUCH**
1

Two
**THE VALLEY OF THE SHADOW**
75

Three
**IN XANADU**
153

Four
**GREAT EXPECTATIONS**
275

Five
**THICKER THAN WATER**
399

# One

# THE MIDAS TOUCH

# 1

'Bloody roadworks!' Francis Appleby banged his hands irritably on the big steering-wheel of his Mercedes.

The senior partner of Chamberlayne's, one of the city of Fernsford's oldest and most prestigious law practices, was not a patient man. As well as this intermittent tattoo, he kept glancing angrily at the dashboard clock and shuffling restlessly in his seat. His usual healthily pink complexion glowed a dull red.

'I shall have words with Mike Peters about this at the Club tomorrow. It's sheer incompetence. You can imagine what's going on, can't you, Sarah? Two lots of bloody bureaucrats arguing the toss. Not to mention the contractors and their insurers.'

'And their lawyers,' I added in reply.

He shot a glance at me, but I remained expressionlessly demure. I knew what was really bugging him. We had a meeting with Trevor Chewton, the Fernsford property magnate, his and, therefore, the firm's most important client, on the site of the enormous new Chewton development. The snarl-up was going to make us late.

Actually that makes it sound much simpler than it was. Rose, Appleby's PA, had explained the situation the previous evening. 'He wants you to go along, Sarah. About time Trevor met his new assistant solicitor, he said.'

She had told me to be ready by ten past ten.

'I thought you said the appointment was for ten o'clock.'

'Yes, but Francis will get there at ten twenty. It's a ten minute drive. He will breeze in, say he had an urgent matter to attend to, but came as quickly as he could. You see Trevor Chewton will have been there only five minutes or so, hoping he was keeping Francis waiting. Games important men play, darling. Who's ahead in the ego stakes.'

Now it was already ten thirty and Francis was going to have to apologize or look seriously rude to his client.

The line of traffic lurched a few more yards and stopped again. Appleby sighed, reached for the car phone and punched in a number so violently I thought he might wreck the keypad. 'Trevor. Francis. I'm stuck on the approach to Free Trade Way railway bridge. County Highways Department and British Rail, what a combination of spastics. I reckon on another ten. Sorry.' He rang off. I winced for his sake at the 'sorry'. It must have been like amputating a finger, Yakuza style.

He was about to put the phone down, then changed his mind and stabbed out another number. 'Thelma. Francis Appleby. Mike there? I see. No, I'll see him at the Club. Thanks.' He slammed the phone down, and rammed his foot down on the gas to catch up the gap which had opened between us and the lorry in front. 'Day off. What bloody right has the Chief Executive got to have a day off when his bloody city is falling apart?'

I sensibly made no answer to this clearly rhetorical question and left him to glower in silence.

I peered through the raindrop-spattered side window at a forest of orange Day-Glo striped traffic cones with red and white chevroned baulks of timber felled in their midst. We were in a line of stationary vehicles, queuing at a temporary traffic-light-controlled one-way system some five hundred yards or so further along. Every few minutes, the line moved up a short distance in response to the very brief green. It was evident from this rate of progress that we would be stuck here for some time.

Free Trade Way cuts through the middle of Fernsford on concrete and steel stilts and from its elevation I could look out over the agglomeration of ancient and modern buildings which had been my home for the past fortnight.

I was still rather amazed to find myself in this West Country burg. Born a Londoner and knowing little of provincial England, I'd not even heard of Fernsford until a couple of months before, when I saw the job ad in the *Law Society's Gazette*.

FERNSFORD: Newly qual. solicitor with London articles to assist senior partner of expanding commercial firm. High-quality work with major corporate clients. Sal Neg. Ref: F/108

My best friend Harriet Weinberg was not impressed. I told her I'd applied and got an interview over dinner in the Cento Cypressi, her favourite Italian restaurant in Bloomsbury, where I made a pig of myself, as usual, eating all of the helping of zabaglione meant for two.

She'd raised her eyebrows and her earrings jingled a bit. For someone as cool and laidback as Harriet, it was the equivalent of stunned amazement. 'Fernsford, Sarah? That's miles west – practically Lands End.'

'Yes. That's the right direction, only not so far. In Westerset. Don't give me that look. I don't have a lot of choice. This is the first interview I've been offered. A commercial firm called Chamberlayne's. A big change from crime and family law. It sounds interesting.'

'It's your life, Sarah. It's not something I'd even get out of bed for. You told me you were all set to stay at Vardy, Leadbetter at the end of your articles. Hasn't that skinflint Pogson made you an offer? He'd be mad not to.'

'He did, as a matter of fact. But that's the point. Fernsford isn't London. I want to get out. I'm sick of the place.'

'Gosh. I never thought I'd hear you say that. I thought London would be in your bones, like it is in mine. I turned down my scholarship at Girton to go to UC because I thought Cambridge was so provincial. Remember Dr Johnson?'

'Sorry, who?'

She laughed, but not unkindly. 'You're not a great one for literature, are you? Dr Samuel Johnson, eighteenth-century writer and lexicographer. Master of the one liner. "When a man is tired of London, he is tired of life."'

'Eighteenth century? He's well out of date, isn't he? Didn't have to travel on the tube, for a start. Or get elbowed around or felt up for the privilege. I daresay he didn't have to work in a rat-hole in Hoxton, either.'

'That's all true. I bet when it comes to it, you won't do it. You'll take a walk across Hyde Park on a bright spring morning, when the city's just coming to life. Or you'll stroll across Westminster Bridge and stop at the far end to look back at the most famous government buildings in the world. And you'll say, I can't leave all this.'

'No, I won't. Because that isn't my world. That's the myth created for American tourists – or real only for people like you with jobs in the media, hobnobbing with Members of Parliament, going out to meals in fancy restaurants. I can't remember the last time I was in Hyde Park, and I've never in my life walked over Westminster Bridge.'

She shrugged. 'There's plenty of time for that. I'll take you there, one Sunday morning. We'll gaze like Wordsworth on the mighty heart and ...'

I drank up my second cup of cappuccino and replaced the cup carefully in its saucer. 'You'll be singing "London Pride" next. It's a different world, yours. Don't you understand? You're a star presenter, running your own independent TV production company. You've got all the contacts: father a merchant banker, mother on every charity going, good school, first-class London University degree, the social whirl. I'm a legal-aid brief in the most deprived borough in England. I'm sick of crime and violence and sordidness. I really thought that was me, you know. The Angel of the Slums. When I was at college, I had this big image of myself as a crusading lawyer – feminist, *pro bono publico* and all that. But it isn't me. I'm sick of my crummy office and the smell of the drains and the bloody zoo that's the Mags Court on a Monday morning when all the sins of the weekend come home to roost. I want to do something clean and abstract. Something where I can close the file at the end of the day and forget about it.'

I stemmed the flood of words, aware that I was beginning to rant. I leaned back in my chair, caught the eye of a waiter and ordered another cappuccino. Hoxton seemed even more repulsive contrasted with the elegant restaurant in which we were sitting. As for Harriet, well she always made me feel like a scruff-bag.

She pursed her full, darkly glossed lips, a quizzical expression on her delicate, pale oval face under the cropped helmet of black hair as she studied me in silence. Her extraordinary earrings glittered in the candlelight.

Harriet's earrings were her trademark. That evening they were matt black triangles set with some fiery white mineral which looked like, and may even have been, diamonds.

To go with the earrings, she was dressed to kill: a sheer black chiffon blouse worn with a bold black and white striped skirt of fashionable length;

around her neck a white gold choker set with more, almost certainly real, diamonds. Her black patent high-heeled shoes had the substantial look of the hand-made article. God, she was chic. She always had been.

In contrast, I felt dowdy in my navy C & A office suit and cheap white blouse. I couldn't afford decent clothes on the miserable pittance paid me during articles by Tim Pogson, my principal, and the senior partner of Vardy, Leadbetter.

The pity of it was I was tall with a good figure, despite my healthy appetite. On the rare occasions when I'd dressed up – in borrowed clothes – I'd looked good and felt good, too. And then there was my hair – the colour of the sunset over Galway Bay, as one of my more poetic boyfriends had, albeit unoriginally, rhapsodized it. It was certainly beautiful, though long and a damned nuisance to look after. And how many times hadn't I cursed the way it had labelled and prejudged me every time I made an appearance? Everyone knows redheads – particularly those of Irish parentage – are aggressive, fiery, impulsive, devil-may-care, thoughtless and irrational. As if non-redheads weren't all those things sometimes as well.

Harriet gave me one of her arch looks.

'"The lady doth protest too much, methinks."'

'What?'

'Sorry. Another quotation. Shakespeare, this time. I don't believe it's your job, or London, for that matter, that's making you go after jobs in absurd little places like Fernsford. To me, the reason's much simpler. It's Colin.'

I turned away, trying to hide the tears which sprang into my eyes at his name. 'I can't deny he's in there somewhere.'

'The Colin thing hit you hard, didn't it? Three years is a long relationship.'

'Yes. As long as I've known you, and that seems for ever. My last term at the poly: that business in New River Place after the inter-college rave-up.'

'Don't remind me. I was completely smashed, wasn't I? And that great hairy medic with about eighteen hands was trying to bundle me into his car. And you and Colin – well you, actually – pulled him off and rescued me and took me home in a cab.'

'Pure chance, wasn't it? Like so many incidents in our lives which turn out so vitally important.'

'So it's finished?'

'Yes. Absolutely. I can't have him back. We had the most awful row. The kind that changes everything.'

She leaned over and patted me on the knee. 'You are sweet, aren't you? Despite doing divorce and domestic violence, I suppose you thought you were immune, like the doctor who never catches the fever. Now you're running away and ruining your life because of a creep like Colin. I shan't ever see you again.'

'Do shut up, Harriet. I don't want to think about him. Of course you'll see me. I'm not running away. I haven't even been offered the job yet. I very much doubt I shall be. And even if I am, I'm not going to hurry to take the first thing that comes along. I'm fed up, not desperate.'

'Here we go, and about time.' I was jerked back into the present by a sudden roar from the engine, as Appleby again rammed his foot on the gas. We hurtled through the lights at amber in a burst of acceleration which shoved me back into the cold leather seat.

He got up to about eighty or so on the straight section after the bridge, braked savagely down to forty and, tyres squealing, took the short slip road down to the mini-roundabout on Brinwell Street. Here he hung a left which threw me sideways with such force my seat-belt reeled me in and hurtled into Canal Street. I felt myself knotting up with anxiety as we shot down the gap between lines of parked cars. After a few hundred yards, we screeched almost to walking pace. Through the curtain of rain, I could see only a high wall of bright red brick, glossy under the downpour.

'The entrance is easily missed. Ah, here it is.'

Ahead, there was a gap in the line of kerbstones, and the wall thickened into a round-edged brick upright. The big car rocked on its springs as he swung the wheel out then sharply back again to negotiate the narrow entry. The discreet whisper of the tyres changed to a dull, oil-drum rumble as it ran off the tarmac on to the cobbled surface of the pavement crossover. I caught a glimpse of rusty wrought-iron gates swung back against the inside of the brick pillars as we passed between. Then we were in a dark canyon formed by tall brick warehouses on either side, their loading bays shuttered with double wooden doors, the dark green paintwork blistered and peeling.

At the last warehouse on the left, a light showed faintly in the gloom. He turned the car into an obliquely angled parking bay in front, alongside a shiny silver Porsche, on the far side of which was a big, and rather grimy, white estate car. We got out. The rain had moderated to a heavy drizzle, and a stiff breeze blew in the funnel-like roadway between the tall buildings.

One ground-floor loading bay had been replaced by large glazed windows, the room within hidden by half-closed venetian blinds. An incongruous wooden portico – presumably put up recently – stuck out several feet over the roadway. White letters on the grey fascia board announced: Friars Haven – Chewton Developments plc. On top, a short flagpole carried a flag, a blue field with a red C, slightly frayed at the ends, which cracked in the gusts.

He pointed up at it. 'Flags. Builders love 'em. Ever see a development without at least one?'

I mumbled a knowingness I didn't feel in reply as we mounted the short flight of concrete steps under the shelter of the portico.

He had calmed down now, his complexion several shades paler again. He pushed open one of the pair of glass swing doors and ushered me in first. I stood looking around, covertly shaking my head to fling the beaded raindrops from my hair. The whole ground-floor area of the old warehouse had been turned into one vast open-plan office space, clear except for white-painted cast-iron columns marching down the middle, supporting the huge central wooden ceiling beam into which were notched crosswise timbers only slightly less massive.

The fluorescent tubes suspended from them were lit only above where we had come in. Beyond the pool of illumination, there was semi-darkness. Except for the unoccupied desk by the entrance doors, obviously intended for some decorative receptionist, and a large, square, grey-painted table directly opposite us, the entire space was empty of furniture. Even after the chill day outside, it felt cold. Appleby gazed about him impatiently, then, with a murmur of recognition, set off over a football pitch of hairy grey carpet tiles to the furthest end, where two figures stood silhouetted against the whitish rectangle of a window.

I followed the elegant back in the dark blue pinstripe.

He was shaking hands with the shorter of the two men as I came up.

'Good morning, Trevor. As I said on the phone, blame the council. Even tried to speak to Peters, but he was on holiday. Says it all, doesn't it? Didn't see you in the gloom at first. Economizing are you?'

The other man gave a short, grunting laugh at this sally. I had observed on a couple of other occasions how Appleby would greet important clients in this aggressively bantering fashion. To unimportant clients or to colleagues he was simply and unapologetically rude.

'Saving up for your firm's latest bill, you know, Francis. But actually, we were looking out, not in.' He turned to me. I saw that his eyes widened coolly, appraisingly. There was something about their baby-blue clarity that at once made me uncomfortable. There was a hardness about them and their scrutiny which didn't mesh with the chubby-cheeked, clean-shaven face and the full, slightly pouting, red lips. 'Well, hello. You must be the new solicitor Francis mentioned.'

Appleby was preoccupiedly riffling through a file he had taken from the briefcase he had given me to carry as we left the office. It was evident he was not going to trouble himself to do any introductions. I smiled and held out my hand. 'I'm Sarah Hartley.'

My hand was engulfed by his. I glanced down at the immaculately manicured object; it had the warm heavy feel of a piece of powerful machinery. As he leaned towards me I caught a whiff of a powerful cologne which didn't quite mask the musky scent of his sweat. 'How do you do, Mr Chewton?'

'It's Trevor, Sarah. No formalities between me and my colleagues.'

I smiled. 'Thanks... Trevor. And I'm really looking forward to the work.'

'Good. Good. That's what we're here for.' He turned to the other man, who during our conversation had been standing slightly awkwardly, holding some papers in his hand. 'Paul. Sarah Hartley. Paul Starling-Richards, architect for Friars Haven.'

'How do you do?' He inclined his head to me. 'Hello again, F-Francis.' He had a slight stammer, I noticed. Appleby looked up, nodded curtly and returned to his file. I shook hands with the tall, dark, nervous-looking man in jeans and a green corduroy jacket. As I did so I saw that the cuff of his brown shirt was worn so that the white lining material showed through.

'Now gentlemen – and lady. Let's get on, shall we?' Chewton's tone became more brisk. He looked at his chunky gold wristwatch. 'Because of the delay, I've got to be away from here in half an hour. Now, the purpose of this meeting is to look at the latest scheme for the main access road.

Last night Paul faxed me a copy of a letter from the planners. You've seen it too, I believe, Francis? Good. Now, Paul, over to you.'

The architect bent down and quickly thrust the papers back into his briefcase. 'I suggest that before I say any more, we should have a look at the place in question, just so we're all clear on what's now proposed.' There were nods and grunts of agreement from the other two.

We trooped out of the warehouse, turned back on the road we had come in on, then right behind the warehouse again, along another narrow cobbled road. There were rusty iron railway lines inset into the paving.

Chewton led the way, with Appleby striding to keep up. The architect and I were a little in the rear. We were both carrying heavy briefcases, as Appleby had given his back to me. But I didn't mind being the bagman. I had a sense of something in the air. For the first time at the firm, I might have something demanding of more than routine skills to get my teeth into.

The architect said, 'A bit of a waste of time, this, but Trevor insisted. You get a look at the place, though. Is this the first time you've been here? To Friars Haven?'

I nodded. 'Extraordinary place. Wasn't this the port of Fernsford at one time? I've read a bit about it in my city guidebook.'

'Yes, it's a good study for the industrial archaeologist. Not to mention the architect. I've studied the history a bit since I've been involved in the project. You see, all this stuff was once the high-technology of its day. State of the art. Now look at it.'

'It does look rather forlorn.'

'Salutary, eh? For anyone with ambitions to build things to last for ever. The Fernsford merchants thought they had the answer in the 1780s. They wanted to grab as much as they could of the new trade in coal and iron from South Wales and the Midlands. The river Fern had been silting up for years, so they went for the Big Idea: a canal direct to the Tarrant estuary at Fernsmouth. They commissioned the great engineer Thomas Brinwell to build it, together with a vast dock basin and warehouses. You can see the money that was invested. No expense spared on them. The best hard red bricks. Terracotta adornments. Temples of commerce, aren't they? They called the style "Fernsford Venetian".'

'It didn't last, did it?'

'No. The railway line to Westhampton and Fernsford from the junction with the Great Western Railway at Swindon was completed in 1842, and that was the beginning of the end of the canal. The railway took a great deal of the trade away. Then the dock at Fernsmouth was built at the turn of the century to accommodate the bigger ships of those days. The inland port has been virtually derelict for years.'

'Until Chewton and Friars Haven. Now it's his turn. And yours, of course. It must be terribly exciting for you.'

He laughed nervously. 'Yes, it is. And a little daunting. I think some people in the city might be surprised, if they're expecting more Fernsford Venetian. I don't believe in pastiche. And nor does my client.'

'The original dock buildings will make marvellous apartments, won't they? The Chewton sales people say they've been inundated with enquiries ever since the scheme was announced. They'll sell like hot cakes. Seems like everyone wants to live in a Grade I Listed warehouse.'

'Maybe. It's the post-industrial fashion. People work in buildings that look like giant cottages and live in old factories. Besides, the conservation people would go crazy if we applied to demolish them. Thankfully, Trevor's housing design people are dealing with the residential side. I'm not terribly interested in fitted kitchens. Over here is my area. That's what you call a clean sheet. Every architect's dream. As you can see.'

I did see. The cobbled road ended at a broken-down chestnut paling fence. Ahead, stretching into the distance, there was an enormous tract of land covered in weeds and scrub: drifts of rosebay-willow herb, the fireweed, and clumps of lilac-coloured buddleia which I remembered from their rapid colonization of vacant lots and derelict buildings in London, huge thistles, docks and nettles, half-grown ragged trees and straggling hawthorn bushes. Amidst the vegetation, I could see stumps of concrete columns, with rusty steel reinforcing rods protruding, and shattered remnants of brick walls. Dotted at intervals were mounds of rubble and earth, like the upheavals of a giant mole; and everywhere there were scattered what seemed like the remains of a vanished civilization: torn plastic and paper sacks, splintered lengths of wood, shattered doors, corroded steel window frames amid the glint of their own smashed panes, bits of broken crockery, a huge metal cylinder studded with enormous rivets, the tractor unit of an articulated lorry, the cab tilted forward and the engine compartment empty, windowless, scorched by fire, the tyres missing.

This was the rest of Trevor Chewton's development site, the one, according to Appleby, he had schemed for, waiting patiently for the railway marshalling yard, the gas works, the factories, the houses to fall into his hands, painstakingly assembling the area on which the phoenix of Friars Haven would arise from the dereliction.

I marvelled at how long it had taken. Chewton had been hardly more than a small-scale builder of estates of houses when he had acquired from a bankrupt landlord the first parcel of the site, a terrace of run-down houses. From the beginning, he had had the ambition not just to build another tacky housing estate but to acquire the whole of this massive area on the fringe of the established commercial centre of Fernsford, a site gradually falling into decay as the works of the first Industrial Revolution collapsed before the onslaught of the second. It had been a gamble. But it looked now as if it was about to pay off. The planning permissions had been obtained – by one means or another, no doubt – to turn this into one of the biggest developments of its kind in Western Europe.

As I gazed for the first time at Friars Haven, I felt a tremor of excitement that my fate had put me here. Here to watch this wasteland blossom into the hard certainties of the twentieth century: a shopping centre to rival the best in the land, a marina, an hotel, a sports centre, offices, flats, houses. And in the thick of it would be me. Drafting the contracts and the leases, the agreements and the transfers, negotiating, arguing, winning. God, how glad I was to get away from the miseries of Saturday-night brawls and beatings, the miserable, half-starved faces of neglected children, the rapes, the murders, the petty thefts which had been life at Vardy, Leadbetter.

I silently reproached myself for my initial reaction to Trevor Chewton. Okay, so he was maybe a hard case, not much better underneath than the villains I had dealt with, but at least his toughness, his ruthlessness and his energy were turned to something constructive. Here was a man with a vision who was on the point of turning it into reality.

We made our way across the site on another old cobbled road, which at one time had been spread with a layer of asphalt. This crust was now lifting and breaking up under the assault of weeds which grew knee-high and left their wet seeds sticking to the bottom of my coat as I passed. Hurrying along to catch up Appleby and Chewton, who had stopped to wait for us, I tripped on one of the potholes. I would have gone sprawling if the architect had not shot out his arm and grabbed mine in a powerful bony grip. As he pulled me upright, I swung in front of him, and reached out my hand to his shoulder to steady myself. We were about the same height and, for a brief second or two, our eyes met. Then I dropped my hand, and he released his hold. I picked up my, or rather Appleby's, fallen briefcase and dusted it off, and put up my hand to push back my hair which had tumbled over my face.

I grinned at him, making my eyes wide with exaggerated amusement. 'Thanks. I nearly went flat on my face.'

He seemed embarrassed and mumbled a reply. I knew why his composure was ruffled, along with his brown hair. In those seconds that my face was close to his I had had the overwhelming feeling that he wanted to kiss me. The desire crackled from him like the electric spark generator in the Science Museum. He must know I had felt it. I suppose if he'd not had Appleby and Chewton as an audience, he would have gone right ahead. I wondered what they had thought was going on. This was turning out to be quite a meeting.

Chewton had a sardonic expression on his face as we came up. He said, 'When you're ready, Paul.' I didn't dare look at Appleby.

There was no high brick wall like the one which edged the Canal Street side. In front of us was a ten-foot steel mesh fence, the tops of its galvanized uprights bent outwards in an overhang and threaded with razor wire. On the other side of the fence were a couple of concrete blocks splashed crudely with red and white stripes which lay athwart the part of the old road where it left the site. Beyond that was what had been an asphalt-surfaced highway, now reduced to half its original width with soil and rubble which had spilled down from the small hill on the far side, the site for dumping some of the excavated spoil for the extension of the ring road, which would run by the top of the Friars Haven site.

The architect had been rummaging in his bag and produced a plan which he unfolded with some difficulty. He jabbed at it with a cheap ballpoint.

'This is the original position for the junction. The Friars Haven access would leave the ring road at the roundabout here – which we have to construct before commencing work on site as part of the planning conditions – and run parallel with the embankment before entering the site where we're standing. Then it would have swung round to the main feeder road, here. They now say the roundabout has to move forward fifty metres – something to do with improving site lines – to here. As you can see, it's a more direct connection, and will reduce the length of the slip road and the curve on the feeder road. The cost implications are therefore beneficial. I think they've done us a favour, for a change.'

Chewton and Appleby exchanged glances. Then Chewton turned away from the fence and stared at the distant warehouses, indistinct shapes in the rainy mist.

His foot, in a shiny black loafer, kicked at a lump of tarry rubble.

'Doing us a favour. That's a laugh. I could tell you about the favours I've done some of those buggers. Fucking servants of the public, my arse. But, in the end, it's all come together. Been a long time, though. When I think of the work I've put in. And Chamberlayne's too. You're in a good firm, Sarah. My lucky day I met your boss. It was through Ralph wasn't it, Francis? The Babbage site. Ralph acted for Babbage. You did the completion. Ralph was off sick. I came along with my lawyer. It was a big moment for me. That was when I decided I'd had enough of my useless brief. The next one, I'll go for that bloke Appleby. And when that site at . . .'

Appleby laughed. 'What a coincidence you should mention that, Trevor. I was telling Sarah only the other day how Welscombe was the first purchase I did for you. We've never looked back, have we?'

'That's right. And Sarah here's going to keep up the good work, aren't you?' He swung his head back in my direction as if it were the turret on a tank. 'Now Sarah, I don't have to say, do I, that everything to do with Friars Haven, down to the colour of the bog paper, is completely confidential? On the legal side you discuss anything you need to with Francis alone. Okay? None of the chats that lawyers have with their mates about "a hypothetical case I'd like your views on". Stumm, completely. Understand? This isn't London. Fernsford's a fucking parish compared with the Smoke. I don't want anyone hearing about my affairs except when they have my leave, clear? You keep stumm.'

I nodded. He hadn't said 'or else', but it was clearly implied. 'Of course, Trevor.'

I glanced at Francis but he was staring fixedly into the distance.

Chewton seemed satisfied. I had thought for a moment he was going to demand a loyalty oath. He swivelled his left wrist to look at the gold watch, which he wore on the underside. 'I said half an hour and it's been three-quarters. I'm off. We'll proceed on the basis of the new road alignment. Paul, you get the details off to the engineers. Francis, you'll need to sort out the licence with the County Solicitor for the works to the public highway. O'Riordan's, the ground works and highways contractor, are down to start in six weeks. Thank you, gentlemen – and lady. Shall we go?'

I took a deep breath. 'Trevor, is it all right if I stay behind here for a while? It seems a good opportunity. I haven't had the chance to look at the whole of the site. It would help to be familiar with it when I'm dealing with the documents. Don't you agree as well, Francis?'

As I'd expected, Chewton didn't wait for Appleby's response. 'That's okay by me. Sounds a good idea. Looking at papers is all very well, but there's nothing like getting the feel of a site. You've got the right instinct there. I'll tell my man at the gate you're still here.' His face twisted into the semblance of a grin. 'You'll be all right – keep to the roadways, there are some nasty deep holes. And by the way, the dog patrol starts at eight, but I doubt you'll want to stay that long.'

Appleby grunted. He was not best pleased that I had outmanoeuvred him – and was setting my own agenda into the bargain. 'I assume your work schedule will allow you to take the time, Sarah. You will also have to find your own way back to the office.'

'I'm free till the sales meeting this afternoon. Judging from the journey here, I daresay it'll be quicker on foot.'

I sat on a heap of broken red bricks and watched them returning to the warehouses where the cars were parked.

It had been a funny sort of meeting, as the architect, Paul, had implied. It could have been dealt with in a quick phone conversation. Why drag us all out here? I'd surely be flattering myself if I imagined it was for Trevor Chewton to give me the once over?

I recalled how at my interview Appleby had made it plain that he considered me a person of no importance.

'So, Miss Hartley, you're twenty-five, nearly twenty-six. You're single. You've spent your articles mainly dealing with, ah, ladies who've made a bit of a pickle of their private lives?'

'I suppose that's one way of expressing it.' I had smiled charmingly as I said this, but I couldn't conceal entirely my irritation with this superb specimen of the professional man, with his suave tongue, his expensive-looking suit and his clearly significant tie. But there was more to Francis Appleby than the tailor's dummy. His pink, well-fed and well-razored face gave nothing so vulgar as a grimace, but there was a tightening around the eyes and mouth, as he digested my riposte. For a fleeting moment the face became harder, a hint of touchiness behind the bland façade.

'Yes, it is, and I'm afraid it's my way. Let me be frank with you, Miss Hartley. This firm is quite different from...' Barely missing a beat – the technique of a seasoned operator in Court, checking a fact in his brief – he looked quickly down to the single typed sheet of my CV, which lay on the spotless, empty leather-bound blotter. 'Messrs Vardy, Leadbetter & Co. We don't deal with Legal Aid cases or so-called *pro bono* work at all. My partners and I reserve our charitable activities for our private lives. If people wish to use our services, then they must be able to pay for them. An increasingly old-fashioned view in these liberal days.' He smiled. 'You must forgive me if I sound unduly dismissive.' He paused, his mouth slightly open, displaying his orthodontically perfect teeth, watching my reaction with interest.

I took a deep breath and smiled in return. 'I want a change. A chance to move on.'

'Good, good. That's what we like to hear. Change is what we're all about here.' He flicked his eyes back to my CV. 'So, what makes you think you could handle a fast-moving commercial environment?'

This was the sixty-four-thousand-dollar question. I said, 'I'm used to working quickly. Emergency injunctions. Habeas corpus and bail applications. I've been involved in complex property settlements following divorce. I've had some experience with commercial property.'

'Indeed. The details?'

'Retail premises, mainly.'

'Ah. And where were these retail premises? Oxford Street? Regent Street?'

I squirmed but spoke defensively. 'Kingsland Road. A jeweller's. But the principles are the same, aren't they?'

He shrugged. 'In essence. But a client who is leasing an office block at a rent in the hundred thousands may not feel entirely confident with a solicitor who's used to dealing with corner shops and lock-ups.'

'I'm willing to work very hard. I can learn. I've had a good training.'

'Ah, yes. Preceded by a little learning. You attended the Charles Pooter Comprehensive School, Holloway until the age of sixteen. You obtained two grade C GCSEs in maths and English. A professional qualification cannot then have been uppermost in your mind?'

'No. I got a job as a junior clerk in a solicitor's firm. I was, er, encouraged by my boss to go to night school to do my As.'

'Ah, yes. Grade Es in law and political studies – whatever they are. Following which, you attended Myddelton Polytechnic, Islington, where you obtained a pass degree in law. Did you choose that institution for any particular reason?'

I squirmed again, but tell the truth and shame the devil. 'It was near home. I had to look after my mother. She was ... ill.'

'I see. A convenient bus route was it? And how does your mother feel now about your venturing so far afield as Fernsford?'

'She died three years ago. Just before my final exams.'

'How sad. The death of parents is so affecting. But also perhaps liberating?'

I met his penetrating stare and said nothing.

He leaned back in his chair with a comfortable creak of morocco leather and steepled his hands in front of his aquiline nose. 'Let me tell you about this firm, Miss Hartley. These are expansive times and Chamberlayne's are moving with them. And anyone who joins us can expect a full share of the rewards of success – provided, of course, they are prepared to work hard. We expect full commitment, but we recognize it in a proper way. Look here. Two of our partners joined the firm as assistant solicitors – only a matter of a couple of years ago. Growth is what we're set on. And we've got the means, believe me. In five years' time, we'll be the biggest firm in Fernsford. And anyone who knows me knows I don't make idle boasts.'

'It sounds very impressive.'

'It is very impressive. Fernsford is what you could call a boom town. It's growing all the time. Banking, insurance, financial services. The major companies are moving here – decentralized management, relocation, whatever you want to call it. No one wants to pay the kinds of crazy overheads of London any more – not to mention the constant hassle with staff, transport, access. Forget London. London is finished. Here, you've got space to develop and expand, countryside just a few minutes away, a good quality of life. That's what people want. And Chamberlayne's is in the thick of it.

'When I came to the firm, what, fifteen years ago, it was old man Chamberlayne – the Chamberlayne family had run the firm since God knows when – and a few clerks. Now there are five partners, and three – soon to be four – assistants. Pretty good going, if I say so myself. And I don't believe in recruiting for the sake of it. Some of my colleagues think that if you've got a secretary filing her nails in a dozen offices scattered across the county, then you're doing well. We don't have passengers. Everyone who works here has to be a contributor. They work damned hard, and they're rewarded.

'We've a good spread of work and it's good quality. Some excellent corporate litigation clients – we even had the London headquarters of one of our clients instructing us the other day: that's what I call a compliment. Company formation, mergers and insolvency: we've an excellent expanding department there: cradle to the grave, you might say. And a pretty good private client base – that's the old Chamberlayne connection – trusts, estates, wealthy individuals, good solid work from the time when Fernsford was just a big country town. But it helps to have that kind of reputation – that's why we kept the name. But the biggest growth area of all at present is property. And there we've got a star. Our own home-grown Fernsford success story. Trevor Chewton. You'll have heard of him, of course? His companies are frequently mentioned in the financial pages.'

It was an awkward moment. I had had to admit I didn't know a damned thing about Trevor Chewton. Or about his ambitious project to transform a canalside wasteland into a huge commercial, residential and leisure project to be known as Friars Haven.

As he had ushered me out through the fancy chrome-and-glass doors, he had shaken my hand with cold formality. 'It's been most interesting to meet you, Miss Hartley. Have an excellent journey back to Town. My partners and I will reach a decision as quickly as we can. I know it's going to be difficult, as we've had so many excellent candidates.'

I bet you have, I thought to myself, as I trudged glumly back to Fernsford's Western Road railway station. I consoled myself that other jobs would come up in time. As I had said to Harriet, I was fed up, but not desperate to leave London.

Not desperate. Not then. That came later.

\*

The rain had stopped and I felt the warm sun on my face. From the scrub which covered the site arose a faint steam, as if it were escaping from some underground devil's kitchen.

Immediately in front of where I sat were the remains of what looked like several small streets of terraced houses. Presumably this was where, according to Appleby, Chewton had made his first purchases. Though almost overwhelmed with encroaching couch grass and weeds, I could make out a network of narrow cobbled streets. I could still see the first few courses of brick marking the curtilages of these dwellings. How tiny they seemed, laid bare like this, hardly larger than the cells of the glass-cased beehive I had seen with Colin at London Zoo. Amongst the hawthorn and the hazel scrub poked up the truncated remains of chimney stacks and scraps of rotten timbers from collapsed roofs.

I walked into the site down one of these flattened streets. Beyond the houses, there were the remains of a substantial brick building – a factory of some kind – the walls of which were mostly demolished to head height. A few window frames remained in situ, their glass smashed so completely that only fragments glinted from the putty like tiny teeth. This must have been quite a playground for the local children, at least until the wicked fence was erected, and if they were anything like I had been as a kid they had probably got through that somewhere.

The overgrown outline of a concrete roadway led past this building into the middle of the site and I followed it slowly, glancing round at intervals to get my bearings. The ground sloped quite steeply downhill. In a matter of minutes, I was alone in what seemed more like a tract of countryside than a piece of abandoned industrial wasteland. The trees here – sycamore mainly – were, some of them, over ten feet tall. Their leaves rustled in the stiff breeze.

It wafted also to my nostrils a faint but familiar acrid smell of coal. I was passing on my right a cleared and roughly levelled area, on which, unusually in these jungly surroundings, no trees or shrubs grew, only tufts of yellowish grass and drifts of dark green nettles. Faded whitewashed letters on a ruined gable end read, Fernsford Gas Light and Coke Co. If that scent could linger for years, God knew what manner of chemical nasties still lay hidden under the acres of smashed brick and clinker-covered earth. This whole place was a reminder of what a sheer bloody mess human beings could make if they put their minds to it.

Unknowingly, I had an audience for these philosophical musings. As I turned away from the remains of the gas works, I found myself staring into the brown eyes of a large reddish animal. Startled, I held my breath. The creature, quite unafraid, turned and trotted away into a patch of brambles, where I heard its scuffling progress.

I stood listening for several minutes, amazed by the encounter. I had never seen a fox outside the covers of dimly remembered children's picture books. And this one had not been wearing a waistcoat or a peaked cap. I giggled to myself as I imagined pursuing him into the bushes to serve him with his notice to quit these premises at eleven o'clock in the forenoon. It seemed odd to meet my first real live wild animal outside of the zoo here, of all places. I was strangely comforted by the sight of other flesh and blood. For I had begun to feel oppressed by the atmosphere of decay and dereliction, by the way in which the comforting sounds of the city had been absorbed by the place, which gave back only sighs and whispers of wind in the trees and among the ruins. If I were the easily spooked person I was not, I might have shivered, despite the increasing warmth of the sun as it grew nearly midday.

Ahead now, I could see the flash of its beams on what must be the water of the canal. When I reached that, I would have crossed the site. I would turn left and walk along the towpath back to the dock basin and the old port. I quickened my pace. I could smell it now, the unmistakable, slightly sewagey, rotten smell of standing water. It reminded me of long walks along the Grand Union in Islington, alone more often than not in the latter days, when Colin would not shift from the computer screen except to pee or make himself another peanut butter and jam sandwich. I was out of all that now. This was a different canal, a different town. There was no Colin, nor any other looming presence out of the past.

I emerged through an arch, the remains, presumably of some kind of wharfside structure, perhaps serving the gas works, the coal for which in the old days would have been unloaded directly from barges on the canal. Lying to one side was a heap of rusting metal, struts and chains and massive gearwheels, which might have been a crane. I stared over the green, still water. It was wider than I had expected. On the far bank, willow trees grew to the very edge, their branches hanging into the water, forming secret pools of darkness. On my side the stone and brick edging was still in good condition, with a clear tow path of crushed cinders. To my right, the canal ran dead straight as far as I could see, its surface mirroring the now white high clouds and the blue of the cleared sky.

I turned left towards the warehouses of the port. It was ten minutes before I was level with the first great block. In the sunlight which shone full on its façade I could see the details of the workmanship which Paul Starling-Richards had mentioned. Each loading bay, with its oblong double doors, was set within an elegantly pointed arch supported by false columns, the whole modelled out of yellowish pink material, presumably the stuff he had called terracotta. It had the effect of making it look more like a palace than an industrial building. Paul had talked about 'Fernsford Venetian'. In the warmth and the light, it reminded me of the travel agents' posters of Italy I used to drool over.

So far I had managed only one trip out of England: the boat-train all night to Paris. Colin hated abroad and had gone only because I had bullied him for months. We had horrible, damp, smelly digs and it rained and Colin got food poisoning and lay in bed groaning and said he would die if I went out and left him. Now I didn't have Colin to hold me back I could go anywhere I liked, even Venice.

I continued past the front of the warehouse, still dreaming of Italy. As I rounded its corner, I came face to face with the real scale and magnificence of the old port. The dock basin, approached from the canal through a lock, was enormous, a quiet oblong pool of water, reflecting the great buildings which surrounded it. They formed a symmetrical group, a pair on each of the short sides, left and right, and on the long far side facing me, another pair on each side of the central roadway which Appleby and I had driven in upon. It was the right-hand one of these in which we had met. I could see the wooden portico and its flag and the glass windows in place of the wooden doors.

I stood on the cobblestones of the wharf staring around, all at once suffused with a feeling of great contentment. All this was something I would be involved in. My work would contribute to the return of this place to life and activity. Once more there would be boats on the canal. The warehouses would be places for people to live and work. And on the wasteland I had just traversed would be built something new and altogether wonderful.

I was rapt with these visions, when, on the opposite bank of the canal, past the entrance to the dock, I noticed a seated figure.

Its hunched posture, its very presence seemed intrusive, alien. I felt a jolt of sudden alarm, a constricting pain in my chest. Sweet Jesus, it was him. What was he doing here? Was he watching me? Waiting for me? And as I stared at him, my heart began to pound and my vision began to blur. I saw him get up and wave his arm at me, and it was like one of those distorting mirrors. His arm, his whole body seemed to stretch and shimmer as it waved towards me, and his mouth seemed to open in a great yell. In my mind I seemed to hear the roar of his voice and he was shouting, 'I'll see you again!'

I shut my eyes, screwed them up fiercely, struggling with the visions that were racing through my brain. I saw in the blackness the coloured lights and swirling shapes that used to terrify me as a child. I opened my eyes, and this time I forced myself to see what was actually before them.

It wasn't him. It was only a man fishing. He was standing, tugging up the rod. Then he drew it back and flung it forward to recast the line. He was young and his hair was not grey, but fair. He wore a short-sleeved checked shirt and jeans. He was surrounded by the nets and impedimenta that keen fishermen tote about. He gave no sign of having noticed my presence. He was innocently whiling away his day off or his unemployment. I didn't know him from Adam. The relief coursed through my veins like a breaking wave.

But, none the less, I felt sick and shaken by the hallucination. I'd had nightmares since my childhood. But never before had their stuff leaked through into my waking life. I thought I had got far enough away from the shadow which haunted me. I had even been planning my new life. Now this had to go and happen. Instead of being banished, the horrible things inside my skull were wriggling to get out even more forcefully. I'd heard of people who'd taken acid, and years after they stopped taking it, vile things would flash back into their conscious minds, sort of hangovers from the bad trips they'd had, like the long-delayed aftershocks of earthquakes.

But my case was worse. My horrors were not chemically induced. They were real.

## II

By the time I got back to the office it was nearly lunchtime. I hoped, wanly, that Appleby hadn't been checking up on me.

I was still new enough to get a kick out of the sight of the classy building I now worked in. It was in the middle blocks of the Horsemarket – the best part of the principal street of Fernsford's commercial district. The ground floor was occupied by a plush branch of the FernWest Building Society, and their corporate headquarters were in the elegant glass tower adjoining.

I rode up in one of the lifts to the third floor. The firm had this floor and the penthouse floor above, as well as the basement floor for storage. There was a panoramic view over the city from the spacious and luxuriously furnished reception area. I could imagine what Pogson, my boss in London, would have said about the glossy-leaved indoor plants the size of small trees which adorned it. 'Plants? I ask you. Is this a solicitor's office or a garden centre? Who's going to pay me for having plants?' At Vardy, Leadbetter what the partners called Reception was a gap between the photocopying machine and the staircase.

I went through the long room which accommodated the typists and the practice admin staff into the short corridor beyond where the assistant solicitors had their offices. Where I had my office.

I loved my office. This wasn't Tim Pogson's idea of an office, a place where you could hardly stand up straight and had to bend down to look through the window. It was quite large and bright, with a pine desk with a tooled leather top, a padded high-backed swivel chair, just like they had in TV ads, a computer monitor screen and keyboard, a state-of-the-art telephone, a decent carpet, a bookshelf, a couple of easy chairs and a coffee table. There was a tall window with a venetian blind with the same view over the city as Reception. The room had recently been redecorated in pleasant pastel colours. Its previous occupant had been Michael Fielding, now elevated to partner and translated on high to the penthouse suite. A good omen, I thought.

'Sarah, sorry to jump on you straightaway. But I've had Jane at Squirrels Patch on to me about Plot 80. Their time extension expires today. She says that orders from above are to chop them if they don't come through.'

Penny, my secretary – my secretary! – hovered by the door to my room. I stopped in the middle of taking off my coat. I saw that the hem was still speckled with tiny seeds from Friars Haven. She was looking at me curiously.

'Are you all right? You look a bit pale and peaky. Nothing's happened has it? I knew I ought to have warned you about poking around that waste ground. They've had all sorts going on there, tramps and gypsies and vandals. Even though it was daylight, I...'

I shrugged out of my coat and flung it on the stand. 'Don't worry. I'm fine. I'm naturally pale and interesting, haven't you noticed? And I didn't see any villains. Only a man fishing. Oh, and a fox. He was lovely, and we had a lovely chat. Now, what was it you said? Plot 80 on Squirrels. Yes, they have been giving us the run-around. Tell her their solicitor has been begging me to keep them in. I'm expecting a call any minute from him to confirm their mortgage is through. I said that was positively their last chance. And what about Plot 10, Green Gables? The punter was supposed to be signing last night, and Bardells were getting back to us first thing?'

'Nothing from them while you were out. Shall I get on to them?'

'If you would, thanks. And Penny, would you...?'

She reached behind her and like a magician produced a steaming mug. 'Da-da! I knew you'd be ready for one.'

'Penny, what would I do without you?'

'You'd do perfectly well.'

'Oh, but would I?'

'You're too modest. Everyone says as how you've got an amazing grip on things. In such a short time too, isn't it? Even the Artful Codger was heard singing your praises the other day for how you got those terrible old B and K Builders files sorted out and billed. Hanging around for ages, they were.'

I grinned happily. The Artful Codger was Mr Dyer, the firm's accountant, who'd been with the firm for years, and who was grudging with his acceptance of newcomers.

She gave a big smile and bustled out to make the calls. I was in love with Penny, I had to admit. I loved her more each day. In a quite non-carnal sense, of course.

Penny was fat and jolly and fortyish and Welsh. She was just right for me who had never had a secretary before: unthreatening and untemperamental. The converse of her amenability was, however, that she knew next to nothing about legal work. I was a little surprised that Appleby had appointed her. He certainly hadn't bothered to give her any training beyond the bare minimum when she was working for him. 'Rose told me what to do and I did it,' she had said on my first day. I was beginning to put that right. She was bright and quick to learn, but as her last job had been working for a senior manager – now redundant – at Westerset Electricity, we had a long way to go. If it had been Pogson, I would have said he'd given her the job because she was cheaper than a proper legal secretary, but Appleby wasn't Pogson and I'd never heard him talk about cutting corners to save money in that way.

Whatever reason he'd had, I blessed it. I leaned back in my heavily padded swivel chair and drank good coffee and stared around at my office. Even now I could hardly believe it. My office. My secretary. My desk. And my workload. Dozens of buff-coloured files with coloured stickers in the right-hand corner, coded according to the development.

The files reminded me, despite my self-congratulation, of the price I had had to pay. It was all very well taking part of the morning for my tour of Friars Haven – which I wouldn't have the nerve to bill for. My little show of independence, which I knew had needled Appleby, had taken me away from the real work, the honest-to-God, fee-earning drudgery that was residential conveyancing for Trevor Chewton's various house-building companies. I had to get to grips with this high-pressure but ultimately boring and routine conveyancing administration, otherwise my head would be on the block. Nor would I, as Appleby had made 'abundantly plain', be likely to get a taste of the more interesting and demanding legal work which would be on offer at Friars Haven. Having seen the place and what it involved I was even more keen to come up to the mark.

Without undue immodesty, I thought to myself that Penny was right. A few weeks ago, the conversation we had just had about plot sales would have been double-Dutch. I had got to grips with things very quickly. I had

had to. Appleby had wasted no time in spelling out what I had got myself into in the session I had had with him at nine o'clock on my first day in the conference room adjoining the partners' suite on the penthouse floor.

We had sat at one end of the long mahogany table, beneath a bulbous-headed, purple-faced caricature version of Lord Justice somebody or other. Appleby had a pile of papers in front of him. I had diligently equipped myself with a new counsel's notebook, which, unlike at Vardys, I had been able to obtain from the stationery store without having to give blood.

He spread his arms on the glassily polished wooden surface and scrutinized me. He was, I had to admit, quite a good-looking bloke and not really all that old, despite the portentously grave manner he adopted. His hair was iron-grey, to be sure, but his blue eyes were clear, without bags, and the flesh of his face and neck firm without sags or wrinkles. I suppose he was in his late forties. He had on what even I could see was a very expensively tailored suit, and the discreetly striped shirt he was wearing had real mother-of-pearl buttons.

Even if I had been brimming over with confidence, what he said to start with would have demolished it pretty sharply.

'Even though we gave you the post, I have to say that the partners in this firm had their doubts about you, Sarah. You are relatively young, very recently admitted to the Roll and extremely inexperienced at the kind of matters with which you will be dealing. Notwithstanding these things, we believed you had certain positive qualities and we have taken the gamble – in the modern phrase, to put our money where our mouths are. I expect you to justify our faith in you, within the contractual probationary period of six months. Otherwise . . .'

The Royal Order of the Boot, I said to myself, and no messing. I gave a bright Miss Goody-Goody grin and said aloud, 'I shall certainly do my best. I'm really keen to get started.'

'Good, good. Now, as I said at our earlier meeting, you will be assisting me in, and in due course taking over from me, many of the matters relating to the activities of Chewton Developments plc. You will get to know the Chewton business in all its aspects. But at the outset you will deal mainly with the sale of properties on residential developments.'

I groaned inwardly. Residential. That was really bog-standard stuff. I wasn't going to be fobbed off with that for ever. I didn't like the sound of 'at the outset'. How long was this outset, then? I said, 'At the interview, you talked about Friars Haven, the big commercial development, not these houses. I am going to be involved in that pretty soon, aren't I?'

He shot me an irritated glance. I got the feeling that this sort of backchat wasn't in the script he had prepared. 'Let us be absolutely clear about this, Sarah. You are now employed by this firm as an assistant solicitor. Your contract, as you will be aware, requires you to undertake such duties as the partners may require. I shall decide when you are ready to cope with the more demanding matters. It's true that on an individual basis the fees for dealing with "these houses", as you call them, are not high, but there is the important matter of volume. It is a not inconsiderable, regular income. More importantly, in this case, house building is currently the major activity of a major client. Chewton is at present dependent on the cash flow from his residential estates.'

'It's not that I want to run before I can walk. I'm just so excited by the whole thing.'

'Naturally. It's an exciting business. When I first met Trevor Chewton he was a small-scale house builder. Now he's one of the major residential developers in the West Country. Quite soon, when Friars Haven takes off, he'll have a national reputation for commercial development – and so will Chamberlayne's. But, I have to emphasize, I don't forget, and no one in this firm should make the mistake of forgetting, that, at present, houses are his bread and butter. He wants them handled properly. If they're not, he looks elsewhere and we lose everything. There are half a dozen firms in this city who are just waiting for us to foul up on Chewton so they can move in. We're a long way from your battered women and petty criminals now. Clients like Trevor Chewton don't walk through the door every day or even every few years. To lose Chewton would be very bad news for all of us.'

I nodded, my face serious. 'I do appreciate that.'

'I'm pleased to hear it. Now, I haven't got all morning for this. Let's at last get down to the details. Chewton builds basically two levels of housing development: cheap stuff, boxes for the proles; and a more grandiose, and hence much more expensive kind of box for the boss, or rather would-be boss class – what's usually called "executive homes". By the way, developers don't build houses. The word is never used. They build "homes". Remember that.'

I nodded dutifully, the pupil at the feet of the great master. He handed me a sheaf of glossy brochures.

'Take those home and study them. They're all the developments you're dealing with. One or two of them have over a hundred boxes on them. They're the prole developments. Executive homes are more exclusive – never more than twenty. And they have more land, bigger plots in the jargon. You can tell which is which because the cheap estates always have cosy nursery-story type names. At the moment, for example, we've got Squirrels Patch, Badgers Wood, Foxes Meadow, The Warren, Green Gables. The marketing people dream them up. They say it invokes the nesting instinct. The executive estates have all got what you might call our-glorious-tradition names, what the salariat thinks will give their lives a touch of class. We've got, amongst others, Buckingham Gate, Castle Park, and Shakespeare Lodge. As for the houses – homes – they build the company's standard types. Each has its own fancy name – the Windsor, the Dorchester and so on.

'Now, the way these things are bought and sold. What happens is this. Mr and Mrs Punter decide they want to move from their present low-grade hovel to a spanking new one. So they go along to their local Chewton site as a result of the huge ad in the paper. What they see is a lot of mud, some unfinished roads and a gang of men in wellingtons drinking tea. The estate on which their dreams are founded has not yet risen beyond foundation level, if that. What there is, though, is a show home, furnished in exactly the right level of revolting bad taste that Mr and Mrs Punter aspire to, which has been thrown up in double quick time. That's what they see. That and these glossy brochures.

'The trick is that Mr and Mrs Punter put down a reservation on a property completely blind. It doesn't exist. It may not even be a hole in the ground. Chewton aims to sell out a development almost before the first bricks have been laid. Essential to keep his bankers happy. And what they reserve is called a plot. Every plot has a number. So when Chewton's sales oik rings you up and says, "What's the situation on Plot 42, Weasels Orifice?"

you are able to answer instantaneously with chapter and verse on exactly when you spoke to their solicitor, what he said, and whether or not you believed him.'

'And there's a time limit on the process, of course. Otherwise...'

He raised his eyebrows. 'Go to the top of the class.' I could sense the genuine surprise behind the exaggerated response. 'Very good. You're absolutely right. The punters have to exchange contracts in four weeks from reservation. You have to keep them to that timetable. To the majority of our professional colleagues it appears a request to construct the Eternal City within a twenty-four-hour period. You have to bully and cajole them into doing it. You keep reminding them that if they don't perform, their clients can be terminated with much weeping and wailing and gnashing of teeth, as well as mutual recrimination.'

'It's all very... businesslike.'

'It is, because it's a business. You're not acting for Mr and Mrs Nobody buying their dream. Don't get sentimental about them. Don't get involved in all the yarns that they'll spin you. Remember, you're acting for a company which makes an enormous capital outlay before it can start to get in a penny. There's no room for time wasters. And this firm has to do what its client wants. Without question. If, Sarah, you've still got the idea that a solicitor is some kind of dispenser of charity, then you'd better get rid of it fast.'

I smiled sweetly. 'Don't worry, Francis, I already have.'

Even at the time I said it, I felt a bit guilty. What was I doing working here, taking part in this contemptuous manipulation of people's hopes and aspirations? But, I reasoned, no one was forced to buy Chewton's little boxes made of ticky-tacky. It was entirely voluntary, attended by a plethora of professional advice. No one would lose from it. Property was the archetyal good investment. Safe as houses. Why should I beat up on myself for making a decent living for a change, where I didn't come face to face with the consequences of crime and violence every working day? I'd spent a fair bit of my life getting what Marilyn Monroe had called, in *Some Like It Hot*, 'the fuzzy end of the lollipop'. Why, oh why, shouldn't I fly over the rainbow? And if working with Appleby and Chewton was the way to fly, then so be it.

*

'Rose,' I asked, putting down the dark green and gold cup of *café au lait*, 'who is Ralph?'

By lunchtime, the weather had completely cleared. We sat outside at a white plastic table. The traffic swirled around the island in the middle of Saxe-Coburg Square, from which arose the tall Gothic shaft of the High Cross, according to my guidebook, a Victorian re-creation of a medieval original destroyed by the mob in the infamous Fernsford 'Reform Riots' of 1831.

I was taking advantage of a break in the, up to now, rather one-sided conversation. She had just completed a violent diatribe against some act of carelessness in the photocopying room, allegedly perpetrated by my colleague Mark Oundsworth.

I watched her hesitate. This was unusual. She was unstoppably fluent on all matters within and without her competence, as I had gathered over several previous occasions such as this.

Lunch with Rose had become a bit of a routine. We invariably went to the same sandwich bar. If it were fine, we sat outside at the tables overlooking the Cross. If not, we sat huddled up in the steamy atmosphere at the benches inside.

I had put together from various things that she had said that lunch had been a solitary occasion for her until my arrival. She had, as the personal assistant of the senior partner, disdained to lunch with the other secretaries, who were mainly in any event younger than she, and there were no other women in the firm. Although I was a solicitor, I was her junior by a good few years and this, in Rose's mind, seemed to cancel out the relative difference in status.

This arrangement suited me at the moment – at least on a couple of days in the week. At other times I could plead pressure of work and eat from a brown bag at my desk, or be on my way to an appointment or simply go shopping. I did, after all, work closely with Appleby and it was therefore necessary to find out as much as I could about what he was up to. In a firm where everyone seemed to be almost as new as I was, Rose, as a long-standing employee was also a link with the history of the firm, which was useful when, as on this occasion, I had something specific in this respect that I wanted to ask her about.

Rose was, I suppose, in her late thirties. A tall, angular woman whose fine facial bone structure was just beginning to show a little too much, and whose complexion, once no doubt pale and interesting by nature, was now becoming dry and sallow, even after the liberal use of creams and moisturizers. Rose knew more and talked more about cosmetics and their eponymous manufacturers than any woman I had known. She would refer to Yves and Jean and Helena and Elizabeth and Estée as if they were intimate friends. I listened sympathetically but silently, much as I would when men talked about makes of car or brands of beer. Rose took an almost perverse pleasure in my appearance, masochistically belittling her own, and at the same time, like a satanist or a druggie, trying to ensnare me in her cult.

'Of course,' she had said at our first tête-à-tête, 'I don't know why I am talking to you of such things. You have youth – the finest beauty preparation of all. I'm just an old hag. What do you use on your face in the mornings?'

'Soap and water.'

'Soap and water! Just listen to the girl! I haven't used soap for years. Of course, you've still got your schoolgirl complexion. And darling, that hair! What on earth do you do with it? Wella is it? Or Vidal?'

'It's yellow, in a big bottle. From Boots.'

I thought she was going into cardiac arrest. 'Oh, my God. How can you? Those things are hardly better than washing-up liquid.'

'I did use that when I was a student. It washed okay but I didn't like the smell.'

She cleared her throat, finally ready to answer my question. 'Ralph, darling? Where did you hear him mentioned?'

I told her, and she nodded, her pale-pink lipsticked mouth pursed in an arch grimace. 'Aha! I wondered how long it would be before you sniffed out the firm's dark secrets.'

'Dark secrets? What on earth do you mean?'

'Just my little joke, darling. They're not secret and not all that dark. But there are some things that one oughtn't to chat idly about. These are sensitive areas still.'

'What do you mean?'

She glanced around us briefly and then leaned across the table. I caught a powerful waft of exotic odour. Close up, her face looked more worn, the make-up as much camouflage as enhancement. She said in a throaty whisper, 'Death.' She tapped my wrist with a long-nailed finger. 'Sudden death. This is an important firm in a town still small enough for everyone who counts to take an interest in what's going on. Solicitors are terrible gossips, aren't they? Not Francis, though. He hates all that. He doesn't like it to be brought up. If I were you, I'd remember that.' She leaned back in her seat to assess the effect of this announcement.

'I'm not likely to do that, am I? I don't know what you're going on about.'

'You'd hear eventually, though. And that's why it's best I tell you. That way, it'll be the truth and not idle tittle-tattle.'

'So this Ralph died. That's hardly a big deal, is it?'

'He wasn't just "this Ralph" as you put it, darling. He was Ralph Chamberlayne. The son of old man Chamberlayne, the last of the line. He was a relatively young man. It was very shocking at the time, I can tell you.'

'So he was a partner?'

'Oh, yes. He joined the firm as a partner when he returned from Hong Kong. He'd been working there in the office of one of those big London firms. When his father finally retired, he divided the partnership. Francis would be the senior man, but Ralph would take over when he retired. It wasn't just that he was family, so to speak. He was a brilliant lawyer.'

'But he died. Was he ill? And why is it apparently such a touchy subject?'

'No, he wasn't ill. He was killed in a car accident. He was driving home from the office one night. He lived in St Oswalds, on the Upper Tarrant. It's a winding road, and he must have taken one of the bends too fast. He went right over the cliff. There's a two-hundred-foot drop to the river. Killed instantly. No one else was involved. It was a fine, dry, frostless night. His Rover was almost new. In tip-top condition. There was no reason for it to have happened. That was what was so awful. It was a bolt from the blue. A man in his prime, with so much still before him.'

I shot a covert glance at my watch. This was turning out quite dull. A car accident. Maybe that was front-page news in Fernsford, but in Hoxton, you had to be shot at point blank range with a machine gun by a hoodlum who then went on to rape your pregnant girlfriend before you got much of a headline. I said, 'That's a sad tale, but why should Appleby get het up about it?'

Rose resumed her confidential posture over the table and her voice dropped back into a whisper. 'Poor Francis was terribly upset by Ralph's death. I do make it my business that everyone understands that. As his personal assistant, I see a side of the man that few others even suspect exists. He was terribly upset. That's why even today, after all these years, he doesn't like people in the office to talk of Ralph. It brings back those awful memories. Because, despite what people might say about their differences, he had a great respect for the man. For his abilities and his delightful personality.'

I suddenly pricked up my ears. 'Differences? You mean they didn't get on?'

Rose waved a languidly dismissive hand. 'Darling, that's just what I'm saying. Francis is sometimes not terribly tactful in the way in which he handles some professional colleagues – he doesn't suffer fools gladly, as you know – and naturally this has created a certain, well, tendency to believe the worst. But I can assure you that there is no truth in their mutterings. The partnership between Francis and Ralph remained totally strong and amicable. Of course in any close relationship, there are bound to be areas of disagreement – policy matters. But that was all. I was close to . . . both of them. I knew that they would get things right between them.'

Again she leaned back to do a quick examination of my face and body language. I maintained the look of inscrutable detachment which I had developed to deal with the horrors that had come my way at Vardy's. There was a certain kind of police officer at Hoxton Police Station who liked to show young female lawyers the most gruesome official photographs of the latest murder or serious assault – 'Just to show you what some of these bastards – begging your pardon, miss – who come through your office are capable of.' These dickheads were agog to see you wince. Dealing with Rose's scrutiny was a piece of cake.

I said, all po-faced innocence, 'Had they had a row then, the night of the accident?'

Rose gave another little airy wave of her paw. 'Row? How can you have got that idea? They were both civilized men. They never did anything as vulgar as row. No, I think I would call it an ever so slightly heated discussion. Voices were raised, but certainly there was no shouting. I have no idea what they were discussing. But I have no doubt that if Ralph had lived, they would have sorted out whatever it was first thing in the morning. As much as anything you know, it was a difference of style. They were like brothers, fundamentally at one, but sometimes distracted by superficial matters.'

'What was Ralph like?'

'He was a charming man. Delightful. Full of wit and humour. He seemed always very relaxed and, to some, he appeared perhaps a little too casual. But he was, in fact, extraordinarily efficient and well organized. He knew virtually everyone in Fernsford. That was the family connection, of course. Ralph always said that he was in the people business. He told me he'd learned that in the East. The ability to get on with all manner of different types, to respect their points of view whilst getting across your own and being willing to let them win a little. Compromise, saving face, I believe it's called. Well, Ralph said that dealing so much with the Chinese and the Japanese had taught him that. And, of course, some of the clients he dealt with could be very touchy. The old gentry, he used to call them. That used to be the majority of the old firm's work, you know. Ralph kept all that up. Francis was always more interested in the commercial side.'

I was getting the picture now. There certainly was a difference in style. Poor Rose's loyal attempt to get Appleby's side in first had merely served to show that there was a great deal to come from the Chamberlayne supporters. By the sound of it there would be quite a few of those. I wondered how long it would be before I heard. Yet also I was touched and not scornful. It couldn't have been easy for her. She spoke of the late Ralph with a genuine affection which I ought to acknowledge. 'Thanks for telling me, Rose. You were obviously fond of the guy. It must have been bad for you.'

She pulled out a lace-trimmed embroidered hanky from her bag and carefully dabbed her eyes. 'Yes. It was. He was such a charming man – so gallant, in a way that most men are not these days. Mark and James are dear boys, but not in the same league at all. The worst thing was that I was almost certainly the last person to see him alive. I remember the date: 8 September 1976. Dates when terrible things happen. You don't ever forget them. A privilege for me, but a distressing one. He had gone back to his office after his, er, discussion with Francis. Everyone else, including Francis, had gone home. That evening, I thought I was the last one to go. Francis had wanted me to type a report for him. He was going to London and would pick it up from the office before he took the early train. I finished it about eight o'clock. Then, as I went out I saw the light still on under Ralph's door. I stuck my head round to say goodnight to him. I quite often did. He was sitting at his desk, perusing some papers. For a second or two when I opened the door, he didn't realize I was there. I remember thinking how handsome and serious – even sad – he looked. Then I rattled the door handle and said I was going home. He glanced up and smiled at me and blew me a kiss, in that way he had. He said, "Ah, lovely Rose, goodnight. This bud of love may prove a beauteous flower when next we meet." He liked to say such things. My name set him off, I think. It was a quote. From *Romeo and Juliet*. It didn't mean anything. He was always quoting poetry.' She took out the hanky again and softly blew her nose. 'I'm sorry. It still upsets me to think about it, even though it was years ago.'

I nodded and patted her hand. It was slightly disturbing to see how brittle was this apparently self-assured epitome of the efficient secretary. She ploughed on, lost in her recollections. 'There was an inquest, of course, and Francis and I had to give evidence. The coroner was old man Forster – retired now, of course. I'd known him since I was a girl when he was the junior partner in my father's practice, so it was all very amicable. But that's how it became common knowledge that Francis and Ralph had had the, the disagreement. Francis was so upset that, as he said, his last words with his partner had been a trivial argument over some matter to do with the practice, the substance of which he couldn't even remember. Then there was the policeman who found the wreckage. There weren't any skid marks. He'd gone clean through the wooden fence. Some of the corners had metal barriers but it hadn't been considered necessary at that one. They put one up soon afterwards, though. And there was the doctor who'd examined him. Poor Ralph had died instantaneously from multiple injuries. No evidence of drink or drugs – as if there would have been.

'The coroner said what a tragedy it was that an accident had deprived the community of such a worthy member.' Again the handkerchief appeared. The dabbing and the blowing were conducted more vigorously as if to dispel the weepy air which had gathered over the table. She rallied and was her office self once more. 'Goodness, look at the time. We'll be shot. And I shall see that arch little person Julie in Reception giggling to herself if I'm late.'

We walked back along the Horsemarket. 'It must have been a shattering experience for the whole firm,' I said, now more intrigued by the matter.

'Oh, it was. Absolutely. But Francis was so wonderfully strong and calm. He held us all together, reassured the clients – we lost a few of Ralph's of course, but not as many as we had feared, and none of the majors. In fact since then, we've gone from strength to strength. We did have some staff leave. Mary, his secretary, she was devastated, poor girl.'

'I'm not surprised.'

'Now, you will remember what I said. Francis doesn't like to talk about it, and he's made it clear he doesn't want anyone else to. It's the past as far as he's concerned. Francis is a man of the present and the future.'

'Don't worry, Rose. I shan't bring it up. I'm the future, too.'

And I really thought I was.

# III

'Still beavering away, Sarah? You know we'll have to start calling you the lady with the lamp: the desk lamp, that is. You know how the song goes: By the light of the Anglepoise lamp, we love to...'

'Thanks for the serenade, Mark. Was there something you needed?'

'Only the gracious favour of your presence at a small soirée being even now assembled by myself and my colleagues.'

'You're going to the pub?'

'They don't call you laser-brain for nothing. Yes. We are about to adjourn after a hard week in the service of our employer to the quaintly named Coffee House Hotel, with the object of consuming alcoholic beverages upon the said premises.'

'I told you before. I don't really like pubs.'

'The Coffee House is not a pub. It's an institution. Come on, Sarah.

You've been here, what is it? Can it be three weeks? And you've never yet joined the Friday nighters. You're not really a *prima donna borissima*, are you?'

I put down the Biro and smiled. 'No, I'm really not. Okay, I'll come. You and your roguish charm have goaded me into it. Give me a minute or two.'

'Great.' His boyish face broke into a huge grin. 'Grrrreat. You've just won me a tenner.'

'What, you had a bet that . . . ?'

'Afraid so. I was the only one with the steely nerve to accept the challenge. Hurry up, now. We'll see you in the lobby.' The head withdrew from the doorway before I could find anything to throw at it.

I was glad that Mark Oundsworth had interrupted me. I was turning into a worse workaholic than my boss. Every day of those first weeks, I had worked late in my new office. During the day the phone rang constantly, post arrived in bundles, demanding instant replies, and there were progress and familiarization meetings with the Chewton sales staff to attend. There was so much to do and to learn. Only in the evenings was there the time to consolidate and record the frantic activity of the day, checking every plot file scattered around my office to ensure that their stages had been entered up on the computer record system, making a list of ones that needed to be chased, weeding out the ones on which all matters had been completed so that they could be consigned to the storeroom in the basement, known in office lingo as Dead Filing.

Already my reorganization of the house sales was paying off. For the first time, the meetings with the Chewton sales director and his assistants were conducted not with reams of useless computer print-out but with properly targeted analyses. I'd discovered that the computer program we used had a much greater capacity to produce management information than had been realized. Now, when I went into the meetings – which always started on time, not at least half an hour late as they had under Appleby – the sales team didn't loll around cracking silly jokes but sat up and paid attention.

I wasn't put out by this workload. I hadn't expected anything else. More than that, I felt I had to prove myself in the macho atmosphere of the firm. So I pestered Appleby constantly to give me more work, more demanding work. He'd look at me curiously on these occasions, his manner oddly hesitant, then he'd fob me off by saying I had enough to get on with. I felt that he ought to have been pleased that I was so keen, that I was willing to work far longer hours than the ones for which I was nominally paid. But he seemed more irritated than gratified.

There was such a thing as overdoing it, however. I deserved a night out. As I brushed my hair in the harshly lit loo, I saw in the glass the dark circles under my eyes. But they were old companions. I couldn't blame them entirely on Chamberlayne's.

When I got out of the lift there was a raggedly ironic cheer from the three men standing in front of the doors.

Mark whistled the first few bars of 'The Entry of the Queen of Sheba', and all three bowed deeply. In return, I inclined my regal brow in stern acknowledgement. Then with each arm taken by the arm of an ardent admirer, with another pretending to carry my train, we swept out into the bright lights of the Horsemarket.

Five minutes later I was sitting on a faded plum velvet bench seat in one of the many bars of the Coffee House and Mark was handing out drinks. 'Tomato juice, Sarah. A bloodless Mary, I suppose? Live dangerously, eh?'

'Don't forget I asked for double Worcestershire sauce. I'm not a great drinker, I told you.'

'Perhaps you're great at something else?'

I ignored this and looked around. 'You were right. This is an amazing place.'

The Coffee House sat like a red-brick ogre's castle, all pointy-topped towers and towering chimneys opposite the High Cross on the end of Corn Street. There had once upon a time been a real Coffee House on the site, where the men of the town had met to conduct business, but there was nothing left of the original building. A few framed black-and-white engravings in the lobby depicted it as it had been in the eighteenth century: cottagey and quaint with funny little windows. It had all been ripped down in late Victorian times and rebuilt with massive high-ceilinged rooms, wide elaborately balustraded staircases and long corridors. I had seen that one of the bars we passed as we came in – the Gleneagles – was got up like a baronial hall, all wood-panelled with stags' heads staring glassily from the walls, and hunting prints and old firearms. We were in the Grand Saloon, the biggest room of all, and everywhere there was the gleam of highly polished brass, the glow of mahogany and the glitter from the innumerable facets of cut glass, on the panels of the many doors, the snob-screens of the bar and the chandeliers.

In the day time, apparently, the professional men of the town still gathered for business lunches, as if in fond memory of the old place's beginnings, but in the evenings commerce gave way to hedonism. It was packed with a predominantly young crowd: smart, self-assured young men in suits and glammy girls in slinky dresses or shiny pants suits, Fernsford's gilded youth who seemed all to be doing very nicely, thank you. Not quite the champagne of the City wine bars, but getting on that way. From somewhere below there rose above the hubbub the thump thump of some heavy rock music.

My other two companions, fellow assistant solicitors James Huxley and David Fromberg, were deep in some discussion about football. There had been plainly some agreement beforehand that the lucky winner got to monopolize my company for at least part of the evening. I sipped the juice and smiled at Mark. 'You were right to winkle me out. I was getting a bit reclusive.'

'You certainly gave that impression. But no, I said, anyone who looks like that can't be entirely dullsville.'

I didn't ask him what he meant by 'like that'. I didn't need to go fishing for compliments. I said, 'How long have you been with the firm, Mark? Rose said something the other day that indicated it wasn't long.'

'Rose. Oh, well.' He seemed about to say more but obviously thought better of it. 'No, only about six months. I was inveigled down from London by an offer I couldn't refuse.'

'London? Who were you with?'

'Dansom and Randall Bond.'

'Really?' I was quite impressed. They were one of the more prestigious City firms. If he had left them, it must have been a good offer.

'What about you? Didn't I hear that you were in Town too?'

'Yes. Vardy, Leadbetter.'

'I'm not sure I've heard of them. Not City, I think. West End?'

'Hoxton.'

He was too well brought up to let his amazement show more than a little. 'I see. Shit-hot conveyancer were you?'

'Not exactly. I did some, but mainly I specialized in matrimonial, child custody and domestic violence. Legal Aid stuff, of course.'

This time he almost choked on his beer. 'Legal Aid. Appleby thinks Legal Aid is the work of the devil. What on earth did you do? Offer special favours?'

I stood up, took out my purse and put a few coins on the table. 'Good night, then. That's for the drink.'

He scrambled to his feet and grabbed my arm. 'Hey, look, that was a joke. Don't get in a huff. Please.'

We had attracted the attention of the soccer buffs. 'Sarah, what's this? You're not leaving already?' said David. 'What have you been doing to her, Oundsworth? Exposing yourself?'

'It can't be that. *De minimis non curat lex*, don't you know,' drawled James.

I laughed, despite my annoyance. 'No, I'm just going to the loo.' I flipped down a few more coins. 'And that's my contribution to the kitty.'

When I got back, James had gone. 'Saw some girl he knows,' explained Mark. 'He hopes you understand.'

'It's hard but I'll try.'

There was a new face at the table. He stood up politely and we shook hands. 'Tom Parsons. I'm at Buckingham's. I have the misfortune to play this character at squash on Wednesday lunchtimes. He always beats me.'

Mark laughed. 'He drinks too much. Look at that flab. A common fault in our profession, eh?'

Parsons was a ruddy-faced, heavily built outdoor type. 'There's no flab. Solid muscle. I was ploughing my father's fields when you poor suburban boys were poisoning yourselves with traffic fumes. Get you on the rugger pitch. That'd show you what's what.'

Mark made a face. 'No, thanks. We could try tennis, though. What about you, Sarah?'

'I'm afraid not. I've spent most of my life under the impression that squash was a drink. As for tennis, netball was the only thing on offer at my school.'

'Oh dear. Deprived childhood, was it?'

'Yes, it was, actually.'

There was a silence. Whoops. There I went again, showing off the chip on my shoulder, gleaming white as if newly cut. I bit my lip. Grow up, Sarah. But that was the trouble. I felt too grown-up. I suddenly felt about a hundred years old, amongst these fresh-faced boys, with their middle-class upbringing and their – it was hard to avoid the word – ignorance of people like me.

Only David Fromberg's searching dark eyes gave a hint that he felt something more than embarrassment at a social *faux pas*. He scooped some money from the table and went off to get more drinks.

It was Parsons the farmer's son who got us going again. 'I say, that Chewton's making big waves these days, isn't he? Big city development projects here, country house conversions there, not to mention housing estates from here to Land's End. Every time I pick up the paper he's done something else. What a man. The Midas of Fernsford. Isn't that what the *Evening Packet* calls him, in all seriousness? Must keep even Appleby on his toes. At my firm, we positively discourage our clients from being so hyperactive.'

Mark snorted. 'I don't think they need much discouragement. They're half-dead, aren't they, all those feudal landowners and widows on their jointures? And there are the ones that really are dead: the trusts and so on. I bet you could work for ages at your firm and not meet a living client.'

'There's some truth in that, on Giles's side of things. But the ones I deal with are very much alive. And there's more to agricultural law than you'd think. But then I would say that, I suppose. I was practically born to it. But anyway, we'll happily leave Chewton to you boys. Giles Matravers thinks he's hopelessly vulgar.'

'Matravers is a fossil. If I were you, I'd be looking for a move. Buckingham's will be as dead as its clients in five years' time. The game's over for these small, private-client outfits. Say what you like about Appleby, he's got his eyes on the future.'

'I say, now, hold on. Not everyone wants to entrust their affairs to the likes of Appleby. He and Chewton are well suited if you ask me. Not to mention some of the characters he's introduced to your firm. Not exactly the cream of society. And does it make such brilliant commercial sense to get so hooked into the work and connections of just one client? I've heard it said that his partners are not so pleased to be dragged down the Chewton road. Perhaps we'll see a parting of the ways before too long?'

Mark had gone quite pale. Perhaps he was thinking fondly of the cast-iron blue-blood certainties of his old firm. 'I should be careful what you say, Tom. No one likes a rumour-monger. And, of course, it's completely untrue.'

'Really? Well, I should tell your man Peterson that. Apparently he was quite tired and emotional at a dinner party the other day. Let slip some of his concerns. Wise up, Mark. The affairs of your firm aren't altogether as hunky dory as the fancy furniture and the shiny computers make them appear. Okay, Buckingham's may not be high-tech, but it's not about to embark on a civil war.'

I spoke brightly into the opening crevasse of hostility. 'Well, I must say I'm finding my work very exciting. Quite different from what I was doing in London.'

Mark grunted an excuse and disappeared in the direction of the loos.

'And what was that?'

I told him. He smiled politely. Then he said, 'That must be useful experience for working for someone like Appleby.'

'I don't understand what you mean.'

'I'll bet you do. But then again, perhaps you don't. Perhaps you haven't seen him unmasked yet.' He looked up as Mark sat down again. 'Mark has, though.'

'Has what?'

'Seen Lucifer in all his glory, revealing why he has for many years been the undisputed winner of the Fernsford Law Society's Unofficial Gold Medal for the rudest, nastiest bastard in the city's legal profession.'

'That's uncalled for, Tom. Appleby can be abrupt, that's true, but . . .'

'That's not what you said last week. You were really slamming the rubber at the squash court, quite uncharacteristically, I thought. An elegant display of athletic advantage is your usual number. I remember I remarked on it and you said . . .'

'I know what I said. I was in a bit of a mood.'

'A bit! Go on, tell Sarah. No? All right, then I will. He said "I wish to Christ this was one of Appleby's."'

I nearly choked on my juice. Mark's face was brick-red with furious embarrassment. He said, 'Look, Tom, let's drop this, shall we? I don't know why you're suddenly coming out with all this. Are you bloody pissed or something?'

Fortunately, at this point, David came back with more drinks. 'Sorry to be so long. It's so crowded. It's like being back in the City.'

He sat down next to me and I turned to him, glad to be out of the gladiatorial combat shaping up opposite. 'You're from the Big Smoke as well, David?'

'Isn't it obvious? How many Jews do you meet in this dump?'

'So why did you move?'

'Sarah, it's a short story. I'm a good lawyer. But I was in the family firm. Same old clients: the companies and the people I'd heard my uncle and my cousins, my grandfather, even, talk about when I was at school. I felt it was all too easy. Here, I'm on my own. No one knows me, no one owes me a living. And there's a lot of money here, and more to come. More and more companies moving here, wanting what they call "quality of life" for themselves and their employees. And I had the promise of a partnership quicker than in Town. My father was, of course, furious. "What do you want to bury yourself there for?" he said. "Fernsford? What's that? Stay with your uncle. It's a good firm. You've got prospects."'

'But Appleby's were better. Do you still think that?'

'Ask me in three months' time. What about you? Are you pleased you made the move?'

I said with genuine, albeit slightly wavering, enthusiasm, 'Yes. It's very exciting.'

To everyone's relief, Tom Parsons swallowed the rest of his pint and waved a chubby hand in farewell. Mark cut in. 'Better than battered women, eh?'

It was what I thought myself, of course, but, somehow, hearing it from the mouth of this cocky son of the establishment, it sounded all wrong. They were my private reasons. I said: 'I'm not ashamed of the work I did. In fact it was a good deal more valuable than helping rich men get even richer. I don't expect you to understand that. Or to appreciate that there was an emotional cost to me. It wasn't a decision I made lightly, you know.'

They both looked uncomfortable again. They weren't used to this talk of emotions, I could see that. Typical bloody woman to mess up a jolly evening. Well, tough. They'd have to get used to having me around.

I looked across at the empty glasses. 'My turn to get them in, isn't it?'

It turned out to be the last round. After a desultory, determinedly non-controversial chat about the entertainments and activities planned for the weekend – a family wedding in Town for David; unspecified loafing for Mark – the party broke up.

We said our goodbyes in the doorway. As I thought he would, Mark said, 'Can I give you a lift home? I'm going your way.'

'I didn't tell you where I lived.'

He coughed nervously. 'Well, Julie in reception sort of mentioned that you'd got a flat near the park, and as I live out on the Welscombe Road...'

I thought, but didn't say, bloody nerve to check up on me like that. But it would save me the cab fare.

We walked back towards his car, which was parked in the multi-storey car park behind the Horsemarket. There was a slightly awkward silence as we turned off the brightly lit thoroughfare into a narrow cobbled street.

'Mark, do you think there's any truth in what Tom Parsons was saying this evening?'

'About the firm? No, I don't. It's simply professional jealousy if you ask me. Have you seen Buckingham's? It's like something out of Dickens. Appleby can be abrasive, and no doubt the partners have their differences, but so what? I work closely with Meredith Jones and he's never said a word about anything major. There's plenty of good work there. Let's forget about it for now. If Parsons continues though, Appleby'll have to get Giles to rein him in.'

We walked into the dimly lit concrete building, and found Mark's GTi. He opened the door for me and climbed in himself. We sat in the dark car, but he made no move to start it up. Then he said, 'I'm sorry about my crass remark earlier – about you and Appleby. It was just a joke, honestly.'

'Maybe I was over-sensitive.'

'I really was surprised though, when you told me about, where was it? Hoxton. I mean, David and I were in the City and even James, who likes to play the hooray Henry, is no fool underneath – a first at Oxford, in fact, and came here from Paston, Porter, Tankerville in Marylebone.'

'So you're saying my low-achieving status doesn't fit the high-flying profile, is that it? Mark, if that's the way you apologize, I think I prefer being insulted.'

45

He reached out and grabbed my arm. 'Oh, hell. I didn't mean it that way. You're taking it all wrong.'

I shook off the arm. 'I don't know how else to take it. Why don't you ask Appleby why he appointed me if you think it's so bloody amazing. I'm sure he'll be only too glad to explain the firm's recruitment policy to one of his assistants. Now, does this pretty car of yours actually have an engine?'

We drove the short distance to Fernsbank Park in silence.

'You can drop me here on the corner, by the postbox.'

He braked, drew into the kerb and turned off the engine. When I put out my hand to the door handle, he reached out and touched my wrist. 'Okay. Am I forgiven now? If you ask me in for coffee, I'll tell you how impressed everybody is by you, despite ... well, you know. That's what I was trying to tell you in my clumsy way.'

For a moment I was speechless at his nerve. Then I laughed and said, 'Yes, all right, I forgive you. But not for long, mind. I'm going into the office tomorrow, so I'm not staying up late.'

'That suits me.'

Something about the smirking alacrity with which he spoke alerted me to how incautiously I'd spoken. I was out of practice in this kind of situation.

I shook off his hand, reached up and switched on the interior light. His face was all smooth curves in the dull glow from the tiny bulb and his dark blond hair had the sheen of old gold. 'Mark. I think we have to get some things straight at the beginning. We are grown-ups and professional colleagues. I admit I may be quite wrong about what you had in mind tonight.' I held up my hand to forestall his attempt to reply. 'No, please listen. But, just in case, I have to say that I don't want my career with this firm muddled up with a sexual relationship, ongoing or finished with. It may be that I'm misjudging you. If so, I'm sorry.'

He shrugged. 'I'm only human. You're an extremely desirable woman. Of course, what you've said is all very rational, you think that in your mind but ...'

I disengaged gently from the arm that was beginning to encircle my shoulders. 'Good night, Mark. Thanks for the lift.' I pushed open the door, slipped out of the car, and leaving it open, I walked quickly – but not too quickly – down the street. Behind me I heard the sound of a car door being slammed, and then after a short pause the roar of an engine. I stopped and turned to see the dark shape accelerate rapidly away, its tyres squealing.

How bloody typical! 'You think that in your mind, but...' But I know what you really want. That's what they all said, wasn't it? Women don't know their own minds. They need a man to help them. To help them give the man what he wanted. Well, to hell with it. I wasn't going to risk my job for the sake of a quick screw. When office relationships went sour, it was never the man who had to leave, was it?

I was too angry and agitated to go to bed. I made myself coffee, kicked off my shoes and slumped crossly in my armchair. But it wasn't Mark's advances which had made me upset. He was a pussy cat, an overgrown kid. Probably he was only trying it on to bolster his sexual ego. Besides, I was on my own in a strange town and he was nice, blast it. In other circumstances...

No, it was the conversation in the pub. That talk of high-flyers from London, the obvious amazement that I wasn't one of them. It reawakened the anxiety I'd felt – that I wasn't up to a job like that in a place so different from London.

When I got back to Hoxton after the interview, my work had seemed comfortingly familiar and my boss, Tim Pogson, whose haphazard working methods used to drive me crazy, a paragon of kindness and reasonableness. I'd begun to think I'd be mad to think of leaving. Even when I'd been kicking myself over a domestic violence case where the client had bottled out at the last minute and left me with egg on my face, he'd been sympathetic, in his paternalistic way.

'You'll get over it. You know what they say, a lawyer's worst enemy is his client. Sarah, I won't tell you I told you so. Blood's thicker than water. When it comes to it, some of 'em, they won't shop the old man.'

He'd leaned towards me over the paper-strewn chaos of his ancient desk, brushing crumbs off his grubby shirt front, and running a stubby-fingered hand through his uncombed mat of black hair.

'Sarah, your articles will be finished at the end of next week. Time's getting on. Have you thought any more about our very generous offer? We made a big investment in you, Sarah, and you've justified our faith and at least some of our money. Who knows, after a few years, you get in some decent work, there might be a partnership. I can't promise, but...'

It was my chance to settle my future. I'd heard nothing from Fernsford.

I didn't expect to hear anything positive. Nor had I had any reply from the other crummy hicksville firms to whom I'd sent my CV. I should stick with what I had.

But despite that, I still hesitated. I said, 'Can I think about it a bit longer?'

With Pogson, there was always a fine line between his joviality and his irascibility and despite my ultra-mild response I had yet again managed to cross it. 'Think? What's there to think about? It's a good offer.' He gave me one of his shrewd looks. 'You haven't had better?'

I'd not told him about Fernsford. I couldn't put it off any longer.

He was genuinely stunned. 'Leave London? Have you gone crazy? You couldn't leave London.'

'I didn't say I was going to. I haven't been offered the job. But whyever not? London's not the world.'

'Sarah. Believe me. It is, as far as the law is concerned. It all happens here. You're a Londoner, like me. You wouldn't feel right in a place like Fernsford. The grass isn't greener. It's only a phase.'

He'd been furious, then sulky like a child, when I told him only a few days later that I'd been made an offer by Chamberlayne's and had accepted. I would leave immediately my articles were over.

'You're making a mistake,' he'd shouted.

And I'd coloured up and been furious and childish too.

'No, I'm not. I'm absolutely not!' Then damn and blast it, I'd spoilt the effect by bursting into tears.

Through my sobs, I heard myself saying, 'I have to take this job, Tim. You can't understand why. I have to. I have to.'

I drank up the coffee. No, I couldn't have told him why.

Stuff Pogson. He was the past. I did have a bright future. Whatever was said about Appleby by those half-pissed boys in the pub, he was my passport to a better life. I had a lot to be pleased with myself about. I was going to stick at it. Maybe I didn't have the flashy public-school and Oxbridge education of the rest of them, but I worked as hard and I was going to work harder. I'd bloody well show them.

And hadn't I already had some of the rewards? I looked around the room.

I had loved the flat in Lochinvar Road the minute I had seen it. It was on the first floor of a smallish late-Victorian house in one of the wide tree-lined streets which led from the Welscombe Road to Fernsbank Park.

The ground-floor flat was occupied by Mrs Carter, a short elderly woman whom I saw only occasionally and never heard at all. She also had the small front and rear gardens. She filled them with miniature conifers, tiny plastic-lined ponds and garden gnomes. This was a pity. I thought longingly of a garden of my own — even a paved courtyard would be nice — but I couldn't have everything at once. What I had was, compared to what I had been used to, wonderful.

I loved the front room. It was this room which had made me want the flat. It was quite large, with a high ceiling with a central plasterwork rose, and an elaborate cornice of intertwined fruits and flowers. It was decorated with, to me, pleasing austerity: white walls, ceilings and woodwork, plain beige fitted carpet without too many stains, brownish and ancient but inoffensively plain curtains and no gewgaws at all.

I had moved the double bed in here from the room at the back. I had no wish to wake up in dark pokiness when I could have light. I stared at the bed in which I now slept alone. Alone.

I was free of London, but the memories still lingered. Colin, oh Colin! How could it have ended like that? How and by what slow degrees had it gone sour? Was it when he had been disappointed of the Research Fellowship at Imperial College, at the same time as I was full of my new-found skills at Vardy's? Was it when his demonstratorship at King's wasn't renewed and I became the breadwinner? Or was it when, unemployed, he became so obsessed with playing and inventing computer games that he virtually ceased to be a communicating human being?

Whatever the reasons, it had ended in bitterness and recriminations. I shuddered as I remembered our final scene. How could we have said such things when we had once cared so much?

But that was what you got from loving and trusting, wasn't it? Why had I thought that Colin was any different? Why had I forgotten the lessons I had learned as a child? Love no one, trust no one. They had been hard lessons. Oh, so hard. I wouldn't forget them again.

# IV

Moonlight silvered the surface of the water, mirror-still but for the ripples from the skeletal fingers of the willows as they dipped and withdrew. The dark figure of a man crouching on the canal bank rose to his feet and slowly moved towards me. I could hear the crunch of his boots on the gravel.

I could only watch as he increased his pace, for I was rooted like the willows, but in terror. Now he was running towards me, panting like an animal. Somehow I was free and running too. But fast as I ran he gained on me. Like the wind I was running, my feet scarcely touching the ground, as if I were flying. But always at my back, I heard the pounding feet and the laboured breath.

Then, at my shoulder, I felt a bony grasp turning me to face him, with his white, strained face and staring eyes. I was screaming at him. Leave me alone. Alone. Then his voice, deep and distant, as if from the grave. I'll see you again. Again. Again . . .

I woke up bathed in sweat. Christ, had I really yelled out? Quite often I did, according to Colin. I threw off the duvet and, shivering, went to the window.

In the street, the ground floors of the houses opposite were in darkness. Only in a few curtained upper windows were lights showing. Perhaps they were nightlights set by parents for their nervous children. No one was leaning out in anxious fascination to see who was being murdered. Not a wakeful sound came from my neighbour below. All was perfect suburban peace.

The tears started to my eyes. I felt like an alien observer, cut off from this quiet humanity. I wept for myself, and for love lost so long ago; it was less memory than dream, love that I would never find again.

I went back to bed but I couldn't sleep. It wasn't only the nightmare. I was thinking about what had happened in London a month before. When the dark figure had stepped out of my nightmares, back into my life.

\*

It was on a balmy and tranquil summer evening, a few days after my talk with Pogson. At the City Road, as I emerged from the tube station, the setting sun gilded the walls of the Angel, Islington, turning its domed turret into the keep of a fairytale castle.

I'd left the bedsit I shared with Colin, and was camping temporarily in a far nicer flat in Duncan Terrace owned by a woman lawyer I knew, who was working in Brussels for three months.

I stood at the top of the steps which bridged the area, fumbling in my handbag for the keys. They had fallen to the bottom and disappeared in a swamp of used tissues, old envelopes and sweet wrappers.

I was so intent on my search that I wasn't aware of the figure climbing up to stand behind me.

Then it spoke.

'Hello, Pippi Longstocking.'

I dropped the bag in my surprise and whirled round.

'Jesus Christ Almighty.' Impelled by some atavistic instinct, my right hand flew up to my forehead. It was all I could do to stop myself from completing the gesture and making the sign of the cross, something I had not done for years, and fervently believed I never would again. I gaped at the dark shape, my heart thudding against my breastbone with the sickening impact of a trapped bird at a window. I could feel that my face had drained of blood to take on the eerie whiteness that had so scared the teachers at school when I went into one of my violent fits of anger and self-loathing.

He made light of the effect his manifestation had had on me. 'That's a fine greeting for your own father, who's come back, as you might say, from the dead.'

The cool arrogance of the man would have been stunning in itself had I not already been made speechless by the shock. I struggled to control the shuddering in my whole body, taking long slow breaths as if I were recovering from extreme exertion. Then I said, in as clear and insouciant a tone as I could muster, 'Is that where you've been then?'

'It was time to see you again. There's been a lot of words said and a lot of things done. But I'm still your dad. Aren't you going to ask me in for a cup of tea even?'

I sank down into a squat to pick up my bag. It was almost dark but in the dim light from the fanlight over the door, I could see the scuff marks on the heavy workman's boots and the earth-encrusted bottoms of the jeans he wore.

I stood up again, taller than he by half a head. I took a deep breath. 'Won't you step in, sir?' I said.

I sat him down on the sofa and then went into the kitchen to make the tea. I didn't want him to see how my hands still shook, making the china rattle on the laminate work surface. But he was ill at ease and restless, and after a moment got up and followed me, stopping in the open doorway of the tiny gallery, and leaning against the door jamb.

'This is not a bad place you've got here. Not done at all badly for yourself, eh? Of course, there's these opportunities these days.'

'If you say so. I can't say as I've had many of them. Mum and I had nothing after you left. Not that we had much before, I suppose.'

'Ah, now, I admit that. There was no great plenitude about the place. I'm full of regret for leaving in that state. For years, I've wanted to make it up to you, but somehow there was never the opportunity.'

I handed him a steaming mug and took my own mug back into the living room. I sat down in the chair by the window. It was just getting dark, the bluish orange-tinted dark of the city. A few pale stars glittered over the rooftops of the terrace opposite. He hovered about, then finally lowered himself into the sofa.

I stared pointedly at the workman's boots, the filthy jeans and the threadbare blue donkey jacket. 'Now you've made your millions, you've come back to compensate me.'

For a moment I thought I had gone too far. The fingers which encircled the mug tightened visibly. But I stared back at him, conscious that I was no longer a little girl, but a tall, strong, grown woman. And as the old fear gripped and wrung my heart, I kept repeating to myself, 'I must never show it. Never. Never.' Why, oh why, had I let him in? Why hadn't I told him to go right back to hell, where he belonged? But my fierce pride was not the answer. If I had done that I would have shown him the depth of my fear, far beyond the superficial alarm at his reappearance. I would have shown him that it was not an ordinary distaste for him that had endured over the years. He would see that I was in mortal terror of him. And if he saw that, he would know why.

'You're hard on me, Sarah, my love. Like your mam was. You know, I suffered too. Oh, you may make mock of my condition, for I'm a poor shambling shadow of the man I once was. For God's sake, I'm fifteen years older. And I've precious little to show for it at the present time. At the present time, mind.'

'What the hell do you want?' I felt my face flushing, and the fear inside was writhing so hard I felt I was going to be sick. I drank some tea and the heat of it inside me drove back some of the demons.

'Want? Is it so surprising I want to see my own daughter after fifteen years? Do you know there was a time when the only thing that kept me from going stark mad and topping myself was that I had a photograph of you? A beautiful little girl, just as you're now a beautiful grown woman. I used to look at that picture every night. It helped me to survive in ... that place where I was, when every night there was screaming and crying and hollering. That picture made me realize what it was I had lost. And I said to myself, I'd come back and find it.'

'You were inside, then.'

'There's no deceiving you, is there, Pippi? You always were a sharp one. You take after me, you see. There was none of that in your mam, bless her. You're my daughter. I've kept that photograph. Shall I show it to you?'

I had no words. I felt my mouth hanging open. I clutched the mug and stared down into the pool of brown liquid with its greasy scum of milk.

When I looked up he was leaning over me, his red hand, its skin so thick and calloused it looked impossible to clench, holding in thumb and forefinger, with as much delicacy as it could command, a small colour snapshot of a little red-haired girl in jeans and a Mickey Mouse T-shirt. It was much creased and frayed at the edges, so I could believe his story of the handling it had got.

'There you are. Four years old you were. Taken at Trent Park, it was.'

As I looked at that little girl, the tears flooded to my eyes.

I felt the big leather hand grip my shoulder and my flesh recoiled so violently I flung myself out of the chair and stood with my back to the window. I said before I could think, spacing each word as if it were a separate sentence, 'Don't touch me. Don't ever touch me.'

He stood watching me; his face, which had once been a full-fleshed oval, bisected by the long nose – my own inheritance – now sunk in, stretched over sharp bones at the forehead and cheeks, with broken veins, dull scarlet tracks in a waste of pale parchment and grey stubble. His grey eyes had always had that capacity to switch from bright openness to hooded secrecy when he was brewing some slight or anger, as if he had withdrawn within to consult some inner prompting. I saw them occluded now, with wrinkled lids like those of an ancient vulture I had once seen lurking at the back of a cage in London zoo. His thin bloodless lips were twisted in a smile of terrible contempt. He took a step towards me and I felt behind me, hoping that somewhere to hand there would miraculously be something I could use as a weapon.

There was nothing. I stood waiting, my legs braced apart, the window sill a hard line against my bottom. I never once let my gaze wander from those half-closed eyes. How long we stood there I don't know, he leaning forward as if his body were arrested in the grip of some contrary force.

Then, gradually, his stance and his face relaxed, and his eyes opened. His smile was now hesitant and rueful. 'A woman does have a way of angering a man my darling. A woman doesn't know what a man goes through when he's provoked. She doesn't comprehend the black bitter tide that rises up and washes away your mind's foundation. You don't understand how hard it is to resist. But you being a child no longer, but a grown woman, you surely must come to appreciate it. Otherwise it'll go hard with you when you join yourself to a man. Maybe it has already. Now I've come back to you in peace and reconciliation and you throw it back in my face. A fatherly hand, and you spurn it. As if I'd ever willingly hurt you, my favourite child. When did I ever do that?'

I didn't reply. Had the jagged, rocky realities of the past really been worn away and dissolved by time, creating in his mind only this pebble-smooth fantasy?

'Well, then. Let's sit down and continue our talk. You know how I love the talk.' He bent down to the carpet to pick up the photograph which he had earlier dropped. He brushed it against his sleeve to remove any trace of dust before tucking it carefully back in a compartment of his wallet.

I sank warily down into the armchair, gripping the upholstery to control my hands, and he again took the sofa opposite.

'How long were you ... ?'

'In prison? In the circle of hell? Nearly seven years. And for what, you might ask? For being on the scrap heap. For having my reputation destroyed by calumny. For being too old to earn an honest penny. For being a casualty of society. For needing a crust and a wet to keep body and soul together.'

'You don't get that long for nicking your dinner from a supermarket.'

'No, you're right. The solicitor is right. But it was not me that carried the shooter or pulled the trigger. And anyway, it was himself Tommy, the stupid fool, shot, in the foot, when that bastard jumped him. And like an even bigger fool I stayed to help.'

'Armed robbery. What was it – a post office, building society? It wouldn't be a bank or a security van, would it? Not for a couple of amateurs.'

'Oh, you think you're smart, don't you? Amateurs, is it? Well, we had a better run of it than some of these so-called professional fellers who end up in the gutter, blown away by trigger-happy bastards in an ARV. Oh, yes, indeed, we'd done banks, security deposits. A real team we were. It was bad luck, that's all. A nice little building society, a holiday, like, in between the hard work. Like we'd done a half-dozen times before. Only this time, the smart-arse behind the desk, a rugby player I don't doubt, vaults clean over and grabs the sawn-off. The judge said that it was only because of his public-spirited action that two dangerous and unscrupulous criminals would be put away for a substantial period. He gave Tommy fifteen, you know. He's still in the Scrubs now. And aren't I counting the days now when he's out.'

It was a story I'd heard at Vardy's a score of times. And thinking of him that way, I began for the first time to relax a little. He was an old lag, that was all. Think of it like that. Nothing to do with me. The horror I had felt when his heavy hand rested on my shoulder was but a memory of another life, a life that was buried deep, like my mother in the polluted earth of Hendon Cemetery.

'So when did they let you go?'

'Three years ago. That was when I . . . when I found out your mam had died.'

'If you wanted to see me so much, why didn't you do that straight away? Why wait until now?'

He smiled, the ends of his wide mouth – my own mouth, I could see – fluttering upwards in self-satisfied amusement. 'Oh, but I have, darling. I've seen you. Many times. True, I haven't been so bold as to request the pleasure of the time of day with you. But I've seen you often enough. And, like I said, I thought the time was ripe for us to start to get to know one another again.'

I spoke quickly, trying to stifle my mounting panic, trying to seem merely interested by the mechanics of his surveillance, half-believing he was lying to me. 'You can't have been watching me. That's not possible.'

'Oh, it is, there's nothing easier to a fellow who's got a mind to it. When I found you hadn't gone back to Ernie Bevin, I dropped into the Railway one evening and there was Mary Flanagan, as ever was, huddled over a gin and lime in the Snug. She was a little surprised to see me, right enough, but after we'd shed a tear together in memory of your dear mam, she told me you'd taken up with a nice young man from your college. She even had your address on a note you'd written to her after the funeral. She was that touched, she'd kept it in her bag. I said not to mention it if she saw you, I wasn't sure whether I was really going to surprise you after all these years. She was impressed by my delicacy – "But you were always a gentleman, Terry, even when your luck was out," she said. Well I went to see your flat down by the old canal basin. Where was it now? St Peter's Place – that was it. I saw you with your young man on many occasions. I saw your name pinned up on the notice board in that college of yours saying you'd passed your exam. Then you went to another law college for a while. I lost track of you after that – I had urgent business which took me out of London, you see. When I came back, though, I was soon in the know again. That's a good job you've got over in Hoxton. Qualifying soon, and being offered an even better one, they tell me.'

'Who told you? How the hell did you know about that?'

'Well, my darling daughter, I have to confess that one morning I followed you all the way to your office – out of curiosity, of course. And then, I hung around a bit more till dinner time and who do I see come out but a likely looking feller. That there is a drinking man, I says to myself. And, sure enough, he goes into a pub, and we get into conversation, like. You know what a powerful man I am for the talk. When I was in the Scrubs I learned it can save your life, being a good talker. A man who can spin a yarn will always be in demand. Especially if you're also a good listener. So people talk to me. Like your man in the office, for instance. People who normally don't talk to just anybody. Now he's maybe a queer kind of fellow, maybe not one hundred per cent in the head. But I get the distinct impression that he's got a soft spot for you, if that's the right expression. I've seen him a few times. He loves a crack and a pint. He keeps me up to date on your doings. Not, of course, that he so much as suspects who I am. Oh, no. I think he gets his own kind of pleasure just from talking about you.'

'Gordon.' I had a sudden vision of the doggy devotion in the eyes of Vardy, Leadbetter's middle-aged outdoor clerk, whom Tim Pogson had got off a charge of indecent exposure and who had slaved for him with pathetic gratitude ever since.

'I believe that's his name.'

My head was swimming. I felt an awful powerlessness stealing over me as if this were all a dream. I reached out a hand to take some tea to soften my stiffened throat, watching the fingers moving as if they belonged to someone else. 'So you've seen me. You know what I do, how I live. You've talked to me. What now? What else do you want?'

'I don't want anything from you. Like I said, I want to make it up to you. I had so many plans for you, do you know that? If I hadn't had to ... go away so suddenly.'

The choking fear was in my throat again as I saw him watching me closely. I stared back at him, my face as expressionless as I could make it. 'What do you mean, make it up?'

I felt a kind of fascination, despite my fear and hatred of the man.

He waved a finger in hideous playfulness. 'Ah, now that would be telling. All I'll say is that I have great expectations. Did you ever read that book? *Great Expectations* by Charles Dickens?'

I shook my head. 'I don't read much except law books. I never got the habit. Unlike you.'

'Much good it's done me, I suppose. But it was remembering that book made me want to come back to see you.'

'And now you have. But I don't need or want your help, whatever it is. You can have absolutely nothing I want. I've managed well enough on my own. Eventually.' I took a deep breath, and stood up, even more conscious of my height as he sprawled on the sofa. 'I don't want you spying on me any more, or talking to people who know me. I don't want to see you or hear from you ever again. Leave me alone. Is that absolutely clear?'

He held up his hands. 'I can see that it's late, and that you want me to get out of here. Let it never be said that Terry Hartley couldn't take a hint from a lady. Of course, what you say is understandable. It's a bit of a shock, seeing me again like this. Just after your young man left, too. There's been neglect and bitterness for you to cope with since you were a slip of a girl. But not any more. Right now you think, "What the fuck can this tatterdemalion old jail bird dad of mine do for me?" But you'll be surprised one of these days. Give it time. I'll see you again, don't you worry about that. And when you're aware of what it is I'm giving you, you'll be interested, that I'll guarantee. That I'll guarantee. After all, you are my daughter, child.'

I said nothing. His last words wrapped my soul in lead. I wanted to scream: 'I'll take gifts from you when hell freezes over.' But deep within a small voice whispered, 'Oh, you will be interested, my dear.'

After he'd gone, I opened all the windows and let the chill of a rising wind sweep through the rooms of the flat.

His mug was still on the low table in the sitting room. I picked it up and took it through into the kitchen, flipped up the lid of the pedal bin and threw it in. Then I washed my hands.

I ran a deep hot bath and lay in it submerged up to the neck, my long hair floating beside me in the water like the seaweed I had seen in a rock pool on the Cornish beach where we had spent the only family holiday we had ever had.

His words still echoed in my head, the soft drip of them, like water in a cave depositing a cold hard dagger of stone. I'll see you again. And once more I was drawn into the dark vortex of the past.

Pippi Longstocking. I hadn't heard that name for years and years. It made me shudder, despite the warmth of the tub. He had called me it after a children's storybook character, a girl with red hair. Books. Maybe that was why I had hated books and all they represented for so long afterwards. They reminded me of him.

In my early childhood, there had been books around. I remembered the piles of them, thick as blocks of timber. Even when I could read the titles, I couldn't begin to imagine what they were about. *The Brothers Karamazov*; *The Open Society and Its Enemies*; *The Age of Revolution*; *A History of Western Philosophy*. My father, unlike my mother, had always been a reader. At the time I remember him best he had, after all, little else to do. He would come home from the Holloway Public Library with a stack of these volumes. And, he would boast, they weren't just detective stories or thrillers. They were 'the great writers and the great subjects': literature, history, philosophy and politics. Oh, yes, he was a great reader and a great talker. He belonged to a circle of working men like himself who met, he told me, to discuss such weighty subjects every Thursday night in a room above the public bar of the Eagle and Child in Turnpike Lane.

He would sometimes take me with him to the library and encourage me to choose from the selection 'for younger readers'. I vaguely remember the look of the place, high ceilinged and gloomy, but I vividly recall the smell – of damp raincoats and the stale sweat of the old men and women reading newspapers and magazines at the long table, and the musty emanation from the books themselves.

When he was in a good mood, or rather in a mellow mood, my father would read a bedtime story. He had a good voice for reading, oddly soft and caressing if he wished it, and which, having a gift for mimicry, he could modulate into the voices of the characters. It was of those times that I suppose I come closest to having happy childhood memories, snug and drowsy in bed, gazing into the pool of light cast by the bedside lamp, the corners of the room in darkness, my father at the bedside, the book spread out on the coverlet, its bright pictures glowing with colour in a way that nothing else in my life then ever attained.

My father was not Irish, at least not directly. He was born in Liverpool, or so he claimed. My father said once that his mother had been killed by a bomb in the war and that he had been brought up by his grandmother. He never mentioned his father.

He met my mother in Islington, in a pub in York Road. She was fresh off the boat-train from Holyhead. She was living in a boarding house in Camden Town, which is, as they say, a short walk with a heavy suitcase from Euston Station. Not that my mother's would have been heavy. All she would ever say of her childhood in the slums of Dublin was that her mother was dead, and that her father had run off with another woman. I never heard tell of any grandparents.

She was working as a chambermaid in the Great Eastern Hotel, by King's Cross Station. My father had recently returned to shore after spending his youth and early manhood as a merchant seaman. He had a job at the

Guinness brewery at Park Royal, driving a forklift truck. They had courted and married in the space of a few weeks. My mother must have thought that Christmas had come early that year: respectably into the bed of a handsome, charming, employed man who, though born English, claimed to be a good Catholic.

For a while that feeling must have persisted. My father's easy, confident manner with other men, his combination of strength and innate mental ability, initially took him some way up the company ladder into more responsible positions, on the fuzzy borderline between blue and white collar – brown overall, I suppose you'd call them. They were on the waiting list for a council house. When my mother became pregnant, they moved into a brand-new tower-block by Manor House tube station. Ernest Bevin House was one of thousands rushed up all over the country in answer to the housing shortage, gleaming, potent symbols of renewal and a bright future.

This time of hope did not last. My mother would refer to it occasionally when she was full of drunken nostalgia as 'that time when we were all together and all so happy'. I had few such memories. By the time I was five, I knew that we were on the long slide into disaster.

My father, for all his much-vaunted reading, had had no education to speak of. And his interests in intellectual matters were too wide and unrooted in the day to day, too cloudily esoteric to go any way to remedying this defect. He had undertaken no course of study in commercial or technical subjects. I think he had not, in fact, the mental discipline to pursue one. So he preferred to scoff at the diligence of other men, mocking them as dull fools who would never amount to anything. Gradually, though, the dull fools passed him by. He remained a junior storesman, nursing a sense of merit unnoticed, of true quality ignored.

My mother was always evasive about what then occurred. Though she berated my father to his face, she was fiercely loyal when speaking of him to others. He had got mixed up with a bad lot. There had been talk of stock going missing, of invoices for supplies being falsified. Then a lorry loaded with the company's products went missing, together with its driver. The man was known to be a drinking acquaintance of my father. According to her it was all circumstantial, he was as innocent as a new-born babe, and 'don't let anyone at that school tell you different', she'd added.

The police were of a contrary opinion. They came to the flat at the crack of dawn, battered down the door with a sledgehammer and took him away. He was charged with a string of offences and remanded in custody in Pentonville. He was there a long time, as the wheels of justice grind slowly in such run-of-the-mill cases. The punishment is carried out before the trial, so that acquittal is an irrelevance. My father returned from the Inner London Crown Court without, as they say, a stain on his character. But the experience had changed him.

Despite the verdict of the court, the verdict of the personnel officer remained unaltered. My father stayed sacked. He was unemployed for a long time, and with unemployment came depression. And with the depression came increasing dependence on what had always been a powerful prop for him: drink.

Ernie Bevin also went rapidly downhill. It was cold and damp from condensation inside, as the fancy electric underfloor heating didn't work properly and was far too expensive to run even if it had. It was a long way to the ground, down fifteen flights of stairs. The lifts were usually out of action and when they weren't, they stank. There was no place for us kids to play. So, out of sight and earshot of our parents, we ran wild in the yards and car parks and streets. We formed tribal groupings – Blacks, Irish, English. We pelted the opposition with stones when it was dry, mud when it was wet and, in winter, with snowballs filled with broken glass.

My father had schemes in the early days. He would keep out of bad company, get back into work: warehouse or stores, or some similar job. When it came to references though, his past dogged him. Inevitably, he was forced to go back down the employment snake much more quickly than he had come up the ladder. The job he had longest was as a security guard – 'A nightwatchman, you mean,' sneered my mother – in an office complex at the Archway. But he took his bottle to work once too often. After that he had nothing but odd jobs in storage depots, humping crates and picking from shelves, to my knowledge, to the day he left.

Sometimes he would come back after being away for days or even weeks at a time flush with cash. Then he was as light-hearted and as charming as could be. When my mother quizzed him about the source of these funds, he would wag his finger. 'Ask me no questions and I'll tell you no lies,' he'd say with his cheeky smile. And my mother would sigh and grimace, but she would take the money. But then the money would be gone and he'd be slumped all day in the lounge with the TV, dangerously unpredictable, to be avoided at all costs.

My mother had to supply the steady income. She worked as a cleaner, at first charring for the up-and-coming middle class who bought and did up the decrepit townhouses on the fringes of gentrifying Islington, then, as she herself became more sunk in depression and took to the drink herself, for cheapskate office cleaning firms, who paid next to nothing and didn't care about the appearance or the sobriety of their operatives.

I don't ever remember having a child's natural faith in grown-ups. Very early on there must have been innocence and trust but what I actually remember is the constant fear and insecurity as I perceived from close quarters the minute day-to-day deterioration in the personalities and relationship of my parents.

He had become, when sober, a moody and unpredictable man, given to unreasoning bursts of savage rage. In drink, the wounded anger was stanched in acts of physical violence. He began to hit my mother about the face and body, as if by so doing he could batter away the frustration and the misfortune of his wretched life. She was by turns sullenly resigned, or provoked to violent rage, in which her voice became shrill and her tongue spat words of savage contempt. Yet at no time was this discord allowed to pass the threshold of our apartment. To the other inhabitants of Ernie Bevin, members that is of our tribe, particularly the women, my father was a man of elaborate courtesy and teasingly raffish charm. My mother never spoke of her true feelings to her friends, but suffered in silence and alone.

The photographs I've seen of them when young – black-and-white snapshots, he almost handsome in a jaunty kind of way, she petite and darkly pretty, with her full mouth and even fuller figure – show how much had changed with them. For physical passion must have played its part. I can remember Mam telling me when she was more than a bit drunk – she would never have spoken of such things otherwise – that she had told my father that he would never get his way with her 'unless there was a priest to bless the union. And didn't he want it that badly that he proposed there and then.' The only advice she ever gave me was not to surrender my precious jewel without a similar guarantee.

Much good it had done her. In my case her admonitions came too late. I'd already finished my early experimentation and had concluded that sex carried a power out of all proportion to the physical importance the act had to me. I knew already that it was too precious a commodity to be traded for anything as insubstantial as the promise of love.

But the greater irony of my mother's philosophy was her concept of her own role and the role of women generally. Motherhood. Mam was contemptuous of the unmarried and the infertile. She never reflected that her daughter might have her own viewpoint on how successfully she carried out her perceived function. Well, maybe, in other circumstances, she might even have been good enough at it. If she hadn't had to struggle with poverty and the degradation of poverty, with a violent, drunken and depressive husband, and her own depression and alcoholism, she might have made a better fist of bringing us up. She might have had her own horizons lifted beyond the mundaneness of mere existence. She might have learned about something other than suffering. If she had been loved herself, she might have loved us.

Us – the word slipped out sometimes when I thought of those days. How much agony and horror it conjured up for me. For indeed, the Hartley family, despite my mother's tendency to miscarry in the first three months, had had two successful live births. And I, Sarah Mary Magdalene Hartley, was not the first born. No, that was my sister Josephine.

That night also, like so many nights before and since, I had lain in bed, sleepless. But how much worse it had been. It was as if all those childhood horrors had become manifest. The grinning figure at the window was not a trick of the light, the ghastly face in the curtains not the product of an over-active imagination, the lurking presence on the stairs really was crouched to spring. All was horrible actuality.

I kept hearing his voice. 'I'll see you again.' I couldn't face that. I would do anything to avoid it. I would run, abandon my career, everything I had worked for, rather than stay where he could appear before me at will. I had wept into my pillow like the small child I had remembered. And from somewhere in the recesses of my memory had drifted the words of the Psalm: 'Yea, though I walk through the valley of the shadow of death, I shall fear no evil: for thou art with me; thy rod and thy staff they comfort me.'

The letter from Chamberlayne's offering me the job had been waiting on the doormat as I left for the office the next morning. If I'd believed in them, I would then have said it was a miracle. I danced out of the house with the single sheet of white paper held high above my head. I was free, I had escaped.

Fernsford was, I believed, a safe harbour and I steered for it with all the desperation of one who fled before the storm.

# V

It was all too short a time before the euphoria of my escape from London began to seep away, before I began to suspect that my translation to Fernsford had been the kind of miracle that turned water not into wine, but into blood.

The first inklings, like fine cracks in the concrete of a dam, appeared the following Monday when Conrad Peterson ambushed me in the photo-copying room.

After my dreadful night, I didn't go into the office on Saturday. I thought Mark might have made a point of being there, and I didn't want him to start pestering me again.

Instead, I decided to go shopping. All work and no play made Jill a dull girl. There were loads of things I needed. I had brought almost nothing from London. All my worldly goods had fitted into a couple of suitcases. I hadn't yet used my shiny new credit card. As far as the shops of Fernsford were concerned, I was a virgin. It was time to get experienced.

I came back from town in a cab filled with parcels: some cushions in bright primary colours, a batik throw for the faded sofa, some more interesting crocks to replace the things which had come with the flat. I'd bought some new tapes as well, and Bach's Harpsichord Concerto No. 1 was playing as I gazed through the pleasantly irregular Victorian glass of the bay window that evening.

The right-hand pane caught the last rays of the sun. The sky was reddening over the distant wooded hills. In the gardens of the houses opposite, people seemed reluctant to go inside and lose any part of the warm summer's evening. Men in short-sleeved shirts were washing cars and mowing lawns. Children were playing on the plastic-and-metal slides and climbing frames set up by their loving parents. Women stood at their gates chatting with their neighbours. Cats lay on shed roofs, waiting to blend with the dusk.

I smiled as I watched. The previous night seemed far distant. The nightmares, the hallucinations might be the last thrashings of a dying beast. It was safe here. I felt an overwhelming relief that I had journeyed so far from London. That here I was out of reach of the threat which had risen up from the shadows of the past. He would never find me here.

'I say, er, Sarah. Do you think you could give me a hand with this machine? Jane usually does it and I'm not terribly good at...'

He made me jump, coming up behind me like that. I thought for a horrible moment that it was Mark. I'd stuck close to my office that morning, having arrived before anyone else, and told Penny to keep all visitors at bay. I ventured out only at lunchtime, when I thought the office would be empty apart from Julie in Reception.

Conrad was next in line to Appleby in the partnership hierarchy. He was corporate litigation. After him came Meredith Jones, the firm's commercial contracts and European law expert. They were assisted by the two junior partners, Michael Fielding and Brian Richardson. The partners occupied their own suite on the penthouse floor. Generally they kept out of the way of the proletariat. As I did no work on any files except Appleby's, none of them had up to that point displayed any interest in me, other than to give me the time of day when we passed on the stairs or stood in the lift together.

Consequently, I hadn't known Conrad was around. His litigation practice meant he was frequently out at Court. Even when he was in, he rarely deigned to come down from the top floor.

In a profession of workaholics, he was an overachiever. His marriage had recently broken up, largely as a result of his impossible personal timetable – out at six a.m. and rarely back before late evening. He acted for various

West Country industrial companies in negligence or employment cases brought by employees or customers, and was, I understood, an expert negotiator in settling claims at the minimum cost to his clients and their insurers. He also had a substantial portfolio of medium-sized private companies, and dealt with their takeovers, mergers and financing needs. It was all stuff that was either completely over my head or in which I would have instinctively aligned myself with the other side. I couldn't ever see myself setting out to screw down the damages of someone blinded by an exploding factory steam-pipe or the woman brain-damaged after routine gynaecological surgery, recent matters in which he had triumphed, according to Mark, whose own part in the proceedings was not neglected in the telling.

But that was because I was a bad lawyer, forgetting that justice inevitably and invariably emerged through the adversarial combat of the legal system, and not as a result of the emotional involvement or moral consciences of the parties and their representatives.

It was only afterwards that I thought of what occurred as an ambush. At the time, it seemed quite natural that he should, in the absence of his secretary, wander into the windowless cubby hole in which the monster machine lived, and batten on to the nearest woman with whom he could play the helpless man.

We stood there as the copies flipped ready collated into the output trays. Like everything at Chamberlayne's, the equipment was state of the art.

He beamed at me as I handed them to him.

'Thank you very much. That was very kind of you. I can never get the hang of these things.'

'That's okay. It comes naturally to me. Women have a gene for photocopying expertise.'

His face tightened as he digested this dig, but he seemed determined to be affable and let it pass. I picked up my own copies and moved out into the daylight and air of the office. He followed, then hoisted himself into a half-sitting position on the top of one of the desks. He seemed in no hurry to go back to his room and seemed to want to detain me also. 'And how are things? Keeping busy?'

Now, 'keeping busy' to a solicitor like Conrad is a phrase which encompasses the whole range of human happiness. What is life if not a well-stocked filing cabinet, a buoyant client-list, an onerous workload? The delights of home and family are but shadows in comparison. I replied that I was busy enough, and likely to be absolutely overwhelmed again quite shortly.

'Excellent. That's what I like to hear. That man Chewton, I suppose. Of course. No time for anything else, eh?'

'Not really. Apart from a few old files that were hanging around and needed sorting out and billing.'

'Yes, I heard about those in a partners' meeting. It's good to tidy things up, isn't it? What about your previous practice? No following there, I presume?'

I wondered what Appleby would have said if the clients I'd had at Vardy's had accompanied me to Fernsford. Or rather, I didn't wonder. 'No, I'd only recently qualified.'

'Of course. And we gathered from what Francis told us that you weren't really a conveyancer. Still he went ahead and brought you on board. He must have had his reasons, I suppose.'

I stared at him. Was he trying to be offensive, or did it come naturally? He had a fat, red face and protuberant, pale blue eyes. He met my gaze expressionlessly as if daring me into some rash rejoinder. I buttoned my lip and gave him a thin smile.

'I should get Francis to introduce you to some of his other people in time. Good thing for you to have some variety. Of course, he gets quite a few of them through Chewton. A good connection, what? Mind you, old Francis likes to play his cards close to his chest sometimes. Would be a bit of a change for him to have someone looking over his shoulder.' He slid off the desk and tugged back his jacket cuff to look at his watch. '*Tempus fugit.*' But he hadn't finished. 'I'm glad to hear you're shaping up. We're too small for passengers, you know. Dog eat dog in the business world now, as I'm sure you're aware. That's why, in a firm like this, we all have to work together.' He waved the papers. 'Thanks again for the help.'

Later that day, I had time to reflect on the incident. As I stared out at the misty panorama from my office window, it finally dawned on me that it was not an entirely casual meeting. I thought back to our conversation. Conrad was not the kind of man to waste time in idle chat. What had he been getting at then? 'We all have to work together.' Meaning my future wasn't entirely at the behest of Appleby? Certainly there was a not too heavily veiled threat to me in what he'd said. I had to shape up or else. Maybe he was implying that shaping up meant I should sneak a look at some of the cards the senior partner appeared not to have let his partners in on? I recalled what Tim Pogson had said about partners, in one of his jovial life-and-soul-of-the-party moods, as he hung an arm round the shoulders of his colleagues. 'Partners? They have to trust one another completely. They have to be like brothers. You know how loving brothers are. Think of Esau and Jacob, Cain and Abel!'

It got me thinking that Tom Parsons might have been right.

There was something else, too. Something I liked even less the more I thought it over. Something that pushed all the buttons already pushed by the evening in the pub. 'Francis must have had his reasons' for appointing me, the fat old sod had smirked. Appleby, on the other hand, had implied that, whilst my appointment had been the result of as much heart-searching and second thoughts as a papal conclave, it had been made by the whole partnership. Conrad had more or less said that they didn't know anything about me. Appleby had not consulted or even informed them until after the event.

So, if the partnership parted company with Appleby, then I too would be out on my ear before you could say 'knife'.

I realized now that what Penny had told me on my first day had been true. At the time, I'd listened with only half an ear as she'd prattled on.

'We had ever such a lot of applications for your job, according to Rose. Not that she really had anything to do with it. She likes to pretend, that one, that she has the running of this firm, always going round giving her little orders she is – "Mr Appleby would like this, Mr Appleby would like it done this way." Talk about power corrupts. Well, in this particular instance, she never knew a thing about it. I got her to admit that finally. Mr Appleby dealt with it all himself – shortlisting and everything. He never discussed it with anybody, not even with Meredith and Conrad, according to Jane, Conrad's secretary. Six people he interviewed, I think it was. Not that we got to meet any of them. But they were all from London, because Mr Dyer in Accounts said that was where he was sending the cheques for expenses claims. Had a lot of competition, you did. You must be really good to have come out against that many.'

Good old Penny. I thought she'd wanted to massage her new boss's ego. I hadn't taken account of the rest. Now it had a much hollower ring. Why hadn't Appleby been more up-front with his colleagues? Had he anticipated that they would think I didn't measure up? And if he thought that, then why did he offer the job to me?

I didn't have any illusions about myself, whatever Penny had encouraged me to think. Both on paper and in actuality, there would have been more impressive candidates. The types like David, Mark and James that the firm had already gone for.

It seemed a particularly strange thing for Appleby to have done, particularly as, according to Penny again, the other partners had strongly had to persuade him to recruit an assistant. It was they who had been concerned that the conveyancing department wouldn't be able to cope with the pressures generated by the massive boom in Chewton Residential Properties. Failure would have been embarrassing and would have put the whole lucrative Chewton connection under threat.

I could partly understand Appleby's resistance. It must have been hard for him to have to admit that he couldn't do everything himself. But once he'd agreed, it seemed quite out of the character of the man I'd got to know for him to pick someone like me for this crucial appointment.

If he had simply made a booboo, as lots of people were now implying, then pretty soon he would realize his mistake and I would be packing my bags. The pressure was on me, therefore, if I wanted to keep the job, to out-perform whatever expectations he might have had. And I did want to keep the job. In the circumstances in which I had come to Fernsford, I had no alternative. I couldn't go back to London. Here I was, and here I was going to stay, come hell or high water.

I drank up my umpteenth cup of coffee and looked at my watch. Ten past eight. Another ten minutes and I would have cleared my desk of the routine stuff in readiness for that night's plum. A message from Appleby. A Führer directive, in office jargon.

It had appeared on my desk that afternoon. It read, in his usual friendly style: 'Re: Smithwood. Have your drafts of the transfers on my desk by 9 a.m. tomorrow.' With the memo was a fat file.

I ought to have been delighted, but I had groaned when I saw it. I somehow sensed what he was up to, the rotten bastard. He thought he was calling my bluff. I'd been pestering him for a piece of the commercial action. So he'd handed me a complex matter for one of his most important clients and given me hardly any time to do it. He thought I would blow it by not meeting the deadline. That would give him the excuse not to entrust me with anything but bog-standard stuff in the future. I knew he didn't rate me. Now he was going to rub it in by humiliating me, by proving to me, as well as to himself that I didn't measure up. If my thoughts this afternoon were at all near the mark, then he was merely fattening me up for the kill.

Smithwood. Not only did he own one of the biggest freezer foodstore chains in the West Country, but also he was a member of the Chewton connection: a rich, influential businessman, first-generation wealthy, without old familial loyalties to a rival law firm. I'd met him briefly in the office. He was as fat, greasy and tasteless as one of the frozen chickens his stores foisted on to the gullible. Mark had told me that there had been rich pickings from his operation on the litigation side. Disputes with suppliers, employee problems, a libel suit against a trade paper which had rashly printed the nickname with which he was generally described by his competitors: Salmonella Sam. He was typical of the kind of wheeler-dealer Chewton knew and encouraged in the firm's direction. But as Mark said, it was the ones who sailed close to the wind who had a regular need for lawyers.

He'd already generated a minor connection of his own: relatives and friends, other business partners. Such connections were as extensive and as fragile as spider-silk – and each strand had to be cosseted. Damage to one part of the web might lead to rupture of the whole.

It was, therefore, doubly, triply important for people like Smithwood to be kept sweet. One of the few Pogson dictums to which Appleby would subscribe would be: a lawyer's worst enemy is his client. Clients never blamed themselves for mistakes, delays or cock-ups. They sued, tore up their bills, and took their business and their connection elsewhere. To be given a share of such a client was to be handed a ticking bomb.

I'd show him, I growled to myself, picking up the file, the poisoned chalice. I'd bloody show him. I started to read.

It was a complex purchase of two parcels of registered land for a new superstore, with the vendor wanting to impose various conditions on its use; and there was a simultaneous sub-sale of part by Smithwood to an associate. There was a number of interlocking matters which had to be reflected in the two purchase deeds, both of which were being drafted by us.

I made myself coffee, dragged my counsel's notebook towards me, and started writing.

I looked at my watch and yawned. It was 11 p.m. Late even by my standards. I swigged the last warmish, sweetish dregs from yet another cup of coffee. I'd finished. The drafts were still in manuscript but Appleby, like most lawyers, was old-fashioned enough not to mind that, or even think it particularly unusual. Though dense and complicated, they weren't all that long. Rose would word-process them in a jiffy. No doubt Appleby would nitpick his way through them, making amendments in his minute, precise handwriting. But not even Appleby would be able to deny that they were a pretty competent piece of work. 'So sucks to you, Francis,' I said aloud to the rubber plant on the window sill.

I gathered the sheets together, took them through to the photocopier and made copies for my own use, the originals I would put on Appleby's desk when I left.

The lift was turned off at night, so I had to use the stairs to the fourth floor. The main landing lights were off, and I could see through the wired glass safety window in the mahogany-veneered door that the partners' suite was also in darkness. I got out my copy of the pass-key which opened all the internal doors in our part of the building and pushed through into the corridor beyond. The heavy panel, tugged out of my hand by the closer mechanism, shut with a soft thump, followed by a click as the thumbblock engaged.

The lights on the staircase hardly penetrated much beyond the small pane in the firedoor. I fumbled around for a light switch and failed to find it. I started to feel my way down the passageway. As my eyes adjusted, I realized that the door into Rose's office was ajar. As I drew level, I could make out that it was dimly lit through its outside window by the glow of the streetlights in the Horsemarket. I remembered then that my pass key didn't open the partners' offices, so I couldn't fulfil Appleby's directive to the letter in any event. I'd have to leave the file and my papers on Rose's chair with a Post-it note of explanation stuck on. I went in, switched on her Anglepoise, and flipped open several of the drawers in her desk-side stationery tallboy before I found the yellow stickers.

I was scribbling my message when I was startled to hear a voice. It was coming through the communicating door to Appleby's office.

Heart pounding, I listened. Then I relaxed. It was Appleby's, not a burglar's. I couldn't hear what he was saying but from the rhythm of it, bursts of speech followed by silences, it was evident that it was a telephone conversation. I knew he worked late, but I was a bit miffed that he'd outdone me that night. He must have been speaking to a client like Chewton who took no account of the hour if there were business to transact.

There was silence. The conversation was over. It was an opportunity too good to miss. I screwed up the note to Rose and tossed it into her basket as I crossed the room and pushed through the door. He always came into me without knocking. If I gave him a fright, too bloody bad.

Appleby's office had two doors – one from the corridor and one from Rose's room. His desk was arranged so that it faced the corridor entrance, the power position. Visitors were supposed to come in this way, to meet the intimidating stare of the great man head on. The way in from the secretary's room was sideways on to the desk. The ministering angel could sneak up discreetly and place papers or refreshments by his elbow without disturbing the course of the main confrontation.

The other result of coming in this way, as I found out, was that he could be taken unawares.

'Good evening, Francis, sorry to disturb you. I didn't realize you were still here. Dropping in the Smithwood papers on my way home.'

I was gratified to see that his shoulders flinched slightly, then he swung round in his swivel chair to face me. At the same time he clicked the computer mouse, wiping off the screen the file which had been displayed there.

He took the sheaf of pages from me. His hand seemed to tremble slightly. My sudden irruption really had made the man of steel falter.

'Thanks. It's very late. Please go home. You're not working efficiently if you're here so late.'

I was about to launch into a cogently argued defence, concerning the demands of my workload and my enthusiasm for it, but he swivelled back to his desk, ignoring me. I was dismissed.

I was really pissed off as I clattered down the stairs. All that crap about the inefficiency of working late. He could talk! Not to mention the praise and gratitude for the work I'd completed!

I should have gone home, but I was interested by what I had seen on Appleby's monitor. It was a development he hadn't told me about. Typical of the man. He liked to keep things back so he could spring them on me, then act surprised when I turned out to know nothing about them. Games, didn't they love 'em. Well, this was one game I was going to learn before it landed on my desk with another Führer directive.

I hauled myself upright in the chair and swivelled the screen, with its blinking cursor, round to face me.

I yawned and blearily consulted the system manual, then punched out the Chewton estate index code on the keyboard. Every development had a reference number which gave access to the files. I was quite used to the system by now. Earlier in the day, I had had a batch of practical completion dates to enter. The program churned out the completion notices for servicing on the purchasers' solicitors. Mr and Mrs Punter could then move in and begin to live their dream, give or take minor annoyances like the unfinished roads and a garden which consisted of nothing but mud and broken bricks. That wasn't my problem, of course. What counted was that the remaining ninety per cent of the purchase price due on completion to Chewton Residential Properties was despatched to us by the Punters' solicitors. Money was what it was all about.

Having shacked up with Colin for so long, computers didn't make me go over all funny as they seemed to other people – including, of course, Tim Pogson. He hadn't a clue about such things and he was too mean either to learn to use one himself or to buy the equipment to let others use them. Typical of his short-sighted attitude. Funnily enough, Chamberlayne's, although they were dripping with expensive hardware, didn't seem to exploit it fully. As far as I could see, it was Appleby who mostly used it. He was rumoured to be quite an expert. He'd never bothered to enquire about my computer skills at interview. I suppose he assumed they were on the level of everyone else. Well, Mr Smarty Pants, you were wrong.

The screen displayed the list of estates. Oak Dean, the one Appleby had been playing with, wasn't there. I looked at the list in the system manual. There was no Oak Dean listed there. It was probably an estate long finished with which had not been deleted. It was certainly there somewhere. I typed OAK DEAN and clicked. The screen blanked out, then threw up one of the things that made the non-computer-literate go, 'Oh, God, what have I done?' ACCESS DENIED ENTER PASSWORD, it demanded. Stupid machine. It didn't need a password for individual estate files, only for restricted access areas like the firm's office account.

Because I thought I was smart, I used a trick which Colin had told me sometimes worked on low-security systems operated by wise-guys. I pressed Return. The machine though would have none of it. It immediately blinked back at me, INCORRECT PASSWORD. And that was that. An expert computer hacker like Colin would immediately have risen to the challenge and tried to break the code, but even if I'd known how, I would have been wary. Appleby might not like that if he had gone to the trouble to restrict access, presumably to himself. Why do that, though? The manual files would be in the office, after all. I yawned again and turned the monitor back to standby. It was late and I was tired. Maybe, though, I would take a peep at the files of this Oak Dean. The computer thing had made me curious.

The plot files were in banks of cabinets in the general office. Each drawer was neatly labelled and the developments were in alphabetical order from left to right along the wall under the windows. There were quite a few non-current estates there awaiting despatch to Dead Filing – one more sign of the way things had not been kept up to scratch – but no Oak Dean. That was strange, because if it weren't current, then why was it occupying restricted access memory space on the computer? I decided to ask about it in the morning. Perhaps Penny or Rose would know and I wouldn't need to bother Appleby. There were so many things I didn't know, so many things I had to learn.

But then again, I didn't want to show more ignorance than I had to. I was still nettled by what Appleby had said about my capabilities that first day. If I didn't need to know, why bother? So I never did get round to asking about Oak Dean. It wasn't until much later that I started to ask the questions I should have asked in the beginning.

# Two

## THE VALLEY OF THE SHADOW

# VI

'Your first time is it, dear?'

I nodded, my legs already stiff and trembling, my arm muscles aching and my knuckles white with tension.

'I thought so. You're all nervous. Relax. Breathe into it. There, that's better. I'm sorry. Is the smoke bothering you? Look, I'll open the window. Gently on this bit. Now stop. It's nice and quiet and we'll try a few manoeuvres.'

Thankfully, I pulled up the handbrake, pushed the gearstick into neutral and released the clutch. I let go of the steering wheel, flexed my finger joints and massaged my right knee. I turned to face my instructor. 'What now?'

'We'll have a little break and I'll finish my fag. How's your Highway Code? Got a copy yet?'

'Yes. I don't have any trouble with the paperwork.'

She laughed. 'No. I suppose not. You being a solicitor. I don't think I've ever taught a solicitor to drive. Watch my Ps and Qs, won't I? Don't want to teach you to do nothing illegal, now. Usually I get middle-aged housewives who think that a woman instructor's going to make all the difference when they've failed umpteen times before with men – the driving test, I mean, of course.'

There was the ghost of a wink in her eye as she said this. I looked at her with interest. There was something about the way she talked that reminded me of something. 'And does it? Make the difference.'

'Actually, I think it does. They seem to pass with me and they tell their friends. It's a declining market now, of course. Most people learn in their teens, as soon as they're old enough. Essential skill, isn't it?'

'It seems so. My boss said I had to. It was different in London.'

'London. I'm from London, myself, originally. Clapham. The feller I was with at the time got a job here. Then he buggered off, didn't he? I managed to get this going, and I do a bit of chauffeuring as well – fetching and carrying visitors for firms, people who've got banned, that sort of thing. I won't do minicabbing though. I want to stay alive. Here, you being in business, you never know.' She handed me her card from a pack stuffed behind the visor. 'Now. Better get going again. Start up. Mirror. Look behind before moving off, you never know, okay?'

'Okay.'

I'd found Womanwheels in the Yellow Pages. It sounded fun, and was cheaper than the others I'd called. Appleby had insisted I get a driving licence. Once I'd learned, I would get a car loan and a car allowance from the firm, but it wouldn't pay for the lessons. 'More of an incentive if you're paying for it yourself, eh?'

Charmaine Potter was a big handsome woman in a sloppy sweater and baggy cords. She had very black, very curly hair and a very brown complexion like a Gypsy. Her car was a clean, three-year-old, bright red Cavalier – 'Be careful with it, dear, I'm still paying for it' – and she smoked Benson and Hedges from an open pack on the dashboard top.

She was also, slightly to my surprise, a very good teacher. A short way into our first lesson, I completely lost the terrible nervousness that had gripped me at the start. She gave clear instructions and didn't yell at me when I did stupid things like hitting the brake instead of the gas, causing the guy in the car behind nearly to swallow his carphone. 'Serve him right, fat pig,' she had said as he had swerved angrily around us and roared off on the wrong side of the road.

I stopped back outside the house in Lochinvar Road, switched off and leaned back in the seat, a big grin on my face. I turned to her. 'How did I do?'

'I think you know. Your first few minutes were a bit wobbly then you took to it very well. You're not quite a complete natural. But then very few are. You won't have any trouble passing, though, after a few more lessons.'

'Thank goodness for that. I was hoping not to have to spend too much. And Appleby will be better pleased if I'm mobile sooner rather than later.'

'Appleby? Is that the name of the bloke you work for?'

'Yes. Francis Appleby. He's the senior partner of the firm. Chamberlayne's. Here's my card. You being in business, you never know.'

She glanced at the card and stuck it behind the visor. Pursing her lips, she stared out of the windscreen. 'I knew someone of that name ages ago. In London. That'd be a coincidence now, wouldn't it? Senior partner, eh? That would be a turn up for the book.' She looked at her watch. 'I can't stay chatting, though. Got to be away for the next lucky lady. Six o'clock next Monday, okay? And pick you up in the Horsemarket, that right? Ta-ta.'

I felt cheered up by Charmaine and the lesson. I had been rather dreading it, and it was nice to think that I wasn't a complete duffer. Soon I would have my own car. Just think of that!

As I sat in the bay window sipping my coffee – I had bought a cafetière, and felt very grand to be indulging in the real thing – it occurred to me what it was about Charmaine that had seemed familiar. I might be wrong and I would never dare to say anything to her in case I was. It was partly the way she spoke, but more the sort of feeling I had – the much scoffed at intuition, I suppose. I would have sworn that, maybe not now, probably in her other life in London, she had been on the game.

One way or another I had known lots of toms, as they were known in police and legal slang. So I had a definite feel for the way they were. And I got that feeling from Charmaine. I'm not in the least saying I disapproved. I had a lot of respect for many of the prostitutes I had come across. The problems they have come not from the social function they perform – men do really appalling things for money and get the praise of society as well – but from the way they are hypocritically persecuted by the law and, as a result, are vulnerable to being battened on to by slimy creatures from the pit who take their earnings, beat them up and hook them on drugs. If I were right about Charmaine, it seemed that she had got out of all that. If so, good for her. But the thing that really got me chuckling was that she might have known Appleby, and that would have cast an interesting, to say the least, light on my boss. A pity that the odds on both being true were so long.

\*

That Sunday afternoon I decided it was time for some fresh air. I'd hardly been out of Fernsford once since I'd arrived, what with getting the flat straight and working.

The good thing about being on my own again was that I didn't have to convince anyone else, or have to argue about where to go. The converse of that was that I didn't have anyone to go with. I wasn't used to the idea of a solitary country walk. It would have to be somewhere with people around. I stared out of the window. The park was too near, too small and too unadventurous. Then I thought of the perfect place, combining business and pleasure neatly and satisfyingly. I would go to Welscombe House, Trevor Chewton's first venture into the leisure business.

'Which do you want, miss? The combined Eighteenth Century Experience and Grounds ticket or just the Grounds? The Wild Animal Valley is separate but you can't go in there without a car. You'd get eaten.'

'Thanks. I'll remember,' I said to the elderly man at the turnstile beneath the huge ornate stone gatehouse, and bought a ticket for the grounds and received in addition a glossy colour print leaflet announcing 'Welscombe House – the day out to remember for a lifetime.' I had decided to stick to the open air and save experiencing the eighteenth century to another day.

On the other side of the clicking steel gate there was a coloured signboard, showing the various parts of the estate. The various trails were marked by little arrows in different colours, and I chose one which meandered through woodland down to the sinuous curve of the Fern.

As I strolled along in the warm afternoon, I looked about me. Into the far distance there was nothing but trees and rolling meadows of spectacularly green grass where plump yellow-brown cows grazed. That must be, as I thumbed through the brochure, the 'famous Welscombe pedigree Jersey herd'.

Hadn't our boy done well? Not bad for someone who, according to what Francis Appleby had told me, had started as a carpenter apprenticed to his father in the tiny family building firm of Chewton & Sons. From a terraced house in the back streets of Bradley, one of the more dismal districts of Fernsford, to being Lord of the Manor of Welscombe.

'It was Welscombe House which brought him to Chamberlayne's, you know,' Appleby had told me one evening just after I had joined. He'd been out all day, and had wandered in looking pleased with himself. He'd parked himself in the chair opposite my desk and seemed disposed to talk.

'This unlikely-looking character walked into my room and said that he wanted to buy Welscombe House by next Friday. The Earl of Anglebury was desperate to sell – the Revenue were hounding him for a massive tax liability. He'd agreed to a very low bid from Trevor. Hence the need for haste. Well, I, we, performed on time, when his other lawyers had said it couldn't be done. And so, we got the lot. The rest, as they say, is history.

'Trevor didn't make the mistake of trying to live in the place as a latter-day squire. He's built a new house for himself on the estate. He always intended Welscombe House to make money. The state rooms of the mansion were made over into what he calls the authentic look of the eighteenth century – no electric lighting, only candles, piss pots behind screens in the corners, live action set-pieces with actors dressed up, that kind of thing. Trevor had seen a similar place in London and decided he could make that work on a larger and more popular scale. An antidote to the National Trust's gentility and tidiness – see the upper classes and their servants as they really were. The fact that the whole place hadn't had a lick of paint for years and was pretty well falling down all added to the authenticity as far as he was concerned.

'He's displayed a similar kind of imagination in the rest. Part of the house has been converted very successfully into a first-class hotel and conference centre, and the old domestic quarters and stables have been made into a very profitable residential development. Then there's the Edwardian funfair, a massive adventure playground, and the Wild Animal Valley. You should take a look. Help you understand the kind of man you'll be dealing with.'

It would give me some pleasure on Monday morning to say that I had done just that.

I was hot with exertion and a little breathless as I descended the last slope of the circular walk I had been on – follow the purple arrows – which had taken me down to the water meadows of the Fern, and then back up along a wide grassy sward through an avenue of huge oak trees. The highest point of the walk was crowned with a tall obelisk commemorating someone or something in Latin, of which I could make neither head nor tail. There was then a steep descent on a zigzag path through woodland. I paused on a rocky platform thrusting out over the valley and surrounded by a semi-circular classical colonnade and I was entranced by what I saw.

Below, in the misty sunlight, was the honey stone façade of Welscombe House. Spreading out before it like a great green pool was a massive expanse of lawn. Beyond that, fringed with huge trees was the serpentine lake created by Capability Brown by the simple expedient of cutting off and rearranging one of the meanders of the Fern. All around were wooded slopes, the splash of the cunningly engineered artificial waterfalls and the shouts and laughter of children hidden amid the leaves.

It was a place of sheer magic. I sat at the base of one of the columns, feeling the warm stone on my back through my blouse, gazing into the valley below, feeling that I could have gazed for ever.

Eventually, though, reality intruded in the form of a frozen bottom and I got stiffly to my feet. A cloud was passing over, draining the gold from the air. The path down was in darkness under the thick canopy of trees. As I emerged again into the light, I heard the raucous sound of Sousa's *Monty Python's Flying Circus* march played on a steam organ in the Edwardian-themed funfair.

I was wandering past the adventure playground when I saw them. The Edwardian theme had been toned down a bit here. There was a steam roundabout with horses which danced to music-hall melodies, but there were also the elaborate climbing frames, rope-walks and slides which provided pretend danger for the kind of well-heeled kids whose parents didn't let them play on demolition sites or in empty buildings as I had done as a child.

It was the jacket I recognized, slightly shabby, baggy and with the cord worn shiny at the elbows. That and the mop of dark, dry dandruffy hair hanging in a ragged fringe over the collar of the Viyella shirt. Next to him was a woman, tall, with darkish blonde shoulder-length hair, wearing a long, low-waisted Laura Ashley-style print dress and white tennis shoes on her unstockinged legs. They were watching and shouting encouragement into the mass of children swarming like insects all over the playground. Presumably in there was one or more Starling-Richards offspring.

Well, this was really turning into a buswoman's holiday of a day out.

What next? Francis Appleby, in a Kiss-Me-Quick hat in the queue for 'real Edwardian-style ice-cream'? I hesitated, wondering how or whether I should intrude myself on the family outing, just to say hello in passing, perhaps, when in response to something the woman had said, he turned, his hand shading his face. I heard him say something like, 'It's over there', and before he turned back, his eyes met mine. I smiled and raised a hand in casual acknowledgement, then he nudged the woman's arm and she turned also. We approached one another.

'Well, hello. As they say, fancy seeing you here.'

'Do you come here often?'

He grinned. 'We do, as a matter of fact. Sarah, this is my wife, Venetia. Darling, this is Sarah Hartley. A new recruit to Chamberlayne's, Chewton's lawyers. We met last month on site.'

I shook her small, cool hand. 'What Paul means is that the children love it here and Trevor Chewton has given us a family season ticket. One of the few perks of the job, isn't it, Paul? It's not an entirely unmixed benefit either, as we've got to have a really good excuse for not coming here, as the children know it's free.'

'It is good for them, though,' he put in hastily as if to dispel the faint ingratitude of her remarks. 'They get bored with the garden at home, and they think the park is dull, except if they want to kick a ball about.'

'How old are they?'

'Michael's six and a half and the twins – Jonny and Alice – are just five. They're a nightmare most of the time. The good thing about this place – ghastly as it otherwise is – is that it burns off some of their endless energy. But you can see for yourself.'

'Mum!' A tall, slender boy with the look of his father about him, and two smaller children had gathered around their mother while we had been talking. Now the eldest was tugging at her arm to gain her attention.

'Michael, please. Can't you see I'm already talking? You must wait for a break in the conversation.'

'Hello, Michael. I'm Sarah.'

He gave me a look of unselfconscious curiosity. 'What are you doing here?'

'Michael! I'm sorry. Michael, you simply don't ask people straight out like that.'

83

'That's all right. It's a reasonable question. I met your father last month, with the man who owns this place. I'm going to do some work for him. So I came here to find out more about his business.'

Michael had lost interest in my explanation halfway through, and was again tugging his mother's arm.

'All right, I give in. What do you want?'

'Daddy says I can't go on the Eagle's Swoop.'

'Daddy is quite right. It's much too dangerous.'

'You always say that. Tom Pattison went on it.'

'Tom's much older than you are.'

'He's only ten.'

'I'm sure his parents didn't know. And you can't.'

'Mum!'

'No.'

'You go on it then. You're older than me. Perhaps you're too old.'

I intervened, I hoped helpfully. 'Michael, what exactly is the Eagle's Swoop?'

'It's this amazing sort of slide. Only it's not the sort of slide that little kids go on. It's really big. You have to climb up a really high tower, then you drop down this kind of black hole and you come out at the bottom really, really fast, and you hit a lot of kind of cushions at the end. Why don't you go on it?'

I looked at Venetia and she shrugged, as if to say, you got yourself into this. 'You show me it and I'll think about it.'

'Great, come on everybody. Sarah's going to go on the Eagle's Swoop.' He scampered off and we followed.

'You don't have to, you know,' Paul said. He was holding the hands of each of the twins, dark-blond like their mother, with the same huge blue eyes. 'I won't. He's been pestering me for ages. I can't stand heights. Stupid, isn't it, in my profession?'

'It should be more common. I used to live in a tower block. Jesus, is that it?'

He laughed. 'I'm afraid so.'

As Michael had said, it was a really high tower, made from an openwork of rough timber poles, with a series of ladders going up the centre to a pitched-roof shed on the top. Attached to one side of the shed was a kind of chute, roofed over with timber boards. If the angle of the chute wasn't actually vertical, then it looked pretty near it. Unlike the rest of the apparatus in the play area it was deserted.

Michael was swarming up the first ladder already. He waved. 'Come on!'

Venetia gave a gasp of impatience. 'Michael, stop, come back! I told you not to go up!' She looked at me angrily. 'I'll have to go after him, I suppose.'

'It's all right. I'm going. Here, someone hold my handbag.'

Paul took it. 'I'll stay down here with the twins.'

I ran over to the bottom of the tower and put my foot on the first rung of the ladder. I felt a sudden jolt of adrenaline. I remembered the night that we had broken into the gas works in North-Eastern Road, me and Jimmy Grant and Eammon Boyle. I was first up that terrifying metal fretwork ladder clamped to the side of the gas-holder. I could hear Jimmy's voice in my ears even now: 'Look at that Sarah. You can see her knickers!' I had crouched on the cold curving metal plates of the enormous cylinder, the wind whistling around me, blowing my hair into my eyes, blurring the yellow glare of the street lights far below. It had been like in the old Cagney movie I had seen on the TV: 'Top of the world now, Ma!' I went up like a monkey.

I caught up with Michael just before he reached the platform at the top. 'Hey, you were quick.'

I grabbed his arm. 'You stay here and wait for your mother.' I looked down and saw her panting and puffing up the final pitch.

'Aren't you going down then? I bet you're scared. Girls are always scared.'

'Don't you believe it.' There was an opening in the side of the shed. I leaned over the low sill and found I was peering down what looked like a mineshaft. Below the sill, the side of the shaft was surfaced with polished vinyl. At the bottom I could see a faint patch of daylight. As my eyes adjusted to the dark, I could see that the bottom side of the shaft had, in fact, a slight curve.

'What you do is you grab hold of those, like, handles up there and you kind of swing yourself out and down. I saw some big kids do it last time we were here.'

I glanced up and saw what he meant.

Venetia arrived. 'Gosh, you're not really going down, are you? Michael, you dreadful boy. I told you not to come up here.'

'I thought you said I wasn't to go on the slide part. You never said anything about the tower. The tower's dead easy.'

I sat on the sill. At least this time I was wearing jeans. They wouldn't see my knickers. I reached up and gripped the metal bars.

'Hey, you're really going to!'

'Do be careful!'

'Here goes nothing!' I pulled on the bars and wriggled my bottom over the lip of the sill, feeling my legs flat against the cold plastic surface. Then, bending my head well forward, I let go.

'Aaaah!' It was the same leaving-my-stomach-behind feeling I'd had when I'd jumped off the old carpet warehouse roof on to a pile of foam offcuts we'd piled at the bottom, magnified about ten times. It was probably like skiing, but I'd never done that.

The coldness under me turned to heat with the friction of my speed. I was hurtling through darkness, faster and faster, my eyes blurring. Then from the blackness of the shaft, I shot forward into light. I zoomed on my back along a long strip of polished flooring like the lane of a ten-pin bowling alley and cannoned into heaps of soft cushions. I lay there for a moment, gasping, exhilarated, aware that my right elbow hurt like hell where I had somehow scraped it in my descent. Above me the sky was an unbelievable blue.

I heard an anxious voice, 'I say, Sarah, are you all right?'

I sat up. He was leaning over the low timber fence which separated spectators from the arrival point. 'It's really amazing.'

'She did it, she did it!' Michael came running from the direction of the tower. 'Did she come out the end?'

I clambered to my feet, suddenly trembling all over. I was climbing over the fence when there was a scream from above.

Michael looked up. 'Mummy! Where's Mummy?'

He didn't have long to wait. She arrived, pink faced and shrieking, her long white legs stuck out before her indecorously apart and her floral skirt ballooning around her.

As I had, she lay there for a moment, flat on her back. Then she rolled over and started to get to her feet. I held out my hand. 'I felt all wobbly. Don't you?'

'Rather.' She pulled herself up against my hold and pushed the hair back from her eyes. 'You see, Michael, I'm not such an old stick as you think.'

She turned to me. Her eyes were bright. 'It takes me back to the time I used to do all kinds of silly things on skis.'

'I loved the whoosh as you come out of the chute. Like being born.'

She laughed. 'Then we're both born again. I think we should celebrate. Come home to tea, to supper if you'd like.'

'Thank you. I'd like that very much.'

The Starling-Richardses lived in Arden Wood, perched on high ground south of the city, its substantial detached houses set back from the gently winding, tree-lined road. I got out of the car on to the shingled drive in front of a huge stone Victorian pile, with elaborately carved gothic windows. To the west, over the side garden, I saw through a screen of yellowing leaves a distant hazy vista of blue hills, and below them the silver line of the Tarrant.

I followed Venetia into the high-ceilinged kitchen-cum-living-room, with another view over the rear garden through the floor-length windows, this time of the city itself. Paul and the children had disappeared.

I stared at my surroundings with frank curiosity. 'This is a wonderful house.'

Venetia was getting out plates and mugs from one of the tall, cream-painted cupboards. 'I think it's rather super. We've been here for years. It was quite a ruin when we first bought it. That was our luck, in a way. Paul could do what was needed when a lot of people would have been put off.'

'Can I help?'

'No, you sit down. It'll be ready in a sec. The other thing was that it had this huge old rambling garage effort at the back – there's a narrow little lane there. The estate agents called it a coach house, in case you happened to have a coach, I suppose. Well, Paul has turned that into his drawing office. He hated having to commute into town. Now he just walks down the garden. You must get him to show you. There's all the Friars Haven stuff in there.'

She went to the door into the hallway and yelled out, 'Paul, children. Tea!'

There was a drumming of feet on stairs and they duly appeared. We all sat round the big oak table. 'Jonny, don't grab! There's plenty for everyone.'

There was. Chunky slices of wholemeal bread. Scones. A plate bearing a hefty slab of yellow butter. Half a dozen different-sized glass jars of jam with neat hand-written labels giving the variety and the date of making. A huge square, shiny brown cake, already cut into, showing an interior richly marbled with dried fruit, cherries and almonds. Mugs of milk for the children. And from a bulbous bone-china teapot adorned with pink cabbage roses, with a chipped spout, delicately scented China tea for the adults.

'This is a feast,' I said biting into a scone liberally spread with strawberry jam. 'And this jam is delicious.'

'Venetia's good at the old preserves. In fact she's a brilliant cook altogether. Cordon bleu. Used to have your own restaurant, didn't you, darling?'

'Paul. It was only a sort of café. And I was a lot younger. BC. Before children, anyway. Now I'm so aged, I can only just cope with you lot.'

'She's too modest, Sarah. The Broad Lea Bistro was a good deal more than a café. It was in the Good Food Guide. And don't pretend you're just a housewife now, darling. What would the practice do without you? I'm hopeless at anything to do with business and admin, you know. I like to stick close to the drawing board. I couldn't ever be like those fellows with dozens of partners with their own jets, designing mega-towers in Singapore or somewhere.'

'Now who's being modest? Listen to him, Sarah. You wouldn't think he'd won the RIBA Gold Medal and goodness knows how many other prizes.'

'Ah, come on now. That really was years ago.'

'Yes. BC. Before Chewton. Since you got involved with him, you haven't had time for anything good.'

'Venetia!' He gave her a warning look. 'I know your v-v-views on the subject.' The slight stammer which had been absent all afternoon had returned.

She looked at me and grimaced. 'Whoops. Speaking out of turn as usual. Sarah, please ignore this Darby and Joan banter. More tea? There we are. Jonny, please don't do that with your bread. Just eat it!'

'S'not bread. Issa spaceship!'

She made a mock appeal to me. 'God. Children, families. Sometimes I want to scream. I was one of five myself. Twins there, you see. Are you from a big family?'

It was a question I always dreaded, but answered truthfully. I would never deny it. 'No. I had one sister, but she died when I was quite small.'

'Oh, how awful.' There was genuine sympathy in her voice.

'Yes. It still seems that way.'

I deliberately turned away and helped myself to cake.

While Venetia bathed the children and got them ready for bed, Paul took me over to the office: 'That is, if you'd like to. I mean it is work, I suppose, and you may not ... well, at the weekend ...'

'That's all right. What do you think I was doing at Welscombe House? It's not too much my kind of thing, you know. But I thought it was important to get to know something about the firm's biggest client without Appleby breathing down my neck or wanting to know how I was going to bill the time.' I stopped myself. Maybe I was being too frank with this man. Perhaps he and Appleby were going to compare notes. But somehow I doubted that and sometimes I had to trust my own instincts.

'I can understand that. Trevor's put a lot of effort into the place. It won't do you any harm if you can show you've taken the trouble to see for yourself.'

We had walked the length of the garden and arrived at a high-gabled brick building, windowless but with roof-lights set into the slate roof. He unlocked a plank door hung on big iron strap hinges. 'Come in. Welcome to Starling-Richards and Associates.'

It was dusk and he pushed a switch, flooding the interior with brilliant neon light. Inside, it was one big room and all white – walls, roof-beams, even white cushioned vinyl on the floor. There were all the usual impedimenta: a couple of big drawing boards on massive steel stands, a range of plan chests under a white laminate counter like a kitchen surface, white filing cabinets, and a big computer monitor in a white cabinet. On one side of the room, a white-painted metal gallery reached by a spiral staircase ran just above head height. I could see shelves – white of course – running the full length, crammed with file cases and folders, and the spines of masses of books, their jackets about the only splashes of colour in the place.

It all looked highly organized and highly austere, a contrast with what I had seen of the house, with its slightly shabby, dog-eared feel, its dark oil-paintings, bronze statues and battered comfortable furniture.

I said nothing of this, but I might as well have spoken out loud.

He said, 'A bit of a contrast, isn't it? With the house, I mean? I leave that to Venetia. Sometimes in my wildest dreams, I pull down that Victorian monstrosity – pseudo baronial tower and all – and build a real house. *Une machine pour habiter*, you know.'

'No, I don't. I'm sorry, I don't understand any foreign languages – unless you count lawyer's Latin.'

'A machine for living in. Le Corbusier. Architect. Swiss, but worked in France. He's rather unfashionable in some quarters now. Blamed for all the "mistakes" of the sixties. Quite unjustified. You can't blame architects for the way in which the buildings are lived in. Social housing can't create society.'

'Social housing? I told you earlier. I lived in a tower block.'

'Student residence was it? I did one of those a few years back.'

'No. It was one of those concrete slums in the sky. We were on the fifteenth. The lifts were usually out of order. When they weren't they were used as toilets.'

'That rather proves my point, doesn't it? It's not architects who piss in the lifts, is it?'

I smiled despite my irritation. 'I don't know. I've never been in a lift with an architect.'

'*Touché.* I can see we're not going to agree. We argue, as Sydney Smith said, from different premises. You know, as we're talking about buildings and arguing...'

'I said I didn't understand foreign languages. I'm okay in English, thanks. Put me down as uneducated but not stupid, please.'

I had embarrassed him. He started mumbling and blushing and stuttering apologies. He was quite sweet, really.

'Aren't you going to show me the Friars Haven stuff? I'm dying to see it.'

He smiled with apparent relief. 'Of course. It's over here.'

When we got back to the house, Venetia, enveloped by a big coarseweave white apron, was in the kitchen frying onions on the Aga. Michael was sitting in a kind of multi-coloured track suit, which I assumed was his pyjamas, at the kitchen table reading a book.

'Hello, there. Paul, go and say good night to the twins or they'll be asleep.' She turned to me. 'Give you the full picture of the glories of Friars Haven to be, did he? By the way, is spag bol okay?'

'It sounds lovely, but I feel as if I've rather sort of imposed on your evening.'

'Nonsense. I'm really pleased we bumped into each other. I like it when things happen spontaneously. Nowadays everything has to be planned down to the nth degree – babysitters and so on. Of course, I forget you're still free of all that.'

'Yes, I'm free of everything right now. I don't really know anyone here at all – apart from the people at work. You've saved me from an evening by the gas fire with beans on toast.'

She turned to Paul who had come back into the room. 'Drink, husband. I'm absolutely gasping. Open some of that burgundy I got from Arnold the other day. It's lovely stuff. All blackberry and appley.'

Back at the stove, she tipped a heaped platter of minced beef and chopped chicken livers into the deep, blackened frying pan with a satisfying sizzle. She stirred vigorously with one hand while with the other she squeezed a garlic press over the bubbling mixture. After more garlic, she swivelled to the chopping board and with lightning speed and a black-handled carbon steel knife she reduced a pile of fresh plum tomatoes, all beaded with drops of moisture on their shiny scarlet skins, almost to purée, then tipped them into the pan. She then picked up a bunch of fresh green herbs from the counter top and plunged them under the cold tap at the oblong, white butler's sink. With the wicked knife they were also chopped into extraordinary fineness and added to the sauce. A wonderful smell filled the room.

I gaped at this, to me, amazing expertise. 'I can't even boil an egg without it being rubbery. And the idea of cooking in public just horrifies me, now. It'd be like being back at school with Mrs Fitzgerald, the Dom Sci teacher tut-tutting below my shoulder. I'd rather do anything than that. Cookery exposes all my incompetence. I couldn't bear even to have Colin watch me in the kitchen. I left it to him mainly, anyway.'

Paul handed me a glass of wine. 'Colin?'

'Oh, sorry. He was the guy I used to live with. In London.'

'Used to?'

'Paul, don't be so prying. Talk about women being nosy. Michael, I know you're doing an awfully good job at being invisible there, but it's time for bed.'

'Aw, Mum.'

'Bed! It's late. Say good night to Sarah.'

The boy grinned at me. 'You were great on the Eagle's Swoop. I'll tell all my mates about it. And you, Mum, of course. Good night.'

'Good night, Michael.' I sipped the wine, hesitantly. What the hell. It was Saturday night, and one glass – or even two – couldn't do any harm. I should have said straight away I didn't drink if I wasn't going to. The truth is that I was attracted by the whole casual lavishness of these people and the way they lived.

Venetia had finished her glass. She held out her hand for more. Presumably she knew when to stop. I couldn't see her getting like Mum, retching her guts out over the toilet bowl with the stink of urine in her nostrils. Venetia's culture had effortlessly absorbed alcohol, in the way it effortlessly absorbed everything: running restaurants, families, big houses, the lot. Was that the definition of civilization or just having money?

I suppose I was jealous. When I lay awake those nights hearing the screech of cars driven too fast in the street, the yells, the occasional crash of breaking bottles or window panes, I used to imagine what it would be like not to live in Ernest Bevin House. I used to see myself looking out at night from the window of the kind of house Mum used to clean in one of those quiet streets in Hampstead or Golders Green where I got taken sometimes in the school holidays. A bay window with a stretch of lawn, silver in the moonlight, surrounded by the black shades of trees. And over me in the dark sky, the glint of countless stars.

And now in Arden Wood I had found my childhood paradise. I gazed around me, at the shabby-beautiful furniture, the woodwork with a deep gleam from years of use, the tilting rows of battered books on the shelves, the wine glasses sparkling on the fine-grained tabletop, and I felt envy no longer, but benevolence as if I too belonged here. I took another sip from my miraculously refilled glass.

'Supper's nearly ready!' called Venetia from the Aga.

'Can I do anything?'

'Oh, could you be a love and set the table? Knives and such in that drawer, mats over there.'

As I moved around, with an ever so slight hint of unsteadiness, I felt Paul's eyes following my every move. His warm, brown intelligent eyes.

# VII

I heard the phone ringing as I went up the stairs and, heart in mouth, I dashed in to grab it. 'Hi, there,' I panted.

But it was a woman, a dry upper-class voice. 'You do sound breathless. Doing your aerobics, were you, darling? Or something more sociable? I mean, is this a Bad Time?'

'Harriet! How marvellous! What a surprise. No, I've just got in from the office.'

'Goodness me. On a Friday. It's gone nine, London time anyway. Does Fernsford stay open so late? I do hope your firm is paying you enough. Or is there nothing else to do? Listen, I know this is short notice, but I have to cover some ghastly political thing in Westhampton next weekend. When I looked at my road atlas I realized that it isn't a million miles from you in Fernsford. Would I be very unwelcome if I invited myself for the weekend? I thought as I hadn't seen you since you disappeared to the Wild West, but you're probably busy or . . .'

'No, I've no plans at all. That would be wonderful, it seems ages since I've seen you.'

'It does to me too. Well that's settled then. This do I'm at will last most of the day, including dinner, so I'll be quite late. I've got your address, but you'd better tell me how I find you. I say, you are all right, aren't you? I had awful visions of your working in some terrible boring office and going home to some lonely flat. It's not like that, is it?'

'No, it's not like that at all. I'm really touched that you were worried. I'll tell you about the new life, don't you worry. Now, it's quite easy to get here...'

I finished giving directions, said goodbye and put the phone down. It would be nice to see Harriet again. How funny that she had been worried about me, particularly as I hadn't given a thought to her. Our lives were so different. She was quite famous. I was as obscure as it was possible to be. I really was touched that despite her awesomely busy life she found time for me.

As I prepared my supper, I wondered what she would think of Fernsford. It wasn't hard to guess. There was rather a contrast between the lifestyle of a metropolitan television journalist and an assistant solicitor in self-consciously provincial Fernsford. I supposed, in Harriet's terms, what she feared had happened to me had actually happened. I did have a boring office job and I did go home every evening to an empty flat in a suburban street with a municipal park at the end.

But the reality was more subtly shaded than this stark outline would suggest. I was getting the job sorted out; Harriet might mock the suburbs, but then she hadn't experienced my sort of inner city; as for being lonely, since I had been living on my own, I had never for one moment felt as lonely as I had done in the depths of my affair with Colin. And more than that, ever since I had got over that early shock of my precipitate flight from London, and despite the occasional lapses, such as my 'funny turn' at Friars Haven, I was finally beginning to feel as if some pressure in my head was being gradually released. In this place, which held no memories for me, either good or bad, I could start to come to terms with what I was beginning to think of now more objectively as my demons. Every day, I felt I was advancing a little towards confronting them, of lifting the lid of the box in which they lay locked up. Every day, I thought of the evening with my father, roaming tentatively over the memories that had ineluctably surfaced, but like icebergs, floated with nine-tenths still below in the dark and freezing water.

Maybe it was the onions I was slicing which had brought tears to my eyes. I reached blindly for a piece of kitchen roll and wiped them. Yes, it was only the onions. I blew my nose and chucked the screwed up paper into the pedal bin. I ran my finger over the glossy page of the cook book.

*Creative Cooking for One.* Now, there was a title. It had sort of leapt out at me in the bookshop a few days ago. Just the thing for the single flat-dweller. Perhaps I would have to hide it when Harriet came or she would laugh at me. But let her laugh at my poor attempts at sophistication if she wanted. I had been pleased with the improvement in the diet I had achieved. I had learned to poach fish and to make a sauce, to cook stir fry and a carbonnade of beef. Tonight I was doing chicken supreme and rice.

I left it all to bubble away, poured myself a glass of apple juice and wandered back into the front room. The book I had just finished reading was on the table in the bay window. I had bought it at the same time as the cook book. It was another stage in what I thought of as the tackling of my fears. It seemed somehow important that I should read this book, and that I should go on to read other books, real books that is, the sort of books that educated people read. Why should I let my father ruin the rest of my life as he had ruined the beginning? And so I had bought a cheap paperback edition of *Great Expectations* by Charles Dickens and I had read it faster than I remembered ever reading anything before.

I saw how it must have appealed to my father's imagination. The convict Magwitch, surreptitiously supplying the funds to make his Pip a 'gentleman' – was that how he saw himself? But it was obvious that he had made no fortune. What did he believe he could give me, what were those 'great expectations' he had spoken of? How could he, after what he had done to my childhood, even think that I would accept anything? The idea was absurd. Absurd and at the same time terrifying. I shuddered. How glad I was that he and his craziness were over a hundred miles away. How deluded I had been that day on the canal to think that he had come after me. He couldn't possibly find me here.

I put the book on the shelf by the fireplace, alongside my law books. Even without my personal involvement, I had been moved by the sheer power of the writing. My mind soaked up the vivid phrases, and revelled in the images conjured up: the mists swirling on the marshes, the cobwebbed remains of Miss Havisham's wedding breakfast, the strange cold girl Estella. Tomorrow, I would buy another of his novels. I didn't know how many there were, but I was going to read them all.

I ate the chicken in front of the news on my newly acquired small TV. I was quite impressed by my newly developed culinary skill. Not that I could ever quite rise to the heights of superchef, superwoman Venetia Starling-Richards. Shit, why did I have to go dragging up her name? But then why shouldn't I? I had no need to feel guilty. Why did I keep trying to blot out the events of that weekend? And why did they come seeping through?

I zapped out the avuncular newscaster. Why was I beating up on myself? Nothing had happened, had it? Not really happened. And nothing more was going to happen. I had made sure of that. Why was it then that I got this eerie tingling every time I heard the phone ring?

In the end I lost count of how many glasses of wine I had drunk at the Starling-Richardses. I was surprised I was still standing. I had stuffed myself with food and we had talked very late. About, amongst other things, London – Paul had worked there after he had qualified and had even had a flat in Islington at one time. About Fernsford – Venetia's family had lived in and around Fernsford 'since the year dot'. This had brought up again the subject of the Broad Lea Bistro – and she spoke of leaving it with a franker sense of regret than she had earlier.

'But even I felt I couldn't do everything: that and the work I had to do in the practice – it was a sticky patch then, wasn't it, my love? We couldn't afford to employ anyone – but it was a bit of a wrench, to let it go just when it had got going nicely. It was a bit of a labour of love, actually. It never made much money, but it was good. And I had created it. So I sold it to someone who made all the right noises and immediately wished I hadn't. It went downhill rapidly and closed after a year. I should have kept the lease and got someone in to manage it, maintained a kind of watching brief. I don't think I had the best advice.' I heard Paul begin to murmur a protest.

'I know, I shouldn't blame Ralph, poor fellow. It wasn't entirely his fault. I don't think I knew quite what I did want to do.'

'Ralph? Ralph Chamberlayne?'

'The very man. My family had always been with Chamberlayne's. I followed in the tradition. Ralph was a lovely chap. He was a friend as well as a lawyer. You're unfortunate not to have known him. He was wonderful company. Many's the time he came here and entertained us with scandalously witty stories about his colleagues. His death was awful.'

'Rose told me about him. He sounded nice.'

By this time she had had a fair amount to drink. Even so, I was taken aback by what she said next. 'He was nice. And he was honest. Unlike the man who now runs the firm. Needless to say – and I'm sorry for your sake – my family's affairs are not now in the hands of Chamberlayne's. Uncle Harold and the other trustees moved to Buckingham's.'

'Venetia!'

'I know, Paul. It's no good glaring at me like that. She'll learn soon enough about Appleby. Probably has already.'

I didn't reply but looked hard at my fingernails.

Venetia got to her feet, looking slightly shamefaced. 'Oh dear, I've put my big foot in it again. I've embarrassed you, talking in such terms about your boss. I can hear my old headmistress now. "Venetia Wooton," she would say, "you have absolutely no sense of when to be silent."' She went over to the drinks tray and started to refill her whisky tumbler.

'She was absolutely right! And don't you think you've had enough?'

'No, I don't, I fucking well don't, darling! He forgets, Sarah, whom he's talking to. I come from a long line of boozers. We Wootons are famous. We have a special gene for large livers, don't you know? My father drank himself to death, the most energetic thing he ever did and not a remarkable feat for a senior Tory politician. When I graduated from the hotel school in Lausanne, I threw a party that is now a legend in that otherwise extraordinarily boring town.'

'Venetia! Stop embarrassing our guest. I think you should take back what you said about Appleby. That's a pretty damning thing to say about a solicitor. Just because you don't like him.'

'No, I don't, and you know fucking well it's not just because of how he treated Ralph. Though, we won't go into that, of course. Ralph loathed him, you know, Sarah. He couldn't understand how his father had given a man like that...'

I coughed in what I hoped was a tactful manner and said as if I hadn't heard any of this, 'Goodness me, look at the time! It's been a wonderful evening. Can I ring for a cab?'

Venetia snapped back into hostess mode. 'God, I'm awful. I'll do it. I know someone terribly reliable. We'd run you home, but I don't think either of us ... you know. The number's in the study. I'll call from there.'

Paul got to his feet as she went out and stood in front of the marble fireplace. At some stage in the evening we had graduated to the sitting room. Over the mantelpiece was a large portrait in oils of a strikingly beautiful young woman in evening dress. Venetia said it was of her great aunt on her father's side. She seemed to be staring down at us out of the frame with amused condescension.

'I'm sorry about all this,' Paul said, awkwardly. 'Venetia always took Ralph's side, and, anyway, perhaps he said things out of bitterness when he'd had too much to drink. I'm sure Francis obeys the law to the letter. What Venetia doesn't like is some of his clients. She's rather snobbish about them, actually.'

'You mean Trevor Chewton?'

'Yes. Strictly between ourselves, she can't bear him. It's professionally extremely unfortunate. I don't really know why she feels like that about him. She does take against people.'

I said nothing and presently Venetia returned. We talked of countryside walks and this filled the uncomfortable time until the taxi arrived.

That night, I didn't go to sleep for ages. I lay awake thinking about the Starling-Richardses. Not about what Venetia had said about Appleby, or even Chewton. But about Paul and what had happened in the office building at the end of the garden.

He had opened the top drawer of the huge metal plan chest and heaved out a thick sheaf of large drawings. He laid it on the central table and turned over the protective plastic top cover. He motioned me over. 'This is the main layout plan. Over here is the canal basin and the existing dock buildings – where we were the other day. And this is what's going to happen to that nightmarish wasteland we wandered across.'

I stared at it in amazement. I'd expected something boring like the site plans I used for selling Chewton's houses, otherwise blank spaces with straight lines drawn around little boxes. In comparison this was a work of art. The buildings, by some trick of perspective seemed to project from the paper. And they were enormously detailed. I could see each tiny window on the old warehouses. Miniature boats floated on the old dock basin and sailed the canal. Even I, unskilled at reading the language of architecture, could get a wonderful idea of the new buildings. As I bent closely over the plan, tracing my finger over the intricate pen-work, I could imagine myself walking through the spaces that had been created.

Along the bank of the canal where I had walked the narrow cinder towpath a few days before was a wide paved esplanade. Facing the water, there were cafés, restaurants and pubs, with tables and chairs set outside to catch the sun. At intervals, wide paved alleyways intersected, breaking the buildings adjoining the canal into regular blocks and leading down into the centre of the development.

Here, in a circular space, like a vast traffic island, except that there were no vehicles, was a huge building, of unusual shape, a plus sign where the arms of the cross were linked by curves, like the webbing between fingers. It was crowned with a vast dome. Around it were other blocks of buildings with crescent-shaped frontages, separated by thoroughfares at the axes of the cross and backed by right angles, so that the cross in its circle was surrounded by a square.

From east to west there was a wide avenue of which the domed building formed the hub. On the western branch, facing the old warehouses of the port across the width of the site, was another structure, whose shape was so extraordinary and yet so familiar, I gasped. I turned to Paul, who stood with arms folded, regarding me with amusement.

'How do you do that, make it stand out like that? I keep thinking I'll bang my nose if I put it too near the paper.'

'It's called an axonometric projection. It's a useful thing to do. It looks very dramatic and it also presents each building at its plan scale area. What do you think?'

'I think it's one of the most wonderful things I've ever seen. I can imagine I'm there, walking round all these amazing spaces. And feeling that it's, well, right somehow. I mean, these aren't great high buildings, are they, apart from . . . ?'

'Apart from the pyramid? My *folie de grandeur*. I'm not sure that will be built. It will need a very imaginative tenant. Trevor has let me leave it in for the last phase. In his words, it gives the development "a smack you in the eye quality". Although a colleague of mine has called it "naïve and presumptuous". I do hope it makes it, if only to prove the doubters wrong. There's no technical problem. It's a shape with plenty of history, not like some of those weird and wonderful ideas that win architectural competitions and turn out to be unbuildable.'

'The great thing is this feeling you can walk round the entire place. There aren't any cars. Where are they all?'

He laughed, with glee, like a child with a secret. 'On the canal side, you see, if you look closely, that long esplanade is raised up on arches. Well, that's the only visible sign of a huge underground car park.'

He leant with me over the plan and pointed with his long finger. 'One of my intentions is for the place to have the same unity as a cathedral close, like Wells or Salisbury. You can't have that if it's full of traffic. By the way, do you know why Trevor called it Friars Haven?'

'Wasn't there something about a monastery here? I remember a reference in the guide book.'

'That's right. Trevor found a rather vague reference to there having been a house of the Franciscans on or near where they dug the canal basin. Presumably it was destroyed in the Dissolution of the Monasteries. But the idea caught Trevor's imagination. The name sort of celebrates the history of both occupants of the site.'

I thought back to junior school stories about Francis of Assisi. 'Wasn't he all for talking to animals, and caring for the poor? The nun who taught us RE was very keen on him, I remember.'

He laughed, a bit uneasily. 'Yes, I suppose he was. Oh well, there are more ways to make people better off than preaching at them. Providing jobs and houses, for a start.'

Oddly enough, there floated into my mind a picture of the fox I had encountered. I hoped my furry friend understood about that when the bulldozers moved in to turf him out of his home.

I stood up from the table, and put up my hand to push back my hair, which as usual was tumbling all over the place. 'Thanks for showing me this. I think it's brilliant. It's everything I longed for it to be. I so hoped it wouldn't be like one of those shopping centre places – like Brent Cross, I suppose.'

'You thought that was what a boring old provincial architect would come up with? A ghastly pile of rain-streaked, sooty concrete, all fake marble and plastic trees?'

'Well, you haven't. I don't think you're boring, Paul. I can't wait to see the details of the buildings. I hope that Appleby's going to let me start helping with the documentation. There's going to be masses.' I glanced at my watch. We had been here for ages. 'Hey, hadn't we better be getting back to the house?'

I saw him looking at me in a way, in that way, and then before I could say any more he drew me to him and kissed me passionately. I didn't resist, far from it, but something inside me was going, 'Oh, my God.'

He stopped kissing me and let his head rest upon my shoulder. His cheek felt hot against mine. 'I shouldn't have done that, should I?'

'You did, though.'

'Yes, and I wanted to. I've wanted to kiss you today ever since you came hurtling down that stupid slide thing. I wanted to scoop you up and hold you. Now I have, I suppose you think I'm just a-another middle-aged man wanting to reassure himself that he's not too old to...'

I struggled out of his arms and pushed him away so I could look at him. 'So, aren't you? I mean it's not ideal, is it? We have to work together, don't we? We have a client in common, a very demanding client. I have a boss who'll be down on me like a ton of bricks if he thinks I'm not one hundred and one per cent committed to the job. I don't imagine Chewton's any different. Oh, and I nearly forgot, you've a wife and three children. Haven't you got a secretary or someone? Your wife's best friend, perhaps?'

'You're right. I deserve that. But you have to believe me. It isn't like that. I don't go chasing after other women. Venetia and I have our differences from time to time, but we have a good relationship. You don't understand. It's you, Sarah. The first time I saw you in that gloomy warehouse. You seemed to glow, your face, your hair all sprinkled with shiny drops of rain, you were so fresh, so young. God, I thought to myself, what would she think if she knew what I was feeling?'

'I did feel it, when we were walking down that road at Friars Haven and you stopped me falling. Right in front of those other two, as well. They weren't born yesterday. Paul, I think you're a brilliant guy. Those drawings you showed me were fantastic. I'm flattered by what you said. Who wouldn't be? But you've got a lovely family and a nice house. And we should go back there right now, otherwise Venetia will wonder what the hell we're doing and it wouldn't be a good idea to get her all hurt and suspicious for no reason, would it?' I marched over to the door and pushed it open as I finished.

'Sarah! Please! All right, we can't talk now. Let me call you. I will call you.'

I was already walking down the path, and he had to hurry after me. I hoped the cool evening air would take the warm flush out of my cheeks.

Over a month had gone by and he hadn't called. I should have been relieved. I wasn't ashamed of myself. I'd been little Miss Moral and done the right thing. Mark, now Paul. It seemed to be becoming a habit. So why did I catch myself wondering whether he would ever call? I'd not been particularly put out when Mark ignored me completely in the office after that disastrous night out. So why did I feel differently about Paul? Because he was no different, was he, from Mark or from the brief, unsatisfactory flings I'd had at Myddelton before I met Colin or the others before that? There was no future in an affair with Paul, but then I'd never thought of there being a future in any of them. For me, there was no future in any affair. Because affairs that had futures involved love. And that would never be on offer. I was sure of that. Only at the beginning with Colin had that will o' the wisp tantalizingly beckoned, only to vanish into the dark night of time.

'Very nice, dear. I think that was a lovely one to end up on. Don't forget the handbrake. Ooh yes, that's right, press the little button on the end and up it comes smooth as silk, never all ratchety. How was it for you?'

I sank back in the velour seat, let go of the wheel and stretched. 'Pretty good. I feel so much more confident than when I started. I was really pleased I anticipated the lorry pulling out before you told me. Mirror, signal, manoeuvre, eh?'

'You've come on so quickly. You drive like that and you'll sail through next week. Then you'll be getting your own car, I expect.'

'Yes, I've seen one I like, in the garage down the road. He's a client of the firm, so he won't palm me off with a heap. As soon as I pass, Appleby'll authorize the loan. And I'll get an allowance for running it. I feel quite excited.' I looked at the dashboard clock. 'Do you want to pop in for some tea? Or perhaps you're rushing off?'

'A quick cuppa does sound nice. I've got to be in Swindon for a pick up ... a parcel, but the M39's not so busy on Saturdays.'

Mrs Carter, the elderly woman in the flat below, frowned when she raised her eyes from weeding around the gnomes to see Charmaine following me up the garden path.

'Ooh, what a smashing flat, all lovely and light. And a nice view too.'

I made some tea and we sat in the bay window, in the warmth of the late afternoon sun.

Through the open sash came the very faint snip-snipping of Mrs Carter's shears. Charmaine nodded in the direction of the sound and chuckled softly. 'I don't think your neighbour approved of me.'

'She's just not very friendly. She's like that with everybody.' This wasn't entirely true. Charmaine would have made anyone look twice.

That day, she had, in a big way, left off her usual scruffy driving gear. She'd slipped out of the black and gold sequin bolero jacket she'd been wearing when she came in, and she looked even more stunning without it. The white satin, low-cut, sleeveless top brought out the rich brown of her wonderful skin and set off her full figure, revealed clearly enough to show that it owed nothing at all to the art of the bra-maker. I wasn't exactly flat chested myself, but I could only marvel. What would Rose have said?

Her long black wrap-around skirt ended in a tasselled fringe, like a flamenco dancer's. The day's only concession to her profession was a pair of off-white trainers, no doubt safer shoes to drive in than the high-heeled gilt sandals which would have gone with the rest of the outfit. To make up for this lack, she wore a mass of jewellery, a gold necklace with dangling jet ornaments, huge earrings to put even Harriet in the shade and, on both arms, a slithering, shimmering array of golden bangles and bracelets.

She drank some tea and then gave me a flashing white smile. 'I bet you're thinking I'm a bit got up to meet a package in Swindon?' She shook her dark ringlets, and laid her head on one side coquettishly.

I grinned. 'I suppose I do.'

'Well, you're right. I think my luck has turned. On the QT, after I do my bit of fetching and carrying I've got a very important date tonight. It could end up very interesting. Do you ever look at the stars?'

I didn't catch on at first. 'What, in the sky?'

'No, not them. In the papers. Horoscopes. I do. And today it says, "Your life is about to take on a new direction. Leap boldly when opportunity knocks."'

'My mum used to read things like that, in the magazines. She'd see them in the houses she cleaned for people. Fat lot of good it did her.'

'You shouldn't talk like that. It's very scientific, you know. You – now, I bet I know what you are. I've got to know you quite a bit. Nothing like driving to reveal the personality. You're definitely a fire sign. But there's something else there as well, something deeper, more cautious.' She looked around at the flat. 'I bet when you moved in here, you were really pleased to have your own place, make it the way you wanted it, eh?'

I shrugged, feeling the beginnings of a blush under her scrutiny.

'I knew it. You're Leo, the lion, but on the cusp, just leaving the watery old Crab behind. Cancer, that's the sensitive, home-loving bit of you, you see. I'd say your birthday was, what, 25 July?'

I gaped at her, impressed. 'It's the twenty-seventh. How on earth did you get so close?'

'Maybe I've got a bit of the second sight, too. My mother always said she had Romany blood. Amongst all the rest. What about me, any ideas?'

I went along with her game and looked hard at her to see if anything drifted into my mind. To my amazement it did. 'I don't know when your birthday is, but I know you're an Aries.'

It was her turn to gape.

I laughed. 'No second sight. Just the ordinary kind. You wear your heart, not on your sleeve but on your shoulder, Charmaine.'

She turned her left arm and squinted down at the small blue tattoo, a ram in a circle of flowers. 'Well, aren't you the observant one. But you're right. I had a... boyfriend once who did this sort of thing. Getting fashionable for women now, at least in London, I hear. Of course, it's normally only revealed to intimate friends. Some of my customers are a bit proper –'d think it's vulgar.'

'I don't.'

'No. You're nice. You're the only nice solicitor I've ever met.'

'Met lots then, have you?' I teased.

'A fair few, but how and why, that would be telling. Now I've got to go. Thank you for the tea. Pick you up outside your office on Thursday at nine-thirty, and we'll have a little practice. Be all over by eleven. And don't worry. I've got one of my feelings.'

At the door, she turned and gave me a big hug. She felt warm and soft against me and she wore no perfume other than her own pleasantly musky odour. 'You're a lovely girl. You're like I always wanted to be. And between you and me, that bit of luck I mentioned? Well you could say as how you'd brought it to me. Oh yes, a real turn up for the book it was the day you came along. It felt like fate – and you have to take your chances in this life, eh?'

I watched her through the window, climbing back into her Cavalier, her amulets flashing in the rays of the westering sun.

# VIII

The Chewton house flag cracked and flapped in the stiff breeze like a sheet on a washing line. I crossed the cobbled road with its inset railway lines and mounted the entrance steps of the warehouse.

There had certainly been changes at Friars Haven since that first visit with Appleby nearly three months ago.

The entrance on Canal Street had been completely altered. Part of the shiny red-brick Victorian perimeter wall had been taken down, rebuilt at less than half its original height and topped with glossy black-painted iron railings. It had been moved back to form an arc-shaped cobbled forecourt in front of the considerably widened entrance, still flanked by the old pillars and their stone carved heraldic beasts, which had been carefully reconstructed. The rusty old gates had been sandblasted, repainted in the same glossy black and rehung. They were now purely decorative, being far too narrow to bar the new carriageway. Indeed, the object of the entrance was now not to keep trespassers out, but to lure in the punters.

Behind the new wall was a huge hoarding, shiny with fresh paint. On it could be read in strong blue Roman capitals on a dazzling white ground:

THE MOORINGS AT FRIARS HAVEN

A NEW DEVELOPMENT OF LUXURY APARTMENTS IN
A STUNNING HISTORIC WATERFRONT SETTING

CHEWTON RESIDENTIAL DEVELOPMENTS

HOMES WITH A HEART

Along the frontage were tall white poles from which hung and fluttered oriflammes in the blue and red Chewton colours.

The quality of the workmanship on the rebuilt brickwork and the relaid cobbles was pretty high and had cost a bomb. But according to Appleby, Chewton was relaxed about the setting-up costs of Friars Haven. It wasn't just another development. It was being built to last – and to impress.

As I strolled through the grand entrance in the autumn sunshine, I was duly impressed. They had certainly got on with it. Mind you, I hadn't been exactly idle either since that first visit. I had spent ages drafting and re-drafting the documents for the hundred-odd flats in the first phase of the warehouse conversions. And that was on top of all the routine house sales I was handling on all the other developments, plus any other little scraps Appleby might throw me from his multitude of other matters.

Some days it had been almost midnight before I finally called it quits, turned off the Anglepoise and staggered out in the cold foggy air of the Horsemarket, making sure that the lock on the glass door clicked home as it swung shut behind me.

I was working too hard, but then I didn't have a great deal to do besides work. I had gone for drinks with the others in the Coffee House a few times, been invited out to a couple of parties – Julie's twenty-first, and Karen, Conrad's secretary's engagement do.

I could have had a more exciting time if I'd wanted. Mark still gazed at me sometimes as if he thought it might be worth another try, and might even have been on the point of saying something but my own eyes looked back at him cool and unblinking, and, without resorting to the pique and unfriendliness of the weeks following his rejection, he took the hint and kept his distance. Perhaps he was playing the long game, trying to find out if I was really as resistant to his charm as I seemed to be. And sometimes I did wonder whether I wasn't being a bit over-scrupulous. He was a nice bloke, really.

But at these times when the hormones made me lie awake at night, thinking of his thick, gold hair, as curly and fresh-looking as that of a child, his slim athletic body, his ready smile and the effortlessly flirtatious banter that he'd been perfecting since public school and Oxford University, I knew that I couldn't let them rule the head. To get involved with Mark would mean that in the end, one of us would have to go and it wouldn't be him. I couldn't allow that to happen. I had got here by some fluke and I wasn't about to give it all up for a few sweaty nights and the kind of thrills I could give myself anyway, if I had a mind to. Because that was all there would be.

So, I worked late, and ate late and watched the TV news and went to bed. At weekends I slept, I cooked food ready for the following week, I listened to music – I was branching out from Bach into Telemann. And I read.

I was well into my next Dickens, *Bleak House*. I'd chosen it because the blurb said it was about the law. And, boy, was it! It all seemed horribly familiar. The obfuscation, the delay, the procedure that was archaic even in those days. But it was about more than that. It was a whole world in which I could lose myself and laugh and cry and rejoice.

I hadn't been back to Welscombe House. I didn't want to run into the Starling-Richardses. Correction: I didn't want to run into Paul Starling-Richards. Clearly he wouldn't want to run into me. It would be embarrassing for him.

Paul wasn't the sort of man I had sexual fantasies about. He had none of the physical glamour, however superficial, of Mark Oundsworth. He was shabby and middle-aged. But he was also brilliantly clever and warm and witty. Despite that, he looked sensitive and vulnerable, liable to be bruised by life without a woman to look after him. But he already had that woman. So it was just as well he hadn't called me.

I pushed open the glass doors under the projecting portico. Inside, too, there had been transformations.

The hairy tiles had gone and in their place were several acres of blue carpet. By the door, at an elegant white desk topped with a computer monitor and mini-switchboard, sat, just as I had pictured her, a blonde and blue-eyed receptionist in a crisp blouse whose interestingly plunging neckline was closed, like a visual smack on the wrist, with a chaste cameo brooch. She turned to me and smiled. Her teeth were better than mine, I noticed, being whiter and straighter. She'd clearly never played games with rough boys at a dentally formative age.

'Sarah Hartley. From Chamberlayne's. Mr Chewton's expecting me.'

I sat down on a blue velvet chair and gazed around. On the big table, empty at my last visit, was an elaborate scale model of the whole of the development. It reminded me once again of how massive it was going to be. The cavernous old warehouse on whose echoing ground floor I now sat was represented on the model by a tiny pink block no bigger than a matchbox. It was dwarfed in scale by the huge central building with its great dome.

I was waiting for my first solo meeting with Chewton. Mainly I did the estate sales meetings every week with the Chewton sales team at their offices on the industrial estate on the Westhampton road. Chewton had come in only once on one of these, arriving unexpectedly and unannounced, sitting quietly at the back of the room, and leaving abruptly before the end. The following day I had heard from the shell-shocked sales manager that a fax had arrived at the Chewton office in Exeter announcing the dismissal of all the staff and the closure of the office 'effective 12 noon today'. This, according to Appleby, had been Trevor in one of his Attila the Hun moods. Exeter had been responsible for several estates which had failed to meet their monthly sales targets. Exeter had, therefore, been blasted into non-existence, the blob which marked its position on the maps in the company's sales literature erased as if it had never been.

Acts like these ensured the continuance of Chewton's awesome reputation. He was not a man to be, as he phrased it, 'pissed about in any shape or form'. I had, therefore, prepared carefully for the meeting, even though it was very largely a routine job which Appleby thought was sufficiently low level – not much more than a delivery job – to let even me tackle unaccompanied.

Little Bo Peep at the desk, after picking up her phone and saying 'Yes,

Mr Chewton, of course, Mr Chewton' three times, tossing her mane – which I was now convinced was dyed blonde – twice, and flashing her pearly teeth – almost certainly capped – at me once, told me I could go up.

The fancy new lift – brushed stainless steel, touch-pressure switches, liquid-crystal displays and big mirrors – made my ears pop as it shot up to the third floor.

There was a small lobby with the same blue carpet. On one side, there was a sheet of roughly skimmed plasterboard, presumably shutting off one side of the warehouse and indicating where the tide of renovation had reached high-water. On the other was a mahogany panelled door. I knocked and heard him shout, 'Come in, Sarah.'

He was kneeling on the floor. The jacket of what looked like a very expensive wool suit was flung carelessly over an upholstered chair, the sleeves of his white silk shirt were tightly rolled up above his elbows, the collar was undone and his striped silk tie was pulled down so hard its Windsor knot had been squeezed to a nodule.

Spread over the thick blue pile were rolls of plans, swatches of material, books of carpet material and vinyls, samples of laminate, ceramic tiles, and piles and piles of paint colour charts. He scrambled to his feet, bent to dust down his trousers, then held out his hand to me.

'Come and sit over here and show me what you've got.'

He gestured to a long white leather sofa on the far side of the room by the window.

I sat down on the cold and slippery edge, opened my briefcase and extracted the file containing copies of the basic draft lease for the Moorings flats. I handed one to him.

'Francis wanted you to see this straight away. We've picked up all the points that were made at the last meeting. And we've included optional clauses for the mooring rights in the dock basin.'

'The Haven marina.'

'Sorry, the Haven marina. Those are only for the ones with the water frontages. Obviously you'll want to read through it in detail. But if there is anything now, I can get it acted on right away.'

He took a pair of gold-rimmed reading glasses from his top pocket and hooked them one-handed over his well-fleshed ears. He slowly turned the word-processed pages of the document, nodding or grunting occasionally.

It ran to more than thirty pages – like all leases it was hardly a masterpiece of concision. But it was as comprehensive and as lawyer-proof as Appleby and I could make it. I had done the original draft and was particularly proud that he hadn't managed to pick more than a few holes in it. It was the first really substantial contribution I had made to Friars Haven, and I waited rather tensely for Chewton to come up with something I hadn't spotted. I had gone through it with a toothcomb the night before, checking the spellings and looking for misprints and omissions and still had the headache to show for it.

He was on the last page. He stopped, checked back a few pages. I held my breath. Then he turned it over and patted the pile of paper back into shape. 'Good. Excellent. It looks very comprehensive. I rely on you people to make sure that the words do what they're supposed to, but all the points I had seem to be covered. I'll read it again later and fax you any observations. Now that you're here, you can help me with something else. Nothing to do with the law. Just a little feminine touch.'

'Oh, of course,' I said, a little warily.

He laughed. 'Don't look so alarmed. I'm not quite the ogre they make me out to be. Not quite. But just like you people, I'm a detail man – but in a different way. I know that you have to have things just so when you're trying to get people to make the most expensive acquisition of their lives. Take a look at this.'

He bent down, plucked one of the sheets of paper off the floor and handed it to me. It was a water-colour sketch of a room. With its heavy beams and supporting columns, it had to be of one of the flats in the development. I waited.

'Well? What do you think of the décor?'

I hesitated, studying his expression to see if there were any clues as to the answer. There weren't.

I looked at the sketch again but more carefully this time, thinking of my own bed-sitting room in Lochinvar Road. I breathed in deeply. 'It looks, well, it looks a bit ... dark and sort of heavy.'

'Go on.'

'The colours. These wine reds and bottle greens in the fabrics. And the chocolate-coloured walls. They're sort of old-fashioned. I'd want more sort of watery colours.' I thought back to my first sight of the sunlight on the old canal basin and the red brick and terracotta. 'And more sunniness.' I stopped, hoping I hadn't dropped some horrible clanger. I'd gone and opened my big mouth again.

But he was nodding. 'You're right. It's exactly what I thought. I've just come out of a meeting with the designers. They want to do the whole group of show flats out in these kinds of colours. I told them it was too much. Too much bloody brown-study. No woman would touch a place looking like that, I said. Okay, maybe we'll get a lot of rugger-buggers, young smart-arses, who'll like that kind of thing. But they'll have girlfriends, maybe even wives. You've confirmed what I thought.'

I started to breathe easily again.

'In this game, you know, Sarah, you have to know about women, and what women like. Everyone thinks that property development is bricks and mortar and planning and doing deals. And so it is, in part. But there's a lot of psychology too. You have to know people. They're the customers. And when it comes to houses, the little woman has the first and the last say. You know the joke? The woman talking to her friend. "He makes all the big decisions: whether we should have a nuclear deterrent, how we view the Common Agricultural Policy. I just make the little ones. Where we should live, what school the kids go to..."'

I smiled dutifully.

'I've gone a long way, Sarah, knowing about that psychology. That's what made me successful. When you go on one of my sites, you won't find a load of prats with their bellies hanging out and bum cleavages you could lose a hodful of bricks down. You won't find trannies blasting out the Top Twenty. You won't find mud sprayed over everything and piles of aggregate in the middle of the road. My sites are tidy, because people come buying in nice clothes. I don't want them to go away thinking they're going to live on a shit heap, if you'll pardon my French.'

'I went to Badgers Wood the other day. Malcolm took me. I thought it looked very nice.'

'It's a good site, Badgers. I know Francis takes the piss out of those names. It's all right – you don't have to make excuses for the man. He's over twenty-one. But it's part of the same thing. Selling houses, you're selling comfort, security, the good life. Cosiness. The names are part of that. No one can get emotional about plot number eleven. We have to warm it up a bit. That's why I thought up our slogan – Homes with a heart. Even Francis, the place he lives in. Do you know what it's called?'

I shook my head.

'The Woodlands. When it comes to it, he doesn't want to live in number eleven either. Likes a bit of class, always did. I doubt there are any number elevens in Ashton St Michael. You ever been to his place?'

'No, I haven't.' I'd heard talk in the office about Appleby's fancy house, but he'd never, as far as I'd heard, invited the serfs to dinner.

'Oh, the Woodlands is very nice, very tasteful, very *Country Life*. Good old Francis has done well for himself. But then you lawyers do, don't you? Everyone expects lawyers to do well for themselves. You're on to a good thing, my girl. Solicitors, they can be rich and honest. What a combination. No one's going to say, "How did he make his money then?" Not when they know you're a solicitor. Pillars of the community, respected citizens, they can be and make their pile too. Keep your nose clean, do what you're told, you'll do okay. What is it lawyers say? "I'm taking my client's instructions." That's it, isn't it? Well, keep taking the instructions, and only the instructions, and you and me will get on famously. Just as we're doing at the moment.'

As he said this, his pale blue eyes bored hard into mine. It was an effort to hold my gaze. I became aware of a change that had come over him. He wasn't the almost-jolly builder he had been a few minutes ago, the self-made man with his 'I did it my way' philosophy, a chubby, shortish fellow in expensively tailored clothes that in some almost comical way didn't look right on him. When he took my hand as we parted at the door of his office, I felt the ruthlessness I had felt the first time I had met him. I felt that he was a man capable of doing harm. That, if he willed it, the large warm hand that entirely engulfed my cool slim fingers would go on beyond the friendly squeeze of farewell and crush them to fragments.

'This isn't bad. And a garden too. And, ooh, those were actually gnomes I saw last night, fishing in the moonlight like the Wise Men of Gotham. They're still there now.' Harriet leaned forward to peer out of the bay window.

'Oh, very funny. It isn't my garden. I can't compete with Dartmouth Park. It belongs to the lady on the ground floor.'

'What a shame. But the flat is lovely, truly. Here's to provincial life!'

She raised her cup of coffee in a mock toast.

'I'll drink to that. So how was yesterday? You looked tired out last night.'

She wrinkled her nose. 'Fairly tedious. We're doing a docu on how people get into politics. Rupert's got a yen for that kind of thing – a seat in the House after he's made his pile. He knows some people in the Westhampton party, including the prospective parly candidate. It's very marginal, so there's a good chance he'll be in next time. We set up interviews. With him: how did he start out and why? And with the chairman of the constituency party: how did they make the selection? That kind of thing. Then the candidate doing the round of women's institutes, local meetings, chatting to local farmers about Europe, ending up with a fundraising dinner with local businessmen. *Très* boring. Not at all what I want to do, even though it is a welcome change of image from the prog I did at the Beeb.'

'So what do you want?'

'You're going to laugh at me.' She seemed much younger and more sympathetic at such moments, and I caught a glimpse of the precociously bright schoolgirl she must once have been, before she acquired her protective glaze of sophisticated self-confidence.

'No, I won't.'

'I want to investigate something, something big and nasty and scandalous. Financial, of course. Where there's brass there's muck. I know a good bit about it. Remember, I read economics. Most of my family are in the financial world. I've got the background and the contacts. All I need is the target to go after. Eventually, I'll find him. I'm sure Rupert would back me. Underneath that Old Etonian hauteur, he's actually no friend of the rich and famous. If I found a decent swindle, he'd let me go after it.'

'I didn't realize you aspired to *Panorama* status.'

'You may not be laughing but you're sneering at me. Okay, I deserve it. Rich Bitch Discovers Social Conscience. That's the headline you've got in mind, isn't it?'

I smiled. 'Not in the least. It sounds very exciting. I lead a very dull life in comparison.'

'It was your choice, darling. But it can't be all conveyancing and driving lessons.'

'If you mean, have I got a lover? No, I haven't. I don't want one either, just now.'

'Talking of that, I bumped into your Colin last week. In Harrods. He looked altogether different.'

'He's not my Colin any more. What do you mean, different?'

'Aha! I detect a stirring of interest despite your pouting disclaimer.'

'Stop teasing me. Why was he different?'

'For a start, he'd shaved off his beard.'

'That's not much of a change. You needed a good light to see he had one.'

She laughed. 'All right. This is the best bit. He's got a job. And not any job. He's got taken on by Kronobyte Corporation.'

'Who are they when they're at home?'

'You're joking. You've moved a hundred odd miles from London, not light-years. Even here they play computer games, surely. It's not really Gotham, is it?'

'I'm not into that sort of thing. I never was. It was when Colin started to get obsessed with it that I knew we were finished. I couldn't share that world at all. To me the computer is only a way of getting a job done. To Colin, it became his whole life.'

'Whatever you think of it – and I can't stand that stuff either – it's a big number for a lot of other people. It's huge business and it's going to get even bigger. Kronobyte is one of the smaller outfits, but rumour has it – and believe me I hear very good rumours when I go home to Mill Hill – that they are pushing hard on the Japanese. If Colin is in with them, he is one lucky games player. He certainly had that appearance. Good suit, handmade shoes, haircut, the complete make over.'

'That's nice for him. Perhaps my kicking him out had a galvanic effect.'

'You're quite hard when you want to be, Sarah. The poor chap was asking after you. Hoped you were all right and all that.'

'Harriet! You didn't tell him where I'd gone, did you?'

I must have seemed very fierce because she suddenly became almost scared. 'I may have mentioned that you'd got a job in Fernsford. It's not a bloody state secret, is it?'

'I'm sorry. I thought I did say before I left that I didn't want him to know where I was. But never mind. He could have found out by himself, probably, if he'd wanted to.'

Maybe I was worrying about nothing. But I couldn't help thinking that it was bad news that Colin had had my whereabouts handed to him on a plate. Who knew who else he might be persuaded to tell? I thought of the figure I thought I had seen at Friars Haven. How relieved I'd been that it was only an hallucination.

'We don't have to go in if you'd rather not.'

'But you said there was a party!'

'It's only Mark's birthday. Just a few people from the office. I said I might not be able to make it.'

'Solicitors with their hair down. I'm absolutely fascinated.'

The Coffee House was even more packed than usual. Saturday night was music night. Disco in the basement, live jazz on the top floor, every juke box in between blaring out the latest hits. We fought our way through into the Grand Saloon. I gazed around in the smoke and the noise to find the Chamberlayne group. I saw Julie and waved. We pushed our way over to her.

'Mark's just getting in a round. Rose has gone to the loo. Penny and Tom had to go early. Amanda's fallen in love and gone off with a bloke from Paignton's. Phil and Heather are discoing. James is chatting someone up over there. Doesn't that make a change?'

I struggled through to the bar and tapped Mark on the shoulder.

He turned round and gave me an old-fashioned look. 'Well, if it isn't the Snow Queen. I'm really pleased you made it in the end. And you've brought a girlfriend, too.'

'Mark. Let's drop all this silliness, please? Would you add a Perrier and a vodka and tonic to your order? Here's a fiver.'

'It's no good. I don't take bribes, particularly small ones. Oh, all right, I shall swallow my wounded male pride. Put your money away. It's my birthday, okay? And, by gum, your friend is rather stunning. Seems familiar somehow.'

Harriet was talking to Rose when I came back with Mark and the drinks.

'Sarah, darling, Harriet and I are discovering all kinds of things in common. We've worked out that Harriet's mother is a kind of distant cousin of my mother. Goodness knows what that makes us. Small world, isn't it?'

'I'll drink to that,' said Mark, raising his glass. He turned to Harriet. 'I do believe we've met somewhere before.'

Harriet didn't blink at the oldest intro in a very old book. 'Have we? How clever of you to remember.'

Julie started laughing. 'You and a few million other people, Mark, you dozy bloke. I recognized her straight away. You are that Harriet Weinberg, aren't you? On the TV? *Wheelspin?*'

'I'm afraid I am. Or rather used to be. The current one is my last series. I've left the Beeb.'

'My dad watches it. He'll be that tickled I've met you. He used to say, that girl can't half drive.'

Mark smote his forehead theatrically. 'Of course. I am stupid. You look different without a crash helmet. Much nicer. But you mean to say you won't be fulfilling every male's fantasy every Thursday night – motoring fantasy, of course. No more Lamborghinis, Ferraris, Formula Ones? No more crashing through forest tracks in the latest four-wheel-drive hairy turbo? I'm heartbroken.'

'I've sort of got away from cars now. A friend and I have started a small independent production company. We're going to do documentaries. We've got one coming up on *World in Focus*. About being a Member of Parliament. It'll have a local slant, as it happens. I've got a company card if you're interested. Spread the word.'

'First Person Productions. A seeing "I" logo. Your idea? Very clever. So how come you know our Sarah?'

They went into a huddle and I half-heartedly joined Rose and Julie in talking office politics and whether Conrad and his wife really were splitting up.

Then James came back with a tall dark girl in tow and announced somewhat drunkenly, 'My friend here is desperately in need of briefs. Although not silk, please.'

'Shut up, James. You're pissed.'

'Tomorrow, I shall be sober and you will still be a struggling barrister.'

'Is he always as bad as this?' said the unfortunate advocate, whose name was Susannah Wolfe.

'Worse!' chorused the entire table.

It was still warm as we bundled out into the night. Below us the heavy pulse of the disco made the stone paving slabs vibrate and the strobe lights flickered eerily through the glass-brick pavement lights.

James said, 'The night is young. Who's for some dirty dancing?'

Mark raised his eyebrows at Harriet but she shook her head. 'Sorry, love to, but I've got to get back to Town in good time tomorrow.'

'Another time perhaps.'

'Never mind, Mark. I'll keep you company,' said Julie, linking her arm in his and pulling him away.

'I'll get us a cab,' said Harriet, pulling out her mobile phone. 'Either of you know a number?'

Rose dropped us back at Lochinvar Road and took the cab on to the house she shared with her widowed mother in Welscombe. Harriet and I tiptoed up the staircase. Mrs Carter's flat was in darkness, as were most of the houses in the street.

I made coffee and drew the curtains across the bay window.

'Are Julie and Mark together?' Harriet asked, throwing off her shoes and curling up on the sofa.

'Good Lord, I don't think so. Julie's not as daft as she likes to make out. She flirts with him and he flirts with her, but Mark does that with everyone.'

'I'd noticed.'

'You made quite a hit. I could see he was really trying. I'd forgotten you did the motoring programme. It wasn't something I ever watched myself, I'm afraid.'

'He was pretty keen. Suggested I show him a few tips – motoring ones of course.'

'And?'

'Sarah, you are a bit thick sometimes, you know.'

'What do you mean?'

'About me – and people like Mark.'

'What, solicitors?'

'No, silly.' She hesitated and drew elaborate spirals on the fabric of the sofa arm with a fingertip. 'Don't you see? It's bloody difficult enough without your going all obtuse on me.'

'Oh, Jesus, yes I do. You mean men. Colin was right, for once, then.'

'Colin?'

'He said to me that you were a d– That you were gay.'

'Dear Sarah, you're the last of my friends to have worked it out. You're quite innocent in your own way, aren't you, despite your lurid past?'

'About that sort of thing, I suppose I am. It's never sort of figured on my agenda at all. Comes of my being so common, you see.'

'You mean you think I'm just a middle-class pervert. Underneath all that sexual bravado, you're a bloody little prude, aren't you? You've gone all disapproving.'

My face had gone hot. I knew that I was blushing in that horrible beetroot way I had. I was cross with myself, at showing my embarrassment, at my clumsy stupidity with her. I think I was still smarting from Mark's sneering references to the Snow Queen and his calling Harriet my girlfriend in that insinuating way. 'I'm certainly not a prude. I'm not disapproving. I'm just surprised that's all. You've had relationships with men. I know you have.'

'So maybe I was trying to convince myself. So there it is. Don't look like that. I'm not going to start wearing tweeds and smoking a pipe.'

'Okay. I got no marks for perception, but why are you being so sort of defensive about it? Why turn it into a sort of guessing game. Why didn't you just tell me?'

'You're right, of course. I have found it more difficult. It was important to me how you reacted. I was nervous just now because, because ...' She had gone back to tracing circles in the pile of the upholstery.

I stood up and went and sat alongside. 'Because you feel attracted to me. Is that what you mean?'

She looked up and her face was ivory pale. 'Yes. I do. I am.'

I got up and went out to the kitchen. I kept a bottle of cheap sherry in one of the cabinets. I brought it back with two tumblers. 'I'm going to have a drink. Do you want one?'

'Is that all you've got? Ugh. At this time of night. Yes, all right.'

I filled the glasses and handed one over. I drank deeply and shuddered. 'You were right, partly, about what you said earlier. I am uncomfortable about ... gays, lesbians. But only for myself. I mean, I just can't imagine myself in love like that, wanting to ...'

'To make love to a woman? I think I've got the picture. Okay, I've made my confession. Made myself look cow-eyed and silly. It's late and I'm going to bed.'

'Harriet. Sit down.' I reached up, took her arm and pulled her down. 'I love and value you very much as a friend. I respect what you've told me. I understand that you have these feelings. I've told you I don't share them. I do hope that they're not going to get in the way of the relationship we have.'

I felt a great shuddering sigh run through her. She stared down at the half-empty glass clutched between her hands on her lap. I took it gently from her and put it on the floor. Then I put my arms around her and held her while she wept. I was weeping too: for I who thirsted had indeed found a well of love but could not drink therefrom.

The next morning at breakfast she was determinedly bright and sparkly. Neither of us mentioned what had happened.

'After all that walking you made me do yesterday afternoon, I feel fit enough even for another week of the crazy hours of television.'

'You couldn't go back to the Smoke without some country air.'

'Mind you, I don't think you meant us to tramp quite so far. I think you were lost – had the map upside down or something.'

'Certainly not. It was all planned. I was told about that walk by experts. That's just your London mindset. Once you're out of reach of an underground station, you get all nervous. Think you're going to fall off the edge or something.'

'That seemed quite likely at one point. That great plunging cliff with the river miles below. If you hadn't kept hold of my arm, I'd have fallen off for sure.'

'No, you wouldn't. You were a bit dizzy, that's all. Spectacular, wasn't it? I'd heard that the Upper Tarrant was worth seeing.'

'What was that place called again?'

'Randolph's Leap. According to some old legend, a knight in shining armour was commanded by a great magician whose daughter he was in love with to undertake three impossible tasks. Only then would he win her hand. Well, the first two – move a hillock a couple of miles, plant a forest in a day – he got through, easy-peasy, because the daughter was no slouch at magic herself and gave him a hand. But the cunning wizard realized what was afoot the last time, and locked her up in a magic castle where she couldn't help. The task was to jump on his horse over the Tarrant, off that bluff we were on.'

'And did he succeed and win the lady?'

'He knew he hadn't the support of magic, but he leapt anyway. He had only his faith in the power of love. As he was about to plunge to his death, the wizard, who'd originally figured this was a handy way to get rid of the troublesome suitor, so he could keep his daughter for himself, saw how gone he was and relented. He cast a spell that carried the bold knight to the other side and released the daughter from imprisonment. She married her knight and they all lived happily ever after.'

'That is a fairy story, isn't it? Love conquering all?'

'Maybe. But why shouldn't we have a happy ending sometimes?'

'Hey, you made it up, didn't you? You were having me on.'

I smiled. 'You've got me bang to rights, I'm afraid. It is called Randolph's Leap on the map, but goodness knows why.'

She stretched out her hand. 'Dear Sarah. I do love you.' She turned the squeeze into a pat, then withdrew. 'I like the story. It shows a nice imagination. You've changed in this place, haven't you? You're happier, as if, well, as if some shadow had left you.'

I shook my head and laughed. 'Shadow? I can't think what you mean. But I can't say I miss Hoxton. That Doctor Johnson of yours was wrong. I'm not tired of life at all. Far from it. It's all happening for me. Now I've passed my driving test, I've got my eye on a little car. With that, I'll be much freer. Appleby promised I can start doing site acquisition investigations once I'm mobile. I know it's old hat to you, but to me it's very exciting.'

'I know the feeling. I couldn't wait. I passed the test on my seventeenth birthday. Mind you, I had been driving for years before that.'

'Yes, I can't hope ever to rival your skills. The way you went down that winding road above the Upper Tarrant yesterday was amazing. I didn't feel scared, just exhilarated. Even though it's got a bad reputation as far as Chamberlayne's is concerned.'

'Why so?'

'Ralph Chamberlayne, Appleby's partner, was killed in an accident there on his way home a few years ago.'

A flicker of interest showed in her face. 'Really? What was it? A head-on? It is quite narrow in places. Or had he been drinking?'

'Apparently not. None of the usual things. He just ran off the road and over the cliff. Rose is too discreet to say straight out, but she implied he and Appleby had had a row. I suppose he could have been upset and lost his concentration.'

'We did a prog about accidents in the last series of *Wheelspin*. There wasn't one where the cause wasn't obvious. Do you know what he was driving?'

I thought for a moment. 'A Rover. A newish Rover, Rose said. Why do you ask?'

'Crude automobile psychology. Not what you'd call an enthusiast's car. Not a boy racer.'

'No, I gather he wasn't the least bit like that.'

'Curiouser and curiouser. You see, I don't go for this lapse of concentration explanation. It may happen on motorways – people nod off or get too involved with a phone conversation. But on a road like that? Particularly one you commute over. You get to know every inch of the surface. You're geared up to do the right thing whether you're fully concentrating or not. Okay, if there had been another vehicle involved – you can always be put out by the unexpected. But otherwise, no. And if you did feel yourself going, then you'd pull it back pretty smartly. Sorry, I'm being a car bore. I can't help it. I adore the stupid things.'

'No, it's interesting. Wouldn't the police have gone into it?'

'You seem to have a naïve faith in them all of a sudden. To think how you used to talk about the Met! To the police, if it looks like an accident, it's an accident. They're far too busy to waste time on speculation.'

'Unlike you.'

'Unlike me. And I mustn't spend any more time speculating idly because I have to be back in town by four. We've got a press preview.'

'Drive carefully,' I said.

# IX

The narrow, double-white-lined road wound down one side of the valley, and between the trunks of the low leafless trees, I could catch vertiginous glimpses of the river which ran at the foot of the ravine. Although I felt, generally, pretty confident about driving, thanks to Charmaine's excellent tuition, this was the first longish trip I had taken since I'd got the car.

At first I had been nervous of this twisting switchback, the very same stretch on which Ralph Chamberlayne had come to grief. I found myself wondering as I rounded yet another almost hairpin bend whether it was there that he had hurtled off the road, or there the crash barriers had, as Rose had said, been installed too late to save him.

His mysterious accident reminded me of my day out with Harriet. I thought, rather guiltily, that I hadn't been in touch with her properly since that weekend, apart from a couple of rather hurried and unsatisfactory phone conversations. I had never been in the habit of writing letters, and I wouldn't have known what to say even if I had been. Since that time, it had been all work and hardly any play. Today's outing, even though it had a serious purpose, was definitely a little bonus.

The damp misty weather of the last week or so had cleared, and although still cold, the sun was bright and the sky was blue. Even in the last days of autumn, the Upper Tarrant was spectacularly beautiful. I had completed the descent and the wide swift-flowing river was on my left, fringed with trees. Every bend in the road brought a new vista of distant blue hills, fronted by the towering cliffs of sheer limestone on the opposite bank, ripplingly reflected in the water, all framed by the massive grey trunks of the ancient beech woods which grew to the very edge of the road, and formed tunnels of branches arching high overhead.

It was good to be out on such a day. I thought fondly again of Charmaine. It was to her I owed my new-found freedom. The warm feeling was tinged with regret that I'd not been able to thank her properly after I'd passed the test and probably now had missed the opportunity. She'd rushed off to another lesson afterwards and she'd only had time to give me a quick hug and a 'Well done, sweetheart. I knew you would.' I'd phoned her when I got back to the office but had got only her answering machine, and she hadn't returned my call. I'd tried again the following day and hadn't even got the machine. That was a pity, as I was going to arrange to meet her to give her the little present I'd bought – nothing much, just some gilt and amber coloured beads that I thought she'd like.

After a couple more goes over the next day or so, I still hadn't got hold of her. I was even getting slightly worried. Perhaps what I had fancifully constructed of her lurid past might have caught up with her. To quieten these probably far-fetched anxieties, I decided I would pop round to her house with the gift. I had the address on her card. She lived in Rosary Street, in the Brinwell district of town. It was only a short step from the office.

So, late one afternoon, returning from a visit to the Guildhall to check a planning application for a private client of Appleby's, I took the opportunity to call on her as well.

Despite its proximity to the Horsemarket and the solid commercial heart of the city, Brinwell isn't the sort of place respectable citizens venture into. This didn't bother me. I wasn't convinced that the villains of a tame burg like Fernsford, even if there were any, came anywhere near their London equivalents.

You reach this den of iniquity by leaving the Horsemarket and going down St John's Street. This is one of the so-called best preserved parts of old Fernsford, where most of the buildings are eighteenth century or earlier, and where the narrow carriageway is still cobbled. If you ignore the parked cars, it could be a stage set for one of those historical TV series.

In actual fact it was as much a front as if it had been built for the films: the quaint half-timbered gabled mansions which leaned their upper storeys over the pavement were building society branches or chain-store chemists and stationers. The narrow-fronted Georgian stucco houses of the merchant classes had long since been gutted and turned into offices. It was in one of these, I had learned recently, Chamberlayne's had spent the first hundred years of its existence.

Appleby had told me in one of his occasional chatty moods that his first act as senior partner had been to move the firm from there into the Horsemarket. I walked more slowly, looking out for it in what was merely idle curiosity. There it was, number 72. It was now I noticed the offices of something that, from the shoddy aluminium nameplate screwed to the doorcase, called itself Barnsbury Investments Ltd. I stared briefly up at the elegant but slightly shabby façade. There were lights on behind the half-closed vertical venetian blinds, an innovation that I was sure had not been there in old Chamberlayne's day.

I put my hands into the deep pockets of the long, rather classy white trenchcoat I had bought myself at the weekend and sauntered on towards the bridge over the Fern. I paused, standing in one of the salients in the wall to let a wide low-slung sports car roar its way across in the direction I had just come from. My hair flew about wildly in my eyes in the wind of its passing. I dragged my face clear of my undisciplined locks again and gazed after it in annoyance. I recognized the personalized number-plate. It was Trevor Chewton's Porsche.

I watched it stop further down the street. It was definitely him. I even saw, in the sun's dying rays, the flash of gold from the chunky watch he wore. Jimmy Maloney down in Maconochie's Bar in Islington, where I used to work during college vacations, would have said, 'One or the other you could forgive, but, bejasus, a fucking Porsche and a Rolex both.' So what was he doing here? He wasn't expected in the office, so far as I knew, and if he were he wouldn't park here but in the space in the basement car park reserved for the most important clients. As I watched, he stuffed the keys into the pocket of his leather coat – Gucci, of course – and trotted jauntily up the steps of number 72. He waited only a moment or two gazing up and down the street before the door opened and he went inside.

It seemed an odd coincidence, but maybe it wasn't. Appleby might well have sold the building or leased it to a mutual business acquaintance. Chewton was a man with a vast range of interests. However, quite where the slightly seedy-looking finance company figured in them was anyone's guess. It wasn't any of my concern.

I stared down at the greeny-brown waters of the Fern. It flowed swiftly, little eddies of turbulence swirling against the triangular revets of the piers. A mist was gathering on the grassy verges of the riverside walk, and the setting sun had been blotted out by a huge dark grey cloud which drifted over the city like the aftermath of a nuclear explosion. I turned up my coat collar and headed over the bridge to Brinwell.

Rosary Street must at one time have been a desirable residence for the Victorian lower-middle classes of Fernsford's first heyday. No longer. The once neat terraces now bore all the signs of multiple occupation and neglect. The small front gardens were trodden mud or rank grass, home for overflowing dustbins and broken furniture. From open, uncurtained windows, rock music bellowed. There was no one about, apart from a youth tinkering with the engine of an old car, his tool kit and various rusty cans spread out over the paving slabs so I had to edge around against the limp leathery foliage of an overgrown privet hedge.

At the number I had for Charmaine, there was no sign of life. I climbed the chipped stone entrance steps. There was a crudely wired-up doorbell, with two buttons, one unlabelled, one reading Potter. I pressed it, and heard a faint buzzing on the other side of the gap-jointed front door. After a few moments, I pressed it again. No reply. Irritated, I glanced back out at the street. There was no sign of the Cavalier amongst the closely parked cars. That in itself didn't mean anything: in this sort of neighbourhood, she'd have been wise to rent a garage. But it wasn't like her to be so unavailable. I'd had no trouble in contacting her when she was giving me lessons.

After another fruitless push at her bell, I jabbed the unlabelled one. Perhaps the neighbour knew when she'd be home. I waited impatiently, about to give up on the whole thing. Then, down on the garden level, I heard the squeak of a sash window being laboriously raised. I leaned over the rusty iron railings. A blonde-haired youngish woman was craning her neck upward. 'What do you want?' The hoarse-voiced challenge set off a burst of coughing.

'I'm looking for Charmaine. It's all right. I'm a friend. She got me through the driving test. I've got a present for her.'

The drawn face lost some of its suspiciousness. 'Well, you're too late. She's gone. Flitted.'

'When did she do that? She never said she was moving.'

'A few days ago? A week? How should I know? I didn't put it in my bloody diary. She packed up her car, and said ta-ta and went just like that.'

'Did she say where she was going?'

'I think she said something about London. Yes, she was from there. Said she'd had enough of this dump and was going back. It's nice for them who've got the option, I said.'

'Did she say where in London? Did she leave an address?'

'No. She never. We weren't what you'd call pals, but I was a bit surprised she went in such a rush. I'd always got the feeling she was doing all right.' This speech provoked another paroxysm. In the room behind, a child started screaming. 'Are we finished? I've got things to do.' She jerked her head back into the room. 'Four of the buggers.'

The Porsche had gone when I walked back down St John's Street to the office, and I didn't think any more about it. I was far more concerned by what I saw as Charmaine's precipitate departure. It surprised me she had gone back to London. I had had the distinct impression from the occasional remarks she had made during our lessons that London was the past for her. She had a nice little legitimate business going. Why would she throw it all up?

But then, how did we fathom other people's motives? Charmaine must have had her reasons — a friend in need or a relative, perhaps. And I had to keep reminding myself that I had probably invented her previous profession. Logically, there was no reason to be worried. But I was. However I tried to rationalize it, Charmaine's doing a bunk seemed odd. But there wasn't, when it came to it, anything I could do about it.

It was hard, on such a day, to stay worried about someone else when I had so much to be selfishly pleased with myself about. Even if it had been a horrid grey day I would still have been chuffed. I was on my first solo mission for Chewton Developments. It had taken me over three months or so of nagging, albeit tactfully at Appleby, to allow me to get involved in the procedures for acquiring development sites. Finally he had agreed that once I had got my driving licence, I could do the first one that subsequently came up. I suspected that he was a bit surprised when I passed the test first time, but he had grudgingly stuck to the bargain and here I was.

He had briefed me on it the previous evening and given me the papers to read over at home.

'Vale View, Woodcombe. That's on the Upper Tarrant. Clavells are the agents. Buckingham's acting for the vendor. One of Matravers's old clients. Sale by informal tender, closing in two weeks. Trevor's had his surveyor have a look, and he's interested in principle, but he wants a full legal report in three days, before they crank up the computer to do all the sums. Here's the stuff they've sent us. Draft contract et cetera. Looks straightforward.

It's a smallish site they're looking at. About a couple of acres or a bit over. Big enough for about fifteen or so of the bigger house types: Marlboroughs or those bolt-on Tudor-beamed jobbies – you know the ones I mean?'

'Salisburys.'

'They're the ones. Six bedrooms. Three-car garage. Mr and Mrs Salesman's idea of heaven.' I was never entirely sure whether Appleby's disdain for this side of his client's activities wasn't a bit put on. The aristocratic style perhaps cloaked some basic social insecurity. I liked to think it did. It showed that he was human – partly, at least. And perhaps that we had something in common.

He'd condescended to take me with him on a couple of previous site visits. I had learned a lot, not because he made any conscious attempt to teach me, but because even he couldn't help showing off to an audience. I had watched him carefully and made notes, hoping that sooner or later, he would send me out. I knew that when he did I would very much be on trial.

In anticipation, I had assembled the things I thought I would need – not that Appleby himself took what he called 'kit' with him, apart from a pair of wellies and an ancient waterproof jacket. But I knew that I would need all the help I could get. So, I had a cheap compass I had bought from a toyshop; one of those instant cameras, second-hand from a stall in the Saturday market; a small torch for any dark corners; a clipboard and marker pen; my dictating machine for doing the notes; my counsel's notebook; and a copy of the documents which Appleby had given me.

I had packed this into a rather garish nylon rucksack. As I came out of the lift, I met Mark going the other way.

He grinned. 'Oh, very fetching. Going hiking? It's nice not to have work to do.'

'Francis thought I needed a day out in the country. "Put some colour into those pale cheeks, m'dear,"' I said in a passable imitation of his languid drawl.

'I know. You're doing a site. Where is it? I could drive out at lunchtime, nice country pub...'

'You're madly busy, remember? Besides, I'm going to be back before lunch, I hope. 'Bye.'

I whirled out before he could reply. I was glad he was finally out of his pique and had stopped the sly hints about my alleged sexual preferences. In a way it was flattering that he was so persistent. In another way, it was just a bore that he seemed unable to treat me straightforwardly as a colleague.

'Woodcombe welcomes careful drivers' read the black-on-white metal sign. Its grey houses rose in tiers up the steep-sided valley. The main road crossed the river by a humpback stone bridge and became the high street of the small town. Scattered along both banks were a few streets of small shops, a couple of pubs, a big old coaching inn with a cobbled yard and a Lloyds bank. Just over the bridge, I parked the car on a single yellow line and dashed across the pavement into a newsagent's shop to ask the way.

The elderly woman behind the counter grumbled to her feet and ushered me back to the door. Through the glass panel she indicated the hillside which hung over the town like a cloud. 'See that big old tree? That's Vale View.'

I followed her pointing finger. The cedar tree stood out dark green amongst the grey-brown mass of trunks and bare branches. I recalled the Tree Preservation Order registered in the search.

'Nunhampton Lane you want. First left back over the bridge. Up the hill. Look for the drive on the left. Mrs Kemble's dead, though, isn't she?'

'So I understand.' I didn't enlighten her any further, but bought a packet of mints instead.

I slowed the car and turned off the metalled lane on to the weed-covered shingle drive, the entrance to which was almost hidden by towering clumps of glossy laurel hedges riotously out of control. One gate pillar had vanished altogether. The other, its stonework crumbling to powder, seemed to be held up by the ivy which coiled around it. Detached and stacked by the side of the drive was the missing pair of gates, their white-painted finely crafted timbers green with mould and showing the cracks and blisters of terminal rot.

I drove on slowly, bumping along the rutted surface. The drive ended in an open sweep before the house. In front, on a wide unmown lawn, was the cedar, at close quarters, vast, its huge plate-like spreads of branches almost touching the side and roof of the house. But as I got out of the car I saw that the lowest of them rested on thick wooden props driven into the ground, like an old woman on a zimmer frame, and the crown of the tree had long since been broken off by a storm or by lightning, leaving a well-weathered but still jagged scar at the top of the trunk.

As for the house, if I hadn't known from the papers that it had been lived in until recently by the late Mrs Kemble, whose executors were the vendors, I would have said it had been uninhabitable for years. As I stared up at the stone façade, I could see the sky through the glassless windows of the top storey. The roof had completely collapsed into the shell. The gable wall on the valley side was leaning outwards at an alarming angle, and from its ruinous upper verges sprouted dry tufts of weeds and small bushes. I could now see that, under the eroded but still spectacular stone shell canopy at the front entrance, the massive wooden door was barred by two rough planks of timber crudely nailed crosswise over it. The ground-floor windows were obscured by closed internal wooden shutters.

I donned my wellies, fished my rucksack out of the car and shouldered it. I might as well start by having a look round the house, even though I gathered that the intention would be to demolish it. It wasn't a listed building and was too far gone to be worth converting. There was probably another access round the back, tradesman's entrance or the like, and the boundary with the lane had to be checked. I walked along the flagged terrace away from the valley side, from time to time almost slipping on the moss-encrusted paving.

The other side seemed no more hopeful than the front. There was the same dereliction; it was worse, if anything. The ground was littered with lumps of fallen stonework, green with algae and fissured with frost damage. Then, as I rounded the corner to the back of the house, I was surprised to smell woodsmoke. It was coming out of the tall brick chimney of an inverted L-shaped range of single-storey buildings facing a cobbled courtyard. In front of me across the yard was a plank door, its blue paintwork blistered and peeling. Appleby had said nothing about an inhabitant. Could there be squatters? I marched a little nervously up to the door and knocked hard.

The woman who opened it was, I guessed, in her mid-twenties, about my own age. She was slightly built and shorter than me, with short blonde hair. She wore a checked man's work shirt and jeans. I noticed that her bare arms and hands were covered in grey muddy stuff, patchily dried to a dusty paleness.

She stared at me with blue eyes wide with hostility. 'Yes?'

'I'm Sarah Hartley. I'm a solicitor, authorized by the vendors to inspect the property on behalf of clients. This is my card. I'm afraid I didn't know that there was anyone...' I tailed off, not knowing quite how to broach the matter of what she was doing here.

She took the card with long grey fingers. 'Chamberlayne's. Fernsford. Who's your client?'

'They are a major property development company, but I'd rather not say at pres–'

'Well, it's none of my business, anyway. You don't have to look so worried. I'll go when the demo men move in. I shan't want to stay when the fucking bungalows go up.'

'Oh, it won't be bungalows – high specification detached homes.' As soon as I said it, I knew it wouldn't impress this angry woman. It didn't.

'"High-specification" are they? Avocado en-suite built-in wardrobes? I don't give a toss what they are. The place'll be ruined whatever.' There was a slight catch in her voice and she turned away quickly and slammed the door.

The encounter with this mysterious person confirmed yet again how wrong I had been ever to think that the sale of land was unemotional paper pushing. There was enough emotion there to fuel a power station. I suddenly realized what the grey stuff on her hands was. Art lessons at school. It wasn't mud but clay. Perhaps she was an artist. She certainly had the temperament. But what was she doing here? Despite her willingness to get out, I should have to get something a bit more definite out of her about her status for my report. But, thankfully, that could wait until later.

'This part of the boundary is very overgrown. According to the survey plan, there's a metal estate fence, but I can't see it. It must be behind these nettles and hawthorns. Ouch!' I clicked back the button on the dictating machine. I would have to ask Penny to delete the sound effects when she typed it up. I checked the tape. I'd used nearly all of it. The business was taking far longer than I'd anticipated. I had been scrambling about for nearly an hour and still hadn't checked the whole boundary. The trouble was that the place was not so much overgrown as a jungle. But as this was my first one, I was going to get it right. Appleby had given me plenty of warnings about looking for things which would not appear on the papers:

encroachments by neighbouring properties, fences moved or walls illegally demolished, evidence of unauthorized rights of way or use, problems of access, unusual or unpleasant uses of adjoining land. That was the reason we made a point of checking over sites ourselves.

Eventually I struggled round the rest of the lower boundary. The drystone wall was derelict but ran where it ought to. I sat down to check the site survey again. It had obviously been prepared for an old conveyance and wasn't very detailed. I had seen and noted the grass tennis court – now almost completely vanished apart from some rotten wooden fence posts and a few shreds of rusty wire-mesh fencing. There was the thick hatching of the central slope. The photocopy was rather blurred, and I hadn't noticed up to then that there was something written in the spidery handwriting of the old surveyor amongst the hatching. I peered at it more closely. 'Grotto' it read.

Grotto? Some kind of ornamental garden structure, I presumed. It couldn't be all that special or the listed buildings people would have picked it up. It was the kind of thing they liked. But the house was Edwardian, its seventeenth-century features faked and of no architectural or historic interest, so it was unlikely that anything in the garden would be different, particularly in its present hopeless state. Still, I thought, it might be worth a look. It even sounded fun.

I climbed back up the slope along what had once been a meandering path through the patch of woodland. Glancing around, I saw big chunks of mossy stone littering the sloping ground, which gradually steepened and rose to the upper part of the site in a low cliff, but there was no sign of the grotto.

I was about to give up when my eye was caught by a clump of sprawling evergreen shrubs at the foot of the miniature escarpment. They seemed to have grown together over a gap, as if at one time they had been planted to frame rather than obscure. With some difficulty I pushed through their thick growth. Emerging on the other side, my hair pulled all over the place and bits of dead bark adhering to my coat and jeans, I found what had to be the grotto.

It wasn't much: a triangular opening in the rock, about five feet high and three wide. I bent down and poked my head into the dark aperture. A damp smell greeted my nostrils and I could hear the faint sound of water tinkling further back in the darkness. At the entrance, the floor of the cave was covered by a thick, carpet-like expanse of spongy moss, and ferns with long, crinkled, glossy green leaves grew straight from cracks in the walls.

It was the water which made me want to investigate further. 'Always be suspicious of springs and suchlike,' Appleby had said. I fished my torch out of the rucksack and shone it into the depths of the grotto.

The cave ended after about ten feet in a solid rock-face, which gleamed faintly in the beam. The spring, if that's what it was, trickled down the back wall. On a sunny day, with the encroaching shrubbery cut back, the grotto would have been less gloomy, more of a pleasant spot to gather for a picnic. As I withdrew my head from the entrance, I saw that the moss on the floor partially concealed a round basin which had been hewn from the stone. Kneeling, I traced its outline with my hand, and found that there was a spillway cut at the front of the basin over which there was still a slight seepage. Presumably, in the old days, the flow had been stronger and the stone basin would have contained a clear pool of glassy liquid which brimmed over into the turf below.

I hunched down on a rock and dictated my findings into the machine. Before I got up, I took a last look into the mouth of the grotto.

Perhaps my eyes had become more accustomed to the gloom, or perhaps the sunlight now shone more directly into the cave – whatever the reason, I saw to the left of the rock wall down which the spring trickled a darker shadow. I don't know why I was drawn to investigate. I bent down and, slipping and slithering on the wet moss and algae, went into the cave, the torch beam dancing wildly over its floor and sides.

There was a narrow aperture where I had noticed the shadow. I shone the torch into it. The light picked out the rough hewn edges of a passageway which doubled back behind the end wall of the cave, preventing me from seeing further than three or four feet. Without pausing to think what I was doing, I turned sideways and squeezed through the gap with my face millimetres away from the rough surface – being scarcely half as wide as a doorway, it was impossible to get the width of my shoulders through, and anyone with more bulk would never have made it even in that awkward fashion. I wormed my way along, feeling gingerly for the ground with my leading right foot, as I had no room to twist my head downwards to see what the torch in my right hand was illuminating.

I soon paid for my rashness. The floor beneath my right boot, which had a moment before seemed crunchingly solid, turned to loose stones at the next step. They began to roll away with horrifyingly sudden slickness under the stiff sole as if they were ball bearings; I heard the rattle as they bounced off rocks far below in the darkness. As my feet shot from under me, I dropped the torch, waving my arms desperately to find something to grab hold of. There was nothing. The enclosing walls of the passageway were no longer there. I fell heavily on to my back, banging my head, all the while sliding downwards with frightening speed. I threw my right arm over my body to twist myself on to my stomach, and my desperate fingers clawed hard into the rock before my face, while I thrashed my legs wildly for a foothold. It was no good, I was hurtling inexorably down what I dimly realized was an almost sheer cliff. At last my right hand closed over a lump of jagged rock and clung to it. It stopped my fall long enough for me to scrabble for a toehold on to tiny ledges of projecting stone. My shoulders and arms burned with the strain of holding me as I clung like a fly, spread-eagled against the damp-smelling rock, my breath heaving, sucking in great lungfuls of air, fighting the dizziness and shock and the tearing pain in my fingers.

I couldn't hang there for long; but which way, up or down? The fall had disorientated me. How far up was the entrance to the cleft I had squeezed through? With great difficulty I pulled my left cheek away from the cold stone against which it was pillowed. I cricked my neck upwards, but the blackness was impenetrable. With my muscles screaming in agony, I swivelled my head the other way. In doing so I looked not only left but downwards in the gap between my arm and the cliff. To my amazement, I saw a faint yellow glow.

The torch. It was unbroken in the fall. And to judge from the size of the light, it couldn't be very far away. The decision was made. I willed my right hand free, and lowered it a couple of feet to a knobby projection. Then with my right leg, I slid down very slowly until my foot hit another miniature ledge and brought my left hand and leg down equally slowly to the same level. I glanced down again. The torch light seemed definitely nearer. I repeated the manoeuvre. Again and again and again.

After what seemed an age, I ventured another glance downwards to the torch. I found I could see part of the orange plastic casing and the silvery gleam of the reflector. And when I lowered my right foot, it met not a minimal shelf, but solid ground.

I was shaking all over as I stood at the base of the cliff I had climbed down. I picked up the torch from where it had fallen between two lumps of stone. I shone it upward, and couldn't restrain an awed gasp.

Above me was about twenty feet of almost vertical rock. At the top, I could just make out the opening of the cleft. I could now work out what had happened. Winding down the cliff-face at a steep but manageable gradient was a narrow ledge of rock, surfaced in shattered pieces of stone and, at the bottom, there were considerable boulders. The ledge twisted sharply away from the entrance to the passageway, so, instead of descending comparatively safely by this means, I had, when I lost my footing, slithered right over it and down the rock face. If I had not managed to get that handhold, I would have fallen the entire distance on to the stony floor. I shuddered. I would at the very least have broken a leg. I doubted whether the woman at the house would have thought very quickly to worry whether I was all right or would have known about this place even if she had.

Gradually, a sense of normality asserted itself. I hadn't killed myself, nor been seriously injured. Apart from a lump on my head, a few cuts, bruised legs and ribs and broken fingernails, I wasn't hurt at all. Now that I was here, I should endeavour to find out exactly what this place was. I shone the torch around. It carved a slim cone of yellow light in the enveloping cold darkness, glinting off the jagged, faceted surfaces of the roof and walls.

I was in an underground chamber. As far as I could judge it was about a couple of hundred feet long and half that broad. At irregular intervals there were thick pillars of rock growing out of the floor like huge trees and, like trees, spreading out curving branches of stone up to the roof. It was these that made me realize that whatever the purpose of this cavern, it was man-made. The rock pillars had been left there deliberately to support the roof when the chamber had been hollowed out around them.

At the far end there were a couple of patches which gave back no reflection to the torch. I surmised that these were tunnels leading to other parts of the cave system. I made no move to investigate. I had no idea how long the batteries would last, and such was the extremely restricted light I had that I had no certainty that I could find my way back to the one place I knew I could get out. I shivered, the chill of the place penetrating the marrow of my bones. I felt all at once the pain of my cuts and bruises. The thought of having to struggle back through the crack in the rock behind the grotto made me feel weak and exhausted. Angrily, I roused myself. It was my own stupid fault I had got into this place and no one was going to get me out. I shone the torch up at the tumbled boulders of the ascent. It wasn't all that far. With my handkerchief I strapped the torch to my left wrist so that I had both hands free. Then, slowly and carefully, I began to climb.

With swollen knuckles I tapped painfully on the blue door of the stable block. After a moment or two the door creaked open, and the woman appeared.

'You again. Finished, have you?'

I opened my mouth to say something, but all that came out was a kind of croak. I saw her eyes widen as she took in my altered appearance.

'Christ Almighty. What have you done to yourself? Are you all right? You'd better come in and clean up. Have some tea or something.'

I nodded limply. All of a sudden I felt terrible, the adrenaline pumped up by my escape from the cave evaporated. She gripped my elbow with a strong clay-encrusted hand to help me through the door, and pulled the door shut.

Inside, I was aware only of a long, cluttered room. On the hearth of a fireplace built of massive blocks of stone stood a black cast-iron woodburning stove. The warmth made me realize how cold I had got. I sat down in a battered leather armchair by the fireside and started to shake and shiver. It must have been shock: I'd seen it on TV medical dramas. I leaned back in the chair and watched my hostess, feeling like an OAP with the WRVS lady.

Under the window by the door was a kitchen unit covered in unwashed pots. On the sill behind, by yellow earthenware jars filled with wooden spoons, spatulas and other impedimenta, stood a clutter of packets of soap powder, and plastic squeeze-bottles of washing-up liquid and scouring cream. I noticed that they were all brands which claimed to be friendly to the environment. I never bought them myself. Not that I had anything against the environment, I just didn't feel the need to be on such good terms as to spend the extra they cost.

I watched her clear a space among the mess, and make tea with teabags in a big stoneware pot. She stirred vigorously then poured it out into a matching mug. 'Milk? Sugar?'

I nodded again, and she handed me the drink, steaming hot and dark brown. I sipped it gratefully. 'Thanks,' I managed to say. I clutched the mug as tightly as the pain allowed and gradually the shaking subsided.

Feeling slightly better, I had to haul myself out of the chair to go to the loo. It was in a kind of lean-to on the other side of the kitchen. There was a discoloured lavatory with a broken plastic seat crammed under the sloping roof, a cracked washbasin and a small mirror. I looked at myself. I certainly was a mess. My hair was thick with stone dust and bits of twig were virtually woven into its thick tresses. My left cheek-bone was raw and abraded. My clothes were coated with yellowish-grey smears from the sticky clay of the cave floor. My whole ribcage hurt when I moved, but I didn't think I'd broken anything. The left knee of my jeans was torn, and underneath I could feel that my shins were a mass of bruises and swellings.

I pushed my jeans and pants down with difficulty and used the loo, but when it came to washing my hands, the cold water made me cry out in agony.

The three big fingers on my right hand were torn and split, the nail of my index finger had been ripped almost in half and the quick had gone quite black. The back was puffy and covered in the raised weals of long gashes. My left hand wasn't in much better shape.

'Are you all right in there?' Her voice came clearly through the thin plank door. She must have heard me.

I fumbled my clothing together somehow and opened the door.

'I'm fine. My hands sting a bit in the water.'

'Sting! I'm not surprised. They should be seen to. I'll get some warm water and clean them up, if you can bear it. I've got some creams that are very good for cuts and bruises. I'm always knocking bits off myself. Occupational hazard.'

I sat down in the chair again. She put water from the kettle into a clean enamel bowl and cooled it at the sink, then she knelt down in front of me and gently swabbed my wounds with tissues.

Although she was gentle, I winced in a good deal of agony. Finally, though, it was done. She wiped them with a dry tissue, and applied soothing creams from different tubes, one for bruises and one for the cuts. I peered down at the labels. 'Calendula, arnica. I've never heard of them.'

She gazed up at me, and smiled. 'They're very old herbal remedies. They stimulate the body's natural healing abilities. I don't believe in modern drugs. They do violence to our inner harmony.' Under the spiky fringe of her rather dirty-looking hair, her eyes were large and a soft grey-blue.

'I see. Judging from the way my legs feel, I could do with some on them.' I gingerly pulled up one leg of my jeans. The shin and knee were red and swollen. 'It's all right, I can do it myself. Ouch!' Even rubbing in the ointment with my damaged paws was painful, so I let her do it.

'There, that's better, I think.' She carefully rolled down the trouser legs, then sat back on her heels to look at me. 'So what were you doing out there to get yourself into this state?'

'I was exploring what the plan I was given calls the grotto and I fell down into a sort of cave – a really big one. And dug out, not natural.'

'A cave? What, under the garden?'

'Yes. Might even go under the house as well. There seemed to be a lot more of it – I thought I could see a couple of tunnels. I don't understand why it's there. There's no coal round here – not according to the mining search, anyway.'

She looked thoughtful. 'No, it isn't coal. I think I know what it is. It's stone. It's an old stone mine. That's what you stumbled into.'

'Stone? I thought you blasted that out of quarries?'

'Not this sort of stone. I remember being told about it at school. Apparently, the kind of limestone round here is found in seams underground. Also when it's in the ground it's soft and easy to work. It hardens in contact with air. There are old mines all over this area. They go for miles underground. Some of them were started by the Romans. Probably many of them are not recorded.'

'So you didn't know about this one?'

'No, why should I? I don't recall anyone ever mentioning anything of the sort. Arabella might have known that sort of thing, but she never mentioned it.'

'Arabella?'

'Mrs Kemble. This was her house. She lived here.' She looked with a faintly rueful expression. 'I know what you're thinking – what you thought when you came to the door when you arrived. You think I'm a squatter. You gave me a very funny look. But then I was quite hostile, wasn't I?'

'A little, perhaps.'

'You were right to be suspicious, I suppose. I'm not a squatter, but I don't really have any proper right to be here any more. I'm sorry, I haven't even told you my name. I'm Caroline Denton.'

I shook her strong hand gingerly. 'So you lived here with Mrs Kemble?'

'She let me use this part of the stable. Years ago, it used to be the gardener–handyman's quarters. It was in quite a state. I did it up, put the Jotul stove in, improved the plumbing. I'm quite good at things like that. She didn't charge me any rent. She was very kind and generous. I would never have been able to afford this kind of space otherwise. She went on living in the house, in a couple of ground-floor rooms, the old kitchen and servants' hall. She wouldn't leave, not until she had a fall and broke her thigh. I had to call the ambulance to take her to hospital. She was furious. "I will not be poked and examined and commented upon by smirking medical students. Cancel it at once!" I had to refuse. I told her she had to go. She would die otherwise. "Once I get to the hospital, Caro," she said, "I shall die anyway. That's what they want old people to do, you know. The decent thing. Die quickly without a lot of fuss." And she did. She developed pneumonia and that finished her off. A bit ironical, wasn't it? Living here in this damp cold place, she was fit as a fiddle. The first whiff of sterile warmth, she's gone.' She looked away and dragged a dirty handkerchief from her jeans pocket.

'Was she a relative of yours?'

'Good Lord, no. She was much too grand for that. I met her by chance in Woodcombe. She was doing her shopping – she still managed to stagger up and down that hill twice a week and she must have been nearly eighty. She got knocked over by a boy riding one of those BMX things on the pavement. She wasn't hurt, just shaken up. I saw what happened from the shop window. I brought her in and sat her down, gave her a cup of tea.'

I smiled. 'You make a habit of being the good Samaritan?' She smiled back. The warmth was having a pleasantly soporific effect and the pain from my various wounds had receded, whether owing to the herbs and potions or the passage of time, I couldn't tell. I felt a great flow of gratitude to this superficially prickly, but kind-hearted woman. 'So, then you got to know her?'

'Yes. She sort of summoned me. "You are an interesting young woman, come to tea." So I did, on one of my days off from the shop.'

'I guessed you were an artist.'

'It was a good guess. I do a bit of sculpture, but I have to have a day job at least some of the time. It's owned by a woman I know. It's called Le Potage. It sells earthenware and terracotta stuff. She imports it from France and Spain and Italy. Hence the joke name.' She saw me look blank. '*Potage* is soup, but also sounds like a pot shop. Silly, isn't it? Well, that's what interested Arabella. The art thing, I mean. Apparently, she was into that in her youth. Went to art school, met people like Augustus John, was even painted by him, apparently. She was beautiful – "and I was wild, my dear." I don't know why she took to me. Maybe she saw me as she had wanted to stay, because she eventually had a conventional marriage into an old Westerset family and settled here. She had no children. Her husband was older and died years ago. She told me he was a director and shareholder of the Westerset Brewery, but he lost all his money on some speculation. She had a small income from her father's family trust, but it wasn't enough to maintain the house. She wouldn't sell it, though. It fell to pieces around her. I remember that first visit. She said, "I'm afraid we shall have to take tea in the dining room as the sitting-room ceiling has fallen in." She simply shut the door on it and left it. It was only because she was Mrs Kemble that the council didn't condemn it.

'When I told her I was living in one room over the shop, and had to beg and borrow work space on sufferance in empty shops and offices or at the college in Bristol where I'd been a student, she said, in that grand way she had, "Space, my dear? I have all the space anyone could need." So I moved in here. I've been here three years. I've done some good work. And I did my bit to help Arabella, difficult though she made it. After she died the lawyer came round to look at the place and remove her papers and her personal belongings, such as they were. I told him the score. A day or so later he wrote confirming that the property was being sold for development and as a former guest would I kindly leave within the next fourteen days. I ignored it. I love it here. But I'm not going to be difficult about going. That wouldn't be right. Arabella was always clear about doing what she called the decent thing.'

'You weren't mentioned on the documents. I think you should have been, but perhaps they assumed you'd already gone.'

'All that explains why I was pissed off earlier. I was wrong to be so rude to you. You're only doing your job.'

'That's okay. I understand how you feel. But, between you and me, I think you can relax. From the Kemble executors' point of view I may have done my job a bit too well.'

'How do you mean?'

'I'm no surveyor, but I would say that having a series of socking great big deep holes under the site – and as far as I could tell the roof covering is quite thin – makes it pretty unattractive to a developer. At the very least they would have to spend a lot more than they'd reckoned on filling it in and making it safe. So it's now worth very much less than anyone thought. I doubt that any developer will think it worth the hassle and expense when there's plenty of other land available.'

'I see. Does that mean I can stay here?'

'That's up to the lawyers. They may still want to kick you out, but probably not immediately.'

'I hope your clients are grateful you'll have stopped them buying it.'

'I think they should be. Eventually they would have done a proper survey, core samples and so on, but even that might not have shown up the real extent of the problem and they might well have gone ahead and bought it by then. Could have been a bit tricky.' I looked at my watch. 'Goodness, look at the time. I have to get back to the office. They'll be wondering where on earth I am.'

'You're not going back to work? You can't be serious. You're not in a fit state to work. And there's no way you can drive straight away. You've had a shock. You need to rest.'

'I'll be all right.' I gripped the arms of the chair to stand up. 'Ow!'

'Everything's stiffened up, hasn't it? Nature's way of telling you to slow down. Here's the phone. Tell them you've had an accident. You must stay here tonight.'

'I can't do that. I mean I'm . . .'

'A complete stranger? Maybe, but you're a guest in my house. It's the least I can do. Don't expect anything very luxurious, though.'

I sank back into the lumpy leathery embrace of the decrepit chair. I was in fact very relieved not to have to move. 'Thanks. I'll do that. It's very kind of you, Caroline.'

'Caro to friends. Look, are you okay for a bit? I'd like to do some work while it's light.'

'Of course. Carry on.'

She went behind the curtain at the end of the room and I heard a slapping noise as she got going again on the clay.

I telephoned the office, punching the numbers out with the little finger of my left hand. Fortunately Appleby was out and I gave the bare facts of the situation – though not the reasons for it – to Rose. 'And please tell him that the Vale View site has big problems. No further action to be taken on it. I'll do a full report when I come in tomorrow.'

'Darling, it does sound very mysterious. I can't wait to hear.'

I had a quick word with Penny to explain, then put the phone down, intending to start dictating the rest of my site report. I hadn't got past the first few sentences when the warmth of the stove and the damage wrought by my exertions combined to make me drowsy and I dozed off.

## X

I awoke to find that the room was in semi-darkness, the only light a small table lamp on a bookcase in the corner. As I looked around, yawning, she came through the outer door, carrying a couple of bulging plastic carrier bags. I was aware of the cold draught from outside and I could hear the wind whistling around the eaves.

She plonked the bags by the sink unit and took off her padded jacket. 'I had to get some supplies from the town. You were asleep so I thought it best not to wake you. It's the shock, still. Sleep's a great healer.'

I roused myself. 'You must let me contribute to, er...' I tried to bend down to pick up the rucksack, but stuck halfway, gritting my teeth with the pain from my knees.

'It's all right. Sit down. You're my guest. I don't entertain very often, as you may realize. I suddenly remembered I hadn't given you any lunch. I don't usually bother myself. I drink tea all the time. Bad for you, but it keeps me going.'

I watched as she unpacked the shopping. Various cellophane packets of grains and beans. A dark bottle with a handwritten label. Brown paper bags from which poked the muddy tops of carrots, leeks and parsnips. An unwrapped loaf of wholemeal bread. A carton of apple juice. I'd been thinking of the lamb chop I'd got in the fridge at home. But when in Rome...

She must have caught me eyeing this fodder with suspicion, because she laughed. 'Sorry, I should have asked. I'm a veggie. It won't do you any harm, you know.'

I smiled. 'I'll eat whatever you give me. I'm starving.'

As she chopped vegetables and put the rice on to boil, I gazed around the room, taking in its details for the first time since I had arrived.

It was sparsely furnished. There was the leather armchair, a gateleg table veneered with wood-effect plastic laminate and a couple of dining chairs with plywood backs and red vinyl seats – junk-shop wares. In contrast, opposite me on the other side of the hearth was a wonderful old grandfather chair, its turned beechwood gleaming with a mellow patina. On its seat was a cushion vibrant with a cobalt-blue and orange abstract pattern.

What gave the room its air of busy clutter were the objects that lined its walls and covered the uneven stone flags of the floor. Hung on the grimy whitewashed walls were a couple of huge canvases, abstracts in brilliant colours of ochre, blue and red. In their dash and movement, they were kin to the cushion cover and to the gorgeous hanging that divided the living space from the studio where she had gone to work. On shelves crudely made from fruit-box timber and piles of bricks, there were set dozens of lumps of wood – either highly polished or still rough with bark – on which were carved wide mouths full of teeth with lolling tongues. Set up in ranks on the flags, like Easter Island statues, were blocks of the local yellow-grey limestone, incised with strange, terrified faces, which seemed to grow from the grain. There were contorted figures of animals and birds. A multi-coloured parrot formed from flattened and beaten enamelled cans of soft-drinks, orange Fanta, red Coke and green Seven-Up, the domestic trash transformed into a strange gem-like beauty; a cat, asleep, made from a coil of thick hawser, its fibres roughened into sun-bleached fur; an enormously elongated heron, its stilt-like legs of thick rusty iron rods, its sharp beak a dagger of bleached wood, its grey body of roughly worked clay. And terrible blank eyes of black pebbles.

In the far corner was a massive construction of more iron rods, hammered and twisted together in the writhing shape of a man, transfixed with huge hexagonal bolts through its feet and hands to a cross fashioned from two sections of steel beams secured together with wire rope. The hanging head of this Christ-figure was a whirling spiral of tightly wrapped and hammered diamond mesh, bound with a crown of barbed wire. At the place in the ribcage where the centurion drove his spear, a thick square-section iron bar was savagely driven between the metal ribs and protruded through the other side.

Disturbing as were all these images in their direct, violent and almost primitive statements of agony and fear, conjured so uncannily out of the everyday materials found in the countryside or salvaged from scrapyards and demolition sites, it was the object against the wall behind me which most seized and challenged my imagination, and at which I looked with almost a sense of recognition.

It was a carving apparently made from a whole enormous tree. Its wide spreading branches had become sinuous arms, twisted, knotted and inter-twined, partly natural and partly sculpted. The spreading roots had become feet with grasping talons. At the top of the trunk was incised a grinning face of extraordinary power, its mouth a vermilion watermelon sliced into the wood, its teeth jagged splinters of white glazed earthenware. But its eyes most of all engaged me. The irises were the bottoms of huge greenish-black wine-bottles set in whites carved deep into the pale heartwood, with a shining eyelash fringe made from galvanized nails. It reminded me of the totem poles I had once seen with Colin at the British Museum, but it seemed far more complex: dreadful, and full of threat and savagery, and in the dark depths of those vitreous eyes there swirled inner pain and lacerating remorse.

Almost hypnotized, I struggled from the chair to run my hands over the smooth wooden limbs and touch with a tentative finger the razor sharp teeth, all the while staring into the strange, pitiful eyes.

'Yes, he's very tactile, isn't he? Treebeard.'

I swung round, almost guiltily to see that she had stopped her food preparation to observe me. 'I'm sorry, I should have asked, I mean you can't usually...'

'All those notices in galleries and museums saying Do Not Touch? I've never taken any notice. I can't appreciate a sculpture unless I touch it. Treebeard, though – remember him in Tolkien? – he's meant to be touched. You see I made him for a nursery playground – one of these advanced educational establishments where they don't allow plastic toys and bang on about developing the imagination. They rejected him. Said he would frighten the little darlings. I realized that, underneath, for all their talk of the freedom and power of the child's imagination, they were trying to deny the truth about that imagination. The world a child inhabits isn't pretty-pretty. It's bloody terrifying. To a child the adult world is full of horror, their emotions are full of violence. I thought that they could handle some of that better if they could scramble about on Treebeard, incorporate him into their games, use him as a focus for their feelings, a kind of lightning conductor for all that raw unfocused power. The function that Bettelheim says fairy stories perform. To act out the conflicts imaginatively and thereby own and acknowledge them. Too bad the people who ran the school didn't ask the kids.'

I felt my head start to swim. It wasn't the references she made to worlds of which I knew nothing: Treebeard, Tolkien, Bettelheim. There was that vehemence in her and in these images she created that made me feel she shared things with me, things that passed most people by. The depthless strangeness of childhood. 'The adult world is full of horror.' How right she was. 'All your work here. It's full of terror and pain, isn't it? Not only Treebeard.'

She turned back to the electric cooker, lifted the lid of the orange cast-iron casserole dish and stirred the contents with a wooden spoon. 'Yes.

So everyone says. If it were more chocolate boxy, I'm sure I'd sell more pieces. Instead, I upset people.'

I was trembling. My mouth parched, terrified at what I was about to say. What right had I to make such assumptions? I said quietly, 'These sculptures. They're wonderful to me in a way I've never known before. They're wonderful because they seem to be saying to me "I know what you know. I know about pain and suffering and horror." More than that, they all seem to me to draw their power from a particular kind of imagination. They reminded me at first of the things I'd seen in the British Museum: tribal things, totems. But now I've heard you speak about Treebeard, I don't think they're primitive, not in that way. I think they're child-like. I think you see things from the perspective of a child. I know that because I felt such things when you did, as a child. When you spoke of a child's imagination, I knew exactly what you meant.'

'We've all been children.'

'Some people had happy childhoods. Like the books I had to read at school. Nice, clean children having nice, clean adventures and waking up in a nice, warm bed. They used to make me laugh. I didn't have a childhood like that. Nor did you, did you, Caro? What's more, it was so awful, you remember it all the time, don't you? Like I do. You can't forget it and it won't go away. Close your eyes and you're back there. That's what all these brilliant, appalling things say to me. "I remember." But what, Caro? What is it you remember?'

She put down the spoon and came over to perch on the leather arm. I stood quietly, my hand resting lightly on one of Treebeard's silky limbs.

'Why do you want to know?'

'Because I can feel the hurt as if it were my own. I can feel it in all these things that you've made. I've never seen anything like them before. I have seen some art. But the art I've seen so far doesn't come right at me in the way these things do. To me, they're expressing a great rage with life. As if something absolutely terrible happened to you as a child, as if you've been robbed of childhood. That's the way I feel. Sometimes I listen to people talking. They might mention how things were for them as kids in passing. Maybe their parents didn't get on, maybe they were divorced. Maybe those people were unhappy, in their own way. I shouldn't judge them. What I know is, I've wanted to scream at them, "You don't fucking know anything! You don't have a fucking clue how utterly fucking deep-down wretched a human being can feel." That's what you know. I want you to tell me why. I know you want to tell someone. Because I feel the same. I want to talk to you. I feel as if I can talk to you. I feel that I'm going to tell you things I've never told a soul. But you have to tell me I'm right. That you feel what I feel, that we do share these things.'

She wiped her nose with the back of her hand, then as an afterthought, fished out the grubby hanky and wiped her eyes. 'You're right,' she said. 'Of course you're bloody right.'

I saw the tears grow in the corners of her eyes. She slid down into the chair and buried her face in the crook of her arm. I knelt down, ignoring the pain which struck white hot knives through my kneecaps, and stretched out my arms to her. Her muffled voice said, 'My dad was a soldier, the King's Own Westerset Regiment. A sergeant. We'd lived in Germany, Mönchengladbach, on the patch, with lots of other families. Then we came back to England, to be stationed in Aldershot. Dad sometimes had to be away, but then he came back on leave and it was great. We'd go on great hikes together, or even to the seaside. Even then I liked drawing and painting – he used to do some sketching himself, army life, and cartoons, quite satirical some of them. He wasn't a typical squaddy by any means. Well, one day – I was nine at the time – he went off on an exercise, and a few days later, an officer came round to the house and spoke to Mum, and she was crying and I knew that something bad had happened to Dad. Then she told me he wasn't coming home on leave ever again. I found out later it had been a live-firing exercise and there had been an accident. That's when my childhood came to an end.' Her voice had become a monotone and her normal pallor had blanched into the greyish white of the dried smears of clay on her jeans and shirt.

'There was some compensation for Mum and a pension. We moved to near Southampton, where she'd come from originally. Mum got us a small house. She had a part-time secretarial job. I went to school. For a time, it seemed as if everything was all right. But Mum couldn't cope with life outside the army. She'd been as dependent on it as Dad. All her structures had gone, all the social life she'd enjoyed as an NCO's wife had disappeared. She felt stuck in a rut, with a kid as well. She was still a young woman – only in her mid-twenties – nearly five years younger than Dad. She'd married him when she was just eighteen. That was when Uncle Billy turned up again.

'Billy was Dad's younger brother. He used to visit us when Dad was alive. He was living in London then, working for one of the councils. He'd come out and stay the weekends. He wasn't a bit like Dad. It was funny to think of them as brothers. Even though Dad was in the army, and he was tough and fit, he was gentle in himself. Uncle Billy was different. Oh, he could be nice when he wanted, but I'd seen him in really nasty tempers. I didn't like him. I didn't like it when he started to visit after Dad's death. I didn't like the way Mum got herself all tarted up when he came down, and the way everything in the house had to be just so and I had to clear off to my own room.

'I suppose I was jealous. But it was more than that. I didn't want him around. I was scared of him.

'Mum was so pleased with herself at her catch. He'd stopped working for the council. He didn't seem to have a regular job because he had time to spend days with us, then he'd go off for a week or so. Despite this, he seemed quite well-off. He said he had his own house in London. He certainly had a fancy car. Oh, yes, Ma thought she was in clover. She told me that she and Uncle Billy were in love. That she might be getting married again.

'By then I was ten. He was always being nice to me. Gave me presents, talked to me, gave me lots of attention. When he stayed with us, at bedtime, he'd come into my room. At first it was only to talk, to say good night. He used to hold my hand and stroke my hair. After a while he started to lie down by me and cuddle me. He called it giving me a cuddle.

'Then one day, when Mum had gone out to work, he came to pick me up from school. We went home and he followed me up to my room. He said he thought I was a very special girl and that he wanted us to do something together that showed us how much we liked one another. It would be our own special secret and I wasn't to tell anyone what it was. Then he unzipped himself, put his arm round my head and pulled me down on to him.

'When Mum came home, everything was so normal, he and Mum joking together at tea-time. It was like I had imagined it. Then that evening when he was saying good night, he gave me a present – a gold bracelet, the sort you fit little charms on – "for a very special girl". A week or so later, when Mum was out in town shopping, it happened again. And I got another present, a charm to go on the bracelet, a little horse. I soon had a full set of the things. Then it seemed like he couldn't wait for Mum to be out – the next time, it was in the middle of the night. He woke me up and got into bed, and then he got on top of me. God, he hurt me so much. I was only a little girl and he forced me. He put his hand over my mouth to stop me yelling, then, when he'd finished, he lay down beside me and whispered in my ear how wonderful it was when people did that together. It meant that they were very special to each other. If it had hurt a bit, that showed how special it was. It went on for about a year. Mainly he put it in my mouth. He didn't risk the other way very often. He was quite careful in his own way.' The strange controlled voice she had been using dissolved into anguished sobbing. Then she struggled upright in the chair, her face now red and puffy, but her eyes were dry and flashing. 'Aren't you going to say, why didn't I tell someone? Why didn't I tell my mother?'

I said nothing. It was as if all the shapes banished to the furthest corners of my mind had broken free and were dancing their wild dance against the backs of my closed eyes.

'At first, it seemed like an awful nightmare, I didn't want it to happen, so I shut it out. Then, after he raped me, I began to feel that perhaps it was like he said, that I was somehow the cause of it. That I was implicated in it. And that what he said was right – it was a special thing. Maybe that's what did happen. So I couldn't tell. I never did. But at some level, I think she knew or suspected. But it was easier for her not to admit it. She was besotted by him, I think.

'She stopped talking about how they were going to get married. He started to visit us less often. He said he had lots of business that meant he couldn't get away so much. Certainly he started to look very well-off – good suits, silk ties, a big gold watch, an even fancier car. Whatever he did was obviously very lucrative. Eventually, of course, he got fed up of both of us. I suppose he reckoned he couldn't push his luck with me not telling. Mum cried for ages when he stopped coming.

'After I was sure he wasn't ever coming back, I took the charm bracelet and all the other bits of jewellery he'd given me into the yard. I got a big hammer from Dad's old tool box and smashed it all to smithereens. Then

I caught a bus down to Southampton and chucked it into the harbour.

'I think in some way Mum blamed me for his having left. And maybe she felt guilty about her part in what had happened. There was always this great shadow between us. There always will be.'

The tears formed again and she bent over and hugged me tightly. I could feel the tremors as her body shook, and the warm wetness as she buried her face in my neck and hair.

She raised her head. 'There. I've told you. I swore I wouldn't ever tell anybody. For years I buried it. I pretended it hadn't happened. Then, gradually, I found ways of dealing with it. But I haven't ever told anyone. Then I go and tell you. I don't even know you.' She put her hand on my cheek. 'You have a most beautiful face. I don't mean only in terms of features, but the look in your eyes. You have deep green eyes. They're full of thought and compassion. And at the back of them, there's pain, so much pain. I can see that. What I've told you, it must have happened to you as well.'

Now I was crying. My mind screamed with the agony of what I was going to say. 'No, no, not to me. Jesus Christ, not me. It was my sister. And my father. My fucking bastard father.'

I pulled away from her and sat facing the fireplace, with its black coffin-shaped stove. 'My sister was what they called ESN. Educationally subnormal. She might have been slightly brain-damaged before or during birth. Mum had difficult pregnancies, and she'd miscarried several times. Josephine wasn't very bright, but she was very loving and trusting. She was three years older than me, but even at an early age I realized that I had to take the lead in our games. I was the nurse and she was the patient. I was the captain and she was the crew. I was the mother and she was the child.

'I felt I had to look after her. Of course, when I started to be aware of things, at four or five, I could see that my father always preferred me to her. It was me who was his little girl. Me he made sure had the pretty dresses and the new toys when he was flush, me he used to read to when he was in a good mood.

'They say that sisters don't get on, but it was different with me and her, perhaps because she lacked any trace of temper or violence. I was pretty aggressive, but never to her. Whenever I got sweets and she didn't, I'd share them with her. Whenever he used to make mock of and scold her, I'd try to take her part.

'He was always going on at her. He'd yell at her when she spilled her food, or dirtied her clothes or didn't do what he expected her to do because she didn't understand. He'd hit her, too. He'd get into rages when he'd been drinking and really take it out on her. He never hit me. Oh, he'd shout and yell at me, but he never hit me.

'Mum, she used to go along with it. She was scared of him when he was in his moods. He used to give her a hiding whenever he felt like it. Partly I think she shared his attitude to Josephine. She was a shame to her, a dirty, snivelling, vacant-eyed child. She didn't like to think that she could have produced that. Anyway, Mum wasn't around much of the time. She was out at her cleaning jobs. Right from primary school, I had my own door key. I got used to collecting Josephine from the special school and taking her home. We'd have sliced bread and marg for our tea and we'd talk and play together and watch the telly until Mum got in. Dad was usually out till late. He went on to the pub after his work, if he was in work. If he was home, he often wanted to read his library books, then everyone had to be quiet.

'When I was eight and Josephine was eleven, she started to change. I understood a bit about it. Josephine was slow in many ways, but not in that. She had her first period, and her whole body sort of bloomed. This seemed to give her more confidence. She started talking about what she would do when she left the school. How she could work in a shop, or even an office and wear clothes like the women you saw on the telly.

'When Dad started to be a bit nicer to her, I was pleased at first. He started to give her lots of hugs and cuddles and say she was a good girl. One night, when we were in bed, she said to me, "Dad likes me better than you, now."

'"Why's that, Josie?"

'"He just does and that's all I'm saying."

'I hadn't ever heard her talk like this.

'Then when I woke up suddenly one night in the bed we shared, I got suddenly frightened – there were always noises in the street at night – and I reached out to her and she wasn't there. I got up and looked out of my bedroom door, but the flat was in darkness. Mum had gone to bed hours before. The only light I could see was coming from the crack around the bathroom door, and I could hear Dad sort of crooning to himself in there. I was going to call out for her, but I thought Dad would be cross to find me awake. So I went back to bed. When I woke up the next morning, she was there again beside me.

'I asked her over the next day or two where she'd been. All she said was, "Special" and "Not supposed to tell." And she showed me the bottle of perfume that Dad had given her. Even at that age I could work out he'd probably pinched it from where he worked.

'So I decided I'd stay awake as long as I could one night, to see where she went. I lay there pretending to be asleep for hours and hours. Then I heard the bedroom door open and it was Dad's voice, saying, "Josie, darling. It's time, my darling."

'And he woke her up and carried her out.

'I crept out of bed and looked out the door. And Dad was just opening the bathroom door, and I could see in the light that he wasn't wearing anything at all, and that his willy was all big and red and swollen. Then the door closed.

'I tiptoed out and stood at the door. All I could hear inside was a kind of soft moaning, and then Dad cried out and said, "Oh, darling, my lovely darling."

'The next day, I got hold of Josie. I said, "What were you doing in there with Dad?"

'I knew about sex, from lessons, and from what the kids at school had learned at home, and from their older brothers and sisters. One girl had to share a room with her mum and her boyfriend, and she described what happened.

'We'd had all kinds of talks from people at school, policemen, priests, all going on about not going with strangers. They never warned us about our dads.

'I knew what was going on wasn't right. At first she said it was her secret. Then when I kept on at her, she started to get doubtful. I said she should tell someone. And she shouldn't do what dad asked any more, because it was bad. And I managed to get her to agree. She was going to tell. I made her promise.'

I stopped speaking and began to cry uncontrollably, my shoulders heaving and shaking, crying in a way I had never cried before. I felt Caroline's arms around me, holding me in a way that no one had ever held me before.

I heard her asking gently, 'And did she tell?'

I buried my face in her lap, and heard my own muffled voice, confessing my own indelible sin, the curse of my own blood. 'No, she never told. Before she could, he killed her. And I stood and watched him do it.'

Three

**IN XANADU**

# XI

'I've put you down for this, young lady.'

I looked up from the letter I had been reading. Appleby had in his usual polite fashion marched into my office unannounced, no doubt hoping to catch me staring out of the window or polishing my nails. Fat chance. I was up to my eyes in Chewton Residential's pre-Christmas sales fever. Now, what else was he going to chuck at me?

He was holding an oblong of stiff white pasteboard. Its edges were dusted with gilt and its corners rounded. 'Don't glare at me, Sarah. It's nearly Christmas, remember. And it isn't work – I do know you're busy – it's pleasure. Of a kind.'

He reached down and snapped the card on top of the open folder with the glee he might have displayed if it were the fourth ace in a hand of stud.

'Francis Appleby Esq', was written in a round feminine hand in fountain pen at the top. Below, the elaborately cursive printing read:

*You are cordially invited to join us in*
*celebrating Trevor's birthday*
*Saturday 10 December*
*8.00 for 8.30 p.m.*
*at*
*The New House, Welscombe,*
*Fernsford,*
*Westerset* FD6 9DL

RSVP Catherine Chewton                                    *Black tie*

'I'm off to the West Indies this year, and the best flight to Barbados is on the Friday before. So, I've made my apologies, diplomatically of course. And I took the liberty of suggesting to Catherine that she invite you in my place. I don't have to say that it's very important that you represent the firm, do I?'

'I'll have to see if I'm free.'

He flushed brick red at my tone. 'Make very sure you are. This is not "drop in if you're passing". It's a command performance. Be in no doubt of that. Particularly as this year it's his fiftieth. Besides,' he gave his wolfish smile, an attempt at ingratiation, 'this is an excellent opportunity for you, Sarah. Think of it as one of the perquisites of your employment. You will be rubbing shoulders with the great and the good of Fernsford. Everyone who is anyone in the district is invited, and such is Trevor's magnetism that few can resist.'

'Except you.'

'For the first time. Remission for good behaviour, shall we call it? I've been to every one of these anniversary jamborees since they were inaugurated ten years ago. Catherine sticks to a tried and tested formula: drinks and circulation for half an hour. Then fireworks. A very lavish display. Nothing but the best for our client. I must say I relish the prospect of not having to stand in the cold for half an hour watching infantile whizz bangs. The culmination is a pyrotechnic tribute which reads, Happy Birthday Trevor. Then the company troops back indoors and is finally allowed to fall upon the baked meats, which are, admittedly, ample and as elaborate and expensive as the starbursts.'

'I don't think I've ever been to a fireworks party.'

'You mean you never stood in your back garden around a smouldering heap of garden prunings whilst your father attempted inadequately to light the blue touch paper on a dud roman candle?'

'No.'

'After such deprivation, then, you will appreciate it all the more. By the way, I hope you've got something decent to wear. It's quite a dressy occasion, you know. No office garb, or weekend casuals. If you haven't the right togs, it'll be an investment. I think we pay you enough for that.'

He left. Appleby didn't waste time on closing formalities. They would blunt the edge of what he had said. I stared at the invitation. It wasn't having to go to the party I objected to – of course I wasn't doing anything else, I'd just been winding him up – it was the way he had had me slotted in as an afterthought and his sledgehammer tactics to make sure I complied with what he wanted. Why couldn't we both have been invited in the first place? I'm sure he could have swung that quite easily. That wasn't his style, though. I was just the office junior to him, until he found some use for me that suited his own convenience. Christmas in bloody Barbados! I bet he hadn't told Catherine Chewton that. Jesus Christ, that man made me mad. I pummelled Appleby's image in the air before me with my fists, then kicked off my shoes and drummed my heels on the carpet.

After a minute or two, I calmed down. I shouldn't let it get to me. I opened my diary and wrote down the date and time – as if I was going to forget. After all, why was I carping? It was, as he had said, a great opportunity, however it had arisen. Cinderella the scullery maid was going to the ball. I had never been to such a do before. Vardy, Leadbetter's clients would have been hard pushed to treat you to a cup of coffee in Gianni's Café. As a result, as Appleby had unsubtly hinted, my wardrobe was not bulging with suitable garments for such an occasion. I smiled to myself. What I needed was a fairy godmother to kit me out. What luck there was one handy. I picked up the phone. 'Rose, I need help only you can provide. Would you do me an extra special favour?'

'This is really nice of you to give up your lunch hour, Rose,' I said as we stood riffling through the racks of dresses that the faintly snooty assistant had pointed out as the right size for Madam, and would I please replace the ones I didn't want to try?

'Darling, it's no trouble. I adore looking at clothes. What about this one?'

I held it against me and gave it a swirl. 'It feels nice. Let's put it on the possible pile.'

Finally I made it into the fitting room with half a dozen dresses of the kind I had never, ever worn before, excluding the one I had borrowed for Mum's funeral, which was hardly a precedent I wanted to remind myself of. This small but rather plush boutique in an alleyway off Broad Lea had been Rose's first choice.

I slipped off my skirt and blouse and slung them on the wooden chair. I picked up the first little number and pulled it over my head. It had that faintly antiseptic smell of newness about it, and the thin silky fabric was cool against my arms. I settled it over my hips and looked at myself in the mirror.

It was dark green, but the material had a faint iridescence about it which complemented the coppery gleam of my hair. I reached behind and eased up the zip. The fit over the bust was snug but comfortable, although the top of my bra showed somewhat over the low, square neckline.

I stared at myself, a little surprised. I looked good, very good. I reached down and turned over the price tag which dangled from the hem. It was high but I could manage it. Think of it as an investment, Appleby had said.

Rose almost gaped as I came out of the cubicle. She prowled around me silently in a feline way, examining me from every angle, making gentle tugs of adjustment to the hang and the fit of the garment. The assistant stood back and let her get on with it.

'How does it look?'

'The brassière won't do, darling. A strapless half-cup, definitely. And you'll need shoes and a good bag – I could lend you one of mine which would be perfect. But you look ... marvellous. Stunning, in fact.'

'Ooh, you're making me blush, Rose. But I do look better than in my work suit, don't I? Yes, shoes. A greeny sort of pump, I thought. And I'd love to borrow the bag. I thought I could do without a bra. I think my bank balance will need the support more than my bosom.'

'Ah, for the firmness of youth! You'll be a sensation. The belle of the ball.'

'Rose, I don't think this is meant to be fun. That's the last thing Francis wants me to have. This is battledress.'

'Maybe. But I'm still madly jealous. You get on and buy the dress, and there's still time for me to try on a small thing I've had my eye on since we came in. I shouldn't really, but I'm going to. It'll be your turn to advise me.'

I felt quite reluctant to get out of my new image, and I watched anxiously as the assistant folded it and wrapped it in tissue paper. I signed the credit card slip without a tremble.

I gave a little skip of pleasure as I took the carrier bag and looked around for Rose. She came out of the changing room in a dazzling laburnum yellow frock. I did my best to be enthusiastic but failed miserably. Rose was nobody's fool. She must have known.

'Don't say it. I know. It's far too young for me, isn't it? It's the wrong length and I've too much tummy and not enough top. Never mind. It is such a lovely colour. I've always doted on this shade of yellow. But it's yet one more thing that looks better on the peg than on the clothes horse.' She dropped her voice so the assistant wouldn't hear. 'Please help me get it off. I think I've gone and jammed the wretched zip into the bargain.' She sounded oddly agitated for such a minor problem.

Back in the cubicle I carefully jiggled the fastener free from where it had become trapped on the seam.

'Feels as if you've got it. It's all right, you can leave it now.'

'No, I'd better undo it completely. Just a sec.'

'I said, leave it. I can do it.' She wriggled away from my hands, trying to turn her back away from me in the narrow space.

I was so amazed at what I thought was her unusual modesty that I remained holding the metal clasp of the zip. Her sudden movement pulled it down to her waist. I gasped as the yellow fabric peeled apart. The bony shoulder-blades which showed above her white silk slip were covered with a mass of reddish-purple bruises.

She pulled away from my touch and faced me, red with embarrassment. 'I told you. I can manage. Please get out.'

I felt like walking out of the shop. But I waited for her nevertheless. When she emerged her composure was restored. 'I'm sorry, darling. I'm a bit sensitive about my body. I had a bit of a bump in my car the other day – thrown back in my seat and I know what a mess it looks. The crash was my fault as well.'

I smiled sympathetically. 'Poor you. I am sorry.'

She gave a quick nervous grin, and we walked hurriedly and in silence back to the office. Rose must have known that I wasn't fooled. Me, of all people. The accident hadn't been mentioned in the office. Those bruises weren't caused by whiplash. No way, sister. They were the marks of angry fists. Somebody, some man, had been giving poor Rose a beating.

I swung the car on to the floodlit parking area in front of the New House. There was already a considerable number of shiny vehicles, more slickly shiny still from the rain which had been pouring down until a few minutes before. Not taking any chances with my new dress, I bundled myself into my long mac before gingerly stepping out on the wet shingle in my thin, dark green pumps. I slammed and locked the door of my grubby Fiesta, noting as I walked away my position sandwiched between a Range Rover and a Jaguar.

I joined other new arrivals as we mounted the steps of the entrance, flanked by startlingly white pairs of Ionic columns. I was tempted to give them a tap to see if they were hollow. They looked to me suspiciously like bigger versions of the fibreglass efforts that adorned Chewton Homes of Distinction's Tara house-type.

But the New House was altogether larger and more elaborate than anything you found on even the most select Chewton development. Through double panelled doors, flung wide for this occasion, was a double-height octagonal, pink marble-floored reception hall. From it rose a cantilevered stone and stainless-steel staircase. A waitress in a black dress and white apron ticked me off the list on her clipboard and directed me upstairs to where an enormous bedroom and adjoining bathroom had been given over to women guests. I squeezed through the crowd to hang my coat on the hanging rail specially provided. Then I waited for the dowager in front to finish resticking her eyelashes and took my turn at the huge gilt-framed mirror in front of one of a pair of sculptured white marble washbasins. There was more marble on the walls and the floor, sickly green like sage Derby cheese.

I washed my hands and freshened up the pale lip gloss I had bought specially. I didn't usually go in for make-up. The band of tiny freckles across my nose used to bother me a lot, and I had, at the age of thirteen or so made earnest attempts to obliterate them under layers of cream and powder. Now I was reconciled to them and to the slightly shiny well-scrubbed appearance of my complexion – what Colin had called, in a rare burst of verbalization, my Irish milkmaid face.

Behind me I could see in the mirror the cream of Fernsford's female society hoisting up their skirts, straightening their tights, or their garter belts, and scratching their bums under their silk and lace pants. The air was filled with the contents of a dozen different scent atomizers. I fought my way out against the incoming surge and carefully descended the amazing staircase, dazzled by the blaze of light from the electric candles of the crystal chandelier. I paused halfway down, gazing over the throng of black-jacketed men and brilliantly gowned women clustering in the vast atrium, on the far side of which were tall double-leaf doors opened upon another huge reception room, equally crowded. I took a deep breath, my annoyance with Francis Appleby long forgotten. This was it. I had arrived. And I would damn well let everyone know it. Then, the fabric of my brand-new dress rustling seductively, feeling for once a combination of Garbo, Grace Kelly and Marilyn Monroe, I glided down that Hollywood stage-set staircase and across the pink marble floor.

Trevor Chewton, chunky in his DJ, looking more like a nightclub bouncer than the host, stood in the doorway of the drawing-room meeting and greeting, accompanied by a shortish, dark-haired woman. He shook my hand warmly. 'Sarah, how nice to see you. The first of many, I hope. I don't believe you've met Catherine, my wife.'

We shook hands and smiled at one another. 'Trevor tells me you're a live wire at Chamberlayne's.'

I lowered my eyes in becoming modesty.

'That's right. We could have dropped a packet on that Woodcombe shambles. Keeping old Francis in line. I gather he can't come tonight?'

'No, he's abroad. He had to be in Amsterdam to advise on a construction contract. He's really sorry not to be here,' I replied smoothly. 'He asked me to give you this from the firm. Happy birthday.' I handed over the package which Rose had given me before I left containing the firm's gift, a small paperback entitled *Fernsford in Old Photographs*, which, I was informed by Rose, was the kind of thing he liked. What else would you give the man who had everything?

'How kind. Thanks ever so much.' He scrabbled at the wrapping of my present like a little boy. 'That's smashing, Sarah. Look, Cath. There's one of the canal and the old warehouses. What would those old fellows on that barge say if they could see Friars Haven in a few years' time?'

There was no answer to that.

'Now, off you go and get a drink. I can see Paul over there. You know him, of course. He can introduce you around. And Giles Matravers is there, too.'

I spotted Paul's tall figure immediately, as if I had radar. I saw his eyes widen as he took in my altered appearance. He gave a slightly embarrassed grin. 'Sarah. What a stunning dress ... You look ... I mean ... er, are you by yourself?'

'Francis couldn't make it. He's abroad.'

'Giles Matravers, Sarah Hartley. But I expect you know one another already. Now, let me get you a drink.'

'Just orange juice, please, Paul.' I nodded to his plump middle-aged companion. 'Hello, Mr Matravers.'

'Miss Hartley, how do you do? It's so nice to see you, er, in the flesh. Quite a change from the telephone.' He drew closer and lowered his voice. 'I say I'm dashed sorry about that unfortunate business at Woodcombe. As I told you, no one at my firm had any knowledge of that dreadful hole in the ground you, er, stumbled into. I've since had very stern words with the surveyors. A most unfortunate matter in all ways. I do hope you're fully recovered. You were at your own risk, of course, in venturing...'

'Of course. *Volenti non fit injuria*, shall we say? I had only a few scratches, fortunately.'

'I gather that weird girl squatter acted the Good Samaritan. I was going to kick her out – just as well I didn't, I suppose.'

'Yes. Are you still going to?'

He shrugged. 'She'll have to go eventually, but there's no hurry and she's not doing any harm as far as I could see. Obviously the place is not as saleable as it was before you er ... Well, anyway, I'm taking my client's instructions. I daresay it won't be back on your desk for a while, if ever.'

I smiled to myself. That was some good news to give Caroline.

Having exhausted our one topic of mutual interest, I could see him casting around for another. He had small shrewd eyes. Finally he said, 'And how do you like Fernsford? Bit dull after the big city?'

'Oh, no. Never that.'

'Francis keeping you on your toes, what? Hard to keep up with, I daresay. Not to mention mine host. He's a phenomenon that man. A Midas. Fernsford's not seen anything like him for years, not since the Victorians. He's done well. Married well too, you know. What a man to have as a client.' He chuckled. He must have seen my expression. 'No, I'm not poaching. Good heavens no. We have quite enough to cope with without our friend there. Room's full of clients. You met our chap Parsons, I gather? Solid man, you know.'

Paul, who had been hovering with my drink during this conversation, took this opportunity to rejoin us. 'One of the things you have to appreciate in a small community like this is the network of relationships which operates. Can be a bit hazardous, eh? Got to know who you're talking to when you feel like being indiscreet. Not that I'm sure that's ever a problem for you, Giles.'

Matravers chuckled comfortably. 'Everyone knows that their secrets are safe with me. Buckingham's may not have the latest technology. We're not flash. But we know the rules and we stick by them.'

He stared at me, his eyes hard under the bushy brows. Somewhere under the flab was a toughie. Then, with a glance around the room, he said, 'Please excuse me. One of the clients I mentioned. I really must go and say hello.' He nodded to me. 'Delighted to meet you, Miss Hartley. Keep up the good work.'

Alone with Paul, the atmosphere became immediately more awkward. I didn't help it. I said, 'You decided not to call, then?'

'You didn't offer me a great deal of encouragement.'

'You didn't sound as if you needed any at the time. I like to know where I stand. I didn't start it, remember?'

'You're right. I didn't know what to do. If only you weren't so ... We can't talk now. After the party?'

'Maybe.' I moved deliberately further away, then said, 'Let's drop it for now. What was Matravers getting at?'

He gave me a pleading look which made me want to kick him. Seeing my expression, he became sulky. 'Getting at? What do you mean?'

I sighed. 'Weren't you listening? Matravers and his talk of sticking to the rules. It was a dig at Francis, wasn't it? Why is it that everyone seems to have it in for my boss? I know he's not exactly charming, but everyone, including your wife seems determined to throw mud. Given my own involvement, it could get a bit personal. What has Matravers against the man?'

'As I said, it's a question of relationships. In the case of Giles and Venetia, the same relationship. With Ralph Chamberlayne.'

'Not him again. But what linked Matravers and Ralph?'

'Marriage. Margaret Chamberlayne is Giles's sister. She took his death very hard, even though when he was alive they had what you might call a stormy relationship. She's never made any secret of her dislike for Appleby. Blames him.'

'For Ralph's death? But why?'

'She said Appleby was changing the character of the firm. Made it much more high-pressured. Heavy commercial litigation. Trevor Chewton. Trevor Chewton's connections. Ralph found it hard to adjust. He became highly stressed. She said that the pressure contributed to what must have been a loss of concentration – and that was why he lost control of his car and crashed. There was no mechanical reason for the accident. But perhaps I shouldn't be telling you any of this. Given my own professional relationships.'

'I don't see why not. Everybody else knows, apparently. Rose told me about Ralph and Appleby.'

'Matravers obviously takes his sister's side, but even without that there wouldn't be any love lost there. Appleby's an outsider still, even after, what, fifteen years. The Matravers family have been here for generations. They're woven into the fabric of the place. Like Venetia's lot. Angleburys, Chamberlaynes, Wootons, Kembles, Matravers, Desboroughs. All the old county families. Intermarried for generations.'

'What I don't understand, given all this history, is why Appleby was taken up by Chamberlayne senior. Surely he must have realized that the two weren't going to get on?' I was intrigued to know more, but we were interrupted.

'Paul, you naughty man. Does the lovely Venetia know what you're up to?'

The speaker was a tall, slim, self-consciously glamorous woman of a certain age, with black, suspiciously jet-black, hair, cut fashionably short. She wore a very low cut, very expensive-looking black dress, with a frost of diamonds around her still elegantly sculpted throat. Rose had confided to me the other day. 'Be careful of your neck, darling. The neck goes first, you know.'

'Er, Margaret, hello. May I introduce my colleague, Sarah Hartley? Sarah, Margaret Chamberlayne.'

We shook hands in a guarded way. Superficially unlike her brother, in her the steeliness was out in the open.

'Colleague, is it? You can't possibly be an architect.'

'He meant in a wider sense. I'm a solicitor. With your late husband's firm. I'm working with Paul on Friars Haven.'

'You don't look like a solicitor, either, actually.'

'How does one do that?'

'You have to be a man, for a start. I'd never trust a woman in that role. Unnatural, like a male midwife. You have to look the part. Ralph, now, was a lawyer to his finger tips. If I could still be surprised by anything that man did, I would be amazed that Appleby had brought you in. I should have said that he thought the same. He certainly did until recently. He must be going soft in the head.'

I was conscious that my mouth had fallen open at hearing this. I closed it sharply, and contemplated a cutting reply, but she had already turned her back on me and was talking to Paul alone. 'And how are dear Venetia and your lovely children? You must invite me to tea again very soon. I've seen so little of you all lately.'

Dismissed, I started to circulate. The room was like an ocean filled with islands of loudly talking, gesticulating men and women, in which I swam, looking hopefully for a friendly landfall. The light flashed on gold cufflinks, sparkled on diamond necklaces. I heard snatches of conversation: 'Do you know, Robert says the house has gone up ten thousand in the last month! A month. Of course, that's St Oswalds for you. The three most important factors in house pricing: location, location and location!' 'I should go for the Mercedes, darling. Even as a second car, it makes sense to have the best.' 'Have you tried Home on the Range? They've got the absolute best choice of Agas anywhere. And the chap who runs it went to school with Harry.' 'I was talking to my broker the other day, and he said you can't go wrong with property. No end in sight to the boom. Things will never be cheaper than they are now.'

So much for being the belle of the ball. I didn't know anyone and no one was taking a blind bit of notice of me. So much for the come-to-bed dress and the heady perfume. It was only in the women's magazine stories that you immediately attracted attention. Besides, most of the men here were as well-fed-looking and sexless as bullocks. And bloody old, too! Grey heads abounded. There wasn't one I'd seen under forty. And if that weren't enough, they had their wives with them.

I thought bitterly of Appleby, sunning himself on a white sandy beach with some exotic drink by his elbow. Oh yes, this was a perk, wasn't it? Listening to the filthy rich talking about how they were getting even richer. A real career opportunity, that. Here was I in my posh dress which had cost a fair slice of my monthly salary, a peasant dressed up like a nob, being made to realize how far I'd got to go before I could be like them.

Having failed through the lack of any suitable conversational passport – not having bought shares or had my kitchen done up lately – to be admitted to any of the merry knots of revellers, I'd ended up at the long white linen-covered table where the drinks were dispensed. Fuck the orange juice. I grabbed a glass of champagne and slugged it down.

Mistake. I was unused to such an exotic tipple. The bubbles went up my nose and the cold did something to my throat. I started to sneeze and cough. God, I was doing well tonight. I could feel myself going beetroot with annoyance and embarrassment. I struggled desperately with Rose's silly little evening bag, which had a catch like the jaws of a baby alligator. I blew loudly and copiously into the lace-edged handkerchief – Rose's again.

A voice at my elbow said softly, 'I say, are you all right?'

I mopped my streaming eyes, and stuffed the hanky away before turning. 'Oh, yes. A touch of cold, that's all.'

He put out his hand. 'I don't believe we've met before. Lambert. Ronald Lambert.'

'How do you do? I'm Sarah Hartley.'

He was tall, taller than me. He had distinguished-looking wings of grey hair over his temples, contrasting with the jet-black hair. He was a bit like Christopher Lee, who played Dracula in those late-night horror flicks.

'I've not seen you here before. I'm sure I would have remembered. I'm a regular. Comes with the territory.' His thin lips smiled. His eyes were steady in their gaze, and very dark.

'What territory is that?'

'The FernWest Building Society. I'm the Chief Executive.'

And a modest man to boot, I thought. Didn't want me to think he made the tea. 'Oh, yes. We've got your head office in our building. In the Horsemarket.'

He cocked an eyebrow. 'You must be from Chamberlayne's, in that case.

Actually, it's the other way round. Your firm is one of the society's tenants. We own the whole block. Appleby, the senior partner. He's usually at these dos. Not seen him tonight.'

'That's why I'm here. I came in his place. We work on Friars Haven together.' I liked the sound of that, even though it wasn't true.

'Really.' He probably knew it wasn't. I must have looked more like his secretary. 'More champagne?'

'No, thanks. I'm driving. So tell me about running a building society. That must be a huge job?'

Most men liked to talk about their work and how good they were at it. I seemed to have picked the exception. He mumbled a bit about building societies playing a vital part in our property-owning democracy – stuff you could read in the ads – then his eyes started to swivel, looking for someone richer and more famous. His gaze connected with someone on the far side of the room. He raised a hand in greeting. 'I say, do excuse me. Chap over there I must speak to. Mention me to Appleby. Haven't come across him in an age.'

I had another glass of champagne to celebrate my extraordinary magnetism.

Catherine's voice raised itself above the hubbub. 'Fireworks! The best view's from the terrace.'

The triple sets of french windows were flung wide and we moved out in a body in answer to the summons. The air was chill on my bare shoulders. I saw that the old party hands had equipped themselves with wraps and stoles.

We all gazed up expectantly into the black sky. There was a whoosh from somewhere down on the front lawn, then a bang and a crackle. Flung across the night like gems carelessly thrown on a jeweller's velvet cushion was a handful of spangles, silver, gold and ruby. From the gathering of Fernsford's great and good came the oohs and aahs of childish delight as sunbursts of red and green and mauve and pink filled up the void in overlapping and intermingled patterns. As their strands and filaments fell earthwards and died in a smoky polychrome mist, more and still more rockets scorched amber trails across the darkness, exploding incandescent sprays of white and gold in thudding teeth-jarring detonations. For several minutes, we stood entranced, transported, all sophistication, all cynicism burned away in this celebration of the elemental mystery of fire.

Overhead the display faded, leaving in my nostrils the faint reek of sulphur, a memory of school chemistry. The crowd was silent, waiting for the finale. Now more accustomed to the dark, I could see over the marble balustrade a silver-grey expanse of grass, ending in a screen of the black fretted shapes of trees. I could see dark figures moving in the obscurity. There was the flare of a match, and then glowing red points appeared floating, as it were, in mid air. All at once, the points shot out orange sparks and then yellow streamers, and there was a fizzing, followed by a roaring as four huge catherine wheels, the corners of an invisible square, began to spin in fierce, dizzying vortices of white, blue and coppery green flames. Unwavering, I gazed at them, as if daring them to draw me into their swirling whirlwinds of fire. In the darkness between, there were new flickers of light, the forerunners of the pyrotechnic greeting predicted by Appleby.

For a moment, indeed there was a ghostly white glow of capital letters, H P Y B    T        Y T      V  R, strangely cryptic, like the incomprehensible code beamed out by a crippled UFO, then all was blotted out in a great roaring sheet of yellow flame, in the light of which the dark figures I had glimpsed earlier could be seen running away at desperate speed into the sheltering darkness. The crowd stirred with the initial joyous realization that something had gone awfully wrong. I could hear mutterings and there was a general and instinctive move back through the french windows, away from the inferno on the lawn. I could now see clearly the framework which had supported the display glowing red hot and beginning to buckle as the fireworks continued to blaze. The mild sulphur of the breeze became a hot wind of vile chemical odours, and I could feel feathers of soot brushing past and settling on my exposed skin. I experienced a pang as I thought of my new dress, but something made me watch to the end.

Figures dashed back out of the shadows, and I could see one amongst them, his visage gleaming like a gold mask in the flames under the silver of his hair. He was waving his arms and shouting at the other men to get back. He stooped and picked up a red cylinder from the grass at his feet. There was a plume of something white which engulfed the metalwork with a hiss and a cloud of steam which ebbed swiftly away into the night, restoring the darkness.

But in the seconds before the last of the fire had been smothered, as I watched the hero of the hour calmly plying the nozzle of the extinguisher, I underwent the same giddy disorientation which had come upon me by the canal basin. Once again I conjured up a face from the past.

Half an hour later, my nervous fit flushed away, along with the smuts on my nose, down the gilded wastepipe of a marble washbasin, I was mastering the delicate art of holding a glass and balancing a plate of food so that I could eat in a precariously ladylike manner, whilst turning a politely interested face to my interlocutor, upon whom I could see I was having some effect.

I had come upon him as I wandered out of the dining room where the buffet had been laid. He was lounging against the wall of a corridor that led to what Trevor had earlier pointed out as the swimming pool and leisure suite. He was a slim young man of about twenty or so, with a mane of longish dark hair, wearing the kind of scruffy-chic casual clothes which only people who didn't have jobs and bosses like mine could get away with at a bash like this. He was very pale, with dark shadowed eyes, with a nervous habit of darting glances around the room as if he were expecting someone to sneak up on him. He had neither glass nor plate.

We were talking about music. Or rather he was talking and I was listening. As he spoke, his pale-fingered hands described fluttering arabesques before his face. He was in a band. He played keyboard, sang a bit and also composed. They were doing really well, getting a good reputation locally and also further afield. They did gigs at clubs and on the student circuit. They had been approached to do an album.

I nodded and smiled in the right places, but the kind of music he was into I had left behind at the age of sixteen, and I was out of touch with the latest manifestations. I wondered vaguely quite what he was doing here. He and I were easily the youngest people present. Finally he asked what I liked.

'Bach, for starters. The classics generally.'

'That's cool. You'll like my stuff, then. Come to my studio and listen to some of my tapes.'

I was wondering how to respond to this invitation when a woman's voice at my elbow said, 'Ah, there you are. I might have known you two would find each other. We must seem an awfully aged gathering to you both.' Catherine Chewton went up to the young man and put her arm round him. She pulled him aside and said in a low voice, 'Your father does appreciate your coming, Robbie, even though he finds it hard to say so. Do try and have a word with him.'

Robbie shook off her arm and glared at her. 'Okay, okay. I just haven't seen him yet, all right?'

'And, darling, you're not eating. Please take something, just for me. Let me get it for you. You don't look after yourself.'

'For Christ's sake!'

I tactfully turned aside, but she was determined to involve me. 'Sarah, you're obviously a girl with a healthy appetite, do try and persuade him.'

'Ma!'

'All right. I've said my piece. I shall go away. But do remember what I said about your father.'

He scowled at the floor until she had gone, then raised his eyes back to mine. 'She still treats me like a kid.'

'Mmm. I hadn't realized you're Trevor's son.'

'Yeah? You don't see the family resemblance? Of course, I haven't got the fucking pighead.'

I drank up the rest of the juice in my glass with pointed determination and started to move away.

'Hey, stick around. I don't even know who you are. You haven't been to one of these dos before. I would have remembered.'

'No. I've only just joined the firm. Chamberlayne's, that is.'

'Shit, a lawyer. You don't look like a lawyer.'

'So everyone keeps saying.'

'That was a compliment, okay?'

'Okay.'

'You look as if you might be interested in other things apart from the law and my father's business. Business. How I fucking hate that word. My father used to try and involve me in it when I was just a kid. Take me on the sites. Get me up on the dumper trucks and excavators. Of course, he was more hands on himself then in the construction side. I was a great disappointment. His only son, and all I cared about was my keyboard.'

'I see,' I said. I really didn't want to get mixed up in the Chewton dynasty's domestic problems. But he obviously wanted to get it off his chest.

'It came to a head when I left school. I wanted to study music in London. He wanted me to do a civil engineering degree at Imperial, and follow it up with an MBA. Get all the chances he never had – I fucking ask you. He even said, "It's nice for you to have a hobby, but you have to work as well." We had a real bust-up. I left home. I got the band together and gave up the idea of being a student. Who needs it? We're doing well. Even on the point of making the sort of money that my father understands. The kids today, they're rolling in it. They really come out with the folding stuff to see us. You know the Coffee House?'

I nodded.

'We've a regular Saturday spot there in the Dregs Club – down in the cellars, you see. You should come along.'

'I'll think about it.'

I felt a light touch on my waist and turned to face Paul.

'Sarah. I wondered where you'd got to. Hello, Robbie. How's the music scene?'

'Hi, Paul. Heading for the big time, you know.'

'Good. Nice to see you again.'

The younger man took the hint, uncoiled from his leaning position against the wall and ambled away.

'Hey, I was having a good chat.'

'Don't waste your time on Robbie Chewton. One of the great no-hopers. I've lost count of the number of times he's told me he's about to break into the big time, as he calls it. He's always just about to make an album, but somehow never quite does. He and his mates bum around this part of the world thinking they're God's gift. If his mother didn't bail him out, he'd probably starve.'

'I'd never have realized.'

He grinned ruefully. 'You're awfully fierce you know.'

'I say, Paul. I meant to ask you earlier. Was this one of yours?' I waved a hand around to indicate the building.

As I'd hoped, he reacted furiously. 'No, it bloody well isn't. I thought you might have gathered the kind of thing I do. And it isn't bloody boudoir neo-classical.'

'Oh, I don't know, I should have thought the pink marble was really you.' Then I gave the game away by starting to giggle.

'I see, I see. What a tease you are. Seriously, this place is restrained compared with the pool room. Have you seen it?'

I shook my head.

'Come on. You shouldn't miss it while you're here.' He grabbed my arm and set off down the corridor.

There were double glass doors at the end and he hustled me through. 'There, now. Beverly-Hills-on-Fern, is it not?'

'Wow!' I exclaimed as I walked around, staring, my shoes clacking on the hard shiny floor. The marble here was white. There seemed to be acres of it, surrounding the enormous, keyhole-shaped azure swimming pool, and panelling the walls. Above was a roof of elaborately curved glass, reflecting the still water. On either side were changing rooms entered through Moorish arches, labelled above in blue tiles, respectively, Warriors and Maidens. The 'Moorish' theme was carried through in the decorative tiled murals, depicting, unsurprisingly, harem scenes and featuring large expanses of undraped male and female flesh unambiguously conjoined. Further along the poolside, there was another arch with a tiled sign, reading Gymnasium and Turkish Bath. The farther end was a wall entirely of glass panels, in which were set double-height sliding doors, presumably opening on to a terrace or garden beyond, now invisible in the darkness. As I gaped about me, I kept shaking my head with incredulity. Finally, I said, 'This must have cost a mint. I didn't think even Chewton ran to this sort of thing.'

'You do now. Our mutual client has done very well for himself.'

In answer, a familiar voice echoed in the big space, with the booming timbre which reminded me of school swimming lessons at Hornsey Road Baths.

The squat, heavy figure of Trevor Chewton strutted towards us along the pool edge. He ought, in these surroundings and with his slightly jerky gait, to have illustrated perfectly why a DJ was called a penguin suit. But, even with the absurdly long movie tycoon's cigar sticking out of his mouth like a beak, somehow Chewton failed to look comical or endearing. I shuddered.

'Indeed I have, my friend. Sarah, you must be a bit cold in here in your lovely dress. We put the heating on when the pool's in use, and then it's real cosy. It was thoughtful of you to show her round, Paul.'

He coughed nervously. 'I didn't think you'd m-m-mind, Trevor. It's one of the sights of Westerset.'

He took a hard pull on the cigar, and expelled the smoke reflectively through his nostrils. 'No, I don't mind, Paul. You don't need to pretend you share my taste, though. Personally, I like a bit of vulgarity. It reminds me of who I am and where I come from. Don't you agree, Sarah?'

There was an edge to this remark which showed me that he was well aware of who I was and where I came from. This information he could have got from only one source. I said, with my most charming smile, 'In my present position, I'm never in any danger of forgetting.'

He barked his short, humourless laugh. 'I like that. You could go far, young lady. Like present company. Look at Paul, now. Set fair to being a famous architect, aren't you? And all because of Friars Haven. That place will make us all. We just need to keep our eyes on the ball and our noses to the grindstone, if you get my meaning.'

Neither of us said a thing. It was like being kids caught in some minor devilry by an old-style bobby and clipped over the ear.

Apparently pleased by the effect of his words, he reached up an arm over each of our shoulders and led us back towards the entrance. 'You must come to one of our summer swim and barbecue parties, Sarah. They're great, aren't they, Paul? A healthy girl like you, I'll bet you're a sensation in a swimsuit.' He let us out of his embrace to push open the glass doors.

'I never wear one. I can't swim.'

'Oh, that is a pity. I am surprised. I thought you were the complete action heroine. It's just potholing then, is it?'

I realized that he must be slightly drunk to be adopting this manner. I looked over at Paul but he was studiously taking no notice of what was being said. He would offer no help to this particular damsel in distress. Of course, Chewton wasn't just a client. He was the client as far as Paul and I were concerned. Even I didn't dare to be offensive back. 'No, I could never learn. I was a complete duffer in the water.'

'You probably didn't have a decent place to practise in. I hated those rotten municipal baths when I was a kid. Now I love the water. You come to our next party and I'll give you a lesson. It's ever so easy; you just let yourself go.'

The guests were beginning to leave as we came back into the entrance lobby. The front doors were flung back to show the rain streaming down again in the floodlit car park. Trevor left us to say his farewells to the mayor of Fernsford, a diminutive elderly gent much encumbered by his gold chain of office.

'I'll get my coat,' I said to Paul, as we stood there, the ebbing crowd swirling around us.

When I came back, he was standing on the now emptied pink marble, wearing his well-worn khaki mac, saying his goodbyes to Catherine Chewton. 'Marvellous, as ever.'

'Well, we try. A pity about the fireworks. I don't know what happened there. Fortunately one of the workmen we brought in from Friars Haven to help reacted very quickly. Trevor will be holding a post mortem, of course. We've never had any trouble before.'

'You coped splendidly.'

'Do give my love to Venetia.'

'Yes, she was sorry not to make it this year. She's had to go over with the children to Westhampton to be with her mother. The old lady's very unwell, you know. Venetia feels she has to be with her as much as possible – especially at Christmas.'

I shook hands with Catherine and with Trevor. 'It was very kind of you to invite me.'

He brushed a few glittering raindrops off his black shoulders and gave his sharp nod. 'My regards to Francis. You're back after Christmas, aren't you? I'll be catching up with the year-end sales then.'

'I'll be at my desk the day after Boxing Day.'

We went out into the night, down the front steps of the mansion. Cars were revving up and queuing to get out on to the drive. 'You've got your own car, I take it?'

'Yes, thanks.'

'Good night, then.'

As he inclined his head to kiss me, I whispered in his ear, 'We need to talk. Come round to coffee – as you've no reason to rush home. Give me a few minutes' start to tidy the place up.'

I hung the green dress carefully in the wardrobe in the back bedroom. It was, to my relief, apparently none the worse for its first outing, despite the ordeal by fire. I had had to get a proper padded hanger for it. I couldn't subject it to the nasties I got from the dry cleaners. Hadn't some Hollywood movie queen crossed off her daughter because she had caught her using wire coat-hangers?

I shivered. I was wearing only pants and tights. Standing in front of the dark-spotted three-quarter-length mirror on the old-fashioned dressing-table, I pulled out the pins and shook my head to loosen my hair from its coils. It cascaded back down over my bare shoulders with its familiar weight and I combed its unruly mass into some kind of order. Farewell, the young sophisticate, I sighed as I hurriedly pulled on a pair of jeans and a thick sloppy jumper, then hurried back into the sitting room to drag the duvet back over the bed and snatch up the bra and knickers drying on the radiator. I lit the gas fire and checked my face, now pinker with effort, in the mirror over the mantelpiece.

Coffee! I ran into the kitchen to slop out and rinse a couple of mugs and the cafetière, and switch on the kettle. Fuck it, there was no milk.

Out in the street, I heard the chug-chug of a diesel engine. The car stopped and the door slammed. I drew the curtain of the right-hand side of the bay aside and watched him come up the front path, then the tinny sound of the door bell. I clumped down the stairs to let him in.

I followed him up the ill-lit stairs. He paused on the landing. 'Go on through.'

We stood in the middle of the room a couple of feet apart looking at one another.

'It seemed silly to wear that dress here and I don't run to negligées.'

Then we moved together to embrace. The first kiss lasted a long time. I felt all kinds of warm and wonderful things happening to my insides, things I hadn't felt for ages and ages. It took quite an effort to pull out of it. I reached out and took his face in my hands, staring intently into those brown eyes. He put up his own hands, clasping mine and drawing me closer again.

'No, wait. I've got something to say. I'll get us some coffee.' I heard my voice small and trembling in the silent room. I gave his hands a squeeze and ran into the kitchen, switched the kettle on to re-boil, and sloshed the water into the cafetière. I carried the loaded tray back into the sitting room. He was standing ill at ease by the fireplace.

'Please sit down, Paul.'

I pushed down the plunger on the cafetière and poured it out into mugs, pushing one in his direction. I still felt chilled and I held mine in both icy hands. 'Paul. I've been here before, and it isn't somewhere I wanted to find myself again. In our case, it's even more complicated, as I said in your office. As our mutual client made plain in his extremely subtle way just now.'

'I know all that, for Christ's sake!' He passed an angry hand over his forehead. 'I don't know what I'm going to do. I've no right to be here. I ought to go.'

I drank some coffee and put the mug back on the tray. I got up and sank down on my knees in front of him, pressing my face into his lap. 'Ever since I met you, I've thought about you. I can't stop thinking about you. That's why I asked you here. To tell you that, and to tell you I'm not making any demands on you. I don't want you to go, but if you do, I understand. If you stay, then that's all I want.' I raised my face. 'The here and now. That's all that matters. I want you so much, Paul. Make me feel you want me.'

I stood at the bay window and watched the rear lights of his car fade into the fog. It was still pitch dark, and bitterly cold. In the soupy light of the street lamp, I could see that rime furrily edged the leaves of the privet hedge alongside the pavement, Mrs Carter's patch of lawn was stiff with frost, and her gnomes had icicles at their noses as they dipped their rods into their frozen pond.

I shivered. I was wearing nothing under the towelling robe. I let the curtain fall back, went to the fireplace and turned the gas fire up to full, kneeling in front of it and watching as the pale biscuit-coloured porcelain elements at first flushed pink then, in the roaring blue gas flames, glowed orange-red.

Behind me the bed was a rumpled, tangled mess. The bottom sheet had acquired two large tackily wet greyish patches – his and hers, maybe. On the floor at the side was a tin tray containing crumb-speckled, butter-smeared plates, two mugs with brownish scummy coffee dregs, and an empty jar which had contained supermarket marmalade.

He'd said he'd had to go and he'd gone. He'd scuttled off home, in the graveyard hours, terrified in case Venetia should ring him early in the morning and discover him missing. Once back in Arden Wood, he'd probably turn up the central heating, and make himself a proper meal – eggs and bacon and sausage and mushrooms – and sit scoffing it, with a big wad of Sunday newspaper at his elbow. That's what he was used to – a warm crib and a fridge full of grub, not my freezing flat, where I'd had to root around to find an apology for breakfast – two slices of toast meagrely spread with orange gunge I'd scraped from the jar.

Venetia would have had fresh brioches in the oven and Buck's Fizz at the ready in similar circumstances. Venetia would...

But other things Venetia wouldn't. It was because of that he'd been here at all. He'd hardly been here for cordon bleu, had he?

I smiled to myself at the memory, got up, and went through the tiny lobby into the minuscule shower room and lavatory. The small window was permanently jammed open and it was absolutely arctic. I twisted and twiddled the shower knob. It was one of those cheap electric ones, where, without a lot of fine tuning, you get either a scalding dribble or an icy deluge. Finally, I achieved a satisfactorily warm flow, stripped off and plunged under it.

My hair grew warm and heavy as the water streamed over me. I lifted up my face and let it wash into my mouth, my nostrils, my ears. I felt it slide over my breasts and belly like a second skin. I turned, bent over and let the jets hose down my buttocks and my loins.

I stood there for what seemed ages, until the stickiness and the sweat of sex was flushed away through the chromium-plated wheel of the waste outlet.

When I got out, I went back to the now reasonably warm sitting room and stood towelling myself vigorously, until the earlier chill had receded and my skin was pink with the effort. Then I put on underwear and dried my hair.

But the raggedness of my emotions was not to be so easily dealt with.

So what did I feel? On the physical level, I felt good, with that lovely sensation of release and relaxation which you get from successful sex, followed by a hot shower.

That was not to be dismissed lightly. I hadn't made love at all for a long time. I hadn't made love with any degree of enthusiasm for even longer.

Paul was good at it. He knew where everything was. He was wonderfully relaxed and unhurried at first. For a long time, we kissed, real kisses with his strong tongue flickering in and out of my mouth, and then cavorting sinuously with mine. I felt my lips growing softer and warmer, more open and more flexible on his. Then we had gently disengaged and he had drawn me up beside him on the sofa. He stroked my forehead and my cheeks, then planted kisses on my eyelids and the tip of my nose.

'You're very lovely.'

'My nose is too big, and my front teeth are crooked.'

'Who wants flawless perfection? Beauty is dappled, said Gerard Manley Hopkins. You have stunningly deep green eyes, and lovely skin. And that hair.' He ran his hands in it and drew it gently away from the sides of my head. 'I knew you would have beautiful ears. Wonderful, sculptural ears. I have longed to set eyes on your ears.' He bent his head and the tip of his tongue traced the inner whorl, and he nibbled the fleshy lobe. 'I could eat you up.'

'It's my ears you fell for then?'

'You're blushing. "Her pure and eloquent blood spoke in her cheeks, and so distinctly wrought, that one might almost say her body thought." It wasn't what I fell for, it was whom. You, my darling, body and mind and soul. John Donne didn't distinguish. That's why he's the greatest love poet in the language.'

He bent again and kissed my throat, and then he was undoing the buttons of my blouse, slowly and carefully. He kissed the tops of my breasts where they mounded over the tight material of my bra. He settled me back against the cushions and ran his tongue inside my navel. I felt his fingers against my stomach as he slipped open the brass stud which closed the top of my jeans. He unzipped and pulled them down and away.

The casual sensuality of him was driving me wild. My whole being felt on fire with longing. He gently eased his hand inside my pants, resting his palm against my mound, while his fingers delicately traced my wetness.

Then he withdrew, stood up, held out his hands and led me to the waiting bed.

Just remembering what happened afterwards made me feel pliant and gooey all over again. I felt his tongue on my breasts and on my belly. His fingers delicately stroking the soft flesh of my inner thighs. His tongue again teasing apart the folds deep in the core of my being, and then, when I was open and moist and oh, so ready, the firm length of him, hot and full and...

Oh, God! I held my hand where I had let it stray until the gasping, surging shuddering was over. I rolled over and buried my hot face in the cool pillow. Christ. I thought with agony of how long I might have to wait for the real thing. And the next. And the...

And then? But I didn't want to think about that. About the inevitable end. The flowers, the note, the 'I think it's best if we don't see each other for a little while.' Because end it would. Always had. Always would. Always. It was better that way. Because I would never have to confess to him the darkness in my soul.

# XII

Luminous grains whirled in the headlight beams and collided with the windscreen in soundless wet kisses. Could it really be snowing? In my mind, I heard the voice of the Old Groaner, dreaming of a white Christmas, and I joined in for a verse or two.

Actually, my experiences of the season were pretty well at odds with Bing Crosby's. I had written no Christmas cards, nor had I heard sleighbells, nor seen glistening treetops. Furthermore, now I thought about it, I sincerely hoped that this Christmas would bear not the slightest resemblance to the ones I used to know. Mum's idea of festive celebration had been to get paralytic on whiskey in front of the TV. Colin had had a similar attitude, except that he drank Australian red in front of a computer monitor, playing endlessly through the stack of new games he had generously bought himself with my money, or hacking for fun into the network of some high-powered corporation or institution.

In fact, the traditional joys of Yuletide hadn't up to now even entered my waking thoughts, never mind my nighttime reveries. I had made hardly any preparations. I hadn't had the time. Far from being eased gently into the festivities, I had been working at full tilt for the last two weeks, consuming the secretarial skills not only of Penny, but also, with Appleby's reluctant consent, of an additional temp, and even, when he'd left for his West Indian jaunt, of Rose herself and anybody else in the office who seemed to have a spare five minutes. I had even got Julie hooked up to a word processor on the front desk to churn out documentation, at which she proved remarkably adept, confirming my impression that she was far more than a pretty receptionist with a pert manner.

Chewton Residential made a big thing about Christmas. It was a powerfully attractive hook to ensnare the punters. Christmas in your own brand new home! went the ads in local papers over the whole of the West Country. There were inducements to exchange contracts and complete purchases within ever tighter deadlines: £500 worth of vouchers redeemable at well-known stores! £1000 cashbacks! A giant hamper of Christmas goodies waiting when you move in! Prices slashed for the festive season! Christmas comes early for Chewton homes' buyers!

The worst thing about this unashamedly tacky appeal to the baser instincts was that it was entirely successful. Families were crowding the show homes and queuing up to slap down their deposits, besieging the offices of building societies and banks for mortgages, and camping out in their solicitors' waiting rooms until the contracts were ready to sign. As for me, I was racing around like a headless chicken, the phone ringing so constantly the switchboard almost blew a fuse. I had never worked so hard or so consistently in my entire life. Like a currency trader in the City, I ended up screaming out the numbers of the plots as they exchanged, so that Penny and the rest of the team could start the machines rolling to print out the deeds of transfer. My colleagues on the other side were also infected with this madness under pressure from their clients, avid for all the special deals on offer. Clerks were being sent out in taxis to pick up mortgage instructions and completion cheques and deliver vital documents in chains of purchase and sale transactions that stretched from one end of the country to another. On one particularly generous come-on – five grand off the price of a Balmoral Home of Distinction on a small private estate outside Plymouth for completion on or before Christmas Eve – the punter, desperate at the law's delays, got the entire chain of buyers and sellers to meet in an hotel room in Exeter for an afternoon to hammer out the problems and exchange contracts.

At last, at five thirty on Christmas Eve, the phones stopped ringing. I had persuaded the firm's banks – it kept accounts in all the main ones, so that money transfers were as quick as possible – to keep the books open to the bitter end. The last of the money was in, the last of the keys had been released, the last of the furniture vans were unloading. I leaned back in my chair and put my feet up on my desk. I whistled as I read on the computer printout the total value of the transactions we had completed in the last few days. I hadn't up till then had a moment to look at the bigger picture. We had broken all the records. Chewton's ought to be delighted. Still, a grateful client was, I remembered the words of Pogson, as common as a vegetarian tiger, and as desirable. 'Do they pay the bills? is all I ask. Can I live on gratitude?'

Why should I worry, then? I had had my month's salary and a personal note from Appleby, thanking me for my hard work and enclosing a seasonal gift of appreciation from the partners, in the form of a not entirely ungenerous bonus cheque. I couldn't expect any more. I pushed the chair back, returning to a sitting position, and slid open the side drawer of my desk. In it were a few packages wrapped in Christmas paper, small gifts for people in the office. I dropped one of them as I fumbled them out – my hands were still shaking with the last vestiges of nervous tension, I noticed – and I bent down to pick it up from the carpet. When I stuck my head back up, a sight greeted my eyes – three grinning faces: Penny, Rose and Julie. And on my desk, a huge wicker basket from which protruded the tops of various cellophane-wrapped goodies: wine and champagne and fruit and coffee and chocolates and a great bunch of exotic flowers. They laughed at my expression.

'There's a card, see,' said Penny. 'Why don't you open it?'

I did. It read, 'To Sarah. A Happy Christmas and thank you from Trevor and all at Chewton Residential.'

'Very well deserved, darling,' said Rose.

'I should say so,' said Julie.

'They've done right by you, my love,' said Penny. Then she winked at the others. 'Come on, then. Let's hear you, now.' She gave a conductorial wave of her plump hand, and they began to sing. 'For she's a jolly good fellow'.

They ended with a majestic choral descant of 'And so say all of us!' But by that time, I couldn't speak for tears.

I felt my eyes pricking as I recalled the scene. It was nice to be appreciated. But now I had to concentrate. The snow was getting thicker, the swirling dots had become heavier flakes and were beginning to clog the wipers. The verges at the side of the road had a pale gleam and I could hear the hiss of slush under the tyres. Even though the road was much more familiar to me than once it had been, I slowed right down for the descent into Woodcombe, turning the wheel with extra care as the headlights gleamed on chequered chevrons and raw metal crash barriers. I didn't want to spend Christmas in hospital.

I looked out for the junction sign for Nunhampton Lane and made the turn. Here, where there was less traffic, the snow had settled quite thickly, and I felt my little car begin to slide and slither as the tyres scrabbled for a grip on the steep slope. At last I saw the great laurel bushes of the entrance, now blotched with snow. The car bounced and bumped and skidded down the icy drive, which was sheltered from a heavy fall by the overhanging trees and emerged into the open space by the house. I parked and clambered out into the freezing air and softly falling snow. The moon, riding high over the Woodcombe Valley, shone through a gap in the heavy clouds, silvering the laden branches of the great cedar tree.

I saw a figure running towards me and I ran to her. We caught each other in an enormous hug. 'Happy Christmas, Caro! Happy Christmas!'

I heard her voice half muffled in the folds of my coat. 'Now you're here, Sarah, I know it really will be.'

\*

I pushed away my plate. 'No, I couldn't possibly eat any more, even of your wonderful pudding. I've already had two helpings. And I had masses of turkey, too. It was all really delicious. I still feel a bit guilty though – I feel I've imposed my terrible carnivorousness on you.'

She laughed. 'Don't be silly. I told you. Even I make an exception at Christmas. That's the definition of feasting, isn't it? Something special you don't have every day. Besides, who'd bother to keep those awful birds otherwise? Those hideous heads like melted candlewax. They'd be extinct.'

'My thoughts exactly. But let's hope our friend on the table there had a short life but a merry one. More champagne?'

'Mmm, all right, then. Did you really get all that stuff as a present? It was very generous.'

'Yes, I was quite touched. Even though Chewton is absolutely mega-loaded, it was still nice of him to do it. I'm glad I had that to contribute. I'm hopeless about food shopping, and I never got round to it at all in the last two weeks. I've been living out of tins and packets.'

'It's my privilege to feed you up, then. You look a bit pale.'

'Do I? Overwork, I suppose, stress.'

'You should try meditation. It clears your mind. Makes you concentrate on being present to the present. Don't look at me like that!'

'I'm sorry. All these things you're into. It's like a foreign language to me. I think I've caught up and then you come out with something else. Meditation. Isn't that like praying or something?'

'It certainly is not. I couldn't have survived without it. I can't explain it. Maybe you should try it.'

'Maybe. Isn't it strange that we've found ourselves together like this? We're so different.'

'On the contrary, the ways that we're different complement the ways in which we are alike. That time you fetched up at the door, all abject and wounded, I felt, even before we got talking, that there was something about you. Something that had been missing from my life which I had now found. It was so strange, because the first time I saw you, I hated you. You looked so glossy and full of authority and pleased with yourself.'

'Was I really? I had that knocked out of me, didn't I? Perhaps you had to see that I was as hurt and damaged as you were before you could respond to me. I certainly needed you then. I need you now.'

'I was thinking of you – and her – yesterday afternoon before you arrived. I walked back home from the shop. The snow was falling, and there was that silence you get with it. I thought of what you told me about Josephine, and how you must be feeling now. It reminded me of a poem. I even looked it out. I'd like to read it to you. Is that okay?'

'Yes, of course.'

She went over to a wobbly bookcase, took down a much thumbed paperback volume entitled *English Romantic Verse*, found a place marked with a scrap of paper and began to read.

I didn't know what to expect, but the first verse hit me with the shock of recognition.

> '"Cold in the earth, and the deep snow piled above thee!
> Far, far removed, cold in the dreary grave!
> Have I forgot, my Only Love to love thee,
> Severed at last by Time's all-severing wave?"'

I listened; her small quiet voice huge in the silent room, its only counterpoint the faintest of crackling sounds from the woodburner.

When she finished, I found that the tears were pouring in hot runnels down my cheeks.

'Read that last bit to me again.'

Her gaze on me was wonderfully warm then, hardly glancing at the printed page, she recited,

> '"And even yet, I dare not let it languish,
> Dare not indulge in Memory's rapturous pain;
> Once drinking deep of that divinest anguish,
> How could I seek the empty world again?"'

For a time I couldn't speak, but sat, my head bowed in my lap. Then I raised my head, feeling my face still wet with weeping. 'How could she know that – how I feel? It was a woman poet, wasn't it?'

She nodded. 'Yes. Emily Brontë.'

'You see, I go for long periods when I don't think about her. Like it says in the poem – "While the world's tide is bearing me along." That's what's been happening since I came to Fernsford. Then, when I do suddenly remember, I feel so horribly guilty, as if I'd betrayed her all over again. And yet I know I should go mad if I thought of nothing else. It's like a horrible loop I can't get out of. Perhaps I should try to forget.'

'No, you mustn't do that. You must remember, you mustn't become obsessed by memory. Put it, and your grief, into a context. Buddhists believe that death is only a stage in life. The dead are reincarnated and live again. And with the living, your work is to deal with your experience, not to run away from it, but to use it. If you believe that then it becomes easier to accept what might otherwise be unacceptable.'

'I can't just accept, though. What about you, then? Have you really accepted what happened to you? I know I haven't. I don't believe I ever will.'

She didn't reply at once to my angry words. It was as if she'd withdrawn herself. Then she said, 'Accepted. That's an awfully big word. No, not probably at the deepest level. There I feel as bitter and angry and hurt as ever I did. But I have learned that I have certain — well, gifts, I suppose — which not only help me to deal with some of those feelings, but have, in the end, grown with those feelings. It's hard to put it into words but I believe that not only are we shaped by our experience, but that we can also shape that experience. What happened to me underlies everything I do. In some terrible, wonderful way, it has made me a different kind of artist, maybe even a better one.'

I stretched out my hand across the table and met hers and held it fast. 'I'm nothing like you. I can't express myself in any way except through anger. All my life I've felt this terrible rage. For years I hated myself and was afraid of myself. Afraid of the fact that I had his blood in my veins. That one day it would emerge in some terrible act of savagery. I still have that fear.'

I felt her grasp tighten. 'I don't feel that in you. You can't inherit evil. Wickedness grows from circumstances. You have expressed yourself. Living can be a kind of art, the best kind. The most creative kind of all. You've made yourself different from what you might have been.'

I stared at her. 'I wish I could believe that,' I said in a whisper.

I lay awake for a long time that night, listening to the faint whistling of the wind, and the creak of the tree branches as if they were performing an avant-garde composition.

What Caroline had said echoed in my mind. It was true that my life had gone in directions the angry, illiterate and self-destructive schoolgirl I had been would never have recognized.

And I remembered the day a couple of months before when I first came to Vale View, when I scrambled out of what might have proved my grave. As if jolted loose by the terror of it, the past had tumbled out and my life and Caroline's had started to flow together. I had told her things I had never told a soul. I had confessed to her things which I thought were beyond confession. And she, bless her, had listened, and gone on listening.

How I longed that something of the burden I carried within might shift, like a grounded ship washed by a rising tide. How I longed for the open sea, for the cry of the gulls and the freshening wind upon my face.

As I lay there, staring up into the darkness beyond the glow of the table lamp, surrounded by the looming presences of Caroline's strange and moving creations, I could hear my own voice, wavering at first and then growing stronger.

'He killed her, and I stood and watched him do it. Can you imagine that? I stood there, sort of frozen. I saw what he did, and I did nothing. At first, I could hardly believe it had happened. I thought I'd imagined it. Then I heard the screaming from below and it went on and on and on, and I knew it was true. I saw the face of my father as he looked over the railing of the balcony, then turned back into the room. The way he looked, I knew he'd do it to me as well if he knew I'd seen him. That was my only thought. To hide, to get away. Look after myself. If he sees me, if he knows, then he'll get me as well. So I told myself that, anyway, the police will get him now. He can't get away with that. He'll be taken away and then things will be all right again. When the police come, they'll lock him up in prison for ever and ever.

'So I sneaked back out of the flat, and down the stairs, and I hid down at the bottom by the rubbish chute. I crouched down and pulled a bin bag over me. Outside, I could hear the screaming, then there was the ambulance siren. Then it was all quiet, so finally I crept out and went back upstairs to our flat, and there was no one there and the door was locked. So I sort of stood there, and the old lady next door came out and she looked ever so upset, and she said, "Oh, Sarah, darling. Don't you know what's happened?" I shook my head, and said that Dad had sent me out to buy his cigs and he was going to be cross because the man in the shop wouldn't sell them to me because he said the policeman had been round checking up on him selling booze and cigs to kids who weren't old enough.

'Then she burst into tears and hugged me and said, "Oh, it's an awful thing, Sarah child. Your sister, your poor sister. She had a terrible fall. From that awful dangerous balcony. She's been took to the hospital, but she was so dreadfully broke up, she's going to die. Your daddy's gone with her and he's so destroyed with the grief. He's blaming himself and saying he shouldn't have left her alone there while he was making the tea. They've sent to your mammy's work for her to go to the hospital."

'I listened to her, feeling my face cold and stiff, but even as I felt her tears dripping warm and salty into my mouth as she held me to her, I couldn't cry myself. What was this I was hearing? My father destroyed with grief? Had I really then imagined what I had seen? They'd always said I had a vivid imagination.

'Later on my mother and father came back together from the hospital, white faced and grim. "You'll have heard what's occurred. It's more than time you were in bed," were my mother's words of greeting. I gathered from what they said to each other that Josephine had died without regaining consciousness. Later in the evening, muffled in the depths of the bed I had shared with Josephine, I heard the knock at the door, the West of Ireland gabbling of the local priest, and then the clink of glasses. The next day, early, the policeman came.

'He was a sergeant, a big man with a red face, sipping tea from a mug, his helmet on the floor beside his chair, full of apologies about the routine inquiries he had to make. "I know you spoke to the Inspector at the hospital, but we have to see where it happened, so we can do our report for the coroner." He noticed me for the first time. "The little girl, was she?"

'My father answered. "No, she was out at the shop. I'd given her a bit of money. To buy sweeties for herself. She didn't come back till afterwards."

'My father told him that he had left Josephine playing by herself in the sitting room, and had gone into the kitchen to get a cup of tea, "and a glass of pop for my daughter". Here he started to sob. My mother had been weeping into her handkerchief ever since the copper had arrived. He nodded in sympathy, and made notes in his black-covered notebook.

Struggling to control his voice, my father said that the door to the balcony had been open, as the washing had been drying there. "I wish to God I'd realized that she would go out there. I'd told her often enough not to climb on the rail, but you must know that the poor child was not entirely, you know, in the head. But I didn't think of it. I heard the screaming. I ran in from the kitchen. I saw that the room was empty. When I looked over the rail of the railing, I saw her poor little body lying smashed on the concrete, and someone bending over her."

'The two of them went out to the balcony, and the sergeant measured the height of the railing, and nodded and sucked his teeth.

'All the time I'm sitting there, thinking, any moment now he's going to take me on his knee like a shop Father Christmas and say, And what would you like to tell me, little girl? Then I'll tell him, when my father can't get at me or give me one of his looks. But the copper never gave me a second glance. I was so scared it was like my tongue was frozen up in my mouth. I couldn't say what I wanted to say. And at the same time I was thinking, what if he didn't believe me, said I was making up stories like I was always doing at school? If he didn't believe me then Dad would kill me as well. So he clapped Dad on the shoulder and said he was sorry, and then he left.

'That night, I couldn't sleep. I had two pictures in my mind. One was the picture of what my father had said. The concerned, heart-broken parent. His beloved daughters. One sent out for a treat, the other playing contentedly. The other was the picture of what had really happened. Or was it that I had imagined it? In that version, my father, drunk and angry at having run out of cigarettes, threw some money at me and said, "Get down to the shop and get me twenty Embassy, you lippy little bitch. And be quick about it."

'I had run out of the door, and down in the lift to the newsagent's across the road from the flats. When the man had refused to serve me, I had got scared, because I knew Dad'd be furious at having to go out himself.

'That was why I sidled back into the flat, hoping he wouldn't see me, and that he would forget about the cigs. I heard a scuffling in the lounge, and then Josephine's voice saying "I won't, I won't!" I crept along the corridor and stared through the half-open door.

'My father was on the sofa. His flies were open and his prick was sticking out, all red and swollen, like the time before. He'd grabbed hold of Josephine, and she was on her knees in front of him. He was saying, "Go on, before that sister of yours gets back. Just a quick one for your dad."

'She was twisting her head away, and struggling. Then she said, "I won't do that no more. It's dirty. I'm going to tell on you and you'll get took away."

'"Why, you little cow!" He lashed at her with his foot, hard, really hard, and caught her on the side of the head. She fell back and there was a horrid thud as her skull hit the concrete floor. She lay there not moving.

'He bent down to her, sort of listened at her chest, put his hand in front of her mouth. Then he picked her up in his arms, and she was as floppy as a bundle of washing. He had this expression on his face. I can't describe it, sort of scared and cunning and mad-looking, all at once. Then he carried her over to the balcony. He sort of sank down on his knees when he got there, and pushed her up on to the railing. He kept on shoving and eventually she tipped over and disappeared.

'Had I really seen that happen? Was the sorrowing, tearful man who was my father the one who had pushed Josephine to her death? Was I the only one who knew, if I did know? Night after sleepless night, I turned this over in my mind, in the bedroom we had once shared, Josephine's few toys and possessions, her teddy bear, a doll, a plastic shopping basket, still lying where she had left them. I would start at every slightest noise, in case it were my father, coming to get from me what he had got from her, or to silence me for what I knew. I thought that he might somehow divine what I had seen just by looking at me, so I avoided his eyes. I tried not to shudder when he brushed against me by accident or touched me on purpose. Once or twice he came upon me in the bathroom, naked, and I felt his eyes upon me. Although nothing untoward happened, I could not relax. When he kissed me at bedtime, I wanted to squirm away from his unshaven face and the breath sweetish with alcohol, or spit the kiss back in his face, but I dared not, in case it showed him that I knew.

'If I did know, then I was the only one, I was convinced of that. The neighbours were universally sympathetic. They had brought gifts and clubbed together to give my sister a proper funeral, beyond what my parents could have afforded. I was not allowed to go, being regarded as too young for such things. I watched as the small white coffin was borne away in the flower-garlanded hearse to the crematorium. Cremation was what my father had wanted, and her ashes were scattered, so there's not even a grave for me to visit.

There was an inquest, which brought in the verdict of accident. The neighbours were keen that we should sue the council for negligence, as everyone knew how dangerous the balcony railings were, although to my knowledge, no one else had ever fallen over them.

'For a long time, I avoided going near the part of the yard directly under our windows. I would take the long way round rather than cross the concrete where her broken body had lain. I hardly had the courage to look down on it from my bedroom window to see, in the days after her death, the flowers in bunches and sprays and wreaths which had been laid there. In jamjars, Josephine's playfellows from the primary school had placed swiftly wilting daisies and pansies. Then one day, all this had gone. The council streetsweeper, a drinking acquaintance of my father's, cleared it all away.

'There were some of the neighbours who said they could still see, ingrained in the concrete the dark stains of her blood, but cars used to park there and it was probably sump oil.'

## XIII

I yawned and stretched my cramped legs in the musty-smelling sleeping bag. It was about a foot too short and I had had to curl myself up to avoid sticking out and getting frozen. The ancient camp bed creaked and groaned as I struggled up into a sitting position. I was in the living room, where I had slept on that first occasion. Because of the stove this was the warmest place to be. Caro had a sort of loft platform over the studio end of the long room, reached by a rickety ladder through a trap door. She said she had got used to the cold, and that anywhere else would seem terribly stuffy. This wasn't hard to believe as the wintry wind blew freely through the gaps and holes in the roof slates.

I looked at my watch. Eight o'clock. As if I were in a school sack race, I hopped, still inside the bag, over to where the pale early morning light shone around the edges of the curtains of the window above the sink unit. I pulled one back and peered out. Despite the gloom, I could see that the snow had almost gone from the yard nearest the stable block, leaving big greyish pools the consistency of thin gruel on the cobblestones. I dragged back the other curtain on its rusty metal runners. The draining board and work-surface were cluttered with plates and pans crusted with the unfestive greasy remains of Christmas dinner.

Yech! I had a big problem with washing up at the best of times, and wasn't at all looking forward to tackling it this time with water made luke warm by pouring in the contents of a boiled kettle and Caro's version of detergent, guaranteed to treat congealed fat in the most ecologically correct, and therefore ineffective, manner. Perhaps we could have breakfast first, if there was anything clean to eat it off. I was hungry again, despite the gorging of the previous evening. It must be the freezing temperature.

I placed a tentative hand on the black flank of the woodburner. It wasn't completely cold, but clearly no inferno was raging in there. I studied the front of it, trying to remember the knack of opening the fire door. I grasped the handle and yanked and twisted and it groaned open, revealing a maw full of whitish ash and a few glowing embers. Please don't go out, I begged as I fed it dry twigs from the pile on the hearth. I was rewarded by a hot, woody smell and a little flare of flame. Emboldened, I piled on small fragments of bark and wood chippings, then, more rashly, a couple of small logs. With another small obeisance, I closed the hatch. From inside, to my relief, there was the sound of healthy crackling and spitting, and a faint bonging from the expanding cast iron.

There was a crash from the studio and a muttered curse, then more mumblings and cursings as whatever it was that had been knocked over was picked up. The resplendent studio hangings parted to reveal the figure of Caro, pale, her blonde hair even more spiky and dishevelled than usual. She was wearing a very old brown felt dressing-gown with a tasselled silk cord. She ran her hands through her cropped locks, raising their spikes into the air and leaving her arms stretched in a pose oddly reminiscent of the Statue of Liberty.

'You look terrible.'

'Thanks. I feel it. It was your bloody champagne. I knew we shouldn't have finished the bottle.'

'It was a magnum, actually. And who wants to drink flat bubbly on the cold morning afterwards? We were celebrating.'

'I know. And it was nice. But I do feel awful. You look really chirpy.'

I did a little dance to rub it in. 'Chirp, chirp. I was hoping there'd be some breakfast.'

'God, how can you? You young people.'

'Who's talking? Go on, how old are you, Grandma?'

'I'm twenty-nine, going on ninety.'

'Are you really? Josephine was three years older than me, just like you. Strange, isn't it?'

She turned her head away and for a moment neither of us spoke. Then, as I had, she gingerly felt the stove. 'Hey. It's going. Did you do that? You must have the gift. When I wake it up it sulks for hours.'

'Do I get breakfast as a reward?'

'You're a greedy beast to feed, aren't you? We ate the eggs yesterday, so today's choice is muesli – or nothing.'

'Muesli, please. Er, what is muesli?'

I chewed reflectively. 'This tastes as if it's very good for you.'

'That's because it is. It's full of fibre.'

'Fibre. As in man-made?'

'Sarah, honestly. Sometimes I think you come from a different planet.'

'But I do. Planet London, where the streets are paved with dog shit, there's a take-away on every street corner, and where no one knows or cares about where food comes from before it's frozen or put into tins and packets.'

'That explains a lot.'

I spooned up the last of the coarse cereal. 'Of course it does. But it isn't just London. Fernsford is virtually the same, give or take a bit of decorative greenery. I'm no more in touch with life's elementals than I would be in

Oxford Street. Maybe it's you who's out of touch. An awful lot more people live in cities than in places like this.'

She put down the outsize mug of tea and smiled. 'True. So we should appreciate it while it lasts. We should go out and revel in it. Look, I think the sun's coming out.'

The path through the wood was slippery with mud, last year's dead leaves and half-melted snow. We had followed the drive back to Nunhampton Lane, then turned in the direction of Woodcombe until a white-on-green sign indicated the start of the public footpath up the steep bank.

Caro was ahead, her slim figure striding easily along, her feet shod sensibly in strong walking boots. I slithered and panted behind, my cheap yellow plastic wellies giving me a poor grip. I thought back to my last country walk with Harriet, when I had poured scorn on her Londoner's distaste for the open air and her pristine trainers. This time I was the hopeless townie. This was a much tougher climb than our gentle amble from the car park along the path to Randolph's Leap. We had turned away from the bluffs along the river and were climbing directly up into the Oxdowns, the rolling hills through which the Tarrant had carved its spectacular way until, swollen by its many tributaries, it reached the plains of Westerset and finally the sea.

The trees ended at a wooden fence with a stile. She waited for me to catch up. 'Come on. The view from up here is really spectacular.'

The last part was the hardest. Away from the sheltering timber, a strong cold wind was whipping up and snow began to fall again in large flakes, which whirled into my face. At this height, it was much colder, the earlier snow fall covering the dry grass in a thin, crisp icy layer, through which tall orange-brown stalks of long-dead weeds poked crookedly. The path was strewn with sharp pieces of greyish limestone, the earth a yellowish clay. At last, the end seemed in sight. Caro raised a hand and pointed, yelling over the roar of the wind, 'There's the trig point.'

We scrambled together up a series of rocky outcrops, like giant steps up to the top of the hill, and together we ran through the crunchy snow to the concrete column and hugged it.

'You're right about the view. It puts everything into context, somehow,' I said when I had regained my breath.

The wintry flurry stopped as suddenly as it had begun. In the clear winter's light, we could see the snow-covered mounds of the Oxdowns, stretching away into the misty distance, interrupted in the west by the line of dark woods which marked the gorge of the Tarrant. The course of the river as it flowed south could just be discerned, and in the far distance, where it made its great bend, was the grey smudge which was all that could be seen of the city of Fernsford.

We huddled together on a flat stone in the shelter of a snow-filled hollow. I was conscious of her at my side, felt her warmth, the rhythmic tremor of her body as she breathed. I knew I had found someone to whom I could tell everything.

Fixing my eye on a candyfloss wisp of cloud high in the steel-blue canopy, I said quietly, 'I never told you what happened after Josephine's death. It was only a few weeks later. I'd got sent to bed early for what my father called being lippy. That was always happening. But this time, he'd taken me to my room, pulled down my knickers and pushed me down on the bed as if he were going to give me a spanking. He'd never done that before. He stood looking at me, as I gazed back in terror, my skirt pulled up to my waist, my pants round my ankles. I could smell the drink on his breath. His face was flushed and I could hear his heavy breathing. He sort of reached out his hands and they were all spread like claws. I watched his face, and his expression kept changing, one moment it was my father and the next there was another kind of look entirely. An ugly look. The same look he'd had when he'd pushed Josie over the railing. It was like he was struggling within himself. Then his hands relaxed and he went out. Then he left.

'I must have fallen asleep, because the next thing I knew it was dark. I heard the front door slam and my father's heavy footsteps on the bare tiles of the hall. He went into their bedroom opposite mine. I crept out of bed and put my ear to the flimsy panel to listen.

'I heard my mother's voice. "What are you doing with that bag, Terry? Where are you going, Terry?"

'Then my father was shouting at her, "I'm getting out of this shit-hole, getting away from you is what I'm doing."

'There was a scuffling sound. "Terry, don't leave me. I couldn't bear to be alone. Don't leave me, for God's sake!"

'I could imagine her clinging on to him, her tear-stained face staring up at him. It would be like all the other times. He wouldn't go.

'There were more scuffles and shouting, then a scream and a sickening thud. I heard him come out into the hall again.

'I scuttled back into the bed and pulled the covers over me, desperately screwing up my eyes.

'I heard my door opening wide, and his footsteps on the bare floor. Oh God, he'd killed my mother, I thought. He would know I had been listening if he saw me still in my clothes. I stopped breathing. I felt his hand on my shoulder, waited for it to rip back the blankets. He was going to do to me the things he did to Josie, then he was going to kill me.

'But his hand rested there for only a moment and then it was gone. I heard his footsteps crossing the room, then out into the hall. The front door slammed. I breathed again. I could hardly believe it. He had gone. Gone for ever. I cried with relief as I lay there. I cried as I waited for my mother to come to take me in her arms and tell me the nightmare was over.

'I heard her coughing in the hall, heard the toilet flush, heard her stumble into her own room. Heard her groans of pain throughout the night. But she never came to me, not then or ever. Nor I to her. We never mentioned Josephine or my father again.'

As I finished speaking I lowered my head to her shoulder and she withdrew her hand from her glove and touched my cheek.

'Do you think she knew? Or suspected?'

'I don't know. All I know is I couldn't tell her. I couldn't talk to her at all. For fourteen years, we lived as if none of it had ever happened.'

'My God. So you never saw him again?'

I turned away to stare at the westering sun. 'I hoped I never would. For a long time, it was as if he'd vanished off the face of the earth. I thought he was probably dead. I used to pray for that. But that wasn't enough. On my twelfth birthday I swore on the Bible that, if I ever had the opportunity, I would avenge my sister's death. I'd let her down, by being too frightened and too cowed to speak out when she was killed. It was too late to tell anyone, so I had to kill him. I think I'd got the idea from that old telly programme, *The Avengers*. I imagined myself dressed up in black leather, seeking him out and beating him to death. Then, when I started to learn about the law, I tried to think of some legal way I could get him. But there isn't one. I was the only witness. There's no other evidence. Everyone would say it was a fantasy brought on by the trauma of her death. It would never go to court. Lots of cases like that never do. So instead, I drove my tutors mad badgering them for ever more information about the defence of provocation. I thought that if I could find a case like my sister's where the same sort of situation had justified a defence of provocation, then I could kill him and be guilty only of manslaughter. That way I wouldn't get locked up for life. I'm not a martyr. I couldn't stand that. But, of course, there isn't such a case. The law relating to provocation is very strictly construed, as many people, mainly women, have found to their cost. Of course, as he'd disappeared, it was, quite literally, academic. A few months ago, however, it became very real indeed.'

'What do you mean?' Her voice was hardly more than a whisper.

'He came back. To see me. He'd been watching me. He appeared one night.'

I felt her hand on my arm. 'Where? What happened?'

I told her.

'Things came together. The end of the Colin thing, the job. Then him. Fernsford was my escape route. I'm sure I wouldn't have come here otherwise. I ran away from my vow. Cowardly to the last. It's funny the way things sort of arrange themselves. If I hadn't fled from London, I wouldn't have met you. Because of you, the darkness seems to have lifted. The more it lifts, the less likely I am to do anything stupid. Since I've been here and found you, I've started to feel differently. But if he tracked me down here, I might have to run again. If I didn't run, then . . .'

'What?'

'Whatever he says, however he behaves towards me, it's because he doesn't suspect I know about him and Josephine. In London, I was terrified that he might guess, that if I looked too frightened, he would know. If I see him again, I may not be able to hide my feelings. Rationally, I suppose, he may realize that there's no way I can hurt him. But I think he's insane – or part of him is. The way he started stalking me shows that. He may not be able to cope with knowing that I know his secret. He may have the same feelings about me as he had about Josephine, accompanied by the same hatred and revulsion. You and I know that even apparently sane men despise women and want to hurt them. He may say that I'm his favourite daughter and that he wants to benefit me, to compensate me for my childhood. That other part of him will want to abuse and kill me.'

I paused and looked into her terrified eyes. 'I'm not a cowed little girl any longer. I won't sit around waiting for that to happen. If I suspect that the mad part has taken over completely, then I'll . . .' I stopped.

'You don't mean that. You can't!'

'I do. I shall kill him. Before he has a chance to kill me.'

The light of the short winter's day was failing as we plodded through the refreezing slush of the drive. The sun had long been hidden behind clouds and more snow seemed threatened. I noticed that the tree branches drooped low already and with another season's growth would begin to make the way impassable unless they were cut back.

'What will you do, Caro, when you have to leave? You will eventually, you know.'

'I do know that. It's hard to think of it, though. I've got so used to this place. But, of course, it's not me, is it? What right have I to be living here? It's been just a brief idyll. I don't know whether I'll be able to afford another studio. My work sells a bit, but it's not what you'd call popular.'

We had emerged on to the gravelled sweep in front of the ruined mansion. The snow still lay in strips where the sun hadn't reached it: against the beech hedge which bordered the lawn, beneath the cedar tree, and up against the front wall of the house, covering the terrace. The house stared at us with its rows of blank windows. I shivered, although there was no wind. She noticed the involuntary movement.

'It can be a bit creepy sometimes. Like the old haunted house in children's stories.'

'It's not that. I don't believe in ghosts. I'm far more terrified by the living. I suddenly felt how vulnerable everything is. To change, to decay. To old age, to death. There's not long, is there, between the first breath and the last?'

She put an arm around my shoulder. 'Come on. All the more reason for living in the moment. We should go in. We're just getting frozen and soon it will be quite dark.'

She led the way round the side of the house, back to the stable yard.

We both stopped in surprise when we saw the lines of footprints in the snow on the terrace.

'It looks like you've got visitors. They weren't there when we went out.'

She didn't reply but started to follow them, walking quickly. I hurried to catch her up. 'What is it, burglars?'

'Look at the size of them. He'd have to be a midget.'

'Kids, then, from the town.'

We had arrived at the back door, the entrance to the quarters to which the late Mrs Kemble had been reduced. Caro was kneeling down, examining the wooden panel. 'No, it's not children. How many children would be out mischief making on Boxing Day? Take a look.'

I bent down to do so. The bottom part of the door was broken away, leaving a gap about a foot high. The timber had obviously been rotten. Dark splinters of it littered the ground, now glowing in the darkness as if phosphorescent.

'Do you smell it?'

'Smell what?' I wrinkled my nose. Yes, there was something, strange and pungent. 'Ugh, what is it?'

'It's a fox. Or more probably a vixen, looking for a cosy winter's bolt-hole.'

'A fox? I thought foxes were scared of humans.'

'They are. The house must have lost its human scent by now. No one's been in it since Arabella died, apart from your Pickwickian legal friend, and he only for an hour or so. I think he was scared the place would collapse on top of him.'

'So the foxes are the new owners then?'

'I know it's silly and the main part of the house is probably infested with all manner of wildlife, but I don't like the idea of Arabella's part being messed up. The first time she asked me round, we sat in the big kitchen in there.'

'So what are you going to do – have a dialogue with the vixen? Get a hound?'

'No. Much simpler than that. I'll go in and make sure that the doors from Arabella's rooms are shut, then burn a few sticks of incense in there, that'll put off our vulpine home-maker. And I'll nail a piece of plywood from the studio over the hole in this door.'

'Now?'

'Yes. I don't want our friend getting time to get too comfortable tonight. But you can go and stay in the warm. Put some supper on, open some wine. You don't have to fall in with my stupid ideas.'

That sounded awfully appealing. I was frozen stiff after sitting so long on the hillside. But I had a sort of feeling I would be missing an opportunity – but for what I couldn't imagine. So I said, 'No, actually, I'd be rather interested, you know, to look inside. That stuff that Arabella told you about her life here was fascinating.'

'Okay, I'll get the key and a torch and the rest of the stuff.'

'Watch out on those stairs!' Her voice floated up to me out of the gloom.

I shone the torch down on to my feet. The treads creaked, but not alarmingly. They were still covered with a threadbare carpet. I was ascending the great staircase from the main entrance hall of the house. I paused on the half-landing. The stairs divided to left and right. I swung the powerful beam around. It caught briefly on a short dangling length of electric flex, the end bristling with bare wires. Presumably, in the old days, there had been a crystal chandelier, like the one that hung in Trevor Chewton's palace.

I took the left-hand branch. At the top, there was a long, high-ceilinged corridor. The bare floorboards were covered with lumps of plaster and plaster dust. I pointed the torch up again. It illuminated patches on which fungus grew and strips of bare lath from where chunks had fallen.

I tried the first door on my left. It creaked open about a foot, then stuck fast. In the gap, I could see the end of a length of squared timber from which rusty nails protruded. The collapsed roof must have gone right through the floor above. I shut the door carefully and crossed to the door opposite.

It opened easily. Here the ceiling was, except for a few patches, more or less intact. The huge room was entirely empty, its great window, which I reckoned must look out over the lawn at the back of the house, covered with the internal shutters. I closed my eyes and imagined what it must have been like in its heyday.

Arabella, Caro had told me during our Christmas dinner, had often talked of her life at Vale View before her husband had lost his money and his hope. They had been rich, and the house had been splendidly furnished. They had entertained a great deal.

This room might have been her bedroom: an antique bed with silk hangings, perhaps, like the ones I'd seen in the V&A. A dressing-table laid with ebony- or ivory-backed brushes, fine porcelain containers, cut-glass-and-silver bottles for cosmetics, a box richly inlaid in coloured woods, from whose velvet-covered trays spilled the chill fire of diamonds, the watery splendour of emeralds and the blood-red warmth of rubies.

I opened my eyes again and shone the torch around. Ropes of cobwebs hung from the ceiling cornices. As the beam passed over the wooden panelling, I could see that it was thickly coated with dust. What must she have thought to see her house crumble around her, her youth and her fortune lost, childless, and becoming old and tired and ill?

I closed the door gently, and turned back towards the landing. That wasn't the entire picture, was it? She hadn't given in, despite old age and poverty. She had been alive enough herself to see life in others. Whatever happened in the future, Caro had benefited from being here. No wonder she felt so much for the old lady. I picked my way back down the stairs.

Caro was crouched by the outside door in the dimly lit kitchen, her mouth full of nails, hammer in hand. She held a square piece of plywood over the hole the fox had made and proceeded to nail it into position. 'That should do it. Until the rot spreads to the rest of the door, at any rate.'

She had set burning a couple of scented candles, and some sticks of incense smouldered in a dish on the pine table in the centre of the room. The fumes made me cough. 'This should frighten any vermin for miles around.'

'Good. Now, let's shut the other door, then we can go home and have our supper.' She went out into the corridor and into Arabella's bedroom opposite. I heard her exclaim with annoyance. 'Come and give me a hand. It's stuck.'

We tugged together at the door, she pushing, I pulling on the round Bakelite knob, but it didn't budge. She bent down to examine the bottom rail. 'It must have swollen in the damp. No, hang on, it's sort of wedged on this floorboard. The light's so awful in here.'

I hurried to get the torch. 'That's better. Yes, look, the edge of that board is sticking up. Perhaps if I push the door further back and then you stand on the board it'll press it down enough for me to heave the door over it. There'll be enough space for us to squeeze through to get out again.'

I did as she suggested. 'No, that's no good. Try jumping. When you thump down, I'll shove the door.'

I put my heels together, sprang up in the air as far as I could, then smacked down. This had considerably more effect than we'd intended. To be sure, the edge of the board dipped under the impact of my weight, and Caro, with a triumphant 'Got it!', slammed the door to. In fact, turning on the fulcrum of the adjacent joist, the board not only dipped but shot downwards into the cavity beneath the floor, having, with a crack, broken free along its ten-foot length from the rusty nails which held it down. Its other end rose seesaw-like into the air. As I overbalanced, then fell full length, narrowly avoiding twisting my ankle, I heard a crash behind me.

Caro hauled me to my feet, shaking with laughter. 'God, that was funny. Are you all right? You should have seen yourself. It was like that trick at school, with a ruler on the edge of a desk and a piece of chalk. You thump the free end and the chalk goes hurtling across the room. Same principle.'

I dusted myself down. 'It's a dangerous place for me, this. What have we gone and done?'

'Nothing much, I think. She flogged all the antiques years ago. Look, the loose end of the board tipped over the bedside table.'

I kicked the dislodged floorboard back into place and took hold of the rectangular mahogany bedside table which had fallen on its front. As I pulled it upright, the single drawer opened. I grabbed it to prevent it sliding out altogether, and set the table level again. I pushed the drawer to close it, but it wouldn't go in.

I said lamely, 'I'm not doing too well here. Now this drawer won't close.'

'Let me have a look.' I stood looking down rather foolishly as her strong capable hands jiggled it. 'Hey, there's something jamming it. There's nothing inside, though. It seems to be hanging down.' She slipped a hand into the half-open drawer. 'I've got it. It's sort of glued to the underneath of the table-top. Here it is.' There was a faint tearing sound of paper being unstuck. Her hand re-emerged holding a large manila envelope, the sort that has one side made of stiff cardboard. She laid it down on the dusty wooden surface.

I stared at it. 'When the table was knocked over, it must have shaken this loose. Otherwise you could have opened the drawer and not seen it was there.'

'So, she must have hidden it. Do you think I should open it?'

'There's no reason not to. It's not even sealed up.' I suppose the most scrupulous lawyer would have gone on about leaving it to the executors and all that, but Arabella, if indeed it was she who had hidden it, could not have had that intention. It had not been meant to be found by the kind of search a lawyer would have made. And, moreover, I was consumed with curiosity.

She wiped her hands hastily on the sides of her jeans, then carefully pulled out the flap, inserted her thumb and forefinger and tugged delicately.

She drew out a single sheet of cartridge paper.

'Wow!' The schoolgirlish exclamation seemed particularly inadequate for the sight at which we both stared in amazement.

It was a pencil drawing of a beautiful naked woman. She lay back on a rumpled bed, her arms stretched above her head, her breasts, full and firm, one leg drawn up, sheltering her crotch. She had long hair which flowed over the pillow. Her eyes were closed and her face bore a serene smile of contentment. There was an ease and sureness about the sketch which conveyed in a few vivid lines an image of abandoned sensuality, an erotic charge which, even in his apparent haste, the artist had conveyed wonderfully. It made me shiver with recognition. I thought of the occasions on which it could have been myself lying there. I remembered the last occasion.

'Is it her? Arabella?'

Caro was staring at the paper and did not reply for long moments. Then she let out her breath in a long fluttering sigh. 'I'm sure it is. It's good, isn't it? I wonder who did it? Yes, it's signed, "E.C."' She reached out and with the lightest of touches turned the sketch over. 'And on the back it says "For Bella." That was what she used to be called when she was young. She told me. Hang on there's something else, very faded.' She squinted at the paper. 'It's in Italian. "*Mia carissima sposa*. Venice, June '35."'

'What does that mean?'

'"My dearest wife". How strange. But it can't have been.'

'Can't have been what?'

'Her husband. The man who wrote that was obviously the artist. It's a love letter conveyed by the picture. But she was married to Arthur Kemble, not E.C. And he was no artist. He was a brewer who lost all his money in a failed business venture, in the fifties, ran away to Monte Carlo and blew his brains out – in a third class hotel, as Arabella pointedly related.'

'Perhaps she was married before?'

'If she were, she never breathed a word of it.'

'Or perhaps she wasn't married. It was an affair in which they pretended?'

'Perhaps he died. It clearly meant a lot. She kept it when everything else had gone. Hidden, too. I think, whoever he was, she loved him. How odd.' She slid the sheet of paper back into the envelope. 'I suppose I'll have to send this to your Mr Pickwick.'

'No, keep it. I doubt it's of any value but I think you deserve something. I have a feeling she would have wanted you to have it, anyway. You'll keep her secret, won't you?'

She grinned. 'You're right – although I hope you don't give that sort of advice to clients. Now let's get out of here. I'm frozen stiff.'

She closed the door of Arabella's bedroom and we went back to the kitchen. The candles had burned low and the flames were dancing in the draught from the roughly patched door. Carol bent over each one and blew it out gently. The incense sticks were grey ash.

Outside, the wind was blowing hard, and borne upon it were stinging particles of icy snow. We ran through the frozen slush of the yard and into the stable block.

The long room seemed cosy and welcoming after the dead chill of the big house. Caro bustled around, turning on the lamps, feeding logs to the stove, closing the curtains. She got the carcass of the turkey out of the fridge and started hacking off slices for supper.

'I suppose you're starving again?' she inquired as she plonked a couple of left-over potatoes on to my plate.

I nodded vigorously. 'What do you think? Country life is awfully energetic. The office will seem a rest cure.'

'I'm sorry you have to go tomorrow.'

'I know. Me too. But I don't have to leave until after lunch.'

'It hasn't been very long, really. There's an awful lot more I want to say.'

'Yes. But we've got the rest of our lives to say them, haven't we?'

'And how long is that?'

'What do you mean?'

'I mean exactly what I said. Life can be very short. Arabella and her artist. Maybe they thought they had the rest of their lives, too.'

'Please don't talk like this, Caro. It's upsetting me. I can't bear to think of losing you as well.'

'I understand. But it's no good. I keep thinking of Arabella. Hiding and treasuring that drawing for over fifty years. I'm here because of what I awakened in her. And maybe that was because of him. She never said straight out, she wouldn't, but I gather from what she did say that the marriage wasn't happy. She told me once when she'd had too much to drink – it was her one indulgence – that she'd always regretted that they never had children.'

'How did that poem you quoted go? "Have I forgot my only love to love thee/Severed at last by time's all-severing wave?" Perhaps it was like you said. It did blight her life, thinking of what might have been. Until she met you.' As I spoke, our eyes met, and the ghost of an impossible thought flitted across the threshold of my mind.

Trying to control the trembling in my limbs and the tingle in my shoulderblades, I slowly put down my knife and fork and went over to the table where Caro had left the drawing. I picked up a wine-bottle-based lamp from the nearby shelf and held it over the picture.

She got up and stood by me. 'What is it? Why are you staring at it like that?'

I pointed down at the reclining figure. 'When I asked you whether she looked like Arabella, you said she did. But doesn't she remind you of someone else?'

Clearly puzzled, she shook her head. 'No. No one I can think of. What are you getting at?'

'You really can't see it? Get a mirror and tell me if I'm wrong, but I think she looks like you.'

## XIV

I went back to the office at the end of the Christmas holiday. The building was largely empty, most of the staff having taken part of their annual leave to extend the break over the New Year. I was saving time and money for a trip to Italy, so I didn't mind coming in to mind the shop. Besides, Chewton had more or less told me to be there. There was the aftermath of the Christmas sales rush to sort out. All of the Chewton team were in: an unoccupied job under Chewton's management philosophy was a redundant job, and his people took leave only with the greatest reluctance.

I had told Penny I wouldn't need her until after New Year and she had gone for an extended visit to Wales. Appleby was still, of course, topping up his movie-star tan on the beaches of Barbados. I didn't know about the other partners. They did not vouchsafe any of the details of their comings and goings to lower beings such as myself. Rose and her mother had gone on a package tour to Madeira. I gathered that none of the other assistants were in. One of the big attractions of Fernsford had, I'm sure, been the more relaxed atmosphere. I doubted that their old firms in the City and West End were so undermanned at this time of the year. Mr Dyer, the bookkeeper was in – had he ever gone home? And so was Marion Wilde, the office manager.

I got on fine with most of the general office staff. Marion was the exception. This was because, to my mind, she still radiated her distrust of me. She was shortish, dumpy and grey-haired, and she wore grey worsted skirts and greyish woolly jumpers, like an old-fashioned primary-school teacher. She had very strong specs, which made her eyes vast and terrifying, reminding me of those of an octopus.

Her eyes had scrutinized me from behind the shiny, rimless aquarium-wall glasses when we had been introduced – could it be? – nearly six months before. Her pale mouth had puckered up a smile in her unmade-up face, and murmured friendly words of greetings in a low voice almost devoid of the local burr, but the eyes had given quite a different message, suspicious and faintly hostile.

Since then I had had little enough to do with her, apart from negotiating with her over stationery and furniture requirements, and once when she had, with extreme efficiency, arranged for the repair of my broken venetian blind. Nothing had ever been said to justify what I thought she felt about me – she had always been politeness itself – but the eyes still swam doubtingly whenever we had our trivial dealings.

So, that first morning back, on my way through the office, I looked in on the fusty old bat's cubby-hole and gave her a top of the mornin' in my best Irish colleen style. We chatted about our Christmas activities. Marion told me about her fun time in Westhampton with her married sister and her nephews and nieces. Marion herself, I knew from office gossip, had been married, but divorced childlessly many years ago, and she now shared her life with an arthritic cocker spaniel in a small terraced house in the Combe, on the lower, darker, less affluent slopes of Arden Wood.

It was quite a surprise, though, when she had stuck her head round my door at about eleven and asked me if I'd like to have coffee with her and Mr Dyer – 'being as we were the only ones around on the third floor'. It was clearly a *détente* in our relations. I quickly finished my dictating and went along to her room.

She was offering a digestive biscuit to Mr Dyer when I arrived. 'Do sit down, Sarah. That's your mug, with the Festival Hall, isn't it? Milk but no sugar? Good. I do like this time of the year – the phone doesn't ring so much and you can get on with the things that need all your concentration. Of course, Mr Dyer, you have to be like that all the time.'

Mr Dyer nodded in acknowledgement of this fact. He was nibbling at the biscuit with his little, nicotine-stained teeth. 'The telephone is a modern convenience I can do without, Mrs Wilde. In the old days, of course, solicitors regarded the telephone with suspicion, rightly. There is nothing like a written word for certainty.'

'That's why I like the fax,' I said, brightly. 'Instant and definite. Best of both worlds.'

'Not everyone has them, do they? Most of the people I deal with don't. They are getting them more, though.'

'In London, they use the fax machine to order their sandwiches.'

They both shook their heads at this metropolitan extravagance.

Mr Dyer took a small, restorative sip of his coffee. 'Ah, London. Everyone has to emulate the capital now. We never used to hear so much about London in the old days. We had our own way of doing things. You know the town even used to have its own time. Many provincial towns did. Fernsford time was nearly fifteen minutes earlier than London time, because of the distance west of the Greenwich Meridian. People didn't move around so much, so it didn't matter. But the railway and its timetables changed all that.'

'Mr Dyer's quite a local historian, aren't you? Had books published, haven't you?'

He waved a self-deprecating, liver-spotted hand. 'Mere pamphlets. And occasional articles for the *Fernsford Historical Society Review* or the *Evening Packet*. I'm an amateur – one of the last of the amateurs, perhaps. Nowadays you have to be a professional for anyone to take any notice. Belong to a university, all that kind of thing.'

'I've started to get interested in history. Because of my job. Land. That's the basis of a lot of history, isn't it?'

'Very true, Miss Hartley. Tussles over land at local, national and international level are indeed the stuff of history, as those of us who have lived through a World War know to our cost.'

'You must know a lot about the site I'm working on. Friars Haven.'

'The amazing Mr Chewton and his plans. I'm afraid I've crossed swords with him on that – on a purely historical level, naturally. I wrote a letter to the *Evening Packet* decrying the lack of historical verisimilitude in the name. Friars Haven, indeed. There was no haven when and if there were friars, and there were certainly no friars when there was a haven. To yoke the two together is absurd, and I said so. Mr Appleby was not pleased, but, as I said to him, facts are sacred.'

'It's sort of symbolic, though, isn't it? At least it acknowledges the place has some history.'

'I'm afraid, in my view, Miss Hartley, history has far more importance than as an aid to what they call the heritage industry – bad history in fancy dress, I call it. As I've said, the very existence of a Franciscan house is in doubt. There is a local tradition, but no contemporary documentation to support it. The case is unproven, therefore. Chewton is merely perpetuating a dubious legend.'

Marion chuckled. 'Mr Dyer is a stickler for accuracy – that's the accountant in him. There's plenty of things about that place which aren't legends, as any old Fer'sf'dian will tell you. Isn't that right, Mr D?'

'That is quite correct, Mrs Wilde. But even Fernsford time obliges a return to the ledger.'

He stood up, slender and frail-looking in his old and rather shiny charcoal-grey suit, saved from sad seediness by the immaculate white of his shirt front and the assertive crimson gaudiness of the paisley-pattern bow-tie. 'A pleasure, ladies. Miss Hartley, if you should like, I will lend you one or two of my little pamphlets. Slight though they are, they may be of some minor interest.'

'Thank you, I'd like that.'

He bowed slightly to us ladies, and moved stiffly to his own cubby-hole next door.

I got to my feet, but Marion gestured to me to stay. She reached over and pushed her door closed. 'Sit down, please, Sarah. I've got something to say to you.'

I sat, my hands demurely in my lap, and waited.

'It's a sort of apology. Not about anything I've said or done. But what I thought. About you.' She paused.

I raised my eyebrows slightly, but remained silent. She was going to have to get it out without any help from me.

'You see,' she went on, turning her amphibian eyes away to stare at the wall below the high outside window, 'I didn't think you were right for Chamberlayne's, not to begin with. I thought you were, well, never mind what I thought. The point is I don't think it any more. I've seen how hard you work, and I've seen the way you work. So have others. Now my brother, he's a legal exec with Paignton's, does the conveyancing that the partners think is a bit beneath them. His clients have bought lots of houses from Chewtons over the years. He said to me the other day, "It's a pleasure to deal with Chamberlayne's, these days. After being treated like dirt by that Appleby, it's nice to have someone who's both efficient and so polite and helpful." That's high praise, you know, coming from him. He's been at Paignton's for over thirty years and there isn't much he doesn't know about the so-called gentlemen of the law.' She paused again and swivelled her head back to face me. 'So what I'm saying is that I misjudged you, out of sheer prejudice, and I'm sorry for it.'

I couldn't help it. I leaned over and gave her a big hug, which I doubt she'd had in many a long day. She went all pink, and she had to take off her glasses to wipe them on the yellow cloth from her old snap-shut spectacle case. Her eyes were quite normal without them.

'Marion, what a nice thing to say to me. I'm touched. I never realized that Mr Oliver was your brother. He always sounds so charming on the phone.'

'I daresay he has his moments. Fight like cat and dog in the old days, we used to. We were much younger and things were different. Sometimes I look at myself in the mirror and think, "Is that really you, Marion?" It reminds me of how things were. That's why Mr Dyer and I enjoy our little chats. We're the last two from the old firm, you know. Not that I've been here nearly as long as he has: thirty-four years, it is, this Easter, to his forty-five. Think of it. Nearly a whole working life in this one place. No one does that these days.'

'It's changed a lot, though.'

'Of course. Especially since Mr Appleby joined. Before that, it was just old Mr Chamberlayne. I remember little Ralph coming into the office – the old offices, that was, not this place, in his short trousers in the school holidays to see where his daddy worked. Just after I'd joined.'

'Rose told me about the accident.'

'A tragedy, that was. For us, as well, between you and me. If you get my meaning.'

I did. I glanced at my watch. My God, had I been nattering for that long? I got to my feet again. 'Thanks for the lovely chat, Marion, but I've got some calls to make before lunch and –'

But she was lost in the past. 'It's hard to think of it, that little boy. I used to feel so sorry for him, his mother being dead and he away at school. And his father, well, I ought not to speak ill of the dead.'

'What was old Mr Chamberlayne like, Marion?'

'Oh, he was a Victorian out of his time. He was so stiff and starchy. I used always to imagine him wearing a wing collar like they do in those old photos. A Tartar, he was. Poor little boy. I remember Mr Ralph telling me once, when he'd had a good lunch with a client, how he'd never been able to please his father. "Puts you off having children of your own," he said. He never had any you know. All that money. She's got it now in trust, but after her it goes to some cousins in Canada on his mother's side, or so I've heard.'

'So the Chamberlaynes were rich?'

'Oh, yes. Mr Ralph's grandfather owned half Fernsford at one time, so they say. It was his great uncle who was the lawyer. He had no children and Mr Chamberlayne took over the firm. So all the money came to him, after his brother was killed in Spain. He didn't need to work as a lawyer, but that was the Victorian in him. I think he liked the power.'

'How do you mean? Being a solicitor, well it's not such a big deal, is it?'

'Things were different then. There weren't so many lawyers. Knowing other people's secrets, it's as good as owning them, so they say. A lot of people in this town were frightened of Mr Chamberlayne.'

'You make him sound like the Godfather.'

She laughed. 'You mean like Marlon Brando in that film? Well, there was a bit of that. Forty-odd years ago when I was a girl, there were a few families who counted, who ran things. Not aristocracy like the Angleburys. Middle-class, well-established people who weren't afraid to work for a living. Mr Chamberlayne, with his legal practice, and his money and his being Chairman of the Board of the building society and dozens of other things. The Desboroughs, who had the paper mill. The Wootons. They'd made their money from stockbroking, enough to make out they were landed gentry, and they got involved in politics, MPs, chairmen of the County Council. The Kembles. They ran the brewery, until the last Mr Kemble had to sell all his shares to pay his debts and lost his seat on the Board. The Whitemans, who ran the bank. The Albrights, they were doctors and ran the local hospital...'

'That was Rose's family?'

'Yes. Her father knew Mr Chamberlayne well. I think they played chess together. He was their family doctor. Practically neighbours, they were. They both lived in Welscombe Road – those great huge houses. Flats, now mainly, or offices. When his father died, Mr Ralph wouldn't move into the house. He told me it was too gloomy and too full of unpleasant memories. Meaning his childhood, of course. He let it off cheap as student bedsits. He was a generous man, not tight like his father. When he died, it got sold, pulled down. Luxury flats it is now. If only he and his father had got on better then, maybe Mr Chamberlayne would never have had to take on an outsider as a partner. But he did and we have to bear the consequences.' She came out of her reverie. 'No point in dwelling on things, is there?'

I nodded sagely and slipped away.

It was funny how I was half assembling in my mind a picture of the long-vanished, almost feudal, society that had been Fernsford before the Second World War, and of the Chamberlaynes, father and son, the sour and the sweet, and the dashing interloper, Francis Appleby. If I'd let myself, I might have got more interested in what had gone on there. But none of it was important, none of it matched up to the problems I was struggling with in the present. That's what I thought at the time.

But I had enough to do to stop me dwelling on it too much.

In the office, the pressure from house sales had eased up. The cold, wet weather turned the sites into quagmires and discouraged the punters. January and February were the dead months of home buying. I spent some time reorganizing the systems ready for the spring offensive, and catching up on the matters which the Christmas rush had pushed out. There was the highways agreement on the new site at Bilton Greville, the documentation for the next phase at Badgers Wood, not to mention the Friars Haven correspondence files which Appleby had thrown at me before he headed for the sun.

'There you are. Some light reading. Correspondence relating to highways, utilities and services, British Waterways Board, British Rail. There's a mass of rights and easements that needs to be sorted before we can start work on the leases. Do a report on what we've got. There's a preliminary meeting with Chewton and the letting agents at head office for the retail units the Wednesday I get back. You can come along to that. But do your homework first.'

The day after I got back, I was beginning to revel in the luxury of spells of productive work uninterrupted by the telephone. Then the phone rang.

'Miss Hartley? I was hoping to speak to Mr Appleby, but I gather he's away on his holiday this moment? Aye. I'm Donald Farquharson, Chewton's Project Director at Friars Haven. The highway and groundworks contractor has turned up a wee bit of a problem.'

'What sort of a problem?'

'They've found a skeleton.'

*

I hadn't been to the site for over a month. In that short space of time there had been enormous changes.

The high brick wall running along the upper end of Canal Street had been breached as if by an enormous explosion. A high, metal diamond-mesh fence, topped by razor-wire overhangs, had been erected in the gap. Through it, steel gates, operated by beefy blokes in uniform, controlled access to the site. At intervals on the perimeter were masts carrying security video cameras.

The street itself was being widened to create two lanes on either side, leading to the roundabout in course of construction on the new, and as yet uncompleted, ring road for the spur road, the details of the placing of which had been the subject of that first memorable meeting at the site. This junction had to be completed within a deadline of three months, as the agreement negotiated with the Westerset County Council stipulated. There had to be a direct link with the ring road for the massive construction traffic which would be generated when the work on the main site started. Then the Canal Street access to the site would be closed. All this served to remind me of the huge complexity and cost of what was going on here.

The access and highways agreement was only one of a number of preliminary stages that had been necessary and ran to nearly a hundred pages, including the technical appendices. Appleby had done this work himself before my arrival. So as there weren't any slip-ups, he had got me to do a précis of these initial documents, so that the client would know at a glance when he was supposed to do what. If he didn't perform, then it wouldn't be our fault.

On the other side of the street, on land owned by the County Council, the new roadways were being gouged through sticky yellow clay subsoil. There were forests of red and white boards and cones rerouting the traffic along the temporary diversion controlled by traffic lights.

I stopped the car at the gate for my identity card to be scrutinized, then drove into the site along the temporary metal-plate roadway, past the scruffy collection of old caravans and battered steel tool-stores that the groundworks subcontractor had put up.

Despite the severe deadline, work seemed to be proceeding in an almost leisurely fashion. A couple of donkey-jacketed man-mountains were having a crack alongside a massive dumper truck, which with its improbably bulbous clay-rimmed tyres and its bright orange body looked like the plaything of a juvenile giant. An excavator was dragging its front hoe into the pile of shattered red brick, which was all that remained of the foundations of the wall, and pouring the result, with ear-aching noise, into the back of another truck. Other than that there wasn't much going on. Perhaps they sneaked back late at night from the pub to do the work when no one was looking.

Near the entrance, Chewtons had erected a double-height row of yellow-painted temporary office modules. These surrounded an area of compacted hard-core, where several dozen mud-flecked cars were parked. A sign on the gates had said sternly, 'Hard Hat Area'. I parked, reached into the back of the car and dutifully grabbed the yellow plastic helmet which made me look like a firefighter in a children's story book. Before getting out, I took off my shoes and put on my new green wellies. I was wearing jeans and a new long black winter coat with brass buttons. Even in these defeminizing garments, I got a couple of the inevitable wolf whistles from a couple of navvies who popped up out of the deep hole they were digging, like muddy terriers scenting their quarry.

I gave them a cheery wave and strode across, avoiding the ice-rimmed puddles, to the main office hut. Inside it was steamily hot from the portable gas heaters. There were half a dozen unoccupied desks strewn with papers and file boxes and topped with the inevitable computer monitors. I helped myself to coffee from a vending machine while I waited for Cheryl, the admin assistant, to buzz round for Farquharson to tell him I had arrived.

I glanced idly at the notice-board and was impressed to see that all the right bits of paper were posted up for the world to observe: Health and Safety at Work Act, Employers' Liability Insurance documents, Building Site Safety Regulations, Company Codes of Practice, emergency procedures and telephone numbers, Fire Precautions, Equal Opportunities Policy.

A blast of cold air announced his arrival. He was tall and broad, with flowing blond hair and beard, like a character in a Viking movie.

We shook hands briefly. 'Thanks for coming so quick. I've rung the police like you said, but they've not arrived yet. Cadbourne is down there, keeping an eye on things.'

I followed him through the rear gate of the compound towards the middle of the site. Heaped on either side of a broad trackway were mounds of brick rubble and piles of broken concrete slabs, where the excavators had torn their way through the tangle of ruins and old foundations. Trees lay on their sides, their branches smashed away, leaving jagged white tears in the bark, their roots brown and skeletal, lumps of earth still adhering as if they had clung on desperately against the machine's embrace.

I was struck by how radically land could be reshaped and rearranged. I had scarcely imagined, when I had looked at the place that first time months ago, that what I took to be its permanent features could be almost casually erased as thoroughly as a sand-castle on a beach. We walked along the swathe of yellowish-brown clay, still shining dully where the blade of the levelling machine had scraped it as easily and precisely as if it were plasticine, and in which were embedded nodules of greyish rock.

Ahead of us, there was finally some more intensive activity. Several excavators stood in a kind of conclave, their front hoes from time to time waving in the air like the heads of giant insects before dipping down to gouge and cram more mouthfuls of spoil into their buckets and vomit them into the waiting dumper trucks.

Les Cadbourne, Chewton's Site Manager, was standing on the edge of this circle of activity, his arms wrapped tightly around his reefer-jacketed figure. Despite being as blubbered as a seal, even he must have been feeling the cold, as, out of the shelter of the compound, the wind blew hard and bitter, promising more snow. I hoped this wasn't going to take long and wished I had put on an extra sweater.

'Hello, there, Donald. How do you do, Miss Hartley? Sorry to drag you out here.'

'So, where is it?'

'Here.'

He bent down and drew aside a blue polythene rubbish sack which lay at the foot of a mound of recently excavated clay.

I stared at the skull. Although I had never seen one in real life before, they were familiar enough from photographs and films and the TV.

'Is that all? You didn't find any more?'

Farquharson shook his head. 'I had the JCB moved as soon as the driver phoned in about half an hour ago. We've left it strictly alone.'

'Have you told anyone else? Apart from Mr Chewton, that is?'

Farquharson bent down and replaced the sack. 'It gives me the willies, that thing staring up at me. I'm very sorry we had to get you in, Miss Hartley. Not a suitable thing for a woman to have to do. No one else knows. Les's been standing guard here. I said I'd have the balls, begging your pardon, of anyone on site who went blabbing it about. Mr Chewton was most insistent there shouldn't be any rumours flying around.'

I nodded. If the two men had expected me to go all wobbly, they were out of luck. Farquharson, despite his massive physique looked far more likely to keel over. He'd gone quite pale. Underneath, he must be quite a softy.

I bent down and again twitched aside the shrouding plastic to study the thing more closely. It stared up at me with its empty sockets. There was a ragged hole in the forehead, perhaps caused by the manner of its being unearthed. There were a few teeth in the upper jaw. The lower jaw was not to be seen. I saw that the bone had a greyish, granular texture and around the hole in the brow had not splintered so much as crumbled away.

I stood up, dusting my hands, although I had touched nothing except the clean plastic. 'I think we're okay. I'm no expert, but this looks pretty old. I don't think the police will shut off the site for a murder enquiry. I suppose the coroner will have to be involved. But the people who'll be most interested, to my mind, will be the archaeologists.'

Les groaned. 'Mr Chewton won't like a load of students crawling around getting in the way.'

'It might be okay,' said Farquharson. 'Yon area won't be needed until the foundation subcontractor starts piling and that won't be for a month or so. I had the digger in there only for a bit of levelling off, so as to have a bit more room to move around on this shite-heap, if you'll excuse the expression.'

'So it could be cordoned off if anyone wanted to excavate?'

'Certainly, as far as I'm concerned.' He turned his head and nodded. 'Looks like Fernsford's finest have arrived.'

The two uniformed constables seemed uninterested in and even disappointed by the find. They were far more concerned at the mud on their shiny boots.

'I don't think we need hurry the doctor on this one. Time of death, what, about three hundred years ago?'

'If he was done in, I reckon they got away with it.'

The tall thin one took out his notebook and scribbled down a few details. 'We'll inform the coroner's office, just to cover ourselves.'

As we walked back to the car park, they became more chatty. 'I thought we had something good there, when the call came through. Bit of excitement, like the old days here. This area used to be a real den of thieves at one time, till they pulled it all down. Always some trouble on a weekend. And there was even a murder a few years back. I was thinking of that as we came here. I don't think they ever caught the bloke, did they, Kev?'

'No. I remember that. An old fellow got his head bashed in. He owned a little furniture factory, somewhere over there, all gone now, of course. Old skinflint he was, by all accounts. Never did anyone for it, though. What was his name, now? Babbage, that was it.'

'What a memory you do have, Constable Iles.'

I climbed in my car and waited for the coppers to turn and drive off. Les Cadbourne leaned in over the top of the door, and looking like Geronimo, with his wind-reddened face and tomahawk nose. 'It's a pleasure to have someone to deal with at your office who doesn't treat you like the dirt under his fingernails.' His head withdrew to avoid seeing any expression of pleasure or embarrassment. His big hand gave a cheerful rap on the car roof, then they both stood clear as I reversed out of the parking space, showering liquid yellow mud from the spinning front wheels.

I drove at a snail's pace through the rutted gravel out of the compound and on to the temporary roadway. I had to hold tight on to the wheel as the car pitched on the bucking steel plates. A man standing by the now stationary JCB, presumably the operator taking a break, was watching me attentively. Perhaps he was getting ready for another cat-call, but he didn't look the type. I could see the white hair at the sides and back of the orange plastic helmet. I drew level and took in the pale and gaunt face, pinched in with cold, and dark sunken eyes beneath the heavy white eyebrows.

It couldn't be. Sweet Jesus, it couldn't be.

I felt something ice-cold clamp around my heart, and a burning sickness in my stomach. In my ears I heard a roaring like the opening of a furnace door. I closed my eyes to blank out what I had seen.

When I opened them, a different kind of terror forced me back to the here and now. Halfway across the windscreen loomed a grey steel gatepost. I was about to smack head-on into it. One of the men at the entrance was waving frantically, and through the thunder in my skull I could faintly hear the words his wildly working mouth was shouting.

I swung the wheel to my right. The tyres squealed and slithered and skidded in the mud and loose stones. Fortunately I hadn't been going fast enough to roll it. The panicky manoeuvre was successful. The car straightened. As I shot through the gate, the security man gave me a very funny look indeed.

I hung a right into Canal Street and kept on going.

I was telling myself to be calm. It was like the man fishing by the canal basin. It wasn't him. It couldn't be him. It was a calmly rational voice. I almost believed it.

But as I walked back to the office from the multi-storey car park, I knew in my heart that the man at Friars Haven was no hallucination. My father had tracked me down, through Colin presumably. Why? Why was he following me? He had said he had wanted to be my benefactor. What did that mean? Was he completely lost in delusion? From what I knew of such things, his behaviour pattern would soon change. He would no longer be content to observe my life from the outside. He would want to be part of it, to share it.

I knew the inner force that drove him, and over which he had no control. I'd seen it murder Josephine. How long would he spend in my company before it turned its attention to me?

A great surge of anger rose up in me, overwhelming my terror at the thought of it. I would be no passive victim. I would do anything to stop him. Anything.

# XV

'Do sit down, Sarah.'

Appleby looked up and waved a hand at the chair in front of the desk. He signed the last letter in the folder, closed it, then capped the gold fountain pen and laid it down on the blotter.

Then he leaned back in the black padded-leather swivel chair and gave me a smile of almost startling affability.

He looked well. Mind you, he always looked well. While the rest of the office had in the run up to Christmas been bent double with hacking coughs, or filling their wastepaper baskets with soggy tissues, Appleby, blast him, remained clear-eyed and clear-skinned, without so much as a sniffle. On that particular day he was in even better shape, having substituted a biscuit-coloured tan for his normal pinkness of complexion, which did wonders for the silvery hair at his temples. If ever a man announced to the world that he had just returned from the Caribbean, it was Francis Appleby.

Outside the penthouse window, the rain lashed down on the roof terrace, an uneven expanse of tarred concrete, largely covered now by a series of linked puddles. Above the parapet, lowered a sky composed of wads of dirty cotton wool.

'Welcome back to Fernsford. I bet the weather was nicer in, where was it? Barbados?'

I think I must have pronounced this exotic word wrong because he started to grimace, but smothered it with another water-melon smile. What was happening? Was he getting Alzheimer's?

'I think you know why you're here.'

'My six months are up.'

'Of course. And how do you feel about us, Sarah? Have we come up to your expectations?'

No, he hadn't gone potty. Here was a double-edged sword for me to handle. If I pronounced myself satisfied, that would give him the excuse to keep me down. If I didn't he could use it against me if I fouled up – 'You did indicate you were ready for this, Sarah.' I remembered the politicians I saw on the TV. Never answer the question in the terms that it's put. I said, 'I've certainly learned a lot.'

'Go on.'

'Well, as I've had such an excellent introduction, I'd appreciate being helped on to the next rung, so to speak.'

'That will depend on whether the partnership wishes to continue the relationship.' He gave his wolfish smile. 'But I think I can relieve any anxieties you may have on that score. The firm is happy to confirm your appointment. You've worked well and done everything that was asked of you. The Christmas figures are extremely good. I know Trevor is well satisfied and he's a difficult man to please. He told me about the way you handled the bones thing at the site. It could have been embarrassing. You got him some good publicity out of it. The *Evening Packet* hasn't always been that kind to our Trevor. Not often you can get that out of a medieval cemetery.'

'It was a plague pit, apparently. Seventeenth century. I got the name of the archaeology professor at the university from Mr Dyer. He was very pleased. Even more so when Trevor said he would sponsor the excavation. They'll have finished and gone by the time the main contractor starts.'

'Happy endings all round, then. And there'll be an appropriate adjustment in your salary at the end of this month – along the lines we discussed at the interview. I've asked Marion to do you a note.'

'Thank you.' I started to blush. 'So, can I get more involved on the commercial side now? I've been doing some research on office leases, so I know basically what we need.'

He held up his hand. 'All in good time. Trevor has been waiting to tie up the last part of the finance. He has now succeeded in securing the support of a group of Japanese banks. I am instructed to supply them with the appropriate documents.'

'I could help with that. I mean any stuff that needed digging out –'

He held up his hand. 'That won't be necessary. We have the package prepared already. Their requirements are similar to what has been provided elsewhere. What you can do, though, is get on to the architect to see if he's made any progress on providing the sort of plans we need – for the shopping mall, in particular. Trevor's instructing London agents to start looking for the two anchor tenants – a food store and a major retailer. See what you can do to hurry him along. Camp on his doorstep if you have to. Starling-Richards doesn't have a lot of back-up. Trevor picked him in spite of his lack of experience on this kind of project.'

'But he's good, isn't he? I mean, I saw the model. It looks amazing.'

'The models always do. And yes, I dare say as architecture, it'll win the prizes – provided it can be built. And that's what attracted Trevor. He had a perfectly good scheme from a London firm, much less costly, but he threw it out. Starling-Richards sent his plan in on spec – knocked it out after reading about the scheme in the paper. It caught Trevor's imagination. He's attracted by the idea of building something extraordinary. He's quite a romantic, is our Trevor. Always was. Now, time we were both getting on.'

He turned his attention to his post. I was dismissed in the usual peremptory fashion. Feeling slightly dazed, I took the lift down to the third floor.

Julie looked up. 'Congratulations.'

'You know?'

'The Führer'd have to be mad to let you go. You're the best thing that's happened to this firm for ages. Everyone says so. Hey, no tears on the furniture, if you don't mind.'

'Wotcher, me old china!'

I looked up at Mark's grinning, slightly flushed face. 'Is that supposed to be cockney? You've been drinking, haven't you?'

'Only a glass or two. A grateful client took me to lunch. At the Anglebury Arms, no less.'

'He must have been very grateful.'

'She, actually.' He paused, to see if this had the effect of raising my interest level. I didn't bat an eyelid. He was so full of himself, he continued anyway. 'As you're so keen to know, it was Emily Desborough. Lady Emily Desborough.'

I couldn't help being curious. I put down the red felt-tip pen with which I had been amending the document in front of me. 'The Desboroughs are with Paignton's. I was talking to Marion's brother who works there the other day and he happened to mention something about one of their matters.'

'Ah, yes, but that's the point. The main Desborough interests are. The pulp and paper mills at Fernsmouth and Desborough Farm Products. But

Emily's a bit of a maverick. She started her own business quite separately from the family a few years ago. Emily's Country Kitchen. Fancy ice-cream and yoghurt, preserves and biccies. Things you get in up-market grocers. Fortnum's, Harrods, that kind of thing. Small-scale but highly profitable. I happen to think that even a distant connection like Emily is better than nothing. These bigwigs talk to each other. You never know what might happen.'

'So you just marched into her country kitchen one day and said, "Hi, Emily. I'm your new lawyer!"'

'What a cynic you are under that innocent Titian coiffure. The very idea of touting for business is anathema to our noble profession, as you know.'

'Now who's being cynical? So how did you fish the old trout?'

'Old trout? Is that the feminist speaking? Emily is not in the first beauteous flush of youth like you, my sweet. But she is neither old nor piscine. And she swam to my hook of her own accord. She needed a lawyer to deal with a problem she had with her ex-associate, whom she'd chopped. With Paignton's the thing got bogged down – and then she heard someone mention my name at a party as an ex-London litigation man. So she called me. I settled the matter out of court very satisfactorily, with a good fee and a nice lunch thrown in. A very nice lunch.'

'Yes, taking you there must have bumped up her costs considerably.'

'I think Emily's canny enough to wangle a deal with the restaurant. She supplies some of their puddings, apparently, though they don't mention that to their clientele.'

'How cosy. You're really getting in with the Fernsford grandees, aren't you?'

'No more than you are. Your own lord and master was there by the way.'

'Chewton? The Anglebury Arms must be like the local corner café to him. He lives very near.'

'Yes. You know, it's a funny thing, but we came out at the same time as he did. He'd been lunching with a bunch of fellows – bankers by the look of them, some of them were Japanese. They all shook hands and the bankers or whoever climbed into a fleet of taxis. Chewton's Porsche was there, but he didn't get into it. Instead, he got into a little beige Fiat, a Panda, which looked as if it had been waiting for him. There was a woman in it, I'm sure. I caught a glimpse of a headscarf. Seems like our client has got a bit on the side.'

I shrugged. 'I don't see why you need to jump to that sexist conclusion. Could have been one of his staff. I didn't realize you went in for gossip.'

'I don't. I thought you might be interested. It never hurts to know what your client's doing – particularly before they know you know it.'

'Perhaps. I should keep quiet about it. Chewton's not stupid. He must have seen you. He'll be able to trace any rumours back to their source. I wouldn't want you to stop being the golden boy.'

'Okay, okay. Let's forget about Chewton. What I dropped by to say is that I feel like celebrating my success. How about dinner tomorrow night?'

I covered my ears with my hands and shook my head wildly. Then I fixed him with my iciest gaze. 'Mark. What on earth do I have to say to you? Is it the lawyer in you that can't understand the word no? Okay. Do you want it in writing? Is that it? A memorandum of disagreement. An affidavit, even? I, Sarah Hartley, make oath and say that I am not going to date Mark Oundsworth ever, ever, ever. Now, go away. I've got work to do.'

He pulled up a chair and sat down. 'This is the bit I like. The point where the negotiation gets really interesting. The point where most people give up. Please don't throw that file at me, just listen. I propose a deal, the conditions of which are as follows. One, you and I will go out together, at my expense, venue to be discussed. Listen! Two, your acceptance of this condition shall not imply any agreement on your part to engage in further meetings or other activities. Three, I undertake not to make any unsolicited advances of a sexual nature. Four, should you, within three days after the fulfilment of condition one, time being of the essence, state that you wish to have no further social contact with me, save for occasions of a professional or quasi-professional nature at which one or more other parties shall be present, then I undertake, with a heavy heart, not under any circumstances to raise the matter again.'

He sat back in his chair and gave me a big smile. A smile which trembled slightly at the corners of his mouth.

For several moments, I held my lips in a steely line, and kept my stare good and arctic. Then I started laughing. 'Mark, you're a persistent sod, aren't you? All right, I agree – with one slight amendment to clause one:

the expenses to be shared. And a rider as to venue, just in case you were thinking you're going to take me to the Anglebury Arms or wherever and get me all gooey with drink – don't look so affronted! I got the point about "unsolicited advances" – I won't go out to dinner or the pub.'

'So where does that leave? The flicks? There's nothing good on this week at the Palace or the Electric.'

'It's your deal, you think of somewhere.'

'I know, the Playhouse. Of course. Grab a quick sandwich at the Coffee House beforehand, one little drinkie in the interval and we can have coffee afterwards at my place – subject as always to the conditions of the original agreement, okay? I'll phone and book for Friday.'

'Hang on, what about the play? Hadn't you better find out?'

'It's *Hamlet*. That's the good thing about Shakespeare, you can't say, "I've seen it." Even if you know it off by heart, it can always surprise you.'

'Mmm. Why you crafty so-and-so, Mark Oundsworth. You had it all worked out.'

'It's a fair cop. Boy Scout training. Be prepared and all that. You're not going to renege on the contract, are you?'

I shook my head. 'No, of course not.' I was really quite impressed by how he'd set me up, but I didn't tell him that. I didn't tell him either that, not only did I not have this *Hamlet* play off by heart, I'd never even seen it before.

I went back to the document I had been working on, but I found it hard to concentrate. Something about that bit of gossip was bothering me. It wasn't Chewton's style to have himself picked up at a swish restaurant by an underling in a cheap car. If he was over the limit, he would have had someone drive him in his own car. Fiat Panda, indeed. He would have gone in that only if he'd had some reason not to be recognized. Perhaps Mark's crude saloon bar phrase had been accurate.

A beige Fiat Panda. I knew someone with one. And so did Mark, if he'd thought about it a bit harder, and wasn't so prejudiced about the person concerned. Rose Albright. She'd parked next to me in the multi-storey car park the other day when I'd had to bring the car in. I had a sudden vision of her getting out of it in her Hermès headscarf, looking like Princess Anne – 'Good accessories are a real investment, darling.'

But Rose and Trevor Chewton? Surely not. What a daft idea. But I knew that Rose had got the afternoon off today. Thursday afternoons she saw her mother in the Nursing Home. She'd told me that.

Rose with Trevor? Had he been the one who'd given her those bruises? I shuddered. What a bastard. Poor, poor Rose.

The king chuckled drily. He reached out and clapped Polonius on the shoulders with both hands, Mafia-style. He held on, staring down at his courtier for a moment, then he wrapped a proprietary arm around the old man and, as he ushered him off the stage, he said, 'It shall be so; Madness in great ones must not unwatch'd go.'

I stared in disappointment as the curtain came down. 'Hey, that's not the end, is it?' I said to Mark, who was on his feet already.

'No, it says in the programme that there's one interval of fifteen minutes. Come on, the bar's open.'

I dragged after him reluctantly, staring at the stage as something called the safety curtain descended. There obviously weren't going to be any adverts.

The stalls bar was packed out. Mark and I stood squashed up by a polished wooden ledge just wide enough to balance our drinks on. I stared with frank curiosity at our fellow playgoers. There was a sprinkling of old-buffer types and their wives, but the rest of them looked fairly normal. The Royal Fernsford Playhouse itself wasn't actually all that grand. It was much smaller than a cinema. It had the well-worn look of an antique chair. The gilded plasterwork of the horseshoe-shaped auditorium was a little tarnished; the pale green paintwork was scuffed and peeling. The velvet-covered seats had springs that had sprung and squeaked and groaned when they were tipped up.

I was relieved at this ordinariness, as I had never been inside a theatre before and hadn't known what to expect. Colin wouldn't go near the theatre, saying it was obsolete and bourgeois.

Why had I listened to him? I was absolutely transfixed by the experience. It was so much more involving, seeing real people going through what looked to me like real emotions. As for Shakespeare, well, for my money you couldn't get more up to date or relevant. For me it was so bloody relevant it was terrifying. To think I had messed about in those English lessons throwing love notes to Jimmy McConochie, and missed my one and only prior exposure to one of his plays, although admittedly it was about some ancient Roman I'd never heard of.

I came out of my musings to find Mark gazing at me in concern.

'What's the matter? Aren't you enjoying it?'

I took a sip of tonic water. 'Yes, I am. It's wonderful. I feel rather overwhelmed by it, that's all.'

'It is a good production, isn't it? It'll probably transfer. Clive Beaumont is fearfully brilliant. He won't be long in Fernsford, that's for sure. The RSC or the National will snap him up. My father used to rave about seeing David Warner at Stratford yonks ago. Maybe I'll do the same about this guy to my children.'

I thought I'd been doing all right and now I was beginning to get that funny feeling. The feeling that although the language is English, and I understand the individual words, I don't grasp the sense of what is being said. Transfer. Good production. RSC. National. Stratford. They cloaked remote mysteries, spoke of experiences I had not had, could not even have imagined. David Warner. I remembered the name from a horror movie on the TV. Could it be the same bloke? I said carefully, 'You know a lot about plays, don't you?'

'I suppose. I was in OUDS. They go well together, the stage and the law. All that theatrical posturing. My client will settle for nothing less than ... Ladies and gentlemen of the jury, the verdict which you are called upon to give ... Particularly barristers. They're actors, reading a script someone else has prepared. What was it that someone said about the main requirements for a silk? A confident manner and a loud voice.'

'Was it the voice that stopped you?'

He laughed. 'Ow. Is that how I come over? No, I never even considered it. You know what the Bar is like. It's a bit more democratic than it was, but it's still largely a rich boys' club. You have to be wealthy or lucky. I wasn't the former and I couldn't rely on the latter. Seriously though, I'm not entirely what you think I am.'

Fortunately, I was saved by the bell from having to respond to this question-begging statement. A voice crackled over the loudspeakers, 'Ladies and gentlemen, the performance will begin again in two minutes.'

He set down the tray on the black glass table. 'Help yourself to milk. It's instant, I'm afraid. I can't be bothered with all the fiddling about. My father drives me mad fussing about his coffee.'

I bent down and selected a mug which bore the legend, Fernsford RFC Centenary. 1887–1987. 'Do you play for them?'

'Good Lord, no. They're one of the best in the country. Club Rugby at that level is more like a full-time career. I used to play for my Old Boys side before I came here, that's all. It's Chris, my flatmate – well it's his flat, actually. He's done an England trial. He's a very part-time accountant in his dad's firm. He's away. Got a game tomorrow in Truro.'

I nodded. There was a slightly awkward silence whilst I drank some of the horrid liquid. I could feel Mark watching me from his seat on the sofa opposite.

'You enjoyed the play, didn't you?' he said finally.

'Yes, I did. It gave me a lot to think about.'

'Good old WS. Even when you've heard those words a thousand times, they still give you a thrill, don't they? "The play's the thing...", "What a piece of work is man..."; "Though this be madness, yet there is method in't"; "That bourne from which no traveller returns"; "Nymph in thy orisons be all my sins remembered". Every line a quote.'

'Mmm. I've a few sins to be remembered, or at least a confession. I've never seen it before. In fact I've never been to the theatre before.'

'I did get an inkling of that. You hid it well. You have that quality of not being thrown by situations.'

'Ooh, thank you, kind sir.'

'God, that sounded awful. I was trying to say something complimentary. I end up sounding patronizing and snobbish.'

'No, you weren't. Or only a little bit. It's hard, isn't it, dealing with someone of my incredible ignorance? But I want to say that I'm ever so grateful we went. I did think it was wonderful. Terrifying, but wonderful. I had an advantage over you, you see, being ignorant. I was on the edge of my seat. Will he kill him? Is the ghost real or just a figment? If it's his imagination, perhaps Claudius's being a murderer is a load of porkies. Not knowing the end was all part of it for me.'

'So you won't want to see it again?'

'Of course I will. I mean, it's a mystery on one level, but it's about his character too. I could see it over and over again. I was willing Hamlet all the time to go ahead and do it. Go on! I kept saying. What are you hanging about for? If you were Hamlet, I mean if you were in Hamlet's situation, don't you think you would want to kill Claudius? Wouldn't you be the avenger?'

He was becoming uneasy and irritated. This would not have been as he had planned the progress of the evening. 'I don't think you can apply it to someone like me. I can't think of myself as other than I am. I'm the product of a sophisticated and legally regulated society. There's no law in Hamlet's Denmark to deal with matters like regicide, particularly as the king himself is the true murderer. Hamlet hasn't anyone to turn to. I'm sure a modern Hamlet would behave quite differently.'

'So what would a modern Hamlet do? Get the cops in? A report to the Elsinore office of the DPP? And what happens if they say, sorry, Hamlet mate, there is no evidence on which a jury could be asked to convict, statements by ghosts being inadmissible.'

He shrugged. 'It's a drama. You're not supposed to take it literally.'

'I don't know how else you're supposed to take literature. The play seems to me to raise an issue that's still relevant. Being denied justice, wanting to get back at someone. A guy's mugged in the street and dies. The police can't find evidence to convict, although they're pretty sure they know who did it. How do the man's relatives and friends think about that? Have they had justice? What if they go out and beat up the mugger?'

'Now you're mixing things up. You're talking about revenge, not justice. We're lawyers, we uphold the civilized punishment of crimes.'

'So, how would we deal with Hamlet if he came to us as a client? Tell him he was going down for life, several times over? I mean, what defence has he got? Self-defence? Provocation? Diminished responsibility? A lot of heavy argument there.'

'Fortunately, I'm not a criminal lawyer. But the principle of the common law is clear: you can't go round killing people because you've got a grudge, no matter how well-founded.'

'That's what they used to say at college. But there are some wrongs the law can't touch. "Murder most foul" as the ghost says. Secret murders. Where the only remedy is blood.'

I was aware that my voice had dropped away almost to nothing and that I was wringing my hands together so that the knuckles gleamed white in the dimmed-down lights. 'Mark, have you ever wanted to kill someone?'

'All the time. You should try driving into town from here every morning. There's one chap in a poxy little Metro who always cuts in from Belvedere Road —'

I shut him up with an impatient gesture. 'No, not that. Really want to. Like Prince Hamlet.'

It came out fiercer than I had intended and I saw his eyes widen in surprise. 'No, I can't say I have. And you?'

He saw the look in my eyes.

'Sarah, what are you talking about? Are you all right?' I heard the alarm in his voice.

'Sorry, I got carried away.' I stood up. 'I have to have a pee.'

'Oh, yes, of course. At the end of the hallway.'

The bathroom had black tiled walls with the grouting picked out in scarlet, and a big mirror in a scarlet-painted frame over the tub. A length of string between two hooks carried drying boxer shorts and T-shirts. The window-sill was cluttered with aftershaves and colognes, half-squeezed tubes of toothpaste and toothbrushes with flattened bristles, bottles of shampoo and disposable razors which had been used and not disposed of. The basin had a grey scummy ring round it and there were crinkly dark pubic hairs in the bath and impressed into the cake of soap. Handily placed on a small table by the loo was a pile of soft-porn magazines.

I peed, then sat there, reluctant to go back. Perhaps he was thinking I was a nutcase. Perhaps I was a nutcase. It wouldn't be very surprising if I were.

I picked up one of the magazines. I'd seen far far worse. One of Tim Pogson's big cases was defending a hard-core importer against those fine upstanding moral guardians in the Obscene Publications Squad. He thought I shouldn't see the samples of the evidence, but I had. At least these were all women. They simpered and pouted at the camera, legs spread apart or stared down in ecstatic concentration as their pearly finger-tips crept towards their vulvas. Pink shots, they were called in the trade.

I pulled up my pants and tights and straightened my skirt.

Mark was standing at the window, peering through the join of the curtains when I opened the door of the sitting room. He turned and smiled nervously, no doubt hoping that my manic disposition had calmed down.

'Hi. I should be thinking of going home.'

'Should you?'

'Yes. Remember our agreement.'

'Oh, that.'

'Yes, that.'

'You don't have to go yet. Saturday tomorrow. I'm not planning to go into the office. Are you? Have some more coffee.'

'No, thanks. What were you looking at when I came in?'

'Nothing really. Well, actually, it was because of the car. There's been quite a bit of petty thieving from cars, broken windows and such and I thought I heard a noise.'

'But all was well?'

'I think so. There was a fellow in the street, but he wasn't doing anything, just hanging around. He wasn't a tearaway type, more elderly.'

There was an odd prickling in my back. 'Is he still there now?'

He put his head between the drapes. His muffled voice said, 'No. He's gone. Wait a bit. There he is. He must have wandered down the road. He's coming back.'

'Let me see.' I joined him at the window, standing close beside him, my right arm pressing against his side, my other hand holding back the thickly lined red velvet. I could feel his warmth and smell the sweetish scent of whatever male fragrance – wasn't that what it was called? – he had selected from the stock in the bathroom. Paul didn't use the stuff.

'There he is.'

I saw the white-headed figure pass beneath the street lamp. He wore a donkey jacket and dark trousers. His head was bent, and there was at this height and angle only an impression of a pale face. I felt myself trembling. I turned abruptly away, into the centre of the room.

'I think I'll have some more coffee after all.'

I was still shivering when he brought the refill. I stood by the gas fire, warming my hands on the mug. He was watching me again. His slightly chubby, tanned face was creased in concentration and his wide apart blue eyes looked soft with concern. He was nice underneath the self-conscious ambition and sexual bravado.

'I'm glad you stayed. I can't help thinking that something's getting to you. You seem quite jumpy. You've been a bit strange all evening. You were quite affected by the play. All that talk of death and murder. There is something rotten in it. You know, there was a famous literary critic who wrote an essay arguing that Hamlet wasn't the hero but the villain.'

'I'm sorry, Mark. I didn't mean to spoil your evening. You're so knowledgeable about things. It makes me feel a complete dunce.'

'Please sit down. I can't talk to you when you're hopping about like that.'

I dutifully perched on the edge of a chair. There was an awkward pause. I wondered how long it would be before I could sneak another look through the curtain without seeming a complete loony. I took another sip from my mug.

'You haven't spoilt my evening. I suppose you think I lured you here, Chris being away et cetera. If you do, relax. I'm not going to leap on you.'

'Mark, I do want us to be friends. I'm so glad we went to the theatre. I'd never have gone by myself. There are all kinds of things I want to learn about. Things that come easy to you. They come so easy you don't know how hard they are to acquire when you've had my kind of upbringing as opposed to yours.'

'You keep saying that kind of thing. But you don't know anything about me. You've such a chip on your shoulder, you can't see beyond it.'

He spoke the words lightly, no doubt with humorous intent, but they got my goat all the same.

'Chip? Is that what you think? A bit of class prejudice I should pull myself together and discard. That first time in the Coffee House. You and the others had to assume I was exactly the same as you were. From a decent, solid home, proper parents, good school.'

I got up and flounced away towards the window. I twitched the curtain aside. There he was by the bus stop.

I went over to my chair and leaned on the back of it, gazing at Mark's ever so youthful face.

'I remember a film on the telly about the sort of school you went to. All straw-boaters and shadows on the cricket field. Mine was the Charles Pooter Comprehensive School. "Poofters" we called it. The teachers were useless. They'd given up and sat dreaming of escaping to the 'burbs or getting early retirement. Because I was red-haired and scruffy and Irish, I was bullied rotten. The only way to stop it was to dish it out myself. And I truanted, went with boys and had screaming temper tantrums. I was public enemy number one. As for my upbringing? My mother skivvied for a living. When I was ten or so, she got me a job washing glasses in a pub after school and at weekends. I was tall for my age, and they didn't ask any questions. It didn't stop me from being propositioned every night by filthy drunks. That wasn't some kind of thrilling work-experience, it was to keep me fed and my mother in drink. The only thing I've had any real education is in law.'

He coloured up, and his full mouth hardened. 'You assume a lot about me. Yes, my father was a member of the professional middle class, a GP, and my mother was a teacher. But they split up when I was twelve. She went off with a younger colleague – to New Zealand. I haven't seen her since. My father did his best, but he was getting on – he's retired now and in poor health from being a two-pack-a-day smoker for years. I went to a comp. We lived in Surrey, so it wasn't as bad as yours, but it was hardly Winchester. I worked bloody hard for what I got, Oxford scholarship, a first, top ten of the Law Society finals, good articles, good jobs. So don't fucking well talk to me as if I'd had it all served up on a gold plate.'

I felt myself flushing scarlet, and yet again went to the window, as if to hide my embarrassment. The figure still patrolled the otherwise empty street.

I swung back to face Mark. 'Okay, I was partly wrong about you, but maybe I would have seen you more clearly if you hadn't been so intent on trying to screw me. I'm a person too, not just a body like those poor cows in your dirty magazines.'

He blushed again. 'They're not mine, they're Chris's. They're just harmless fun, anyway.'

I sighed.

'You're wrong about me there, as well. I didn't ask you out to get you into bed. Haven't I stuck by our agreement?'

He had such a look of entreaty, like a little kid, that I couldn't help laughing.

'Oh, yes, you certainly have. Not even a finger laid on me the whole evening. That could give me a complex.'

'What?'

'Perhaps the office rig put you off? I can easily alter that.' I slipped out of my jacket and kicked off my shoes. 'There now.'

He was goggling. 'Do you mean you're ... What about the agreement?'

'Oh that. The agreement stands – but let's say you can, well, insert a rider. By the way, if you're unprepared with the thingies, I've got some in my bag.'

'Sarah?'

I felt his breath tickle my ear. 'Mmm?'

'If your schooling was so awful, how did you manage to get qualified?'

I turned to him and propped myself up on my elbow, the air of the room chill on my naked shoulders. 'Why do you want to know?'

'I'm interested in you. All about you. Haven't you gathered?'

'Somehow, I got a dogsbody junior clerk's job at a solicitor's. I was treated like shit by the smart secretaries. I got angry. Why couldn't I be like them? I realized I would be on the scrap heap if I didn't buck my ideas up. Then I twigged that one of the younger partners fancied me. I said I'd let him screw me if he helped me to get the education I'd missed at school. It was a good bargain for both of us. He got me into night school, helped with the books, the fares, coached me in the work. He was keen on classical music, and he got me to appreciate that as well. I did better than either of us expected. I got a place at Myddelton Poly. The rest is, as they say, history. Shocked?'

I felt his body stir against me. 'You're truly amazing,' he said.

I smiled, but inside, I was going, 'Oh, my God!'

I couldn't see anyone in the street when I went out, leaving Mark asleep and closing the door softly behind me. It was a very cold dark morning. As I drove home along the Welscombe Road, the frost on the parked cars was turned the colour of Cornish ice-cream under the amber street lights.

I sat in my bay window, drinking my coffee and watching the dawn whiten the wintry sky.

I was not proud of my night's work. I had taken the coward's way out. Confrontation with my father was inevitable, but I had ducked out of it. Sooner or later, though, I should have to face him. I vowed it would be the next time.

The next time he appeared, I should tell him to get right back to hell where he belonged.

And if he wouldn't go? If he wouldn't go? I remembered what I'd said to Caro on the windswept icy summit of the Oxdowns. If he wouldn't go, then I'd send him there myself.

## XVI

'May I speak to Sarah? Sarah Hartley?'

I didn't recognize the nervous-sounding voice. 'Speaking.'

'It's Robbie. Robbie Chewton, you remember we met at my father's birthday . . .'

'Yes, of course. Hello, how's things?' This routine politeness had a dramatic effect. His voice tailed away into a whisper and I could barely catch the words. 'I need to talk to you. Alone.'

I hesitated, but only a second or two. This didn't sound like a pick-up line. 'All right. I could see you this afternoon. You know where the office is?'

'Please, this is very urgent. It can't wait that long. It's got to be this morning. But not in the office. Can you meet me down by the riverside walk? The Broad Lea end. There are some benches. Do you know it? Please help me.'

This time I hesitated a good bit longer. But it wasn't just nervousness in his voice. It was desperation. 'Okay. Calm down. I know where you mean. I'll be there in half an hour.'

There was a sigh which might have been 'Thank God', then a click as he put the phone down.

Oh, shit! Now what had I gone and done? It had sounded like trouble of the Hoxton kind. And my Vardy, Leadbetter habits of immediate and caring response died hard. I picked up the phone to tell Appleby the score.

Then I remembered he was out and put it down again. If I waited until he got back I might miss the appointment. And by accepting it I'd implied to Robbie that he was my client. A duty to a client always came first, as Pogson had forever dinned into me. So, what the hell did he want? Robbie Chewton in some seedy music-biz imbroglio was all I needed at present. But at least it would get me out of the building for a bit.

Quite predictably, the aftermath of my night with Mark had been dire. I'd made a point of being out a good deal at the weekend, and when I was in answered neither the phone nor the doorbell. But I couldn't avoid him in the office. He'd bounced in on the Monday morning and started talking about our plans. I stared at him, frozen-faced.

'Plans?'

'Yes, for this week. I mean now that we're ...'

'Now that we're what?'

He started to get upset. 'I should have thought it was obvious. Or did I imagine Friday night?'

'Mark. This is Monday morning. Friday night is gone, finished with. Now, please go away. I've got a great deal of work to do.'

'Go away? You're joking, aren't you?'

'No.'

He sank down into the chair opposite. 'Please, Sarah. Don't be like this. What's wrong? I thought you ...'

'Ever since I arrived here you've been trying to screw me. Well, you have, so now you can leave me alone. Please. Go and make up your scorecard.'

'Scorecard? That wasn't what fucking happened and you know it. Why are you being like this?'

'Mark, don't make this even more difficult than it is. Friday night was a mistake. It shouldn't have happened. It was a one-off, a dead end, okay? Now please get out before the whole fucking firm starts yakking about us.'

He gave me an imploring look, but I bent my head to the papers in front of me.

I heard the door slam. I swivelled my chair round to the window. You stupid, horrible bitch, I said to myself, as the view of the Fernsford skyline blurred with my tears.

In warm weather the riverside walk was a popular place for tourists to stroll and eat ice-cream. At this time of year it was deserted, apart from the inevitable elderly man pulling a decrepit dog and a couple of schoolkids leaning on the railings, smoking fags. They nudged each other and pointed at me, muttering something smutty, no doubt. I gave them a V-sign and stalked on.

It was a still, cold day, with a damp mist already coming off the river. Not being a tourist, I didn't care for the riverside walk even in summer. The council had done its best to posh the walk up with tasteful street furniture, and signposts with gilt lettering pointed the way to it, but, particularly in that day's half light, it had the shabby look of a place to leave dustbins. The scruffy blocks of council flats and factory units over on the Brinwell side dominated it and made it look, as the water level sank with the receding tide, like a big ditch.

If it hadn't been for Chewton's son, I would be back in the warmth of my office doing the work for which I was paid. I pulled up the collar of the white trench-coat, and adjusted the silk scarf at my neck. But then, of course, if it hadn't been Chewton's son, I should never have agreed to this clandestine meeting. That's how it felt. Secretive and furtive. A bit like that spy serial I had seen on the TV, the one with Alec Guinness. Robbie had better have a good reason for dragging me out, and not just want to sell me tickets to one of his gigs.

I had to walk a fair way before I saw him. He'd chosen a bench in the middle of the long stretch between the alleyway down the side of British Home Stores from Broad Lea, the way I had come, and the steps up to the Jubilee Bridge. There weren't any other ways of getting down to the river between these two points. Alongside the tarmac surface of the walk itself was a strip of grass backed by trees and thick shrubs, so you could hardly see the backs of the stores and offices on Broad Lea. It was almost as if he'd deliberately chosen the most out-of-the-way bit of the town he could think of on a wintry day.

In the quiet he must have heard my heels clicking from some way back, but he didn't raise his head from its position on his knees until I had come right up to him.

'Hi, Robbie.'

His dark straggly hair was plastered down with wet, like a dog that had got left out all night. He was wearing black jeans, black T-shirt and a black leather jacket. His face looked unhealthily pale against all this midnight gear, his eyes sunk in hollows and rimmed with red.

'Thanks for coming. I'm sorry it had to be here, but I couldn't come to the office. You'll understand when I tell you about it.'

'Okay. So tell.'

'I'm in trouble. Smoke?' He waved a packet of Gauloises under my nose.

I shook my head. 'What kind of trouble?'

He pulled out one of the cigarettes and lit it with a disposable lighter. His hands were shaking.

Uh-oh, I said to myself. This was like old times. 'What is it?' I prompted. 'Dope? Coke? Speed? H?'

He blew pungent plumes from his nostrils, then shivered, a gut-deep shudder which the chill of the day and the thin unsuitable clothes could not explain. 'I wish. Yeah, a drugs bust would have been bad, but I don't keep my stash where the cops would find it. No, this is mega-bad. If only I'd...'

'Robbie. Don't beat up on yourself. If you want me to help, just tell me what it's all about.'

'I met this chick, girl, after a gig. A club on the Fernsmouth road. UFOs. She was kind of hanging around afterwards. Said could I give her a lift. You know how it is. We went back to my place, you know. She was tall, and you know, mature. How was I to appreciate that...?'

'So how old was she?'

'Not old enough, as it turns out.'

'If you thought she was over sixteen, there's a good chance she's more than thirteen. And you're what? Twenty-two, twenty-three? Under twenty-four anyway. Okay, so if you haven't done this sort of thing before and you can convince the Court that it was reasonable to think she was old enough to consent, then you've got a statutory defence. In that event, whether a jury believes you is going to depend on what they think of the girl, if they think she looks...' I saw he wasn't listening, his head was back down on his knees, and he was moaning softly. 'Robbie? Robbie?'

He thumped the sides of his thighs, shaking himself as he did so. He pushed his angry white tear-stained face at mine. 'You don't fucking understand! It's not the fact I screwed her under-age. She's saying I raped her.'

Pogson once told me that lawyers have to be like doctors. They shouldn't jump to conclusions or express opinions without examining what appear to be the facts. Nor should they panic. Just as medics don't go, 'Oh, my God, that sounds like cancer', when the patient comes in with a lump, briefs have to maintain a similar calm demeanour when faced with clients who, in the worst scenario, may be spending a fair slice of their naturals doing porridge. Particularly when, like Robbie Chewton, they are major dickheads into the bargain.

I'd already ignored this sound advice twice in this conversation and put my big foot in it, so when I finally responded I was, with a great deal of effort, icily analytical, the great criminal lawyer in action.

'Robbie, I know you're upset, but I'm really not clear where we are in all this. She's saying. Who's she saying it to? The police?'

'Yes. The stupid little bitch told her parents first. Then they all marched off to the police and said I raped her. But I didn't. She didn't just consent, she was begging for it. I swear to God she was. Oh, God, I should have realized. You've got to help me. I can't go to prison, they'll fucking murder me in there.'

'Please, Robbie. I know it's hard for you, but we have to get things very clear right from the beginning. First of all, what about the police? I assume from all this hidey-hole stuff that you've done a runner?'

'Too right. I got the hell out when I heard what was happening. That was this morning.'

'So how did you hear?'

'The father. He rang me up. I'm in the book, worst luck. He said I'd raped his little girl. She was going to the police. She was just a kid. That he was going to make sure they crucified me. And if the law didn't, he would. That was when I realized she was jail bait. I legged it straight away.'

'When did you and the girl . . . ?'

'Saturday night.'

'And you went to your place?'

'Yeah. I've got a flat in Kemble Square.'

'Did she stay all night?'

'No, I drove her home. She lives in Brinwell. I suppose by then it was about three thirty in the morning. We smoked a joint afterwards.'

I stifled a groan. It got better. What else had he done? Pinched her dinner money?

'So, how many times did you do it?'

'What? I don't remember.'

'Listen, Robbie, you'd better start remembering every detail of this little get-together. Please. For your own sake. If you want me to help, you've got to. So how many times?'

'Once.'

'Was she a virgin?'

'No.'

'You're sure about that?'

He gave a smirk of sexual recollection. It was the first remotely cheerful expression I had seen. 'Oh, yes. I mean I've had virgins...'

'Okay. Now tell me exactly what you did together.'

'What do you mean, all the details?'

'Yes, everything.'

'Hey, are you getting off on this? I mean are you enjoying it?'

For two pins I'd have slapped him in the kisser. But the Law Society discourages that kind of behaviour. I took a deep breath. The river was only a vague presence beyond the dripping iron railings, and I could hardly see the next bench along the walkway. My hair felt heavy and clammy and my face felt cold, and I knew it had that dead-white mask look that I get when I'm stressed.

'Robbie. You came to me with a problem. I'm trying to help you. I'm asking you the kinds of questions that need to be asked. Technical questions, not fun questions. Okay?'

'Okay.'

'You went back to your flat. You said she asked you for a lift home. Whose idea was the detour?'

'Mine, I suppose. But she was going on about how she'd liked the band – and me in particular. I said something like, we have to go right past my place, why don't you come in for a coffee? I think I said something about listening to some demo tapes we'd made as well.'

'What did she say?'

'She said that was a great idea.'

'And did you make coffee and listen to the tapes?'

'No, because she started kissing me once we got through the door. A real tongue sandwich.'

'Was there anyone else in the flat? Anyone see you going in?'

'No. I don't share it. It's only a studio.'

'So she kissed you first? What did you think?'

'I thought, Christ, you're in here.'

'So normally, with a girl, you'd make the first move?'

'Normally it's fairly mutual. Isn't that how it is with you?'

'So, when she kissed you like that, how did you think she was feeling?'

'Very turned on.'

'Very turned on by you? She hadn't been drinking?'

'Plenty of women are. They don't have to be pissed to fancy me.'

'So, she wasn't pissed?'

'Not that I was aware of.'

'What happened then?'

'We got on the bed, took our clothes off and screwed. What do you think happened?'

'I wasn't there and that isn't detailed enough. Please try and see that all this is crucial. You started off by the door. How did you get on the bed?'

'I don't know, we just got there. I told you, it's a bedsitter. The bed takes up nearly all the room.'

'So there wasn't anywhere else to sit?'

'Not really.'

'Were you still kissing?'

'Yes.'

'So how long before you moved on to intercourse?'

'Christ, I don't know. I wasn't looking at my bloody watch.'

'But you must have got some kind of idea of how fast things were going.'

'I told you she was very turned on. Yes, it did happen quite quickly.'

'What was she wearing?'

'One of those skimpy tops and a short skirt. Typical disco outfit.'

'It's January. Didn't she have a coat?'

'Yes. She was wearing it in the car. It had a fake fur collar. She must have taken it off straight away.'

'What were you wearing?'

'Jacket. Chinos. T-shirt. Pretty much like now.'

'So, you're on the bed, kissing. Lying down?'

'Yes. We kind of rolled around.'

'Then what?'

'I put my hand on her breast.'

'Did she try to stop you?'

'No way. She held it there, rubbing it around. She was hot for it. I slid my hand under her top. She wasn't wearing a bra and her nipples were rock hard. Then I slid my hand down between her legs and she was wet there.'

'Was she wearing pants and tights?'

'Yes, both.'

'So did you take them off completely? What about the skirt?'

'Christ. I don't know. No, I think we were both pretty excited by then. I just pulled them down and pushed the skirt up. I undid the buckle of my trousers and unzipped myself and got right on with it.'

'You undid your zip? You're sure about that?'

'Yes.'

'Did you put a condom on? Did you ask if she was on the pill or had a cap?'

'No. I guess not. I mean it all happened so quickly.'

'Did she at any stage try to stop you, or say anything that might have indicated she didn't want to go on? Did she struggle or try to turn away from you? Did you have any feeling that she was not a willing sexual partner?'

'No, absolutely not. It's like I said. She was panting for it.'

'And did you penetrate her?'

'What?'

'Did you have an erect penis which entered into her vagina?'

'Of course I bloody did. Right in hard.'

'Was there any resistance at the moment you attempted to penetrate? Did she clench up? Was it difficult for you to get in?'

'No way. It was all as smooth as silk. She was ready, I tell you. When you're as experienced as I am, you can tell the difference.'

'Did you come?'

'I certainly did. Wow, did I!'

'Did she?'

'I suppose she must have.'

'You mean you're not sure?'

'Yes, no, I don't know. What the hell does it matter?'

'Robbie. I'm asking the questions. Did she have any of the signs of orgasm? Did she cry out, were there rapid intakes of breath, did her body give spasmodic shudders, did her vagina contract?'

'Do you think I don't know what an orgasm is? Maybe there was a little bit of that. Ah, now I see what you're getting at. But women don't always, do they? I mean not like men. It doesn't mean they don't want it. It's quite rare, isn't it?'

It was hard to stop myself blurting out that it would have been a bloody miracle to come with a creep like him as a lover. But there was no accounting for the tastes of others.

'Afterwards you said you smoked a joint. Did you share it equally?'

'She had a couple of puffs.'

'Did she put her clothes back on?'

'Yes, she sort of pulled things back together.'

'Did she go to the loo? Have a shower?'

'No, she just lay on the bed. We talked while we smoked the joint.'

'What about?'

'I told her all about the gigs we'd got lined up. About the album we're going to do with these guys in Town who're just starting up with a new label. She was really interested.'

'Did she tell you anything about herself. Her name? What school she went to, for instance?'

'Whose fucking side are you on? I told you I didn't know she was under-age. I don't know a fucking thing about her. It's not my fault if she didn't say much, the stupid cow.'

'So you drove her home, to Brinwell. Did you take her to her front door?'

'Not likely. She lives in one of those stinking council tower-blocks. I dropped her at the end of the street.'

'Did anyone see you?'

'Not that I know of.'

'And that was the last you heard of her until this morning. Had you arranged to see her again?'

'I sort of said, you know, see you around. Like you do.'
'Like you do,' I echoed.

'I can't fucking believe I'm reading this!'

Appleby flung down my handwritten notes. His face was the colour of an overripe tomato. He put his hands on the desk and half rose in his chair as if he were going to jump right over and throttle me.

'What was I supposed to do? Tell him to piss off and sort it out himself? So he goes home and tells his dad what wonderful legal advice he got from Chamberlayne's?'

He sank back slowly into the buttoned leather upholstery, taking deep breaths. When he spoke again it was with his familiar expletive-free pomposity.

'Sarah, please do not compound the seriousness of your position with vulgar insolence. Can you not appreciate that Chewton senior might himself not want his son's grubby social life being dealt with by the same solicitors as a prestigious development costing hundreds of millions? There will undoubtedly be publicity. I tremble to think of the reaction of, say, the Bank of the South China Sea if it discovers that Chamberlayne's, far from being an exclusively commercial firm, deals with criminals of the most despicable kind. Such a delicate matter should have been referred to me immediately. That it was not has made a difficult situation much more critical.'

I gave a bit of a gulp. It was a fair point, but I wouldn't let him steamroller my own case without a struggle. 'First off, I didn't know what he wanted, but he sounded as if he really needed help. Secondly, as I've already said, it was because he was Chewton's son that I went straight away. Thirdly, I did intend to check with you, but you were out. I didn't know when you would be back. I thought it would be negligent if I failed to keep the appointment once I'd made it.'

'Precisely. You shouldn't have made it in the first place. Robbie Chewton is not our client. You should have found out what he wanted before you agreed to see him. If he wouldn't tell you, then you should have smelt a rat and said you had to get my authority as you dealt only with property matters. Then it would have been my decision as to what to do about it. As it is, through your misplaced confidence in your skill at criminal law, you have embarked on a frolic of your own and in so doing embroiled this firm in a case of extraordinary sordidness. I thought I had made it clear to you that we do not deal with such things. Your own evident predilections in that respect do not override that policy. And, let me say, it's not the only occasion in the last week or so on which you have taken an unwarrantedly independent line. It is something which I have been intending to raise with you. The fact that your probation is over is not *carte blanche* to do whatever you feel inclined.' He held up his hand. 'I don't want to discuss the detail of those matters now. They can wait. It merely gives further illustration to the point. I am rather afraid that you are in danger of becoming a loose cannon, Sarah. Please recall that the fate of a loose cannon is to explode prematurely and fall overboard.'

The nautical metaphor was contrived, and possibly inaccurate, but the message it carried was clear. It was time to pop the frozen halfway humble pie into the microwave.

'I'm sorry if you feel I've caused embarrassment. As I've said, I acted in what at the time I considered to be the best interests of the client and the firm. I realize now that there are two ways of looking at that, and that I did possibly make a mistake. I do think, however, that I gave him sound advice. I told him to go back to his flat and act normally. The police probably hadn't made up their minds to arrest him yet. They'd still be interviewing the complainant, having her medically examined and so on. Therefore there was no need for him to surrender himself voluntarily, as that might be construed as an admission. When he was arrested, he should use his phone call to inform me. If for any reason they wouldn't let him contact anyone, then he should stay completely silent through any interview.'

Appleby's face had returned to a less apoplectic shade. He shrugged. 'I defer to your more recent experience of such matters. The only thing I care about is to get out of the mess. I don't give two hoots what happens to Robbie Chewton and, between ourselves, I doubt that Trevor does either. He's been nothing but trouble and disappointment. The bane of the parent.'

Did Appleby have children? Was that bitter experience talking, or just relief? Was he even married? I knew nothing about him, a contrast with my last boss, whose domestic travails I knew to the minutest detail. Pogson, the least discreet or embarrassable man in town. Pogson...

I said, 'As I have, on one reading of the situation, got us into it, I may have a way of getting us out.'

'Go on.'

'I can suggest to Robbie that he needs to go to one of the best criminal law firms in the country, and one who will have no objection to liaising closely with me. They're in London, but that's even better to keep Fernsford gossip to a minimum. It will look as if it was natural for me to make the connection.'

He gave a thin smile. 'Vardy and Leadbetter, I presume?'

I nodded. 'I'll tell Tim Pogson it's a late Christmas present.'

I met Pogson at Westhampton Junction station and drove him into the town.

For most of it, he didn't speak, unless you count his grunted greeting. He quite often, in between the loquaciousness, had periods of stony silence. It used to bother me. I'd tell myself he was distracted by thought, or even shy. Now I knew it was a kind of compliment. He was treating me as he would treat a male colleague.

He sat munching his way through a packet of chewy mints, without offering one, clung theatrically to the dashboard whenever I went round a bend, and glanced covertly at the speedometer whenever the road was straight. I was itching to put the stereo on, but knew he would tell me to turn it off again.

I hoped he'd spent the train journey reading Robbie's statement which I'd sent him, and my summary of subsequent events.

Robbie had, as I had advised him, gone back to his flat where the police had picked him up later that day. He had been interviewed, in my presence, and again as advised, declined to answer any questions. The police had hung on to him as long as they legally could, hoping a session in the cells would soften him up, but he had kept stumm. They charged him with rape anyway. When he went up before the magistrates, I got counsel to ask for bail. Given the seriousness of the charge and the circumstances, this was refused, particularly as neither of his parents offered to stand as sureties. He was remanded in custody pending committal for trial to the Fernsford Crown Court.

I had, of course, been given the task of telling the Chewtons about their baby boy before it hit the papers. Appleby had washed his hands of it. His story was that I had acted all along as the agent of the criminal practice in London which had taken the case.

Catherine had been distraught. Trevor went literally white with fury, and spoke for a considerable time only in expletives. When he did come down from the ceiling, he asked me to 'Tell the bastard he's on his fucking own this time.' On hearing this, Catherine had slammed out of the room, saying she was going to stay with her mother. Trevor turned to me in that friendly way of his and said, 'Piss off out of it now, would you?' Talk about shooting the messenger.

Pogson, who'd been staring fixedly ahead through the windscreen during our slow, traffic-curdled progress through Westhampton town centre, turned to me, breathing minty fumes, and said with heavy irony, 'This is an improvement on Hoxton?'

I was about to retort that I didn't live or work here, but he knew that full well and was only winding me up, so I took a leaf out of his book and didn't reply.

If pushed, I would have had to admit he had a point. Westhampton looks a lot like the pictures of Belfast you see on the TV, only worse. The fact that the Victorians chose to site one of their most forbiddingly designed gaols – Fernsford would have none of it – in one of its suburbs does not add to its classiness as an address.

We had arrived. I parked the car on the forecourt, looking up at the West Country's version of an ogre's castle.

HM Prison, Westhampton, has high brick walls with round towers at each corner, and a great big arched gateway between more towers. Set in the iron-bound main gate is a small door. In a fairy story, you'd need the password for it to be opened. In our case, I had our letter of introduction ready.

Despite the medieval trappings, the atmosphere inside was the same as all the other prisons I'd ever been in. It never failed to give me the creeps. The air seems to hum with a scream you can't quite hear, like one of those whistles that only animals respond to. There's a stink beyond the smell of stale cooking, sewers and disinfectant which you can't quite detect, a stink of abstract qualities that shouldn't have any odour: corruption, degradation, violence.

We waited in the guardroom within the main tower for an escort. You don't go wandering about by yourselves in a prison. Because we were solicitors, they didn't subject us to a search but that was because those were the rules, not because they trusted us. Behind the desk was a blackboard with the number banged up chalked on it. Every time a prisoner left, or another one came in, the number would be changed. Below it a circle of coloured tin hung on a hook. The day's alert status. Black. They must have known something we didn't.

A fat prison officer appeared in the doorway and beckoned to us. We followed his elephantine behind. He carried a bunch of keys on a thick steel ring. We waited as he laboriously unlocked the steel-barred inner gate, then waited again as he locked it behind us. Never leave a door unlocked. Those were the rules. On the other side of the yard, below the rows of identical grilled windows, he went through the same process with another metal door. Then along a corridor, finally through a wooden door inset with a wired-glass observation panel, again unlocked and locked.

The room beyond, the remand prisoners' interview room, had been recently decorated and smelt of fresh paint. Fresh grey paint. There were grey formica tables, grey plastic chairs and a grey streaky vinyl tile floor. On each table was an aluminium ashtray. On the far side, another brief and his client, whom I wouldn't have wanted to meet on even a very bright night, were in earnest conclave. We sat down at the indicated place and waited yet again. Pogson had earned a packet in waiting and travelling time and he hadn't even met the client yet.

Robbie finally arrived sandwiched between two prison officers, dressed in jeans and plain white sweatshirt. He was already prison-pale. Having regard to the alleged offence, they were keeping him on the Rule, but he must still have been shit-scared most of the time.

The screws withdrew to their cubby-hole. I did the introductions and we sat down. Pogson produced a packet of Capstan Full Strength with the cellophane already off and offered one to Robbie. He then put the open pack on the table. I fished out the disposable lighter I always carried in my handbag, a habit from my days at Vardy's. Robbie bent forward for the light. When he leaned back again, the packet of smokes had gone. He was learning quickly.

Pogson went through the situation. We hadn't yet had from the police the girl's statement. We didn't know whether they would try to get away with putting a written statement in at the committal hearing. If they did, we would insist she gave an oral deposition, so that she could be cross-examined. Pogson turned to me. 'One or the other they have to do, surely? There's no other evidence, is there?'

I shrugged. 'I shouldn't have thought so. Medical, obviously. People at the gig. The parents. But that wouldn't establish a prima-facie case of rape. They have to have her evidence. Mind you, there isn't anything we can do to force them to have her at the committal, if they do rely on other evidence. *Epping and Harlow Justices ex parte Massaro* is on all fours with this.'

'Sarah, you're so impressive when you want to be. Why did you ever leave?'

'Look, fatso, would you mind telling me what the fuck is going on?'

Pogson regarded Robbie over his glasses. 'Mr Chewton, you would be advised to address me civilly, otherwise our relationship will not prosper. Our object at this stage is to get the rape element of the charges thrown out at committal. In that event they may not proceed with the other matters. The evidence of the girl is crucial. I suggest we engage leading counsel. I shall have to obtain the consent of the Legal Aid fund.'

'Stuck in this fucking shit-hole, begging for bloody charity. My father's worth millions and he won't give me a penny. He wrote to me and told me that. And he's persuaded Mum not to use her money. Most of it's tied up in bonds and things, anyway. The bastard. If I ever get out of here, I'm going to settle the score, I can tell you.'

The mention of Trevor Chewton reminded me of our last encounter.

'Robbie, when I saw your father, he said, "He's on his fucking own this time." What did he mean?'

He looked nervous. 'It never came to court.'

'Was it drugs?'

'No, it was a girl. At school. She said I . . . but I never. She was the class scrubber. She went with everybody. That's what everyone said. Dad, you know, spoke to her parents. Asked them if they didn't fancy a move to one of his new estates. It was ages ago, anyway.'

Pogson and I looked at one another. His expression was deadpan, but I knew what he was thinking.

\*

'So what do you think?'

My question hung in the steamy atmosphere of the Westhampton Junction station buffet while Tim Pogson bit into a Danish pastry, a vast cartwheel of cholesterol, with relish, then slurped a mouthful from the giant-sized mug of coffee to wash it down before he was ready to reply.

'We're in some difficulty. You were quite right to get him to keep quiet in the police station. It will be counsel's decision, but my view is that we shouldn't let him anywhere near the witness box. A cross-examination would destroy him for a jury. We don't know about the girl yet. If she comes on in gymslip and white socks, then he could go down so far you won't hear the splash.'

'You'll be doing your best to find out all about her, poor little bitch. As the only issue is consent, so the only object of the defence is to make the complainant seem like something you scrape off your shoe. In which the court happily assists.'

'That's an exaggeration. Rape is a serious charge. It needs to be seriously addressed. It can wipe out the man convicted.'

'Which they hardly ever are. That's on your side.'

'Our side, remember? Don't blame me, Sarah. It was your idea to involve me, the most brilliant criminal lawyer you could think of. You dragged me all the way down from London. So that our mutual friend could have the best defence. And you did the right thing. It was your duty as a solicitor to give the best advice you could.'

I remembered my session with Appleby. 'I felt at the time I was in an awkward position. If he went down, there'd be a lot of bad publicity. The firm have got a big investment in the father's business. Do you want another coffee?' In the office, Pogson drank the stuff in relays. A fresh mug was always waiting when he finished the last. I'd seriously thought of getting him an intravenous caffeine drip.

'Please.'

I went over to the counter to get one. When I came back with it, he'd fished the Chewton papers out of his battered Gladstone bag and was staring at them intently. His grimy glasses were pushed down his nose: he'd had an unimplemented prescription for bifocals in his pocket for years.

'Impressive this, isn't it?'

He hadn't been looking at the notes I had sent him on the Chewton case, but the covering letter on the Chamberlayne notepaper. He was pointing at the letterhead.

'I was looking at your boss's full name. Francis W. Appleby. Any idea what the W stands for?'

I shrugged. 'I've no idea.'

'It could be Walter then?'

'I suppose so. Why?'

'I knew of a Walter Appleby years ago. It could be him. I wish you'd told me about him before you left. You mentioned an old-established firm in Fernsford, not Walter Appleby.'

'What would you have said if I had?'

'I would have said, watch your step.'

'Come on, Tim. I know there were a few sour grapes about my leaving. So, did you once lose a case to him? It isn't like you to bear a grudge.'

'Let me tell you a story of far away and long ago. My old friend Arthur O'Riordan, who practised on his own account in Holloway and would be practising there to this day if he'd kept off the booze, had a criminal client, an estate agent, who was charged with deception. His MO was to approach elderly owners of largish houses in North London – Highbury, Islington, Camden – mainly widows, and purport to give them independent advice about the value of their houses. They'd be the sort on fixed incomes, not able to maintain their old homes, but not being very clued up about the alternatives. You can imagine what followed.'

'They were valued very low, though it would seem like a fortune to the old dears, then it turned out that the agent had found a potential purchaser at just that price. Presumably it was the agent himself wearing another hat?'

'Very good! What a loss you are to crime, Sarah. You think like a criminal. Yes, the agent and his partners in crime turned the properties at a good profit. In fact the diabolical refinement was that they sold the old women they'd swindled out of their homes flats they'd converted from properties fraudulently acquired earlier – and at inflated prices. It was a nice little fiddle. Of course the amounts involved look now like peanuts compared with the way the market has gone, but they made a good living.'

'How does Walter Appleby come into this?'

'The firm who did the conveyancing on the swindled properties, acting for the old ladies, was called Redwood's. They weren't the type to have lawyers of their own, so they were very pleased to be introduced to charming young men who charged very reasonable fees – or claimed they did. Now, according to Arthur, his client was always very clear that Redwood's knew quite well what was going on. He also claimed that the firm who acted on the side of the company which bought the houses was in fact a dummy firm which looked independent but was in fact nothing more than Redwood's under another guise. Have a guess who was a member of the Redwood partnership?'

'Walter Appleby?'

'A hole in one! Yes, indeed. Your man, it was. So what a fine stew it was. Criminal conspiracy. Deception. Not to mention the breach of every one of the Solicitors' Practice Rules, in spades.'

'What happened?'

'Aha, I think you have an inkling. Did justice triumph? Were the old ladies restored to their castles? Were they, hell. No, the prosecuting authorities dropped the case. It was too difficult to prove, despite all the circumstantial evidence. No one made any admissions. How do you establish that a valuation is given in bad faith? It's an opinion, after all. And doesn't the whole of the trading business turn on buying cheap and selling dear? So the case was quietly dropped. I daresay the parties regarded discretion as the better part of valour. I'd guess the estate agent, if he's still in business, probably makes enough money now from the legitimate property market. He's no need to think up elaborate frauds. As for Appleby, he's clearly doing all right out here in the sticks. A respectable man, now, no doubt. I only remember the name because Arthur agonized to me for ages about his duty to the profession. He hated bent lawyers, but there wasn't anything he could do. I feel the same. I won't employ anyone who's made the tea at a bent firm.'

My brain was boiling. How much of it was true? How much was the drunken gossip of Pogson's unreliable friend? And where did it leave me?

Then, infuriatingly, the public address gave its admonitory wheeze and the voice of the announcer, so thick with Wes'set cream it was fit to curdle, chummily informed us that the next train to 'arroive at Platform Wun wuz the seventeen-ten Inter-City Express fur Lunn'on Paa-ddunton only.'

Pogson gulped down his coffee. 'And I wouldn't knowingly let any of my staff go to work for a crook. In your case, though, you left in such a tearing hurry. If you'd asked me ... But there, you made the choice of your own free will, which is your privilege. But I shouldn't worry about what I've told you. Ancient history. It was all, what, fifteen years ago.'

'Of course you've bloody well worried me. What about one of your other favourite sayings, the liberal, enlightened one that goes, once a thief ... ?'

There was a rumbling outside the buffet. 'Hey, there's my train.' He scrambled to his feet and shook my hand quickly and awkwardly. 'Take care. Call me. Okay, Sarah?' He ran surprisingly quickly to the glass swing doors and barged through.

I stood up, my mind reeling. Hell and damnation! What was I letting myself get all het up about? Besides, there probably wasn't a firm in England that Pogson thought lived up to his own standards. Screw him! I wouldn't call him. I didn't give a stuff about Appleby's alleged past, if it was the same Appleby, which I doubted. I had a good job and I was going to keep it. No matter what.

## XVII

'Have you heard the news, Sarah?'

I looked up to see Penny flushed and excited at the door.

'What news?'

'About David. He's leaving.'

'Oh? How the hell do you know?'

'I overheard Meredith just now tell Amanda to get out the file for his job-description and to make sure to get the ad in next week's *Gazette*. Why else would he do that?'

'Dunno. I expect you're right. You usually are. Tape here for you.' I pointed at the spool on the desk.

She gave me one of her looks – the kind she usually reserved for Appleby – and scuttled off back to the general office.

I sighed. I shouldn't be taking out my anger and frustration on Penny. Poor woman. I had been a cow to her lately. I'd buy her some chocolates to make up. That's what men did, wasn't it?

I couldn't concentrate on my work, so I filled my mug with coffee and strolled along the corridor to David's office. I saw little of him in the working week and hadn't really talked to him at any length since that first time in the Coffee House all those months ago. It might be my last opportunity.

The door was ajar, a sign that he was not with a client, so I walked in.

David's desk was even more cluttered than mine. He was on the phone, so I cleared a stack of paper off the only chair and sat on it, drinking the coffee and flicking through that week's *Law Society Gazette*. I hadn't got round even to taking off the plastic wrapping from mine. As I scanned the reports of the hearings of the Disciplinary Tribunal, to see who'd been struck off or been given a whopping fine and why, I listened in to his pugnacious telephone manner.

He was saying, 'Am I hearing this right? You won't accept "use best endeavours" in para seventy-two? There's no way my client will agree unconditionally to guarantee the action of a third party. No, we must have "reasonable" and not necessary, yeah? Okay, I'll take instructions. Give me an hour to get hold of him. He's on a mobile but it's patchy.' He put the phone down and started scribbling in the counsel's notebook in front of him. Such enthusiastic energy was depressing.

I coughed gently.

'Sarah, where did you spring from?'

'I flew in through the window. Didn't you hear?'

'Sorry. I was miles away. I've been trying to tie up this business sale for weeks. I think I'm almost there. You'd think it was a plc and not a potty little PR outfit. What can I do for you?'

'The grapevine says you're off.'

'The grapevine is right, but I only put in my resignation this morning.'

'Bad news travels fast.'

'It's not bad for me.'

'So where are you going?'

'Back to London. On a partnership. My uncle finally made me an offer I couldn't refuse. Mind you, I was going to leave anyway. I've had enough of this shit-hole.'

'I didn't know you felt like that.'

'I didn't want to admit I'd made a mistake. Fernsford is not my kind of town. It's dull, damp, and full of fools.'

'Thanks.'

'With honourable exceptions. Sarah, you're wasted here. And exploited.'

'I don't have an uncle to offer me a plummy alternative. That's why I came here in the first place.'

'You won't stay. There's no future here, for people like you and me.'

'And what's that?'

'People who speak out of turn. Who don't kowtow. Who think for themselves.'

'Hang on. You said I was exploited. Now I'm a free spirit.'

'You are, basically. You won't stick it. One day, you'll wake up and see it like I did.' He got up from the desk, went over and closed the door. 'You'll see that this place is a sham. That the work is crap. That the partners are incompetent.'

'Come on now.' I waved a hand vaguely at the room. 'You're snowed under. It can't be all crap.'

'Not all, and that's the point. Meredith shunts all the difficult stuff on to me. He can't hack it. He can't make decisions. Whenever he has a real problem, he goes snivelling to Appleby. I'm fed up of doing all the work and getting none of the credit. Whenever I've mentioned partnership, Appleby goes all smooth and evasive. I've seen the writing on the wall, and it says, piss off, Jewboy.'

'Perhaps you need a break.'

'Not a break. A permanent fracture. No, I've made my decision. You should do the same if you've any sense.'

'You're not right about having no future. What about Michael and Brian? They were assistants until quite recently.'

'Michael and Brian? Prove the point, don't they? When did you last hear them say one thing that was interesting or controversial? When did you last hear them say anything at all? The reason they work so hard is that they're too stupid to do anything else.'

'What about Conrad? Don't you rate him?'

'Okay. I have some time for Conrad. He was a bit tired and emotional one night and he let slip a few things. Like he can't stand Appleby for a start.'

'Really? I can't say I've noticed.'

'That's because you're always working in the office. You don't get out, except to your cruddy sites. You don't meet other lawyers. If you did, you'd hear things.'

'Like what?'

'Like Chamberlayne's is notorious for hiring bright young London-trained assistants, promising them the earth, then chewing them up and spitting them out. Unless, like Fielding and Richardson, they have the right kind of bland *apparatchik* mentality. Which they usually don't. The only recent exception to that seems to be, I mean –'

'You mean me. Because I'm stupid and because I'm a woman. I seem to remember I've had this conversation before.'

'I've never said anything of the sort. And what I've already said shows I don't think it. No, what I was trying to say is that Appleby, unlike his partners, has never gone in for assistants, unless you count Rose. You're the first one he's had. And he fought the idea of it tooth and nail. The way I heard it, the others ganged up on him, for the first time ever. Led by Conrad. Appleby was thought to be spending far too much time on routine conveyancing, under pressure from Chewton, and not enough big-ticket stuff. They were worried. They didn't want to lose out on the lucrative matters – that's the steady income that pays for the Mercs and the BMWs. They wanted Appleby to magic up some more. He got the brewery, not Meredith. They know he's the only one who has the Midas touch. The Chewton connection.'

'I heard a version of that from Penny. Frankly, I was always a bit surprised he picked me. He could have had anyone.'

Before David could reply his phone rang. He waved in a gesture that meant 'this is a long one'.

Back in my office, I groaned aloud. That was what I needed on top of everything else. To be told, by someone I rated, that I was in a crap firm with no future.

Then another horrible thought occurred to me. If Appleby, as Pogson had implied, was bent, he wouldn't pick one of the best and brightest, would he? He wouldn't like anyone working closely on his files, except a secretary of cast-iron loyalty, like Rose, or an ignoramus, like Penny. Certainly not a smart alec. So, if he were forced into getting an assistant, he'd go for someone who, he would reckon, would not pick up on what was going on – an under-educated cockney-Irish scrubber.

Why was I thinking like this? David hadn't said anything of that sort. What he had said might accrue to my advantage. The more I could shine above my colleagues, the more likely Appleby was to take me seriously. Already I saw him looking at me occasionally with a grudging respect. I'd be like Pinocchio. The wooden puppet would come to life. One day, I'd really surprise him. Fromberg could piss off back to London. Me, I was sticking around.

'I can't believe the prices you're asking!' I exclaimed to Martin Vernon, as we stood together under the pillared porch of the new Lansdown housetype. Vernon was Chewton's new Sales Director – the old one having been recently, in Appleby's phrase, 'taken out and shot at dawn', following an altercation with his lord and master.

Vernon, a slim, superfit thirtyish type with a button-down shirt collar, flashed a set of perfect teeth. 'With prices escalating as they are, in a few months, they'll seem cheap. You have to stay ahead of the game in this market. You don't do our sort of customer any favours if you underprice. The more they shell out now, the more they'll make when they sell. There's no problem with mortgages for the right punters. We've had the FernWest practically begging us to put people their way. They're awash with money. We could sell this lot ten times over. They'll all go under reserve in about five minutes tomorrow. This,' he waved a hand at the assembled throng, 'is pure PR. Not sales. Trevor is giving notice that he's playing with the big boys. Wimpey, Barratt, Tarmac, watch out. And he's got a spectacular planned, you hang about and see.'

I was at the launch party for the new site at Bilton Greville, a snobby bijou village off the Westhampton road. Appleby had of late tended to send me along to this kind of thing, which he made no bones about despising. It showed I was beginning to have my uses.

Rectory Fields was one of Chewton's most up-market developments.

The glossy brochure called it 'a classic English setting', and for once the hype was somewhere near the mark. No expense had been spared on the show home. A design consultant had been hired for the interior décor, and Carlyons, Fernsford's most upmarket store, had supplied the furnishings. The garden was planted with flowers, shrubs, even a couple of largish trees. These had been brought in by lorry the night before. Workmen bussed in from other sites had been slaving on it since dawn, and the last stray crumbs of earth had only in the last hour been swept from the freshly laid bowling-green turf of the lawn. It gleamed under the sprinkler like an expanse of emerald Axminster.

The place was buzzing with free-loaders lapping up the champagne and scoffing the canapés at the trestle tables laid with dazzling white cloths in the marquee set up on the driveway. I sipped fizzy mineral water, and introduced myself to Jemima, the debby-looking site sales rep.

'Hi. Heard about you,' she said. 'Word is you're a bit good.'

'A bit,' I admitted modestly.

I had on my new office suit, dove-grey, which had added alarmingly to my mounting credit card balance, and I looked, I thought, fairly formidable.

I was about to pop one of the teeny sandwiches into my carefully lip-sticked mouth when I saw a tall white-haired figure in a donkey jacket stride across the top of the drive carrying a case of wine.

I froze for an instant, then as Jemima had her eyes on me I forced my hand to continue with the action.

It was as if I'd crammed in a handful of gravel. I started to choke.

Jemima, with the unflappability of her type, grabbed me round the middle from behind and squeezed hard. I spluttered bits of half-chewed bread over my jacket front. She handed me a paper napkin and I cleaned myself up.

'You know, I've always wanted to do that manoeuvre, ever since first-aid training. Works okay?'

I nodded, weakly, and drank mineral water. 'Thanks. Went down the wrong way.'

The figure recrossed the tarmac.

Controlling the tremor in my voice, I said as carelessly as I could, 'That bloke looks a bit out of place at this do.'

She laughed. 'Him? He's not a guest. That's Terry. He's a real charmer.

So helpful. Turn his hand to anything. I think he's at Friars Haven most of the time. One of the chaps Trevor roped in here.'

I mumbled a reply, then drank up the water. 'I must look for the loo.'

My heart pounding, I headed for the temporary lavatory. I walked quickly, not thinking what I was about to do, conserving my resolution before it ebbed away. I had to do this. I had said I would the next time he made his appearance.

I skirted round the cabin then, out of sight of the reception, I dashed to the back of the show-home garage. I could hear someone moving about.

I slipped inside, grasping the door handle to control the trembling. It was him. Of course it was him. He was filling a crate with empties. He looked up when he heard me enter. He said, his pale face devoid of expression, 'Well, talk about coincidence.'

'Fuck coincidence. You came after me,' I whispered. 'We have to have a serious talk. When do you get off?'

'The minibus'll get us back to town about eight. We have to clear up.'

'I'll meet you at ten past in Saxe-Coburg Square, the corner of Victoria Street, outside the Planet Federation offices. Okay?'

He nodded.

When I rejoined the party, my colleagues were too preoccupied to notice my dead-white face, which even a splash of hot water in the loo had done nothing to alleviate. Vernon was checking his watch nervously.

I raised an eyebrow at Jemima and she chuckled. 'Not in on the secret? Like in the film. Watch the skies.'

At that moment, there was a roar of engines from above. Everyone threw back their heads to see a blue and red helicopter zoom in over the surrounding woodland, and then float down as lightly as a dragonfly to land in the adjoining field. The chunky figure of Trevor Chewton emerged from the machine and, bending low under the thrashing rotor blades, ran towards us. Vernon had hurried forward to open the gate from the field, and as they came up together, Trevor brushing back his hair with the flat of one of his enormous hands, said curtly, 'That reporter here?'

A weedy fellow with a camera duly appeared and Trevor posed, the captain of industry.

I heard Jemima at my elbow murmur, 'God, it's like the White House lawn.'

With cracks like that I couldn't imagine she was going to last long.

At last I managed to slink away, pleading pressure of work. Trevor was in his element, playing the big tycoon.

On the way home, my mind still churning at the thought of that evening's meeting, I was irritated to find myself stuck in a traffic jam on the main Westhampton to Fernsford road. I couldn't bear the idea of grinding along behind a string of HGVs until the accident or whatever it was up ahead had cleared, so I dived impatiently down the first side turning, imagining it would miraculously take me back to the highway at a point beyond the hold-up. What I didn't reckon was that I would immediately be plunged into a warren of Westerset's famous deep lanes, worn down over centuries between high banks and massive, gnarled overarching trees. It was not long before I had completely lost my sense of direction. In these gloomy green tunnels I couldn't even see the sun to help me head west, the right general direction. Also I had been going downhill, which wasn't right either. I should have been following the high ground above the valley of the Fern, if I were to have any chance of reconnecting with the Fernsford road.

I dragged the map out of the side pocket. I wasn't much good at maps. It was on too small a scale, and I wasn't entirely sure on which of the white squiggles I had set off. I could be almost anywhere. I peered out of the windscreen. I could see a flash of white that might be a signpost, the first one I had seen. I restarted the engine and drove up to it. It pointed downhill to the right. The black letters read, Ashton St Michael 2. I fished out my map. I could see now where I must be. Follow the road down to Ashton, cross the Fern, and then I could join the M39 motorway and enter Fernsford from the north. It was a long way round, but it was better than being stuck in these dark and oddly threatening lanes.

I took the turn and followed its twisting course. I soon began to wonder whether I had made a wise choice. It wasn't exactly a trunk road. Clumps of weeds had broken through the mossy crust of metalling at the crown of the road, and the overgrown hawthorn hedges compressed it from either side.

It was with some relief that I rounded yet another blind right-angle bend, then skidded to a halt at a junction with loose gravel rattling in the wheel-arches; the motor stalled.

I had arrived at an altogether more sensible-looking stretch of asphalt with a broken white line in the centre. To my right was a sign which read, Ashton St Michael welcomes careful drivers. Ashton St Michael. I remembered now why it sounded familiar. This was Appleby's home turf.

I felt the need for some distraction. It was several hours until the meeting with my father and there was no way I could get any work done before it. The events of the last few days had served to make me curious about what made my boss tick. Now I had blundered upon his manor. It seemed an opportunity too good to miss.

There were rumours about him in the office, of course all of them conflicting. He was a womanizer with a string of mistresses the length and breadth of the county. He was gay – James Huxley told me he'd heard on good authority that Appleby had been seen with a rent-boy in Bold Knights, the gathering place for queers and S & M types in the basement of a crummy hotel by the Western Road station. He was divorced – this was Penny's theory. 'Five minutes, I bet the marriage lasted.' He was a widower. He'd never been married. Everyone had their own story. Everyone that is, except Rose. She was the only one who might reasonably be expected to know the truth, but being the perfect personal assistant, she offered no confirmation or denial of any hypothesis, giving only her tight-lipped, noncommittal, polite smile. That, presumably, was the way Appleby wanted it.

I stopped in the narrow village street and wound down the window. An elderly man sat cuddling his belly and dozing in the evening sun on a wrought-iron seat outside the open door of his cottage.

'Excuse me, I'm looking for the Woodlands. Can you help me?'

He came to with a jerk and stared at me with narrowed eyes in the mahogany face.

'The Woodlands?' I asked again.

He leaned forward, hawked and spat on to the pavement between his spread-apart legs. 'Who wants to know?'

'I've some papers to deliver. Legal papers.'

He nodded. 'First right. Big house through the gates on the left. He's not there, though. Not come home yet. Not heard my windows rattling.' He gave a phlegmy chuckle. 'You can tell him that if you see him. Not heard my windows rattling.'

The entrance-drive to the Woodlands was barred by a pair of handsome wrought-iron gates, black, with gilt spikes, set between tall stone pillars surmounted by stone pineapples. A high stone wall surrounded the property on this side. I got out of the car and peered through the bars.

A shingled drive, weed-free but rutted by vehicles, curved away, flanked by magnificent banks of rhododendron bushes, laden with the buds of pink and white and scarlet flowers, the turf beneath carpeted with fallen, brown-edged leaves. I stood by the left-hand pillar, trying to see the house. Through the shrubbery, I had an impression of a grey stone-columned portico, with carvings in the triangular space above, and steps leading up to tall double doors. I could see the back half of a big green estate car which was parked at a careless angle on the drive in front. Even if his lordship were not at home, someone else was.

I drew my face away from the cold metalwork. The gates were firmly shut. Discreetly bolted to the inside of each leaf was a steel bar. A chain glistening with oil led from the bar and passed through a steel-rimmed eyelet on the inner face of each gate pillar. It was an opening and closing system. In answer to some electronic command, from within the car or the house, the gates would open and close mechanically. It was the sort of thing you might expect to see on a London ambassador's residence or on some security-conscious millionaire's place in Surrey, but a bit unusual in this neck of the woods, where they hardly shut their doors at night, never mind locked them.

To live in a place like this, with this level of gizmos, was the mark of someone seriously rich.

I hadn't ever thought of Appleby like this. This was more on the Chewton scale of living. Did running Chamberlayne's pay so well? I thought of what Pogson had told me. Once a thief . . . As I drove back to Fernsford on the M39, I dismissed the worm of doubt wriggling in my mind. The distraction was over. I had more important matters still to address.

The pub was called the Britannia, I remember. It was just busy enough at that hour for us not to attract more than a cursory glance from the barmaid, even though we were an oddly assorted couple.

We'd found a corner in the most dimly lit end of the big room, away from the entrance doors with their cut-glass panelling and the back door with the metal sign reading Toilets.

I sat watching him as he took a swallow from his pint. His adam's apple, prominent in his thin neck, rose and fell. Below it was the open collar of a checked work shirt and the ribbed band of a navy-blue jersey. He'd kept on the donkey jacket, and its PVC yoke gleamed faintly under the fake gas wall lamps of the public bar.

I had to force myself to look directly at his face, its grey-stubbled pallor, the broken veins, the washed-out pale grey eyes. He didn't meet my scrutiny, but applied himself to the plate of pie and chips I'd bought him.

We didn't speak for quite a while. My father ate his supper with some relish, and polished off the pint. In between covert glances at him, I stared at the glass of tonic water on the marble tabletop in front of me in which a slice of lemon floated, as pale and thin as a communion wafer.

Finally he aligned the knife and fork on the plate and pushed it away from him. He looked up and at me. Then, his eyes hooded, his mouth curved into what might have been a smile.

'Time for you to get it off your chest. But first, I think I'll get another pint. No, don't disturb yourself. I'll be fetching it myself. It was pay day today. I'm not short.'

I watched him at the bar. He was having a joke with the barmaid. I saw her nod in my direction, as if to say, does your ladyfriend want anything? He shook his head and told her to have one herself to make up. He paid with a twenty-pound note, peeled casually off a roll dug out of his back pocket, and swept up the pile of change without so much as a glance at it. My mother's voice drifted into my head: 'Treating your mates as if you were Croesus.'

He came back, the pint already well started, a grin on his face. 'I was well in there, did you see? I might pay another visit here, when I'm not otherwise engaged.'

'You've really made yourself at home, haven't you?'

'I've been far worse. The foreman at the Haven's not too bright, and he'd just lost his JCB driver in an accident. It didn't matter that I was a bit older than the average. It was one of the things I learned in gaol, you know, at the end, not in the Scrubs. They sent me to one of those open prisons, in the country. And I'm willing to do overtime and extras whenever they want, at the Haven mostly. Stores, bit of night security work, weekends and that. And the sort of thing I was doing this afternoon. Mr Dependable, I am.'

'You found out where I was and you followed me, didn't you? Why? Why are you doing this to me? I told you in London, I don't want anything to do with you.'

He grinned slyly, but did not reply.

I stared straight at him, my eyes wide. 'I'm not getting through to you, am I? I don't want you to stay here. I don't want you watching me, following me, spying on me. Is that so unusual? Can't you understand that? How many times do I have to say it?'

'I understand how you feel. Of course I do. I was a bastard to you and your mother. But I told you. I want to make it up to you. I owe you. And soon I'll be able to. Very soon. That's why I came here after you.'

'Was it Colin who told you where I was?'

'It might have been.'

'I thought so.' My head buzzed.

He finished up the pint. I hadn't touched the tonic water. The slice of lemon had curled up and sunk.

'So, are you going to leave me in peace?'

'I told you. I'm expecting something that'll make it all different. Not long now.'

'And I told you. I don't want anything. All I want is to be left alone. And not to see you again, ever. Ever.'

I got to my feet. He gazed up at me, and this time his pale eyes were wide with what I was sickened to see was a kind of appeal. Then he turned away again, and his voice was lower even than the throaty whisper he had been using to avoid being overheard. 'I can't leave you. Not now. I have this feeling I've got to see you're all right. You and me. We're flesh and blood. Whatever you think of me. There's that bond between us. We're alike, aren't we? When I see you're really all right, when I've given you what I'm expecting, then I'll go. Meantime, I'll stick around. I'll stick close. I have to. I have to, Sarah, my love.'

I couldn't believe he had said that. I felt the bile rising in my throat.

I virtually ran out of the pub, pushing past a party of OAPs coming in. I fumbled in my bag for the Fiesta's key, but as my suddenly shaking hands tried to fit it to the lock, I leaned my head against the cold metal of the roof and vomited. I remained there for several moments, retching drily.

As I lifted my head, I saw out of the corner of my eye that the last couple of the crumblies' night out who'd not managed quite to stagger inside were watching me with amazed fascination. The woman gave a contemptuous sniff.

I sat in the car, my head buzzing, my whole body filled with aches and pains, as if I were stretched on one of those torture machines in the Chamber of Horrors.

I'll stick around, he'd said. He'd be there, all the time, when I expected it and when I didn't. I couldn't stand that. I couldn't stand waiting for him to realize why I hated him so much, waiting for him to decide whether he was going to destroy me. I'd have to talk to him again, think of something to make him go. I was certain of one thing. I wouldn't run any further. Here I was and here I stayed.

The third floor was pitch dark when I let myself in. No one else kept my schedule. I'd come here, rather than go home. To force myself to work might still the voices in my head.

There was a pile of messages on my desk. I spent a couple of hours dictating things for Penny to deal with, flagging up files I would have to make calls on myself the next day and typing out and sending by fax the things that I thought couldn't wait. It always helped for a nasty fax to be waiting on some poor bastard's desk when they staggered in bleary eyed from the traffic jam. It sort of set them up for the day.

I'd almost finished when the phone rang. I picked it up automatically. I had no fears that it would be my father. Phones weren't his style. It wasn't that unusual to get a call late in the evening. Appleby had plenty of clients besides Chewton who relied on him to be available at any hour. The board was switched through at night so that any extension could pick up and transfer calls.

I was engaged in my usual bad habit of chewing the little plastic nubbin in the end of my ballpoint – it saved my nails – so that my response to the caller emerged as a strangled grunt.

'Appleby! You're fucking late, as usual. Get over here right now and bring the Oak Dean stuff with you.'

By this time I'd got the pen out of my teeth. I said, 'I'm sorry, it's not Mr Appleby you're speaking to, he's –'

Before I could volunteer any more, the line went dead. Thanks and good night. It still pissed me off that people would talk only to the great man himself. I was pleased, though, that if he eventually turned up at this meeting he appeared to have forgotten he was in for a bollocking, judging from the tone of the client. I wondered who it had been. Only Chewton among the clients I knew would have dared speak to him in that manner. But I knew Chewton's voice all too well and it definitely hadn't been him. He did sound an equally nasty piece of work. Appleby specialized in the type. However, there was something about the nasal voice and what it had said that seemed slightly familiar, but it floated on the fringes of my memory and I couldn't grasp it.

I yawned. I really was shattered. I couldn't put off going home any longer. If my father had been hanging about to serenade me, he'd've had a long wait. I'd pick up something unhealthy to eat at the chippy by the Western Road roundabout.

I slammed the outer door behind me as I emerged into the Horsemarket. It was, to my relief, deserted. This part of the street was mainly offices. The shops didn't start until nearer Saxe-Coburg Square. I walked the short distance to where I had parked the car. I'd returned after the end of restrictions, which saved me from having to brave the multi-storey car park.

As I unlocked the driver's door, I looked up at the Chamberlayne building. I noticed idly that someone else was also still tied to his desk. A light glimmered high up on the top floor of the FernWest tower which adjoined and for its lower storeys was contiguous with the Chamberlayne block.

Another workaholic, like me, like Appleby, burning the midnight oil. Then I remembered Oak Dean. Oak Dean. The property development that I had seen that night long ago on Appleby's screen. The one I had looked for in vain amongst the firm's records.

The oddest thing was that there was not and never had been a Chewton development called Oak Dean. Of that I was now absolutely certain. I had seen no other reference to the estate whatsoever until that evening.

And the mystery caller had put the phone down straight away when he discovered he hadn't been talking to Appleby. As if Oak Dean was a subject not to be mentioned elsewhere. But why? Where was this Oak Dean? And why was it apparently being kept a secret?

'More wine?' I stretched across Paul's chest to get at the bottle on the bedside table.

'That's lovely, the way your breasts sort of ripple over me when you do that.'

'Yes, I can feel your hairs against my nipples.' I bent down and kissed him, with a wide mouth, hungrily. The bottle tilted alarmingly, slipped out of my grasp and fell with a thunk on the carpet. 'Oh shit!' I pulled away, leapt out of bed and went round to his side to mop up the spill with a handful of tissues.

He swivelled his head down. 'Good job it was white. Leave it and come back to bed. I didn't want any more anyway. I've got to drive. Wouldn't do to get picked up for drunk driving in Fernsford. I'm supposed to be at a RIBA dinner in Bristol and getting back too late to be phoned. Venetia's gone to her brother's in London.'

'Paul, I don't want to know.'

'Hear no evil, see no evil. Keeps you whiter than white, is that it?'

'Paul! I'm not trying to pretend she doesn't exist. It's purely practical. The less I know about your movements, actual or supposed, then the more the chances of my dropping a clanger if I run into Venetia are reduced. If I let slip something you've told me, I'd have to lie my way out, and then everything gets very complicated.'

'Is our affair purely practical then?'

'What do you mean?'

'I mean that sometimes you seem so detached. We make love with passion, but I don't feel as if I've really reached you. It makes me wonder why you asked me to stay the night after Trevor's party.'

'There's no mystery. I wanted you and I knew that you wanted me. You hardly made a secret of that. It seemed a logical next step.'

'There you go again! Do you always go to bed with someone out of logic? Perhaps it's a generation thing. People your age. You want something. You go out and get it. Sex as a consumer product. No worries about costs or values. Is that how it is? What happened to love?'

'Love? You want the sweet music, the walk in the woods, the slow motion chase through the cornfield, the ecstatic cleaving together as the geese rise from the lake and fly off into the sunset? I've seen the movies, Paul. They were my education. I used to bunk off school to get into the Odeon, Holloway Road. I found out how to trip the mechanism of the fire-exit doors from the outside. I wasn't very old before I found that there were films and there was real life. It seems to be taking you rather longer to shed the illusion of the ideal relationship, somewhere just out of reach.'

'Maybe. I do believe in commitment. I've risked a good deal for you. Put my marriage on the line. That's what I mean by commitment.'

I allowed him to haul me upright. I leaned against the buttoned padded plastic of the headboard. I put my hand up to touch the line of his jaw, roughened with dark stubble. 'Yes, you've taken a kind of risk. But you haven't committed yourself by telling her. Or are you going to? Are you really in a movie where you leave Venetia for me? Leave your comfortable home and your children?'

'It happens.'

'Yes, it does. Some men go off with their secretaries, start another family, ruin more lives. Can't you understand? If I thought you were going to do that, I'd hate it. I wouldn't stay there for you.'

A look flickered in his eyes before he suppressed it. Relief, perhaps? 'But, darling Sarah, I do love you. I –'

I put my finger to his lips. 'No more of that stuff. You don't, can't love me. I want us to be together as much as we can. These last few months have been wonderful. I don't want them to end, even if I know that sometime they must. Let's accept that that's the way they are.'

He started to speak again, but again I laid my finger against his mouth. 'Shhh!' This time I did not take it away, but drew it down over his full lower lip, making it wet with his saliva. Then I slid two fingers slowly into his mouth, rubbing them along his gums and teeth, gently stroking the sides of his tongue. I felt the waters begin to flow in his mouth. I took my hand away, and bent my lips to his to lap them.

I slipped my spit-wet fingers under the sheet, and trailed them over his belly to where his cock was beginning to reawaken from its lair of wiry pubic hair. As it grew and stiffened I ran my finger tip up and down the tender fleshy tube that ran the length of its shaft.

As I kissed him, I settled him back against the scattered pillows, at the same time softly with my thumb and forefinger pulling his prick up and down. I heard him begin to groan softly and pulled my hand away. I rolled away from him and, leaning on the crook of my elbow, smiled down at him.

'Don't go away!' He started to reach his arms to me and I tenderly laid them back at his side. 'Wait!' I commanded. 'Just lie there. I'm not ready even if you are.'

I threw back the sheet which covered him and giggled. 'My, my, you are ready.'

I knelt and straddled his legs, then bent and planted a kiss on the swollen, straining head of his prick, its delicate skin stretched to a translucent glossiness.

He wrapped his arms around me but I pushed them off.

'Down, Sir!' I ordered, laughing. 'No touching.'

I raised myself again, still kneeling over him, pushing my pelvis towards him, so that he could see what was happening between my parted thighs. Slowly I ran both hands over my breasts, squeezing them gently, and encircling the hardening nipples. I could see his eyes beginning to bulge. Yet again he tried to lever himself up and reach his arms up to me. Again I pushed him back and smacked his wrists. 'Wait, I said!'

'Are you trying to drive me crazy?'

'Yes.'

I left my breasts and ran my hands down over my belly and down my thighs to my knees, then I drew them back up the inside to rest against my pubes. I smiled, as I saw his eyes goggling.

I slid a finger inside me and felt my wetness. I had hardly touched myself before I felt myself begin to tense and shudder. I threw myself down upon him, and felt his stiff length enter me, then all the control I had enjoyed exercising deserted me, and for a few moments the world seemed to dissolve in a glorious warm blossoming explosion which rocked the decrepit bed till it too added its own agonized squeaks to our cries and groans.

I giggled as juice spurted out, ran down my chin and between my breasts. I watched as the pinkish liquid coursed over my belly and turned my navel into a glimmering upland tarn.

'These are delicious. Don't you want one? Here.' I picked up another peach and waved it at him.

'No thanks, I could manage the juice, though.' He ducked his head down and I felt his tongue scouring out my belly button. Then it moved further down. I reached out and grabbed a hank of hair. 'Hey, you. Where do you think you're going? No more. I have to get up early tomorrow. Things to do. Work.'

'But it's Saturday.'

'So what? Chamberlayne's is a hive of activity at the weekends.'

'Scratch a lawyer and you find a workaholic.'

'What do you get if you scratch an architect?'

'Ow! What are you doing? That hurt. Okay, you find a bit of a dreamer. Now the dreaming has to stop. Friars Haven is taking over my life. I've had to recruit more staff, get an office in town. I spend my life in tedious meetings. I've finally had to realize that I can't wave things into reality like Kubla Khan.'

'Who?'

'Don't you know the poem by Coleridge? I learned it by heart at school. That was when I first thought of becoming an architect.'

'Let's hear it then.'

'What, now? I don't know that –'

'Come on. I bet you can remember it.'

'Oh, a challenge! All right. The first bit I think I can. Here goes.

'"In Xanadu did Kubla Khan
A stately pleasure-dome decree:
Where Alph, the sacred river, ran
Through caverns measureless to man
Down to a sunless sea."'

He paused. His voice had changed as he had recited, the clipped matter-of-factness became less evident, the vowels longer and more melodious.

'"In Xanadu did Kubla Khan".' I rolled the words around in my mouth as if they were wine. 'That's wonderful. But what does it all mean? Who was Kubla Khan?'

'He was the Mongol Emperor of China, master of all he surveyed. The legend is that he had built a great palace, just as it says in the poem.'

'So little Paul thought he would like to build a palace too?'

He smiled. 'Silly, wasn't it? At least I didn't dream of being the emperor, only the architect. I was a practical chap, even in my dreams. But that stuff about creating a pleasure-dome. That was what inspired my imagination, what, nearly thirty years ago. The idea of doing that myself. I still get a shiver when I recite the words.'

'You know, I've heard that name somewhere before.'

'Kubla Khan?'

'No. Xanadu. I've got it. It's a film. *Citizen Kane*. Kane calls his house Xanadu. He fills it with art stuff, but it's never finished.'

He frowned. 'I remember. But that Xanadu was satiric. A symbol of the futility of wealth. It was a folly, like Beckford's Fonthill or Ludwig II's Neuschwandstein.'

'Whereas your work is not at all foolish. But it's funny how apt that poem is. You have ended up working for an emperor of a kind. Your dream came true.'

'Yes. Don't remind me.' His lips thinned and his eyes narrowed. 'They say there's only one thing worse than not getting what you want in life. Do you know what that is?'

I shook my head.

'Getting it.'

It was almost dusk. Canal Street was already bathed in the amber glow of the sodium street lights. It had been raining and I could hear clearly the watery swish from the tyres of the cars which passed the Fiesta's half-open window at my right shoulder.

The ragged edges of the hole torn in the brick wall, the steel post and mesh fence and double gates erected to cover the gap showed up in silhouette against the blaze of the arc-lamps within the site. They shone down from gantries, making it look like a football stadium. I looked at my watch. Five minutes to knocking-off time.

I shuffled impatiently in the seat, and stretched my hands above my head to touch the clammy plastic of the roof lining. There was some movement at the gates. A dark figure appeared and I could hear even at this distance the rattle of metal as he unshackled them and pulled them open. A car nosed out, its headlight beams bobbing up and down as it negotiated the potholed surface. Then it shot smoothly out into a space in the stream of traffic and accelerated away towards the city centre. It was replaced immediately by another. The gate keeper bent down to this one and I heard a snatch of conversation.

He wouldn't come out in a car. Only the project management and office staff were allowed to park on site in the compound. The workmen had to use the surrounding streets. He wouldn't have his own car. My main worry was that he would get a lift with a mate. That would really mess things up. I would have to follow them through the evening rush-hour traffic and take my chance to catch him before he went inside wherever he was living.

Figures on foot appeared at the gates, about a dozen of them, as I had reckoned. There was some laughter and horse-play. Then they were out of the brightness of the lights and merging with the darkness of the street. This was the crucial point of the business. I had not dared to watch before this night. He might have seen me before I was ready for him, and I could not put myself through another inconclusive meeting.

Would they separate immediately and which way would they go? I had parked on the opposite side of Canal Street, a little way up from the contractors' entrance, in the dark pool between two street lights. This wasn't a bus route, so he would have to walk. At this end of Canal Street, there was only access to the junction for the ring road and the motorway. He would be bound to walk back into town. That meant I would be facing in the right direction to follow him.

The group of men was splitting up. Two or three peeled off with shouts and waves and walked in my direction. As they passed me, I heard one of them jingling car keys. I looked them over carefully, but they were all of them too young.

There was a sound of car doors banging from the darkness where the rest of the men had disappeared. Then headlights came on in a Cortina and in another car further down the street. I had to get closer. It was time to move.

When I turned the ignition key, the engine's firing seemed so loud that I feared they would hear it and scatter in alarm like soldiers before an incoming shell in a war film. I slipped into first and, barely pressing the gas pedal, I nosed out into the street. Most of the traffic was going in the opposite direction, out to the ring road, so I could drive slowly past where the Cortina had half pulled out, waiting for a break in the stream of vehicles. There were about four men still standing on the pavement. As I passed them, I caught my breath. One of them was taller, gaunter than the rest. He wore no cap and his head shone silver. Him.

At the end of Canal Street, I pulled in to the kerb on a double yellow line, turned off the lights, but left the engine running. The heater was spewing out nauseously hot air – one of the sliding controls had broken and it was stuck on full blast. I was glad of the chilly breeze from the wound-down driver's window. There were no turnings off Canal Street, so he and his mates would have to come this way. I squirmed round in the seat to look behind. There they were. Still all together, two by two on the narrow pavement. I could hear their voices. They drew level and I ducked down, hoping that none of them would notice the sound of the engine turning over in a car without lights.

Luckily, at that moment the speeding cars on the far side congealed into a stationary line at some obstruction further up, and the irritated revving and hooting effectively drowned out the noise. I raised my head again carefully and saw that they had passed me and reached the end of the street, where it joins Carpenter Road. There's a mini roundabout where the traffic from the east side of the town comes through on Brinwell. They all waited at the zebra, then crossed together. On the other side, they stood for a moment, then three broke away and set off down Carpenter into town. The fourth man gave a perfunctory wave at his retreating mates, shrugged up the collar of his jacket and turned the corner into Brinwell. As he passed under a street lamp, his hair gleamed.

With a quick glance in the mirror, I slid forward over the junction in pursuit, driving dead slow on side lights only.

Brinwell Road had few houses at this end. It was mainly factories and warehouses, set behind concrete block walls or chain link fences, several unoccupied, plastered with agents' boards and the signs of guard-dog outfits. After the first few hundred yards, where the traffic slowed and backed up for the intersection, impeding my view of the figure walking along on the opposite pavement, and incidentally hiding my halting progress from his view also, there were longer spaces between the homeward-hurrying cars and I could observe him clearly. I pulled in to the kerb.

It was far better than I'd hoped. The ideal place to surprise him. I had rehearsed over and over what I was going to say. That if he didn't leave, I'd use my influence to get him fired. I'd tell the local police he was a convicted armed robber I'd known professionally in London whom I suspected of planning a job here. They'd keep an eye on him then. Make his life a misery. Run him out of town, I shouldn't wonder. If I did it right, it would work. It would be good to put fear into him. If he turned nasty, then I had the car in which to make my escape.

He walked quickly, his hands thrust into the deep pockets of the donkey jacket, not looking around, but eyes downcast to pick out his way, as the asphalt surface was churned up into ruts by heavy vehicles, and the water-filled craters glimmered with reflected lights.

I would let him get well ahead into the most deserted and derelict part of the street, but not out of sight, then I would pull out and roll up alongside. 'Hello, Dad. Time for another little chat.'

There were no pedestrians, and even the traffic had tailed away to almost nothing, as the early rush-hour motorists dispersed from the nearby industrial buildings. There were still a few lights showing in them. I sat gripping the steering wheel, feeling it tremble with the vibration from the idling engine, staring down the straight, wide, empty, dimly lit road at the tall figure hurrying along into the distance.

At that moment, I didn't want to talk any more. I no longer believed in my plan. I hadn't admitted it to myself until then, but I hadn't come after him like this to cajole or threaten. I had come looking for an opportunity. And now it had presented itself.

It would be the matter of a second to swerve the car across the road and on to the pavement, to send his body cartwheeling through the air to smash against a wall or a concrete post, a matter of another second to get back to the proper side of the road, a matter of minutes to be back at the office, having first given the offside of the car where it had impacted a good scraping on the side of one of the awkward ramps of the multi-storey car park.

It would be so easy.

Quietus.

I turned the headlights to full beam and let in the clutch. The car leapt forward with a jerk. I jammed my foot right down on the gas. The engine screamed into top revs. I was doing nearly sixty as I came up behind him.

He turned his head towards the sound. His eyes were wide with surprise as he saw the car veer across the road towards him. He stopped and hesitated, not quite believing what was about to happen, perhaps knowing that to run was useless. One more flick of the wheel and that would be that. His face was as pale as ivory, his eyes blinded, his long-fingered hands beginning to flutter upwards and outwards in a futile gesture of defence, as if it were the white blaze of light itself which threatened.

It looked like supplication.

Four

**GREAT EXPECTATIONS**

# XVIII

'Sarah! What a nice surprise!'

Hearing her voice made me jump. I felt a tingle in my cheeks that I hoped to God wasn't the beginning of a blush. Whatever I'd said to Paul, I'd always dreaded bumping into her like this.

'Hello, Venetia.' I put down the teacup with scarcely a rattle, closed my book and held out my hand. 'I'm having a greedy tea, all by myself.'

'Well done, you. Is it all right if we plonk ourselves on you? I'm with Margaret. Margaret Chamberlayne. You met her at Trevor Chewton's bash, I think? She's fighting her way through now with the tea. Over here, Mags!'

Her powerful voice rang out even over the hubbub, but she was quite unabashed by the swivelling heads at the other tables. We were in Frederique's Tea Rooms – the Fernsford answer to Fortnum's or the Ritz, and not, consequently, somewhere I parked myself except when I needed to feel pampered. I might have known it would have been one of her haunts. She'd hardly go to Hamburger Ranch.

She rapidly emptied her tray of the two plates of cake and cutlery, then went to assist Margaret's wobbling progress through the tightly spaced tables. 'Now, you're China, there. And that's my Indian. And you're the chocolate. And I'm this lovely almondy creamy thing. Now Mags, sit down, dear. I'll get rid of these. You remember Sarah, of course?'

She whisked off to replace the trays on the pile by the counter. Margaret Chamberlayne and I eyed one another for a moment. Then she said, 'Not at the office? Not ill, I trust?'

I treated this arch remark as the most tremendous piece of perception. 'Good heavens, it must show more than I realized. But I'm not ill, just exhausted. I've had the most killing schedule for weeks, Saturdays and even

Sundays. I thought I'd earned a break. So I've taken the afternoon off and I'm going away for the weekend.'

Venetia returned and flopped into her seat. 'What's that? Away for the weekend? Somewhere super? Lucky you. Gosh, I remember when Paul and I could just throw a few things in the boot and up and off. The Lakes. Cornwall. Even Scotland. Now getting away is a bloody military operation. So we hardly ever get the urge to mobilize except for Christmas or the summer hols.'

'Well, I'm not going far. Only Woodcombe.'

Margaret raised her carefully pencilled, seriously plucked eyebrows. 'Really? Do you know people there? That's my part of the world, you know.'

She was so possessive about it, I felt like asking her if she handled the visas. But that was how people like her talked, wasn't it? As if they owned every bloody joint they ever went near. 'You must try my hairdresser, my manicurist, my little man' – they were never full-sized – 'who does my garden.' Bourgeois bitch, as Colin would have said. But I was getting that way myself, and was even proud of it. So I said, 'A friend of mine, an artist, lives there.'

'An artist, how interesting! Who is she and where's her studio? I might know of her.'

I hesitated. I doubted somehow that Caroline's squat was on Margaret's social round. But it wouldn't hurt for her to become known in the kind of society which had real money to buy real art, not just Tretchikoff prints. 'She's called Caroline Denton. She lives and works at a house called Vale View.'

Venetia, who'd been busily digging into her Linzertorte, looked up sharply. 'Vale View? Did you say Vale View?' I saw her and Margaret exchange glances and then they both stared at me.

'Yes, she was a friend of the owner, an elderly lady who died. I met her when I went to look over the place, which was being sold. I, er, had an accident, and she helped me.'

Venetia's expression had quite changed. All the jolly-hockey-sticks schoolgirlishness had been replaced by a shrewd hardness about her eyes and mouth. 'You obviously don't know that I'm well acquainted with Vale View, though not with this Miss Denton. You see, Mrs Kemble was my great aunt, my grandfather's sister. She was a Wooton. She had a life interest in the house under a settlement created by her father. It would have gone to her children, if she'd had any. Now she's dead, it, or rather a share of it, belongs to me. My sisters and I are the only surviving relevant issue. So I'm really quite interested to know where exactly this friend of yours comes in.'

It was all very Fernsford. Was there anyone in the place who wasn't married to or related to everybody else? I should have kept my mouth zipped, and remembered the lawyer's maxim: loose talk costs. Now I'd gone and got a member of the property-owning classes with a pain right in her sporran, the most sensitive part of her anatomy. I put on my most deadpan face. 'Mrs Kemble let her live there. She's going to move out when the place is sold. Didn't Giles Matravers tell you about her?'

'Why would he tell me? I'm only one of his clients. Actually, I suppose I'm not even that, but a beneficiary. Uncle Harold and one of my cousins are the trustees of the settlement. The last thing I heard was that the sale had been put off for "the resolution of site engineering difficulties", whatever that means. I don't suppose you know anything about that?'

I shook my head. 'I'm afraid I can't really discuss it with you. Professional etiquette, you know.'

'You know, but you won't tell. Typical of a lawyer. Margaret, how I miss dear Ralph! It's not the same having to deal with Giles, shrewd though he undoubtedly is. We don't have the same rapport.'

Margaret pursed her thin lips. She'd had a good go at making them thicker with a bright scarlet lipstick. Mistake, darling. 'Better him than that Appleby man. Harold was quite right to take the trust business away. But I'm embarrassing Miss Hartley, taking his name in vain. I do apologize. Look, I really am sorry. As you're going to be in the area, why don't you and your friend come to lunch on Sunday, if you'd like. I have a sort of open house every month. Here's my card. You don't have to decide now. Just turn up.'

Her drawn, sallow face brightened into a smile. I sensed the charm of the woman that she'd hitherto held in reserve. Now, for some reason, she was wheeling it out.

I put the card away in my wallet. 'Thank you very much. I'm sure we'll be able to come.'

I stood up to go, picking up the carrier bag with the new underwear I'd bought from Ooh-La-La in the High Street – a see-through black bra and pants set, and black stockings with lacy stay-up tops. A bit of fun for Paul. As I said my goodbyes, I felt a pang of pity for Venetia. But it was mixed up with other feelings that, if I were honest, I was rather ashamed of. Feelings of triumph that I had taken her husband away from her, that I gave him what he wanted.

I thought as I made my way home in the car how well I had handled that little scene. I had been discreet and charming. I had even been invited out to a posh lunch with the county set. What would Margaret have said if she had known that only a matter of weeks ago, I had so nearly committed a murder?

The fact that I could deal so calmly with such an encounter seemed almost a benediction. It reminded me that today I felt once more in control of myself. That night on the Brinwell Road, I must have been quite mad.

I remembered nothing of the drive back to Lochinvar Road. The next thing I had been conscious of was staggering out of the car and up the front path, my hand shaking so violently I could hardly fit the key in the door.

I had undressed and stood in the shower, trying to wash the memory out of me, scrubbing furiously at myself as if I were splashed with blood. Then I had sat, wet and naked, on the edge of the bed, shivering and sobbing, watching as my hands writhed and twisted around each other as if they were small hairless animals over which I had no control.

What had intervened? What had stopped me from running him down? Was it that, in the glaring light of the headlamps, I saw him so clearly, his face ravaged and hideous, but human like myself, sharing the same blood? Would a flick of a switch have made the difference? Would I, in the darkness, have felt the same urge to mercy? Whatever the reason, I fervently thanked the God I did not believe in for it.

The car had rocked on its springs as I wrenched back the steering wheel. There was a teeth-crunching jolt as the front wheel hit the raised concrete kerb and then thudded back on to the road surface. The tyres screamed, and there was a horrible sort of scuffing noise as their sidewalls scraped along the pavement edge, but I didn't spin out of control or stall. Outside

I heard the sound of running feet, a voice yelling. 'You fucking mad bastard. What the fuck did you think you were fucking doing?' I swung the wheel out and rammed my foot down on the accelerator.

In the rear-view mirror I saw the dark figure standing at the kerbside gazing after me, his hair shining in the amber light.

Whatever the reason I had spared him, I was glad of it. Glad that no matter what I felt from now on, I would not wake – if I ever slept – at the beginning of each day to the thought that I had killed him. For I knew now that his death would not relieve me as once I had thought it would. He no longer had that significance. He was nothing to me. Perhaps in time I could forget his very existence. To have murdered him would have made him a part of my life for ever.

After that encounter, he seemed finally to have left me in peace. Had he known I was the driver? Had that made him more circumspect or even afraid? Was he even now planning his next appearance? Somehow it no longer seemed to matter. I no longer felt that it was my role in life to be my sister's avenger. And she, the gentlest of creatures would, I now acknowledged, have wanted no part in my thirst for blood. I knew now that revenge destroyed the avenger as surely as it did its victim. Malice was corrosive to the soul no matter to what end it was directed. All these things I had been aware of rationally for years. But I'd truly felt them only when I turned the searing headlights away from my father's terrified face.

And what of Josephine? I heard myself repeating Emily Brontë's poem, which I found that I now knew by heart.

> But when the days of golden dreams had perished
> And even Despair was powerless to destroy,
> Then did I learn how existence could be cherished,
> Strengthened and fed without the aid of joy.

That I had not yet learned. I had lived with my fantasy of revenge for so long, mistaking its death-force for life, that I felt bereft over again. It had been my only companion, and now I watched it drift away on an ebbing tide, leaving me alone on a desolate shore.

'Sarah, let's go home. I'm not into this kind of thing. I look all wrong, I know. I'm not me.'

'Nonsense. You look absolutely wonderful. That colour is perfect, it goes with your eyes.'

It was true. She did look amazing. I had never seen Caroline look like that before. It had been a struggle to achieve it.

I had told her when I arrived just before lunch on Saturday that we were bidden to Margaret Chamberlayne's at home in St Oswalds the following day. She had refused point blank.

'I hate going out. I've nothing to wear.'

'I don't believe you. Show me your wardrobe.'

She pulled open the rickety upper doors of an old pine clothes press that stood at the bottom of the ladder up to her sleeping loft. 'There. I told you so.'

It was almost true. On the warped shelves were a pile of denim work shirts, another pile of smocks and sweaters and several pairs of jeans stained with paint or clay or both.

I rummaged around. I found a very crumpled blouse which had once been white, a pair of khaki Bermuda shorts and, at the very bottom of the heap, a package wrapped in tissue paper.

'Aha, what's this?'

'Oh, God, I'd forgotten about that. I thought I'd slung it out. Well, I can't wear it, I won't wear it. It doesn't fit.'

'It feels wonderful, even through the paper. Do let me look.'

She turned away and sulkily started to chip at a lump of stone on her work-bench with a cold chisel. 'You can look if you like, but it's no use.'

I carried it through to the living room away from the dust and mess of the studio.

I put it on the sofa and carefully peeled back the Sellotape-secured folds. Then I lifted it up and shook it out in the light from the window. 'Oh, Caro, it's lovely.'

It was a dress, in a soft, warm material, with a cornflower-blue background and a complex interlaced pattern of golds and greens. The skirt was slightly flared, and there were long sleeves with ruffled cuffs, and a modestly scooped neckline. I held it against me. It was too short and slimly cut for me, but it would fit Caroline perfectly. It might have been made for her.

'Caro, where did you get this? How can you leave it mouldering away in that awful cupboard?'

I went back into the studio, holding it against me, the lightness and the softness making me want to pirouette on the stone flags.

'I'm not going to wear it. I never have and I'm not going to. It isn't me. It's for someone else, someone who never existed.' She threw down the chisel. The steel rang on the paving with an ear-jarring clang. Her eyes were bright with anger, the kind of anger that is near to tears.

'Caro, what's wrong? What are you talking about?'

'It's easy for you, isn't it? To you it's just a dress. You don't have any problems about yourself – in that way, at least.'

'What way? Sexually, you mean?'

'Yes, of course. I mean no one could mistake you for anything but a real woman, could they?'

'I'm not gay, if that's what you're talking about.' I looked at her sharply, then blurted out, 'Are you gay? I'm sorry I don't understand what this has to do with . . .' I ended lamely, feeling how foolish I must look holding the frock.

'No, I don't suppose you do.' She bent down to pick up the chisel and set it back in the rack at the back of the bench. 'It's not your fault, Sarah. It's the way I am. I expect you'll soon get fed up with me as everybody else has. You couldn't have known about the dress.'

I draped the delicate fabric over the back of a reasonably clean-looking wooden chair, admiring the way it hung there. 'Known what?'

'How it brought the thing to a head for me a few years ago. It was a guy at college. He fancied me. He was always pestering me to go out with him. He gave it me for my birthday. He did a sketch of the dress, bought the material and had one of the girls in the fashion school run it up.'

'Wow, he must have been really keen to go to that kind of trouble.'

'You see, it doesn't raise any problems for you.'

I shrugged. 'He might have been a complete creep.'

'No, he wasn't that. He's actually become quite well known. But I told him to get lost anyway. I didn't want him or his dress. A dress! I hadn't worn a dress, not since, not since . . .'

I rushed over to her and put my arms round her shoulders. I felt her shrink slightly under my touch.

'I see, I'm so stupid. Of course it's hard for you to think of yourself as a . . . as a sexual being. But won't you have to come to terms with it?'

'Maybe. I don't know. I'm frigid, I suppose. It's classic Freud, isn't it? Childhood rape leading to a fear and hatred of sex. But it is actually the case that I can't bear the idea of being touched sexually by man or woman.'

'I've never felt the least problem about sex. I enjoy it. Not that that doesn't lead to complications. The last time, I said to myself, no more married men. But what does that leave? Only men who've been married seem to know anything about women. I've had enough of the other kind.'

'You make it sound like visiting a supermarket. I don't like that brand, I'll try this. I don't think you're that shallow, are you, Sarah? You must realize that, after your experiences, you've got the same problems with trust and self-worth as I have. You may not think you have a problem with sex, but, like me, you have a problem with love.'

I blushed deep crimson. 'Okay, you think I'm a tart. I don't have your self-control. But you're not as cold as you think. You kept the dress, didn't you?'

'Yes, but...'

'Well, maybe nothing in life is ever accidental. Come on, try the dress.'

'Turn your back.'

'For goodness sake, Caro!' Then I saw how scared she looked. I lifted the frock from the chair and handed it to her. Then I did as she asked.

There was a scuffling and panting behind me, then a soft slithering.

'You can look now.'

'Jesus, Mary and Joseph! Aren't you a wonder!'

And so she was. The fabric clung to her slim, softly rounded figure. I had never seen her in anything but trousers. She had strongly-made yet slender legs, with beautiful ankles.

I cast my eye over this revelation. As I smiled into her small apprehensive face, I couldn't resist a Rose-ism. 'Darling, what are we going to do about your hair?'

St Oswalds was a couple of miles out of Woodcombe, to the west of the old Bristol road which threaded its tortuous way through the spectacular gorge of the Upper Tarrant.

We drove past a big village green with a verandahed cricket pavilion, and a long, low pub, the Rose and Crown, with wooden benches flanking its porch. This picture-postcard rustic appearance was, as often these days, a bit misleading. St Oswalds had a reputation in Fernsford as the poshest suburb in north Westerset. Well-off Fernsfordians of the professional classes commuted from there into the city. They had modernized and extended the former homes of the country tradesmen and farm-workers to form their bijou residences.

The heavy-timbered five-barred gate was propped open on its treetrunk-sized post and I turned the car into the shingle driveway of the Old Bakery. Opposite was a clapboarded cart shed in which a dark green Mercedes estate car stood alongside a fancy lawn tractor.

I parked the Fiesta in decent obscurity by a stand of evergreens.

It was a fine bright day, with a hint of spring. The pale green plank door under the trellised porch stood ajar. Within was a glimpse of stone-paved hallway. A delicate warm scent of cookery drifted out. I gently tapped the brass clenched-fist knocker.

There was the click of heels on the flags, then the door was pulled wide.

She was wearing a wine-coloured wool dress, at her neck was the glow of what were probably real pearls. Her sallow complexion was slightly flushed. She gave us a smile of welcome and gestured us in.

'Well, hello! How super you could both come. Let me take those coats. It's Caroline, isn't it? And I'm Margaret. I've heard such a lot about you. Tell me all about your work.' She hung my black greatcoat and Caroline's beige Oxfam mac on a rack behind the door and, seizing Caroline by the arm, bore her away, leaving me to follow in their wake.

Margaret's sitting room was wide and sunny, with a low ceiling criss-crossed with massive honey-coloured wooden beams. At the far end was a closed stripped-pine panel door. The wall by the door through which we had entered was taken up by a stone fireplace, in which a log fire blazed, and to one side of which was a black iron latched door, presumably the old bread oven. It seemed odd to think that the local baker had sweated and laboured half the night here. Despite the ancient structure, it had been given a strikingly modern treatment, cool, elegant and minimalist in the manner of one of those glossy magazines, stark white walls, furniture covered in fabrics in pastel shades, bookshelves painted pale aquamarine, the books interspersed with sculptural ceramics in red and yellow.

The light came in not only from the small leaded light windows we had seen at the front of the house, but from three sets of french windows which looked out over a stone terrace and a sweeping expanse of shrub and tree-bordered lawn.

There were three other people in the room, a tall white-haired elderly man in a sports jacket and cavalry-twill trousers, a plump middle-aged female in a tight green suit and a girl of about sixteen, with long blonde hair.

Margaret gathered us together to introduce us. The old gent was Professor somebody or other. The other two were mother and daughter, from the village.

Margaret was still monopolizing Caroline. The venerable geezer, who had risen creakily to his feet to give my hand a tremble or two, subsided into the cushions of the cream corduroy oversized sofa and motioned for me to sink with him.

'What is it you profess, then?' I enquired politely, sitting up demurely, with my skirt pulled down over my knees.

His eyebrows wobbled about a bit at this introit, then the laugh itself emerged.

'Very little, I'm afraid, these days. I'm what they call emeritus. Every so often they wheel me out, meet some dignitaries, that sort of thing.'

I'd been smiling and nodding my head like a good little girl, but I'd been thinking as well. '"Emeritus." That's Latin, isn't it? Sounds like something to do with merit? I bet you're famous, really. You still haven't said what you were professor of.'

'Not famous, my dear. Academic lawyers are never famous.'

'Law? Of course! I know who you are.' The name Margaret had mentioned floated back into my memory, fraught with significance. 'You're Weighton's Law of Real Property. I read your book. It was set, so I had to.'

'I can't imagine that it would be read without compulsion.'

'I didn't mean it like that. You did actually make it interesting.' I paused, wondering whether he had swallowed this fib. But he was smiling, the old bighead. 'Just as well I took some notice because that's how I'm earning my keep at the moment.'

'How kind of you to say that. Ah, yes. Margaret did mention. You're at Ralph's old firm. Dear Ralph. He was one of my star pupils at the university. That is how our acquaintanceship began. When I retired from Oxford, I returned to my roots, so to speak.'

'He was a nice man, Ralph, wasn't he? Everyone speaks well of him.'

'Delightful. It was a great source of regret to me that we lost touch for those years when, so to speak, he exiled himself. And when we did re-establish contact, it lasted but a short time before that dreadful accident. A great loss.'

He was silent for a moment, then recollected himself. 'So you're now in Ralph's shoes as a property lawyer. A lively time to be in that world, is it not?'

'Yes, I'll say. One of our clients is a big housebuilder and developer. He keeps us very busy.'

'Ah, yes. Mr Chewton, I believe. The local man of the moment. How fortunate for men such as he that the wheel of fortune has turned so decisively towards them. I can scarcely remember a time when the mere possession of bricks and mortar has been sought so ... voraciously – and encouraged, one might add, by the powers that be.'

'Do you still get involved in that kind of thing yourself?'

'Yes, indeed. The wonderful thing about academic life is the marvellous contacts you make – rather like politics. When I first left the university, I had many generous offers for my services, but I decided to serve on the board of the Fernsford and Westhampton Building Society, the FernWest we have to call it now, non-executive, naturally. You're familiar with them, of course.'

'Yes, their office is in the same building as ours. A lot of Chewton purchasers go to them for mortgages.'

'Indeed. They are now one of the largest of the second-rank provincial societies. You know, your firm can take some credit for their extraordinary growth.'

'Chamberlayne's? Why's that?'

'Don't you know your firm's history? Ralph Chamberlayne senior was Chairman of the Board of what was then only the Fernsford Building Society. A sleepy, one-office, local society doling out mortgages to its savers when it judged house-purchase appropriate for their moral well-being. Ralph had the vision to appoint the present Chief Executive, Ronald Lambert.'

I remembered the sallow Dracula-type at Chewton's party. 'Oh, yes, I've met him. At Trevor Chewton's party.'

'Really? I wish I had been able to be there myself. I would have had the pleasure of meeting you sooner. But regrettably I was indisposed. A bout of the flu.'

I looked around for rescue, but there was none. At least his nibs hadn't switched to his health. But the bloody FernWest was almost as bad.

'A splendid fellow, Lambert. The ideal man to head the society. Since his appointment, there's been nothing but successful growth: the swift merger with the Westhampton Permanent, the introduction of imaginative new saver accounts, the delayed payment mortgage for first-time buyers, the roll-up payments scheme. Not to mention the engineering of a new corporate identity. The FernWest logo and design scheme is first-class, don't you think?'

I can't say I'd really taken a lot of notice, which was pretty poor considering I passed a FernWest office every day. 'It's green, isn't it? And a kind of leaf?'

'Yes, indeed. A fern, an appropriate symbol of vigorous growth.'

I nodded, vaguely. He reminded me of some of the college tutors. Once you wound them up, they never stopped. I'd always regarded building societies as in the same interest league as table football.

'Fascinating things, building societies, don't you think? They mirror our changing times so well. One of the engines of the transformation of the financial status of everyman. A chap wants to borrow more money for a better house and a better life, let him. If he can afford it, he affords it. If he can't, too bad. Personal responsibility. I've preached it for the whole of my life. Now the powers that be have loosened their bureaucratic controls. It's glorious.'

He downed the contents of his glass and blinked around for more. I grabbed a bottle from the table behind me and glugged some out. 'Thank you, my dear. I envy you, you know. You'll see the final shape of the future, of which I've only helped a bit with the foundations. And you're in the right place. Chamberlayne's. A great firm. I'll mention our meeting to Lambert at the next board.'

I had nodded so much my head felt it was going to fall off. When Margaret came by and shepherded us into the dining room, I almost cheered.

'Lunch is ready. Do come and help yourselves.'

I forgot all about boring building societies as I heaped up my plate with quiche and pâté and salad. I felt quite pleased with myself, chewing the fat, or rather the gristle, with an Oxford professor, with no clangers that I could remember.

'How's it going?' I whispered in Caroline's ear. She'd been finally left alone by Margaret, who'd gone into the kitchen to work more culinary magic.

She actually had a smile on her face. 'It's better than I thought. You were right. Margaret is very interested in the arts. You know she's on the committee of the Woodcombe Festival? It's not exactly Edinburgh, but quite a big deal around here. There's usually a couple of exhibitions. And she has a friend who has a gallery in Hampstead. She says she'll introduce us.'

'You see, I said it was worth the effort. And the hair mousse.'

'Maybe, but I'm still a scruff-bag at heart.'

'That's what I used to think about myself. Now look at me. Knocked 'em in the Old Kent Road!'

We both started giggling. The fat woman turned a disapproving glance in our direction.

There was a choice of fruit salad or cheesecake for pudding and I chose both.

We had coffee in the drawing-room. I got into a conversation with the fat woman, who turned out to be a consultant gynaecologist at the Westerset Royal Infirmary. Close up, she wasn't really fat at all, but big and powerfully built. She had strong opinions about crime and punishment. What else was new?

'It's a pity they ever got rid of the rope. The only thing some of those thugs understand. Don't you agree?'

I started to feel queasy, and it wasn't the fact that I'd stuffed myself. I spoke in my most carefully detached voice. 'I'm no criminologist, but the argument that capital punishment is a deterrent is fairly discredited. Most of the States has capital punishment, and the murder rate is about the highest in the world.'

'And Singapore has it, and the crime rate's one of the lowest. I think you lawyers are too soft-hearted. Now, I know you're going to say what about the medical duty to preserve human life. But I don't find any inconsistency. When a surgeon finds a tumour, she doesn't say, let's give it a second chance to see if it's going to turn non-malignant. She cuts it out. Human society is like a body. You have to get rid of the nasty elements, permanently, otherwise they get nastier.'

I shrugged. 'Lawyers make mistakes. Don't doctors?'

'Oh, that old chestnut! We haven't abandoned the practice of surgery because of a few wrong diagnoses. I used to have this conversation with Ralph. He'd always find some other argument to switch to. Typical lawyer, poor man.'

I was glad of an opportunity to escape the noose. 'You knew Ralph. He's very much around still, isn't he?'

'Yes. You don't forget a man like that easily.' She lowered her voice. 'I was in the hospital when they brought him in that evening. My colleagues did all they could for him. He was very badly smashed up. They never did find out what happened. Ran off the road, you know. So strange. He'd driven that way thousands of times. And he was no boy racer. Far from it.'

I excused myself and went to the loo. As I was coming back down the stairs, I heard the sound of piano music coming from behind the half-closed door of a room opposite. My curiosity got the better of me. I pushed the door gently and slipped inside.

The room beyond was dominated by the shining ebony bulk of a concert grand piano. Margaret sat at the keyboard, the music stand empty, lost in her power over the instrument. I stood behind her listening. Close to, I could feel as well as hear the precisely struck chords as their vibrations resonated from the Steinway like heat.

Suddenly she stopped, the last plangent note seeming to hang in the air. She looked up and caught my eye.

'Don't stop. It was so beautiful.'

'No, that's enough. I didn't mean to abandon my guests. I suddenly felt the need to play.'

'It was the "Waldstein" sonata, wasn't it? The slow introduction to the final movement. You stopped at the point where it starts to gather pace, and sort of slides into the rondo.'

'Yes. How clever of you. Do you play?'

'No. Only the tape machine. You're wonderful. You must be a professional to play such difficult music with such perfection.'

'Thank you. I wanted to be, but I knew I was never quite good enough, and then I was married and ... not that I regret it, of course. There were amateur concerts, charity things. I loved to play for Ralph. The "Waldstein" was one of his favourites.'

I became aware that the room was quite different in style from the drawing-room, the colours more subdued, the feeling more old-fashioned, more masculine. The walls were lined with mahogany bookcases, which were full to overflowing. Modern paperbacks rubbed shoulders with worn leather-bound tomes. There were series of volumes ranked like soldiers in uniform on the shelves. The blue of the *All England Law Reports*. The brown of *Halsbury's Laws of England*. The massive certainties of well-fed men in horsehair wigs.

By the small stone-mantelled fireplace stood a winged armchair with a tattered blue velvet cover, by its arm a round table on which lay a copy of the *Conveyancer*. In the window was a knee-hole desk set with a well-used blotter, a green-shaded lamp and an old cigar drum full of pens and pencils. Drawn up to it was an ancient swivel chair with a collapsed leather seat reinforced with a brown-covered cushion.

I gave her an inquiring look.

'Yes, this was Ralph's study. I suppose it looks a bit of a shrine. Or like something in a birthplace museum. But I couldn't bring myself to change it. I redid the drawing-room the way I wanted it. But not this. All I did was to have the piano moved in here. So I could remember him as I played. Sentimental, wasn't it?'

'I don't think so.'

She pushed back the stool, got up, and carefully closed the cover of the keyboard. I helped her lower the heavy lid of the case.

As I faced the fireplace to do this, I noticed for the first time the portrait which hung over it. It had the dull gleam of an original oil-painting. It showed the head and shoulders of a young man wearing an open-necked white shirt. He was tanned and dark blond, his hair cut short in the style you see in those old ads for Brylcreem. He smiled out at me sardonically.

She watched me as I returned the smile. I turned to her and asked, 'Is that Ralph?'

'No, although there is a slight resemblance. It's his uncle, Edward. Ralph senior's younger brother. Poor fellow. He went missing, presumed killed in action, in Catalonia in 1936. It was only after the war that his death was confirmed and his place of burial established.' She saw my uncomprehending expression. 'The Spanish Civil War.'

'Ah, yes. Of course.'

She looked unconvinced by my pretended recall. 'Edward was with the International Brigade. He knew George Orwell. He was only twenty-five. A tragedy. Ralph used to talk of him sometimes, although he died before Ralph was born. He told me that, in his boyhood, he thought of Uncle Eddie as a stainless hero, the first to see and fight against the menace of Fascism. But not only a man of action, an artist. That,' she indicated the painting, 'is a self-portrait.'

'So he wasn't another lawyer?'

'Oh, no. He was at the Slade, then tried to make a go in London. His father gave him an allowance. I never knew him, of course, but by all accounts he was a quite different character from his brother. Wild, and extravagant, and strong-willed. You can almost see that, can't you, in the picture? He knew that about himself. He was rather a good one, I think. A tragedy that his life was cut short, when he had so much to achieve.'

The catch in her voice showed it wasn't just Edward she was thinking of. I said, more out of politeness than genuine interest, 'Was he famous, then, as a painter?'

'Good Lord, no. He'd hardly started. There are a few things of his in the Municipal Gallery in Fernsford. Landscapes, portraits of his family. He's buried in Spain. Ralph and I visited the cemetery once, just before Ralph died. I remember that he was very upset. That was unusual. I'd never realized that he felt like that.' She stopped her flow of reminiscence suddenly, as if reminded of the circumstances, how she was relating family history to a complete stranger. 'I'm sorry. How boring of me to buttonhole you like this.'

'No, please, don't apologize. It's fascinating. Really.'

'I must get back to my other guests. But I do like the portrait. I like to think of it as another part of Ralph, the part that wasn't his father. Edward, by all accounts, took after his mother. He did have a talent. There's another rather fine picture by him that Venetia has. If you've visited her house, you may have seen it. Her great aunt as a girl in evening dress.'

I nodded. 'Yes, I remember it, although I don't think she mentioned the artist.'

'Odd how we were talking about her the other day, in Frederique's.'

'Were we?'

'Why, yes. Arabella Kemble, née Wooton. It's her portrait.'

'She knew Edward well, then?'

'But of course. Don't you know? In spite of opposition from both families, they were engaged. They were to marry when he returned from Spain. Poor Arabella. In some ways, I think, she never recovered from the shock of his death. That may explain her later eccentricity. What pain there is in love! One day, my dear, you will surely know that.'

# XIX

'That's loopy.'

'I don't think so.'

'But can't you see? You're supposed to be the lawyer. What happened to evidence? What happened to caution? Isn't that what lawyers are supposed to be like?'

'So you've got mixed up with the exception. It's the hair, you see. What can you expect?'

'Don't be silly, Sarah. But you're really not serious, are you? About me being Arabella Kemble's grand-daughter? And this Edward Chamberlayne being my grandfather?'

'I'm completely serious. As for my not having evidence, I may not have got chapter and verse yet, but I've got enough to be going on with. According to the official version, Arabella Wooton and Edward Chamberlayne are engaged to be married. Neither family are very keen on the match – Edward is a bit of an artistic type with no means of support apart from a parental allowance. His father is rich but hale and hearty. I asked Margaret Chamberlayne, and she said that Edward Chamberlayne senior died in 1950 at the ripe old age of eighty. He would have had a long wait for his share of the inheritance. And Arabella's own family fortune, which consisted, in effect, of Vale View, was only a life interest, unless she had issue.

'But, consider what we know: Arabella is the "*carissima sposa*" of an artistically talented man with the initials E.C. In other words they had married secretly – as no one seems to have known about it – perhaps somewhere abroad in 1935. It might even have been Venice, in 1935. He goes away to the civil war in Spain and disappears, presumed killed. What more natural than that Arabella should have got pregnant before he left? They didn't have all the stuff that we do – and maybe she was keen to have a child. She must have been nearly thirty – quite old in terms of a first baby in those days.'

'But you can't prove that they had a child. Never mind that that child was one of my parents.'

'It would have to have been your father. You told me your mother was only in her mid-twenties when your father died. She's too young. He was five years older, so his dates fit. He must have been born in 1936.'

'Yes. But it's still ridiculous. You're basing it entirely on resemblance to me. I wouldn't say either of us had very distinctive features.'

'No. Not entirely. You told me yourself your father wasn't a typical squaddie. He had an artistic streak, didn't he? Did he come from that sort of background?'

'No, my father grew up in poverty, in a miserable home. He joined the army to escape that. He never spoke of his parents. I never knew them. I think they were both dead. He never talked about his childhood or about his brother. The army became everything his own family had never been.'

'Well, then. He could have been adopted. Adopted children often react against their adoptive parents. Arabella might not have wanted the child around. He might have made it more difficult for her to remarry. Doesn't that make sense?'

'Absolutely not. That's the part I find least convincing. The version of Arabella you've given me is not the woman I knew. I can't imagine her having a child, a son, and abandoning him. I told you how affected I thought she was by the fact that she didn't have children. Arabella was conscious of her duty, of doing the right thing. She wouldn't have put him in such a home. For goodness' sake, Sarah. You spring this on me and expect me to be transported by the idea. But the whole thing's crazy. You can't prove it. Why stir up things like this? I don't want to think any more about my childhood than I have to.'

'There's something else. If your father was Arabella Wooton's son, then he couldn't have had a natural brother called Billy. The man who abused you would be no blood relation of your father, the father whom you loved and admired. You said how unalike they were. That's why. Wouldn't that be worth proving? That you didn't share a drop of the same blood?'

For a moment she stared at me, her blue eyes wide and moist with unshed tears. Then she swung violently away. 'Yes, blast you, it would.'

Oh, Christ, I thought, what am I doing, raising the emotional stakes like this? And why? Because I've got a bee in my bonnet and want to prove how clever I am – to myself.

But it wasn't that. I wanted desperately to help Caroline. I knew what she did not appear to realize: that if this were untangled in the way I was suggesting, there would be money for her. A great deal of money. A share of the Chamberlayne fortune, not to mention Vale View. She was the only person I'd ever known who genuinely wasn't interested in money. She might even think the worse of me if she thought that this was one of my motivations. But money and lawyers are inextricably bound to one another. I was certainly no exception. And whatever she thought, money would be something that, in the end, she would be grateful for.

She sat, turned from me, staring at her hands. She'd changed out of the beautiful dress as soon as we got back and was once again in one of her pairs of tattered, clay-stained jeans. Then she got up, went over to Treebeard and caressed one of his smooth limbs.

'You're really serious about this, aren't you? So. You're the lawyer. And the law is about documents. Can't we prove this thing one way or the other? I mean, if you're adopted, aren't there papers or something? Dad would have had something, wouldn't he? Or there are court records?'

I smacked my forehead theatrically. 'God, I'm so stupid. Of course, there is proof. If your father were adopted, there must have been an order of the court. If he weren't, then there would just be his birth certificate. That would show his mother, at least. That would clinch the matter. Perhaps your mother has those.'

She gave the sculpture a last stroke, then moved listlessly to sit in front of me by the stove again. 'Mum doesn't have Dad's papers. I've got them, such as they are.'

'You have? Where?'

'Here. It isn't much. A few old brown envelopes. A few photographs. In the end I never wanted them. I only wanted to get them away from her.'

'Your mother?'

'Yes. When I went away to college, I suppose I must have had a kind of breakdown. In the long vac after my first year, I went home to Southampton and had a horrible row with her. I got out all the hate and anger I'd felt about her in my childhood and never expressed. How she'd brought Uncle Billy into our lives. How she had polluted my father's memory by sleeping with his brother.'

I stared into her face seeing only more of myself, as in one of those fairground illusions where a pair of mirrors in front and behind reflect their own images in endless diminution.

'After that, I went round the house, collecting up everything that was mine. Pictures, books, everything of my childhood. I took all my father's papers, too. I couldn't bear for her to have them any more. I even took his framed photograph from her bedside table. I couldn't understand how she could have that by her, seeing what she'd done. Then I walked out of the house and drove away. I haven't had anything to do with her since.

'I've never even glanced at them, you know. Not once. You may find that hard to understand. But it was enough to have got them away from her. I put them away in a suitcase. I'll go and get it.'

She went through the curtain into the studio and I heard a banging and scraping as she moved things around.

Finally she returned, carrying a small leatherette overnight bag. She put it on the low table and sprang open the lid. It contained, as she had said, a number of brown envelopes. 'There you are. Papers. What you lawyers love to get your hands on. Dig in, enjoy yourself.' She sat back in her chair, furiously rubbing her eyes with the back of her hands and sniffing. She'd drawn up her legs, and curled up in the ramshackle armchair, her face haggard, on which the fresh tears shone in the lamplight. 'Go on, get on with it.'

In the first envelope, there was a bundle of school reports, including a glowing testimonial from the headmaster of Carpenter Road County Secondary School, Fernsford dated 14 July 1951. 'To Whom It May Concern. Thomas Denton is a fine young man who has made the most of his opportunities at this school. He is disciplined and conscientious in everything which he undertakes, and strives to the utmost until the work is complete. He has told me that he intends to make application for a career in the army. I have no hesitation in recommending him in the highest terms to this service or to any other employment to which he may address himself.'

The next envelope contained photographs, snapshots, and others in stiff vellum folders, presumably wedding pictures. I didn't look at these but put them on one side.

The third contained a letter from Colonel Richard Hawley, King's Own Westerset Light Infantry. It was addressed to Mrs Anne Denton and began, 'Dear Mrs Denton, May I, as Sgt Denton's commanding officer, express my sincerest and deepest sympathy and condolences...' I read no more, but put it to one side.

The birth certificate was in the last envelope at the bottom of the case: a narrow pale manila, brittle with age. I gingerly slid out the folded slip of paper, opened it out and smoothed it flat. It had the familiar heading in the familiar red printed lettering.

CERTIFIED COPY of an ENTRY OF BIRTH

Pursuant to the Births and Deaths Registration Acts
1836 to 1929

*Registration District* FERNSFORD

I didn't need any more confirmation but I read the clerkishly handwritten entries with a sinking heart.

Caroline was slumped in the chair, watching me expressionlessly. 'Have you found it?'

'Yes.'

'So, he wasn't adopted?'

'No.'

'So, he wasn't Arabella's son?'

'No.'

'So, that's it then. Bit of a waste of time, your speculations. All your dreams of my aristocracy vanished into thin air.'

'I'm very sorry, Caro.'

'You know, I think it's those Victorian novels you've been reading. *Bleak House*, wasn't it, the last one? Missing heirs and lawsuits and concealed births. Quite why you had to go and involve me in your fantasies, I don't know. Perhaps you're compensating for your own background. You need to accept what you are. Nobody, like me.'

'Caro, please. I've said I'm sorry. Let's leave it. You're right. I've been letting my imagination run away with me – on all sorts of things actually. Perhaps I'm going crackers.'

She yawned. 'I'm going to bed. You should too. You've got to drive back to Fernsford tomorrow at the crack of dawn. Good night.'

She disappeared behind the hanging. I heard the squeak of the ladder as she went up to her loft.

I lay awake in the sleeping bag. I had promised to forget all about Arabella Wooton and Edward Chamberlayne. They were dead, without issue. Caroline's father was the son of Frederick Denton, builder's labourer of 12 Shelley Road, Fernsford. His mother was Edna Mary Denton, whose former name was Hawkins. He had been born on 10 March 1936. All this had been certified by M. Smythe, Registrar.

That was it, then, as Caro had said. Except that there was something a little unusual about the certificate. Although clearly of no significance, it lodged in my memory.

The person who had informed the Registrar of the birth of Thomas Denton was not, as was usually the case in those days, the proud father, Frederick Denton. It was the mother, two weeks after the date of the birth. And the birth was stated to have occurred not at home or in hospital but at the Firs, Welscombe Road, Fernsford, which had been, as Marion Wilde had told me, old Ralph Chamberlayne's address.

I crossed with silver the palm of the gnarled old crone who flogged the *Evening Packet* on the corner of Broad Lea in front of the sheltering portico of Barclays Bank, and got the usual snaggle-toothed grin in response.

I'd got into the habit of buying the local rag. It was something I had realized could be useful to keep up with in a place like Fernsford.

I glanced at the headlines as I weaved my way through the homeward crowds and thought for a moment I had hit a time warp and ended up back in Hoxton.

A typical splash in the *Packet* would be something like 'Council in Cracked Pavement Row'. Today it said in socking great black letters:

MURDERED WOMAN'S NAKED BODY FOUND IN RIVER

It was so untypical, so startling it was compulsive. Instead of stuffing the paper into my case and hurrying on my way, I stopped in the doorway of the Planet Federation building to read the story.

Workmen carrying out routine maintenance this morning on a jetty at the port of Fernsmouth discovered the naked body of a woman trapped below the waterline against one of the piers. The body appears to have been in the water for only a short time. Full forensic tests are to be carried out, but police sources state that she was battered to death with a blunt instrument with such violence that her features were unrecognizable. A sexual motive for the murder cannot be ruled out. The victim had been completely stripped before entering the water. No items of clothing or other personal possessions were found at the scene. Local waterman Emmett Richie, an expert on tides and currents, in an exclusive interview with the *Evening Packet*, stated that in his opinion the body could have been dumped into the Fern at almost any point below the Brinwell Weir and swept by the current downstream until becoming entangled with the wharf. Richie told our reporter, 'She would have maybe been washed loose by the next tide into the Tarrant, and from there into the Bristol Channel. No telling where she would have ended up then.'

The victim is stated to be about 5 feet 5 inches in height, well nourished, deeply tanned with black hair and brown eyes. The only clue as to the identity of the murdered woman is a small, blue tattoo featuring what appears to be a goat on her upper left arm. Detective Chief Inspector Frank Sedgemoor who is leading the enquiry told our reporter, 'This was a savage attack. There is no doubt we are dealing with a vicious killer who may strike again.' He appealed for anyone who had any information to contact Fernsford Central Police Station where an incident room has been set up.

They say that your heart doesn't actually stop when you have a shock, but it bloody well feels like it. My heart has done a fair bit of stopping in its time, so I know what I'm talking about. It did again.

I went all dizzy, and cannoned into someone walking in the opposite direction. He apologized to me with old-world courtesy. 'I say, are you all right?'

I nodded, and staggered on. Men were strange. Some of them bashed you on the head for no reason. Others apologized when they hadn't done anything. A vicious killer who may strike again. Why did the police always say that when they didn't know why he'd struck the first time? Why did I suddenly feel involved? I was wrong. It couldn't be. There must be thousands, millions of average height, black-haired, dark-skinned women around. But the tattoo clinched it. Fernsford was not teeming with tattooed women. That was a metropolitan fad, no question. The distinctive design which had clearly puzzled the incisive minds of Fernsford CID was not a goat, but the zodiac sign of Aries, the ram.

I knew with a sick chill of certainty that the woman in the Fern was Charmaine Potter.

'Are you all right, miss? There's a ladies here down the corridor.'

'No, I'm okay.'

'It's the smell in there. That's what used to get me at first. In the end, though, you can get used to anything.'

'No, really. I'm fine.'

'That's it. Take a seat there. So you are sure it was her, Charmaine Potter. I mean the face was...'

'Yes, yes, I'm as sure as I can be. It's her. I knew it as soon as I read about the tattoo.'

'And you last saw her alive, when?'

'As I said earlier. It was around the end of October. The last lesson before I passed my driving test. I kept ringing her, and getting no reply. Then about a week later I went round to her flat to give her a present, and the woman in the basement told me she'd left, saying she had gone back to London.'

'She may well have done that. She certainly wasn't in the river all that time. Only a day or so at the most by the looks of her. So, if she did go to London, she came back. There must be someone in London who saw her while she was there and might know what she was doing here. We'll get on to the Met. See if they can come up with something. Now we know who she is and what she did, we can talk to the people she might have known in her line of business. If she'd come back from London, perhaps her car is still in the area. Cavalier, you said it was? Colour?'

'Red. I remember the number. I drove it often enough.'

He wrote it down. 'We'll do a PNC check. It'll turn up eventually.'

'She did also talk about a man she moved down from London with, but he'd apparently long gone. I don't know his name or anything about him.'

'Well, we'll jog some memories. There must be loads of people who knew her. Through the driving and so on. Not that any of them came forward, except you. Without your help, we might have been stuck for a while, at least. You must be very observant.'

'Maybe. Perhaps I'm not as unwilling to get involved. But I don't want my name in the papers. The firm is a bit touchy about the wrong kind of publicity.'

'It's a piece of luck your being in the business. I don't have to explain to you how to write your statement.' I reached automatically into my bag.

'Thank you. Chamberlayne's. Mr Appleby's your senior partner, isn't he? I thought so. Well-known to us for his motoring skills, is Mr Appleby. Perpetually in a hurry, which hasn't always helped him to get there any faster, if you know what I mean. Mind you, he does play golf with the Chief. But as I'm sure you're aware, the law is blind as to status.'

I smiled wanly. What was this? A plod with a sense of irony, as well as indiscretion. I'd learn to be more careful if I were him. I'd remember the name, though. DCI Frank Sedgemoor, a good earthy Wes'set moniker.

There was some chilly sunshine as I walked down the front steps of the ugly, modern Fernsford Central Police Station in the redeveloped area on the south side of Broad Lea.

Despite my show of coolness, I had felt the bile rise in my throat when I had seen poor Charmaine's mutilated body. I'd never seen a corpse in a mortuary before. The copper was right about the smell of disinfectant. It would hang in my clothes. I'd have to have them cleaned.

It had been so much worse than the photographs in Hoxton. Her face was an unrecognizable mass of wounds and contusions, hideously swollen, the teeth and jawbone smashed, her eyes burst and missing, only her mass of thick black hair and her dark gypsy skin to remind me of how she had been.

Over the next few days, I looked through the *Packet* for evidence of the progress of the murder enquiry. It was depressingly familiar. 'Investigations were continuing' and 'various leads' were being followed. In other words, they hadn't a clue. Then, 'a man was helping police with their enquiries'. That would be the boyfriend. Predictably, the paper reported the following day that a man had been interviewed and 'eliminated from the enquiry'.

Towards the end of one afternoon, I rang Fernsford Central and spoke to Sedgemoor. Probably because he regarded me as being in the business, he was chatty. Charmaine Potter had a criminal record – soliciting, obstruction, assault on the police. Surprise, surprise. The Met had come up with a lot of information about old contacts. He was optimistic. Then he said, 'You're taking quite an interest, aren't you? Can you think of any reason why someone should murder her?'

I was quite taken aback. 'No, I've no idea, Chief Inspector. She wasn't really a friend, but I liked her. I very much want to see the man who did it caught.'

After I put the phone down, I sat staring out over the rooftops of the city. I had a strange, anxious feeling. A feeling that it was down to me to do something about Charmaine. That there was something I knew but couldn't remember.

But what could I do? The matter nagged at me all day. In the end I packed it in early, and drove out to Fernsmouth. Didn't amateur detectives always start with the scene of the crime?

It was sunny and warm and I played Mahler's First on the stereo with the window down.

Unlike the river, which meandered apparently aimlessly through its flood-plain of flat pastureland, its course edged with willows, the New Fernsmouth Road was uncomplicatedly straight. 'New' as in at least fifty years old. After its brief heyday, the port of Fernsmouth had fallen into decline, and was still declining. Meanwhile heavy lorries thundered to and fro along the crumbling concrete to the Fernsmouth factories, the inheritors of the mantle of the river and the railway.

And how. I jerked the wheel instinctively as a juggernaut, too wide for its narrow lane of the highway, roared past, its slipstream buffeting my flimsy car.

I followed the road out past a dreary estate of semis. The houses ended abruptly. Beyond a flat, marshy-looking field was a brick wall topped by galvanized steel railings. I could see the jibs of cranes and a cluster of long, metal-clad warehouses. The way forward was closed off by a steel pole hung with a stop sign. A brick building to one side bore a notice which read, Port of Fernsmouth No Unauthorized Admittance.

I stopped the car in front of the barrier and waited. A uniformed security guard popped out of the gatehouse in response, like a toy weatherman. He was brushing crumbs off his fancy epauletted jacket. He probably wasn't keen on having his tea interrupted. He was in his fifties and overweight.

I climbed out of the car showing quite a lot of leg and gave him a cheeky smile. 'Hi. Sorry to be late. Sarah Hartley, Chamberlayne's.'

As you might expect, he gave a blank look at this sally.

'What, didn't they tell you? Typical, isn't it? I expect it's too late to check with the office. I bet they've all gone home. Here's my card.' I flashed it at him, but didn't let him take it.

He peered at it doubtfully. 'Solicitor, are you?'

'Yes. My clients want me to check out the site. I expect you read about it in the paper, although, of course, it is highly confidential. You know how it is, I'm sure.' I gave him another warm smile.

'I'm not supposed to without authorization...'

'Come on, now. You can sort it all out tomorrow. Make a report. I don't look like a terrorist, do I?'

He grunted and sucked his teeth for a moment, and grinned. He liked my sense of humour. 'No, you don't, miss. I expect it's all right. No one tells me anything.' He went chuntering back to the gatehouse and a few seconds later the metal barrier rose into the air. I gave him a thumbs-up sign and drove off as if I knew exactly where I was going.

When I was well out of sight of the guardpost, I slowed down to a crawl, looking out for the place described in the newspaper. There was no alternative but to follow the main access road. It led in front of a huge concrete grain silo, under a footbridge and along the deserted quayside of Fernsmouth's enormous dock. It then bent sharply to the right, where the dock ended at a pair of massive steel lock gates, topped by a metal walkway, with a timber and glass cabin for the operator on the far side. A few yards after the turn, further progress was barred by another metal pole. This one had a sign reading RWYC Members Only.

I stopped the car and got out, the chill wind ruffling my hair. I was standing on the bank of the Fern. The sluggish river ran in its channel in the midst of a milk-chocolatey waste of mud and sand, streaked with runnels from streams and drains that flowed from either side and printed with the footmarks of gulls. The far shore was covered in scrubby bushes and trees above the steeply shelving cliff of oozing clay.

The stone quay on which I stood was of similar vintage to the one at Friars Haven, inset at intervals with iron bollards. Fifty yards upstream of where I stood I saw a timber structure which jutted out into the course of the river. It was a pier or jetty. It had to be what the report in the *Packet* had referred to. There were clear signs of building work going on. A stack of timber decking. A pile of aggregate. A concrete mixer. A metal toolstore. A compressor for a pneumatic drill.

I walked past the barrier along the uneven cobblestones, stepping over coils of orange nylon mooring rope. Access to the jetty was denied by red and white plastic boards slotted into the tops of traffic cones. I noticed in one of the clefts a shred of blue and white plastic. I recognized it as a piece of the tape the police used to cordon off what were known in the jargon as incidents.

The workmen had been replacing one of the huge wooden struts underneath the platform. I could see the pale brown of the new oak, and the glint of the not yet rusted coach bolts which secured it. Part of the wall showed fresh stonework and pointing. There was a stack of rotted planks, stuck full of twisted rusty nails which had been removed from the platform and not yet replaced. The structure was supported on blackened timber legs, sunk into the ooze of the channel, each one surrounded by a pool of residual river water trapped in the dimple in the muddy sand created by the swirling of the incoming and receding tides.

Now I had got to this point, the purpose of the structure became clear. On the other, upstream side, the quay followed a steep inward curve, creating a marina for pleasure craft. Listing crookedly on the river bed or bobbing in the river shallows further out were dozens of yachts and cabin-cruisers, attached to mooring buoys lying on the mud, or to the bollards on the pier and along the quay by weed-draped ropes. Directly below me on the ridge of muddy shingle at the foot of the harbour wall were secured the dinghies by which, presumably, the owners of the pleasure craft out in the river got on board when the tide was in.

On the other side of the road, behind me, was a plate-glass and concrete building, with a curved central section, apparently modelled on the bridge of a ship. On top sprouted a crop of metal prongs and masts, and a flat thing that was slowly revolving – radar or wireless or something of that kind. A large and highly polished brass plate read, Royal Westerset Yacht Club. On the first floor, there was a wide balcony, with white plastic tables and chairs, reached from inside the building by french windows, through which I could see lights. I could hear the faint sound of the kind of music played in bars. No one was brave enough this evening to sit out on the terrace, which must have had a marvellous view of the whole estuary. As I squinted up at the windows, I thought I could see a couple of figures looking out, perhaps wondering whether I was up to no good.

What was I up to? God only knew. I had seen the place for myself. What now? Was I hoping to come up with something the police would have missed? It seemed unlikely. No doubt they had thoroughly checked out whether the yacht-club types had seen anything. It was the sort of thing they would do. The killer must have intended that the body be swept into the Tarrant by the ebb, and from there into the Bristol Channel. Instead it had got caught up in the jetty through some chance swirl of the retreating river.

Had the body been dumped here? It seemed a stupid place to do it. The security guard almost certainly logged daytime vehicle movements. At night, the most obvious time, it would be impossible to get in without a special reason. Maybe there were places upstream where a body could be put in the river. I wondered if the police had checked them out.

I realized I had been standing for a long time, looking out over the wintry river. I felt chilled, and not just by the icy wind. I turned and started to walk back along the quayside, casting a final glance at the marina and the rich men's toys littered there. Furthest out in the river was a real beauty, to thrill any weekend dinghy dabbler, a long white powerboat with two huge outboard motors. From the flagstaff on its raked bow hung a blue and red flag. I stopped and stared hard. A blue field with a red C. The Chewton house flag. I strained my eyes to read the name on the side of the cabin. *Catherine*. It was only to be expected. The man who had everything was bound to have a yacht as well. I remembered that he had a private landing stage upstream at Welscombe.

I shrugged my shoulders and walked back to the car.

As I drove home, I wondered why on earth I had been acting like a character in one of those private-eye programmes? It wasn't as if Charmaine was a friend exactly. What was Charmaine to me, or I to her, that I should weep for her? Another woman? I thought again of her battered body. No one should die like that.

I thought back to that conversation I had had before Christmas with her neighbour in Rosary Road. Had the police been to see her? I'd bet she hadn't told them anything. Was there anything to tell? Did she know more about why Charmaine had left? I flattered myself that she would be more likely to speak to me than the cops. I had a kind face, didn't I? Perhaps I would go along for another chat at lunchtime the next day.

Rosary Street hadn't changed. What looked like the same bloke was still tinkering with the same car. Out of one of the houses blasted the same kind of music.

This time, I didn't bother with the front. I went down the broken cement steps into the area, avoiding the pile of dog shit at the bottom. I banged on the glazed door. There was someone at home. A warm smell of fried food wafted through the hole where the letter box had been and I could hear a kid crying. Then a dog started barking.

A face appeared at the window behind the grubby nets, giving me the once over. I saw her behind the door. It squeaked open a crack. 'What do you want?' Behind her the barking and the crying grew louder. 'Shut it, both of you!'

'I can't talk through the woodwork. It's all right. I was here before. I was a friend of Charmaine's.'

'I remember – your hair, anyway. The coppers were round, not long since. Asked me questions about the poor cow. It was on the telly.'

'Please, I'd like to talk to you. Just for a minute or two.'

'I don't know any more than what I told the police. Like I told you before.'

'Please. There might be something in it for you.'

'I bet. Like the fucking coppers, looking sideways all the time they were here. "That's a nice video, Tracey. That's a nice three-piece suite, Tracey. Had 'em long?" Practically asked me for the fucking receipts.'

I dug in my pocket and fished out the twenty pound note I had put there earlier. I flourished it near the door jamb. 'I'm not interested in your furniture. All I want is a quick word about Charmaine.'

There was silence for a moment or two, then a rattle as she took off the chain. The door opened stiffly, scraping on the bottom step. 'Come in, then.' She backed out of the doorway to let me through, holding tight to the collar of a brown mongrel dog, which yelped and struggled in her grasp.

Although it was almost midday, she was wearing a short white towelling dressing-gown. Her legs were pale and mottled blue and red like a supermarket chicken. A child of about eighteen months with a dummy in its mouth, its round eyes bright with weeping, peered at me round them.

She dragged the still struggling animal across the floor. I could hear its claws on the slippery vinyl. With her elbow, she shoved down the handle of a door on the other side, kicked it open, threw the dog inside, and slammed the door shut. The dog whined and scrabbled but, at a shouted threat from Tracey, went quiet.

I stood by the softly roaring gas fire, taking in the piles of children's clothes, the litter of toys, the unwashed dishes in the sink, the potty full of urine, the TV showing some kind of cartoon flickering soundlessly in the far corner. It took me back to Ernest Bevin House, where there were plenty of women who looked too old for their age, like Tracey. There but for ... not grace, but something.

She pointed at the flowery-patterned newish sofa and I sank down into its foam embrace. She pushed the child out of the way and it toddled over to the TV. 'Keep him happy for a bit. Thank Christ the rest of them have gone to their nan's for the day. Do I hate school fucking holidays. Go on, then.' She stared hard at the crumpled note in my fist.

I smoothed it out and laid it on my knee. The smug face of the monarch regarded me. 'I was very upset by Charmaine's death. I saw what had happened to her, you know. I was the one who identified her to begin with. It was horrible.'

'Christ, I can imagine. But I don't know nothing more than what I told you before. She went home to London, back of last year. That's all I know.'

I started to fold up the money. 'I bet the police started talking about your having to go to court to be a witness, if you knew anything. Give your name and address in public. I bet that sounded really scary. Especially if you didn't want someone to know where you lived.'

She said nothing, but I had her attention.

'Me, I'm only someone who had driving lessons. Anything I heard, I wouldn't write down in a black notebook. I wouldn't tell anyone. It would just be woman to woman. So what did Charmaine say when she came back to see you?'

Before she could stop herself, she said, 'How the fucking hell did you know that?'

'I didn't, but I knew Charmaine. She wouldn't have lived in the same house as another woman without getting friendly. Look at me – and I only saw her for driving lessons. And if she came back to Fernsford, as she must have, she would have popped in to see you. And your kiddy, he's wearing a very fancy pair of rompers. Osh-Kosh or Gap, I shouldn't wonder. Just the thing that a generous pal like Charmaine would have brought as a present, if she were in the money.'

'I'm not standing up in no court.'

'Don't worry about that. Trust me. Tell me what happened. I bet you've been wanting to tell someone, ever since you heard about her.'

'It was about two weeks ago. She turned up one afternoon. She looked really great. New clothes, hair-do, the lot. Like you said, she brought some smart gear for the kids. She gave me a fifty note. Treat yourself, she said. Have you come into money, I asked? And she winked and said, You could say that. But I've only just started. I've come back for a top-up. And then she talked about how she was liking being back in London, going out and having a good time. Better than the old days, she said.'

'So had she gone back on the game?'

Tracey gave me another of her looks. 'Are you sure you only had driving lessons?'

'We chatted a lot. Had she?'

'No. She once said to me she wouldn't. Too old, and too many flash pimps more interested in pushing drugs than looking after their girls. No, it wasn't that.'

'So what was it?'

'I don't know.'

'Come on, Tracey. You're not daft. She must have given you some idea.'

'All she said was, "Men. One minute they can't get enough of you. The next, they wish you were on another planet. Particularly when they get respectable. Well, respectability costs, don't it?"'

'Respectability costs? What do you think she meant by that?'

'I think she had hold of some old punter's dick and was giving it a bit of a pull. But he didn't like it, did he? When she came back for more, he did her in. You see now why I didn't let on to the coppers. A right bastard like that, and living in this town. No way am I going to be the one who has to point the finger. I mean he might get here first.'

'So who is he?'

'I don't know.'

'You can trust me, Tracey. Honest. No one will know.'

'She didn't tell me his name, of course. But she mentioned a place she was going off to. Perhaps she was meeting him there. It weren't Fernsmouth, where she was found. It was a funny name, like they are round here. It was Combe something. That was it.'

I made encouraging noises, but Westerset was stuffed with places called Combe Something.

'Then just before she left, she said, "I could tell you a lot of stories about these blokes who are supposed to uphold the law. They're worse than the poor criminals." I mean, she as good as said he was a policeman. And I should talk to the coppers?'

I nodded calmly, trying to control the sudden trembling in my limbs. I handed over the twenty and she stuffed it down the front of her robe. 'You were absolutely right. I should keep stumm if I were you. Forget we ever spoke, eh?'

'So what are you going to do?'

I shrugged. 'Not a lot, in the circumstances. Looks like Charmaine's murder isn't going to get solved in a hurry.'

She looked relieved.

'As I said, I should forget all about it.'

I was going slowly and carefully up the area steps when she stuck her head out of the window. 'That place. I've remembered. It was Combe Ecsipi, or something like that.'

The car mechanic had gone in for his lunch when I walked back down the street, and even the heavy metal had stopped. After the fetid gloom of Tracey's basement, the weak sunshine seemed dazzling, and the polluted city air as fresh as the heights of the Oxdowns.

But I was in no mood to enjoy them. I remembered what Charmaine had said to me the day she had had tea at the flat. I'd brought her luck she'd said. That had puzzled me at the time. It was only now that I connected it with what she'd hinted about knowing Appleby in London. If she'd renewed the acquaintance, that might not have been too welcome to a pillar of Fernsford's insular high society. Tracey might have been right. The old trick she'd been blackmailing who upheld the law: he could have been a policeman.

But he might have been a lawyer.

Hang on, now. Francis Appleby, a murderer? That was ridiculous, wasn't it?

## XX

'Good morning, Miss Hartley.'

'Good morning, Mr Starling-Richards.'

Paul turned to the assembled group. 'Gentlemen – and lady. I think we're all here now. Shall we get on? A few introductions first, perhaps?'

I shook hands and exchanged grunts of greeting with the burly middle-aged men, all wearing yellow hard-hats which gave their business suits an oddly skittish look, as if they were going to a fancy-dress party. There was the contractor's site manager, the man from the planning department, a couple of bods from the highways department, the man from the Fernsford Canal Trust, the structural engineer, the council's estates surveyor.

Then, with the tall and faintly bohemian figure of Paul in the lead, his longish dark hair spilling out of the back of his helmet like a schoolboy's under his cap and waving in the stiff spring breeze, we set off across the site.

It bore no resemblance to the wilderness I had first explored some nine months before. The trees, the undergrowth, the ruined walls and buildings had disappeared. Instead, on the cleared plain there had sprouted a forest of scaffolding, hydraulic jacks and moulding boards in which, like dinosaurs, roamed the massive machinery of the modern construction industry.

We were walking down a man-made canyon. On either side reared walls of rough concrete, hoops and prongs of steel reinforcing bars as thick as my wrist protruding from their tops. The surface we walked on was slick with the grey slurry of Portland cement. Pools of brown water surrounded the bases of giant concrete columns which lined the route like the grotesque stumps of fossilized trees. The air was thick with dust and debris.

Above all, there was the noise. Not one noise, but a whole dissonant symphony of sound, of which a composer could only dream: the bass ground-heaving percussion of pile drivers; the treble scream of a cutting tool; the whine of the cable gear on excavators; the screeching of Caterpillar-tracked scrapers and levellers; the roar of heavy diesel engines; the intermittent shouted instructions of the construction workers; and the clanging and hammering from the riveting guns of the riggers, as steel beams were lowered into position by several tower cranes, one of which, erected for the construction of the great domed central building, was reputed to be the tallest at work in Western Europe.

As we walked, I tried to fit my memory of the site plan to the apparent chaos I could see around me. The wide, newly formed road, with its gentle gradient, was the main vehicle access to the site. It would become a tunnel when the ground-level deck was constructed to cover it, supported by the forest of vast pillars. It would be, according to Paul, the largest underground car park in the UK. The place garnered superlatives wherever you looked. But not only the largest, also the most impressive: the tall shapely columns would give it the shadowy resonance of the ancient mosque, now the cathedral, of the Spanish city of Cordoba.

He'd got annoyed when I said that it sounded a right muggers' paradise. I'd got a stern lecture on how the design would give the lighting a high priority, and anyway it wasn't the job of the architect to keep out the riff-raff. Dear Paul. I sometimes thought he was a bit too idealistic to be designing car parks and shopping centres. Give him a real cathedral to get his teeth into. Unfortunately I couldn't see Chewton or his backers spending hundreds of millions on a palace for priests.

The one thing that was the same on this ant heap was the canal. We assembled on the tow-path and stared at its green wind-ruffled waters. On the other side, the overhanging willows were bright with new leaves, their trailing branches dipped and withdrawn by the gusts like the chilled toes of nervous swimmers.

I willed myself to stop day-dreaming and pay attention. Paul was saying, 'The proposal is that the footbridge should start here, linking on the other side with the resited tow-path and walkway. It would connect with the development at the plaza level. You've all seen the preliminary design. It's in keeping with the style of other similar canal structures.'

There were nods of concurrence. It was my turn to pipe up. 'My client has generously agreed to pay for the design, construction and installation of what will become a public asset, even though it was not envisaged in the original scheme.'

Someone murmured, just loud enough to be heard, 'What a benefactor!'

I ignored it and continued, 'There will, of course, need to be a document confirming the various rights and obligations involved with the Canal Trust and the local authorities, in particular for access to the opposite bank during construction. My firm are in the process of producing a draft which I will circulate for approval by the beginning of next week.'

I liked that. It sounded so clear and efficient, amongst all these ponderous-looking bureaucratic types. They looked like children's story-book elephants, with their big fleshy heads and yellow hats. They hadn't thought to wear sensible clothes, so their dark suit trousers were splashed with mud and cement. Mrs Elephant was going to have a fit when they went home on the range.

There was a bit more pachydermatous mumbling and grumbling. One of them produced a tape measure and waved it around. Another made copious notes on his clipboard.

Finally we were finished and went trooping back through the noise and the muck. I kept at the back, and Paul gradually gave up the lead walking slower and slower until we were together and the rest of the herd were wallowing along several yards in front.

'And how is Miss Hartley, today?'

'I am very well, Mr Starling-Richards. You don't have to rush off now, do you?'

'Well, I've got a lot of things on in the office. What's the alternative?'

'I've got a key. A key to the new show flat in Galleon House, which, as you know, is the one on the end overlooking the marina. Very private. Miranda Bettiscombe will no doubt have pissed off for lunch by now. I thought we might, you know, check out the progress of the building works?'

I got out of the Fiesta. Good. Miranda, the sales rep, had, as I had predicted, gone early for a long lunch. It was a slack time for her. Argosy House, the first phase, had all been reserved. There had been a bit of a delay in releasing Galleon House, as the show flats had fallen behind schedule, so she was finding time for a fair bit of manicure these days, not that there wasn't a regular stream of gawpers to dish out brochures to.

There was the sound of a car, and Paul's dirty white Renault Savanna bumped over the pavé and parked as we had arranged outside the Chewton offices in what was now known as Brigantine House. Fortunately Trevor had gone off to Truro today to tour the Cornish retirement-homes operation and put the fear of God into the regional director, prior, probably, to his eventual execution.

I opened the door into the lobby of the sales office. Paul followed and I locked it behind me. Once inside, he attempted to kiss me, but I gave his hand a little smack and flourished an imaginary fan. 'Mr Starling-Richards, I think you are a little presumptuous. You must be patient. Shall we stroll a little to the upper floor?'

The show flat was warm but smelt of damp plaster. In the main living area, the second fix of the electrics was mainly completed, and the area cleared. The bedroom was full of sheets of plasterboard, sacks of thistle plaster and unopened tins of paint. In the galley kitchen, the units hadn't been fitted, and stood against the wall in their plastic coverings. Trevor would do his nut when he saw this mess.

It certainly wasn't very welcoming. It was a good job I had brought some home comforts. I opened my holdall, shook out the folded double blanket and laid it on the rough chipboard which covered the floor: the specified Scandinavian polished stripwood had not yet been laid.

Also in the holdall was a hunk of supermarket Cheddar, a french loaf, a bottle of Irish whiskey and two plastic cups. I set these out by the blanket.

Paul was watching these preparations in amazement.

'Mr Starling-Richards. It is a little close in here. Would you kindly assist me to remove my blouse?'

'Certainly, Miss Hartley.'

I felt his trembling fingers at my neck.

I flexed my shoulders. 'I find my brassière is a little tight. Would you assist with that also?'

A shiver went up my spine as I felt his hands fumbling with the clasp. Then the tension went out of the material and I slipped it off, letting it fall to the floor.

'Ah, that is better.' I flung out my arms in a balletic movement, feeling the air swirl around my breasts in their unaccustomed freedom. Biting back the temptation to laugh, I pirouetted up to him.

'Mr Starling-Richards. I find I am encumbered by my skirt. Would you be so kind?'

He stooped to jiggle down the side zip. The suddenly limp material swished softly to my ankles. He remained, knees bent, gazing at the junction of my thighs. I took his hands and raised them to my haunches and together we peeled down the nylon of my tights, collecting my pants as they slid over my buttocks.

I hopped back a pace or two, disentangling my feet from my underwear.

Then, quite naked, I danced with myself, twirling and whirling around the room, feeling my heavy hair fly around my ears, as I heard the strings of an imaginary orchestra play the waltz from the *Merry Widow*. Finally I sank, panting, on to the blanket.

'Mr Starling-Richards, you may kiss me if you wish it.'

He certainly did wish it.

'It's so beautiful. It's strange that Gaudi is the only architect I can think of right now who's dared to use unashamedly feminine shapes. Those plastic, almost melting forms of the apartments in Barcelona. Other than domes, of course. Yes, the dome is about as far as my male-dominated profession goes in paying tribute to the uniqueness of the female form.'

I came out of my nice doze and hoisted myself up on my elbows, feeling the rough flooring through the thin blanket. 'What are you going on about, Paul?'

He was kneeling between my spread-apart legs, obviously fascinated by what he saw there.

He rested the heel of his hand on my mound. 'This. The neglected beauty of form that's found here. The whorls, the folds, the crevices, the capacity to swell, to change colour, to exude. I suppose the nearest you'd get is a cave. A sea-cave on some Adriatic shore. Hot and dark and wet, and smelling of seaweed, overlaid with the salt-tang of the sea. Perhaps that's the answer. Architects don't design caves, because, by definition, they don't stand out. They're inward. Secret. Buildings must be statements. Hard, erect announcements of piety or power or wealth. Perhaps that's why domes went out of fashion. It was all towers. Now we're shifting back. More curves, more irregularity, functions exposed. Buildings which hug the ground. Tent-like structures. Feminization and the Post-Modern. There might be an article in that.'

I laughed. 'Is that the definition of the intellectual, Paul? The man who looks at a cunt and thinks of a treatise.'

'Cunt? Is that how you..?' He was almost blushing.

'It's as good a word as any. You're not embarrassed, are you? You've been quite happily staring at me, and building up some theory about my anatomy. It isn't that I mind your doing that. But when I open my mouth, when a coarse flesh-and-blood woman emerges, you go all evasive. Perhaps you prefer me silent. I'm less likely to embarrass you that way.'

'I don't know what you mean.'

'No, you don't. But I'm not entirely a person, am I? A body to have adventures with and in. But you don't share anything with me. You haven't, not since you showed me the plans of Friars Haven.'

'I thought that was how you wanted it. No commitments.'

'You don't understand. Isn't there a relationship in between romantic love and pornography? I know most men seem to function quite happily with that emotional range, but I thought you were different. Now I'm not so sure.'

'I am different.'

'Prove it.'

'How?'

'Tell me something. Share something with me that's important to you. Something you might tell a close friend. Not about us, or sex, but about you. Let me believe you trust me enough to do that.'

'I can't think of anything.'

'You mean you won't. Okay. I'll ask you for a confidence. What do you really think of Chewton?'

'Trevor's a remarkable man. He's going to make my reputation as an architect. He took a chance on me. I respect him for that.'

'Come on, Paul. Save that for the after-dinner speech. Tell me something real. Tell me about what you feel.'

I could see him hesitating. I sat up and knelt facing him. I reached out and took his hand in mine. 'Please, Paul.'

'I despise him. I despise myself for getting mixed up with him. He's a vulgar tyrant. I curse the day I ever sent him those sketches for Friars Haven.'

'But Friars Haven is one project. When it's finished, in what, two, three years, then you'll be free to do whatever you want. Design a cathedral – or a cave. The commissions will flood in.'

'They may or may not. But I'll be bound to do whatever Chewton wants. He'll have priority until I fall out of favour. Then if he has a mind to, he can ruin me.'

'What do you mean? Paul, what is it?'

He was silent for a long time. When he spoke his voice was icily clinical, as if dictating a specification.

'When I sent him my ideas for the Friars Haven scheme, he told me how much he liked them. I think he thought they would reflect well on him. He's got a hankering to be grand, you know. That's why he bought Welscombe House. That's why he goes in for those parties. Well, he flattered me solidly for about half an hour. Then he said, "Of course, for you to get this commission would be a real leg up, wouldn't it? You've not done anything on this scale before. I like to know all about the people I'm working with." Then he opened a file on his desk and started to read. "Paul Edmund Christian Starling-Richards. What a lot of names! This is your life. Educated Eton and Oxford University. Married in London – St Luke's, Chelsea, no less – Venetia Charlotte Amelia Wooton, daughter of the late Lord Wooton of Westhampton, life peer, former minister in the Macmillan government. You moved to Fernsford, your wife's home territory, in 1974. She started a successful restaurant. That was when the glittering progress of your life took a bit of a hiccup, didn't it, friend?"

'What did he mean, Paul?'

'Venetia. She used to drink a fair bit. Running a restaurant, it's an occupational hazard. She'd had a couple of convictions for drink-driving several years before, in London. She used to say that she'd been unlucky and drove better drunk than most people did sober. She and I were driving back from a lunch party. We'd had a bit of a row. She hated being driven, so she insisted on driving, even though she was pretty tanked up. God, I was stupid. I should have insisted. I'd been feeling off-colour and had been on mineral water. But I wanted to avoid another row. We had an accident on the way home. A very serious accident. We skidded on a bend and killed a pedal cyclist. I knew then, with her record, and being drunk again, there was a good chance she would go to prison. I couldn't let that happen. So I moved into the driving seat. There weren't any witnesses. We said that the cyclist had been riding erratically. Swung out on the bend. That was easy to say. He was a ten-year-old boy.'

'Christ.'

'I had a clean record and got off. The police were sympathetic, as I was obviously very upset. The inquest returned a verdict of accidental death. I still remember the faces of the boy's family, staring at me as I left the coroner's court.'

'And Chewton knew about this?'

'Yes.'

'How?'

'Venetia insisted on making a written statement of her involvement – saying I only did it to protect her. It was in case it ever did come out. She sealed it up and gave it to Ralph Chamberlayne, stating it was only to be opened on her instructions. She has this idea that one day she'll own up. I suppose he filed it away. He was killed a month or so afterwards. Then it came into Chewton's clutches.'

'Appleby?'

'That's why Venetia hates him so much.'

'You can hardly go to the Law Society, can you?'

'Every day for the last ten years, I've thought about telling the truth.'

'Maybe Chewton will let you off the hook when you've done Friars Haven.'

'No, he won't. The man likes having people in his power. If he can't dominate you, he'll smash you. Don't get too close to him, Sarah. Don't cross him. He may seem like a caricature of a self-made man but he's much more dangerous than that.'

I reached out and took his hands. For a moment we gazed into each other's eyes, naked and vulnerable in the dusty emptiness of the huge room.

'Why did you tell me that, Paul?'

'Because you asked me to. Because I wanted to. Because I wanted you to understand. About the whole mess. Venetia, me, Chewton, we're locked together. I can't break free. It must make me seem despicable. Weak. Pathetic.'

'No, Paul. I'm not one to make moral judgements. All I know is that you trusted me. I can tell you what I haven't dared to tell you. I love you very much.'

And at that moment I did. How could I not? He had placed his whole future in my hands. In the space of half an hour this afternoon, I'd ventured so far it was too late to pull back. I'd lost my certain foothold on the solid ground of cynical suspicion and fallen into the dark unknown of love.

He threw his arms around me, then drew back to look at me as he felt my body wracked with sobs.

'Why are you crying?'

'Because we've no future. Tomorrow, we'll be back in our separate worlds. You have your work, your children. This is a kind of bubble in time.' I saw the look on his face. 'Please don't deny it. This isn't a romance, remember? This is real. This is what real people do. They compromise. They go on with their lives. They don't die for love.'

'I do love you, Sarah.'

'I told you before. You can't.'

'What do you mean?'

'You don't know who I am, what I am.'

'Then tell me.'

So I did.

\*

I went over to the window, pulled up the venetian blind and stared down into the Horsemarket. It had rained, and the wet street gleamed gold under the lamps.

Paul and I had made no arrangement to meet again. It was best that way. We'd reached a point where we could go no further. But I had watched his face as I told of the terrible secret of my blood and saw no wavering there. Only unalloyed sympathy. As I had with Caroline, I felt the warmth of trust requited, of hope fulfilled.

But life went on. Behind me, my desk was littered with papers, the result of hours of work. It was late again. Why was I doing this? Why, night after night, did I end up in the office, when everyone else had gone home? Home? I didn't have a home. I'd never had more than a bed where I slept. I lived on coffee, sandwiches and take-away food. So much for the healthy diet of home-cooked food I'd embarked on after I'd met Caroline. Away from her influence, I'd reverted to type.

I hadn't seen her since the weekend of Margaret Chamberlayne's party. Neither had we recently had any of our interminable late night phone conversations. I felt a shadow had fallen over our relationship, temporary perhaps, but distressing while it lasted. It was my fault. I shouldn't have insisted on trying to make her the heroine of a missing heiress melodrama. But I'd only done it because I thought she was owed something by somebody for what she'd gone through. I'd only succeeded in stirring up the blackest days of her past. We needed a break from one another. I also had the feeling that somehow the business of Caroline's parentage was not finished, despite her adamant insistence to the contrary. Sooner or later, I was sure that some vital piece of information would come my way. And if it did, I wouldn't be able to ignore it.

I sat down at the desk and shuffled the papers around. Actually one reason I was still here was because I had been 'at lunch' until gone four o'clock. Penny had raised her eyebrows when I'd floated into the office. She had lowered them again quickly when I glared at her and rattled off a stream of instructions about matters to be chased and calls to be made.

Then I shut myself in my room and, with guilty urgency, started going through the pile of messages. Only when I had attended to the urgent but routine things could I get on with doing what I had confidently announced at the meeting that morning was well under way, the document relating to the canal footbridge.

As expected, it was quite a saga, a true piece of Fernsfordian legend. The file on it was bulging already, thus conforming to my own dictum, fat files mean fuck-all action. Appleby, such things being beneath his eminence and in the absence then of an assistant, had delayed doing anything about it. When the pressure mounted from all the parties involved, he finally threw it at me. Which was why I was slaving under a hot Anglepoise on an evening when I'd far rather have gone back to the flat and dreamed impossible dreams.

I wasn't concentrating and hadn't got very far. Now I had hit a problem which I hadn't anticipated. At the Friars Haven end, the Trust had to be granted rights to have the bridge supports on Chewton land. I had thought this would be straightforward but it was not.

Friars Haven had been built up over many years from a patchwork of land acquisitions, some big – the gas-works site, the old dock – some very small – the individual terrace houses of the former Poets' Corner, the warren of tiny streets at the western end of the site, now demolished.

In order to simplify the conveyancing problems of having to deal with dozens and dozens of individual title deeds, the entire site had been registered at the Land Registry in two blocks – the warehouses and marina, and the rest of the land – reflecting the distinction between the residential and commercial conveyancing requirements.

What I had in front of me that evening was a photocopy of the Land Registry document showing the main Friars Haven site. It was so simple that even a non-lawyer could understand it. It rendered the countless bundles of the original title deeds waste paper. There was a plan, with the land edged in red to show the extent of ownership. The owner, Chewton Developments (Friars Haven) Limited was printed on the first page.

Unfortunately, the red line on the plan delineating the Chewton land had a wiggle just where the bridge was going. This meant, according to the architect's drawing that one of the bridge supports would rest on Chewton land, the other would rest on land belonging to someone else, possibly the Canal Trust, as it abutted the tow-path which belonged to them, possibly not. It was impossible to tell from the Land Registry filed plan. What I needed to sort out who owned that land were the original title deeds.

All the Chamberlayne deeds, including the ones I wanted, were kept in the fireproof strongroom in Dead Filing in the basement. This strongroom wasn't as grand as it sounds. It wasn't secured by eight different locks with umpteen different combinations. It wasn't linked by alarm to the police. It wasn't controlled by a time switch. You didn't need a 20mm rocket-propelled grenade and Clint Eastwood to open it. You needed the key that Mr Dyer kept in the old tobacco tin in the top left-hand drawer of his desk.

The general office was in darkness and Mr Dyer's office was locked. I opened it with my pass-key and got the strongroom key out of his desk. Then I hesitated. I was about to commit a capital offence. Appleby had made it, in one of his favourite phrases, 'abundantly plain' that only Mr Dyer was allowed to open and close the safe. He kept a ledger which recorded which deeds were taken out and who had them. Appleby was known to check this regularly to see who was doing what and whether they ought to be. Deeds had to be returned to the safe every night at close of business. If you didn't remember, the Artful Codger chased you and snitched to Appleby and you were bollocked. This had happened to me on a couple of occasions, as I had been brought up in the Pogson attitude to deeds, which was that you left them lying around the office to use as coffee mats or took them home where they were eaten by the dog or peed on by the cat. Appleby ranted and raved and said that if I did it again he would fine me a day's pay. Thereafter I had been a good little girl.

Until today. I sighed. I did so want to resolve the bridge document that night, if I could. But I knew that Appleby would be incandescent if I went opening the strongroom out of hours.

I picked up Dyer's phone and buzzed Appleby's office. No reply. I buzzed the conference room, the library and then Rose's room. Unless he was in his washroom, he was safely out of the building. I buzzed his phone again. Still no reply. He'd gone. I made my decision.

The basement was reached down a flight of spiral stairs behind the lift shaft in the entrance lobby. At the bottom was a steel door, double mortise locked. I opened it with the other two keys on the ring from Dyer's desk.

I closed the door quietly behind me. The room seemed completely dark. As my eyes adjusted I could see that some faint amber illumination came through the glass-brick pavement lights at the Horsemarket end of the room. I fumbled around on either side of the door, and found a line of switches.

The room flickered like a disco as the lines of fluorescent tubes sprang into life. I made my way along one of the corridors between the file-laden dark-green metal shelf units. The strongroom had been built across the back end of the room. A grey steel door with a chrome wheel was set into a concrete block wall. In a movie, this would be when the creepy music would start.

I flipped up the keyhole cover and stuck in the dull phosphor-bronze key. It turned slickly. I grasped the wheel, rotated it anti-clockwise and pulled. Half a ton of door swivelled open under my hand. I threw a light switch to reveal a room ten feet or so square. On similar metal shelves to those in Dead Filing were hundreds of files, bundles and parcels. On the concrete floor beneath the stacks were dozens of black japanned deed boxes and trunks.

I sighed. I hadn't the foggiest idea where to start looking. This was old Dyer's territory. He knew all this stuff intimately, knew where it was without thinking. But when I looked closer, I realized I'd done him a disservice. The bays of shelving had letters and numbers fixed with sticky tape, and pinned on the wall behind the door was a catalogue in his neat old-fashioned cursive handwriting.

Using this, I found the Friars Haven acquisition files in Bay F8. There were dozens of them. I took one down at random. It wasn't the right one, needless to say, but pasted on the inside of the front cover was a very useful feature. Someone, Appleby perhaps, or more likely Rose, had done a key to the whole of the Friars Haven site. Each component parcel of land was inked in on a large-scale plan and given a file number. In the case of the one I held, the appropriate parcel had been crayonned in red as a reminder. All very efficient.

I quickly found the one I needed on the bottom shelf: No. 3/25 Land adjoining the Fernsford Canal – Higgins (Coal Merchants) Ltd. I knelt down on the cold floor and riffled through it. At last I came upon what I was looking for, the original conveyance of the land to Chewton's company. There was a handsome surveyor's plan, on a much larger scale than the one on the Land Registry Certificate, with the land involved coloured pink. There was the boundary with the canal. The reason for the kink in the boundary line was to avoid an oblong hatched black, presumably a building. I peered closer. There was a label in tiny lettering: Boat-store, B.W.B.

Some you had to win. I stuffed the documents back in the file and put it back on the shelf. Mystery solved. The land had to belong to the Canal Trust. It would have been conveyed to them by the British Waterways Board. I sat back on my heels, feeling pleased with myself. I could go back to the office and finish the draft.

I started to get to my feet, but the chill of the place and the awkward position I had adopted had given me an awful cramp. Yelping with pain, I lunged at the metal upright of the unit to stop myself from falling. In so doing, I disturbed the equilibrium of the files on the middle row and one after the other, like dominoes, about half of them tipped over and slithered off the shelf. I managed to grab a few, but the rest spilled out their insides all over the dusty floor. I stood staring at the mess, massaging my knotted calves and cursing pointlessly.

I crouched down again and started to retrieve and reshelve the scattered papers. Several of the files were so old and well worn that the thin cardboard wallets had burst open at the seams and would no longer hold their contents. I should have to take them back up to the office and mend them. If I just shoved them back, old Dyer was the sort of stickler who would notice their state of disrepair and make a fuss about unauthorized entry to the strong-room, to which I should have to own up.

I bundled them into my arms, securing the pile with my chin, and staggered out of the strongroom, blipping the light switch with my elbow. I daren't leave the safe open while I did my first aid upstairs – it would be Sod's Law that at that precise moment a fire would break out – so I had to put the whole lot down while I closed and locked the door. I had to go through this rigmarole again with the basement door and then with the door into reception. Finally I got the old files in a cleared space on my desk, and went to work with the big adhesive tape dispenser and scissors from the post clerk's desk in the general office.

I've never had any talent for any of the traditional intricate and painstaking female skills like needlework or dressmaking, so I ended up taking ages and using yards of sticky tape. Nor would I have received any marks for neatness. If you didn't look at them too closely, though, the repaired slip-cases would pass muster and hold their contents securely once more.

I peeled the stray bits of tape off my desk and junked them, scraped the lank tangles of hair out of my face with both hands, piled up the files once more, collected the strongroom keys and made my way back out into the darkened reception area. I put my burden on the floor to hoick open the spring-loaded door, when I heard a noise on the stairs outside. I looked through the wired-glass spy-panel.

Christ Almighty! It was only fucking Appleby himself, wasn't it?

He was descending from the penthouse floor with a cardboard box in his arms. He was wearing his outdoor coat. He must have come back into the building when I was doing my repair work. He was concentrating on manoeuvring himself and the container down the stairs, so he didn't notice me peering at him. This was as well. It was silly to be acting like a guilty schoolkid, but I didn't want to be caught with the deeds from the safe and given a right royal telling off. Thank God I'd turned everything off and locked up in the basement. What the hell was he doing? Had he gone or was he coming back?

I stealthily pulled open the door, stopped it from banging shut by sliding the files in the aperture with my foot, and crept out on to the landing. I leaned over the balustrade to listen to what was happening two floors below. I could hear nothing, so I slipped off my noisy half-heels and, carrying them in one hand, went on tiptoe down the stairs to the empty lobby. The glass entrance doors opposite the staircase, made mirror-like by the darkness outside, reflected my crouching form, showing how ridiculous I looked. Where was the sod? Had he gone out to his car?

From below, I heard a familiar slamming bang. The door to the basement. He must have taken the box down to Dead Filing. I had no time to reflect on why he had chosen this particular time of night to carry out what was in any event a clerk's function, as his heavy leather-soled shoes could be heard clattering up the bare concrete of the steps.

I didn't wait for his head to appear from behind the lift shaft and spot me, but ran softly back up the cold marble treads to the third floor. Once again I leaned out into the stairwell. This time, I distinctly heard his feet in the lobby. Then, as the lights on the stairs went out, there was the creak of the glass panel as he opened it and the thud and click as it swung to behind him.

I waited for a few more minutes. The fact that he'd turned out the lights seemed to indicate he was not returning, but I wanted to be sure. Finally I breathed a sigh of relief, switched on the lights again, slipped my chilled feet into my shoes, collected the files and returned to the basement. What a farce this had turned into.

I wrenched open the strongroom door and started to put the files back in their right places. To do this I had to read the index numbers on the white pasted-on labels. I had been so busy with the tape upstairs that I hadn't taken any notice of what I'd got. I squinted at the last one. The label had yellowed and the typing had faded. Finally I made out the number and very carefully made a space for it in the correct place in the row. I was about to slot it in, when the name jumped out at me. Elmdale Furniture Factory: P. L. Babbage.

Babbage. That name rang a bell. Chewton had mentioned him in that first meeting at Friars Haven. He'd been Ralph Chamberlayne's client. An important man, Mr Babbage, given that he brought Chewton to Chamberlayne's. I wondered wryly how much he'd taken Chewton for. A lot, I hoped.

I was dead curious. There was something that was beginning to fascinate me about the way in which Chewton had accumulated the land for Friars Haven. I'd wasted so much time that evening, I might as well waste some more. I sat down on the floor with my back against a hefty deed box, set the file on my knees and opened it.

There wasn't much. The land had been owned by Babbage's for over a century. There was a very old manuscript marked Abstract of Title, the summary of deeds and documents of title, and a conveyance on sale by which one Thomas Alfred Babbage – the grandfather – acquired the land for his manufactory from the Fernsford Gas Light and Coke Company in 1879. The land had since been passed through the next two generations by vesting assents from the grandfather's and father's executors. Then Percival Leonard Babbage had conveyed the land to Chewton Developments on 23 September 1976.

I was surprised that the consideration was pretty small even for ten or so years ago. Old Babbage couldn't have been that shrewd a negotiator. Looking at the plan drawn on the conveyance, the land occupied a crucial position in the centre of the western end of the site that Chewton had eventually acquired. Babbage must have known that Chewton had already been acquiring land in the area. I'd gathered from Appleby that he'd started at the beginning of the seventies. Babbage would surely have realized that Chewton needed his site both for his own scheme and to block the existing owners on either side – the Gas Board and British Rail – from linking their landholdings together. By 1976, Chewton's intentions to build a strategic landholding must have become evident, if not to Babbage then to his advisers.

Had old Babbage been out-manoeuvred, negligently advised? Chamberlayne's, in the shape of Ralph Chamberlayne, had been the advisers. Ralph was a nice guy, maybe, but no great shakes as a property lawyer if he hadn't spotted what was going on.

Then I remembered Chewton saying that he'd been dissatisfied with his own lawyers over the Babbage deal. That was why, having met Appleby through the transaction, he'd switched to Chamberlayne's. What had they done wrong? It seemed that Chamberlayne's had been the ones who'd been out-manoeuvred. The only explanation might be that Babbage had had some kind of cash side deal with Chewton, a consideration over and above what appeared on the documents. That way he could avoid capital gains tax. Men handing over paper bags of money at 'pre-completion' meetings had been not unknown in the Vardy offices. Pogson didn't like it, but he'd been savvy enough not to object. But maybe Chewton's lawyers had. So who were these unparalleled paragons of virtue?

I riffled through the documents in the file. There was no tagged or clipped sheaf of correspondence. The only papers in the file were the pre-registration deeds, which would have been sent to and then returned by the Land Registry. The reason for that was, of course, that this wasn't the acquisition file. Chewton's scrupulous lawyers would have kept that, and handed over to him only the deeds of the property he'd bought. Our correspondence would be on the Babbage side.

Now I'd started, I might as well get the whole story. It was interesting to see how these things worked. I went out into Dead Filing, rubbing my rump, numb after sitting on the cold concrete floor. Here, everything was in alphabetical order by client name. I soon found Babbage. It was like the family vault in a graveyard. Here were many files relating to several generations of the Babbage clan. Business deals, wills, tax advice, property purchase. But nothing on the sale of the factory to Chewton. Nothing after a codicil to Babbage's will in 1970.

Odd, that, when everything else about the Chamberlayne system was so organized. I went back into the vault and again thumbed through the file. I found what I had been looking for and extracted it. I smoothed out the crumpled, buff-coloured, folded double sheet. It was the agreement for the Chewton transaction, a standard form Fernsford Law Society contract.

I looked down to the foot of the first page to where the names of the solicitors for each party were recorded. Babbage, the vendor, had of course been represented by Chamberlayne's of 72 St John's Street, Fernsford. Reference R.C. Chewton, the purchaser, was represented by Redwood's of Camden High Street, London NW1.

Redwood's. The idea that they would have objected to a cash-under-the-table deal was laughable. They were the bent firm Pogson had told me about. The bent firm that Walter Appleby had been a partner of. Chewton must have been operating in London. And if Chewton had been a client of Redwood's in London, how could he have avoided knowing Appleby?

I stopped short, stunned by the enormity of the implications of what I had discovered. Chewton and Appleby must have known one another in London, long before they claimed to have met one another in Fernsford. Chewton had lied when he said he'd met Appleby for the first time when Appleby had stood in for Ralph Chamberlayne at completion, because Ralph had been ill. Appleby had told me that the Welscombe transaction was the first in which he'd dealt with Chewton. He was lying too, but it was a different lie. They hadn't got their stories sorted out beforehand.

Why lie about such a matter? Could it be connected with Pogson's hints of Appleby's shady past? Was Chewton part of that shady past? Had Chewton been part of the conspiracy? Pogson had said that the scam involved flat conversions. For that you'd need a builder. And Chewton was a builder.

That afternoon Paul had said that Appleby had given privileged information from Venetia's file to Chewton, for Chewton's advantage. This was one of the worst kinds of unprofessional behaviour, for which he could have been struck off. Appleby would have done that only if Chewton were not just another client but a colleague. A partner in crime.

Oh, shit! What was all this? Was this web of suspicion justified? On the basis of an unsubstantiated allegation by Pogson, I had embroiled two of Fernsford's most prominent citizens, acquainted with the great and the good of the city in a conspiracy – to do what? That was the point, wasn't it? Okay, so they might have known each other in the old days, and might not want that to be known – because, because they were both reformed characters. Give or take Appleby's handing to his old mate the heads of the Starling-Richardses on a platter. Unpleasant, deeply unprofessional, but not actually criminal.

Then I saw the date of the Babbage contract. 9 September 1976. Rose's voice drifted into my mind. 'The eighth of September 1976. Some dates you never forget, darling.' Up to that moment I had forgotten. Ralph Chamberlayne had been dead when the contracts for the furniture factory were exchanged. He had been dead for over two weeks when it was completed.

Chewton had implied that, up to the date of completion, it had been Ralph's matter. Appleby had only stepped in, as was natural, in the place of a sick colleague, for completion. But death was rather more than indisposition, so why describe it as such?

But why the unnecessary lie? To deflect any suggestion of impropriety in the deal? And if that was the intention, then that meant that some impropriety was surely involved.

I stared at Babbage's signature, the wobbly script of an old man between the pencilled crosses which, by hallowed tradition, the solicitor places in the correct place to guide the client. Heart in mouth, I scrabbled again at the file, looking for the conveyance. There again was the same shaky signature between the same pencilled crosses. Witnessed by F. W. Appleby, Solicitor.

We'd had forgery cases at Vardy's, and I knew a little about graphology. One thing I'd learned was that signatures are never exactly the same. But this one was. I looked from one to the other and they might have been carbon copies.

Had Percival Leonard Babbage signed one or neither of these documents? The only person who could truthfully answer that question was Babbage himself. Then I remembered the conversation with the two plods at Friars Haven the day the skeleton was discovered, the day I had recognized my father. They'd talked of an old skinflint murdered nearby. Until now I hadn't recalled his name. It was Babbage. It must be the same man. They'd even mentioned the factory.

Had Appleby and Chewton decided to take advantage of Ralph Chamberlayne's accidental death to get control of land owned by his old client? Had

Babbage been unwilling to sell? And had they been so desperate to secure the land that they had forged his signatures to the documents and then, to keep him quiet, had they...?

Murder? Was this serious? Appleby and Chewton, murderers? Surely this was fantasy. It had to be.

As I slid the papers back into the wallet, another even more fantastic idea floated into my mind. Ralph Chamberlayne's accident had got him out of the way very conveniently if Chewton and Appleby had been planning to defraud and murder his client. Very conveniently. Too conveniently. Had Ralph's death really been an accident?

The basement was unheated, but it wasn't only the cold which was making me shiver. With a trembling hand, I replaced the file on the shelf carefully. Appleby would be bound to notice anything amiss. He'd been poking about down here only an hour ago.

I was about to turn off the lights when I saw that one of the japanned deed boxes on the floor was sticking out from underneath the shelving unit. Had I moved it somehow when I'd been scuffling around after the files tumbled? Concerned, I bent down to push it back into line. It wouldn't budge. There was something behind it. I pulled it out to peer underneath the bottom shelf. Hard against the wall was a cardboard box, the kind that contained photocopying paper. There were always a few around. We used them to store estate documentation. It was the kind that Appleby had been carrying when I saw him on the stairs.

I reached under and dragged it into the light. It was heavy. The flaps weren't sealed, just folded down. I peeled them back. It was full of paper. I scrabbled out a bundle of photocopied sheets stapled together at the top left-hand corner. It was a set of title deeds, together with a summarizing list, which lawyers call an Epitome of Title. Land at Combe Episcopi in the county of Westerset. We prepared such things for all estates which were not registered land. So what had Appleby been working on? I knew of no development at Combe Episcopi, a village a few miles north of Fernsford, not far from the service area on the M39. One of Appleby's little surprises to wrongfoot me perhaps. Games important men play, darling.

This one he wouldn't win. I grabbed the first bundle of documents, wadded it up and shoved it in my jacket pocket. Bedtime reading. Then I thrust the box back into its place and carefully locked the strongroom door behind me.

I crumpled up the paper which had contained the fish and chips and dropped it into the waste-bin. I licked my fingers and dug out the set of papers I'd pinched from Appleby's box. I hoped he hadn't counted the copies. What had the devious bastard been cooking up to spring on me?

I stared in surprise at the latest deed listed on the Epitome of Title. Conveyance made between Barnsbury Investments Limited (1) Chewton Residential Property Limited (2) dated 5 November 1986. What the hell was this? Land bought only last year, obviously being currently developed – otherwise why all these sets of documents? – and no mention of it to me, supposedly in charge of all residential property sales! What was the bastard playing at?

I turned to the site plan included with the conveyance, an extract from a large-scale map with the land edged on the photocopy with a thick black line – presumably red on the original. It was quite a big site – a hundred acres or so. It was on the outskirts of Combe Episcopi, bordering the main trunk road which linked Westhampton with the motorway. The map showed the line of a track from the road. There was a scatter of hatched squares and oblongs – buildings, presumably a farm. Yes, in small italic print, there was a name. Oakdean Farm. I read it again in amazement. It couldn't be a coincidence. This had to be Oak Dean, the development I had seen on Appleby's monitor, the one the anonymous caller had mentioned.

I scrabbled at the rest of the pages. Who were these Barnsbury Investments? From whom had they acquired this land? I thought I'd by now come across most of the development companies operating in this area, but obviously not.

Here it was. A conveyance dated 31 October 1986 by Reginald Thomas Hargreaves, Michael John Hargreaves and Francis Walter Appleby of the one part and Barnsbury Investments Limited of the other part.

Hargreaves? I'd heard of the Hargreaves brothers. Together with, as was not unusual, their solicitor, they were the trustees of the Hargreaves Will Trust, one of the biggest the firm handled, a hangover from old man Chamberlayne's days. The farmland at Combe Episcopi was trust property.

330

The property had been sold out of the trust to a development company. No doubt the trustees congratulated themselves on a good deal. Barnsbury Investments had sold the land on to Chewton, who then proceeded to develop it, with the assistance of Francis Walter Appleby.

All above board, if a little coincidental, provided it was what was known as an arm's length transaction. If there were any connection between Barnsbury Investments and Chewton, then Appleby might be in the firing line for conflict of interest and breach of his duty as a trustee.

Barnsbury Investments? I was sure I'd seen the name before. Then I had it. The brass plate on the offices in St John's Street. The offices that Trevor Chewton had been visiting.

If it was above board, why hadn't I been told anything about it? Why was the computer record of the transactions barred to everyone but Appleby?

Questions, questions. But no answers. Not yet.

## XXI

'What date did you say, duck?'

'September 1976.'

'I shan't be a sec. They're up here, not down in the cellars. That's quite recent, compared with some we get asked for. Started in 1821 we did. Not that I've been here that long.'

I laughed dutifully. She disappeared into the room behind the old-fashioned shop-type counter. I had a glimpse of green metal industrial shelving. More dead filing.

The offices of the *Evening Packet* were in a bow-fronted stuccoed building in Regent's Place in the touristic part of town. I'd taken a wander in my lunch hour and, on the spur of the moment, had called in. Maybe it wasn't so accidental. What did I think I was doing? What did I hope to find in the back numbers of the world's most boring newspaper?

The elderly assistant returned a few minutes later with a hefty volume bound in black leatherette which she thumped down on to the mahogany.

'This is September. Take it over there to look at.' She indicated a table with a sloping top of the kind you see in public reading rooms. 'Be careful. It's a real ton-weight. I'm always on at them to get them microfilmed, but they won't spend the money. Doing research are you?'

'It's for my college course. I'm examining the treatment of national stories in local papers. The date's arbitrary.'

This seemed to satisfy her curiosity. I could feel her watching me as I carried the mighty tome over to the lectern. Then I heard someone come in to order some photographs and she lost interest.

I flipped through the dry, yellowing pages. They might well have been a hundred years old.

There was nothing on the eighth, of course. They'd gone to press long before the accident. Here it was: 9 September.

Tragic Death of Local Solicitor

Only a brief item. Even the *Packet* couldn't milk much out of the story. I scanned the opening sentences. The facts were there as I knew them already. The clear, dry conditions. No other vehicle involved etcetera, etcetera. What else had I expected?

Then I reached the middle paragraph.

> A police spokesman informed our reporter that a green Rover 3.5 similar to the accident vehicle was reported by several persons as being driven fast along the Old Bristol Road at about 8 p.m. that evening. It was likely that excessive speed on a dangerous bend was the cause of t' ...cnt.

The conclusion the alert reader was meant to ... was clear. Except, of course, that speeding did not appear to be an element of the laid-back Ralph Chamberlayne's character. I thought back to what Harriet had said about road accidents. Would stress make you drive much faster and with less care than you did normally on a road you knew to be full of double bends and hairpins? She didn't think so and neither did I. Of course, if the car on the Old Bristol Road was being driven not by Ralph Chamberlayne, but by someone else, someone who habitually drove too fast, then that would explain the discrepancy.

No one had questioned that it had been an accident at the time. No one now had any reason to suspect anything different. Except me.

If Ralph Chamberlayne's client Babbage was, say, being pressured to sell his land to Chewton, then his lawyer would know about it. He might even make a fuss about it. He might even have had a flaming row with Appleby about it. He'd had such a row the night he died. Had he died because of that row? Had Chewton and Appleby decided that the only way to pressure Babbage into selling was to get Ralph out of the way? It would have been so easy for Appleby to lie in wait for Ralph in the gloomy multi-storey car park, on the pretext that he wanted to talk to him again. A matter of seconds to knock him unconscious and drive the car out unobserved. The carpark was a pay and display and the barriers were unmanned. He could stop at a call-box and get Chewton to meet him on the road. They could push Ralph's car through the fence and over the cliff. The perfect crime, unpremeditated, opportunistic.

And that, of course, was the point. I had no way of proving, after the lapse of time that that was what had happened.

I flicked through the rest of the pages looking for the other item. I found it in the issue of 27 September.

### Vicious Murder in Keats Street

The body of Percival Babbage was found today at his house in Keats Street, Fernsford. He had been savagely beaten to death. Neighbours had alerted police when it was realized that Mr Babbage, 72, had not been seen since the previous day. The dead man regularly took his dog for a walk along the derelict canal near his home. From evidence at the scene, it is believed that Mr Babbage may have disturbed a burglar. The surrounding community has been shocked by the tragedy. The victim, a reserved man, who is understood to have had no close living relatives, was for many years the proprietor of the Elmdale Furniture Works, which ceased to trade on his retirement several years ago.

I continued to turn over the pages looking for a follow-up item. I found it in the last edition, of 30 September.

### New Developments in Babbage Murder

Fernsford police today released an artist's impression of a man seen acting suspiciously in the vicinity of murdered retired businessman Percy Babbage's house in Keats Street on the evening of the incident. He is middle-aged, of short, stocky build and dressed in jeans and a dark, donkey-type jacket.

I looked at the picture. It could have been Chewton, but then it could have been almost anybody. Those things were useless. I carried on reading:

Officers are now convinced that the motive for the brutal killing was robbery. Mr Babbage was distrustful of banks and was believed to keep considerable sums in cash in his house. Furthermore, local property magnate Trevor Chewton has revealed that Mr Babbage had recently sold him the former premises of the Elmdale Furniture Factory. Mr Babbage's solicitor and executor Francis Appleby of Chamberlayne's, the well-known city solicitors, confirmed that the proceeds of the sale which Mr Babbage had insisted on having in cash could not be traced.

A cash transaction would mean that it wouldn't show up on the firm's client account as monies received and disbursed. How convenient. That is if there had been any money. Babbage's signature could have been forcibly obtained to the contract and the conveyance or forged at any time up to his death. The dates on the document were arbitrary. Conveyancing documents were always dated by the lawyers. The whole transaction could have been a sham. The firm had held the deeds. It had been only a question of adding a few more bits of paper for Chewton to become the owner. That was what conveyancing came down to. Trust and bits of paper.

Ralph Chamberlayne's file on Elmdale was missing. It might have contained correspondence or notes which indicated that Babbage didn't want to sell. Ralph Chamberlayne was dead. Babbage was dead. The title had been registered, which effectively hid the history of its acquisition. My suppositions were unprovable. The trail was cold. It was the past and who'd care about that?

I was about to heave closed the massive volume, when a voice at my shoulder said, 'Miss Hartley. What a coincidence! But a very pleasant one. Allow me to help you with that.'

A pair of thin hands on gaunt wrists took hold of the bound newspapers and hoisted them away over my head. I looked up at the weatherbeaten walnut features of the Artful Codger.

'Mr Dyer. How nice. You can walk me back to the office.'

He nodded a farewell to the woman behind the counter as we left.

'And did you find what you were looking for?'

'Oh, yes. Just a thing for one of Appleby's clients. A news story about a boundary dispute. Checking the date.'

'They are most helpful to researchers. Some more self-important journals impose fees, can you credit it?'

'Were you looking up something?'

'Not on this occasion. Delivering an article. On the construction of the Fernsford sewers subsequent to the Public Health Act of 1875. It will be published in next Friday's edition.'

'I'll watch out for it. By the way, I've been meaning to ask you. I'd be very honoured if you'd come to tea on Sunday. We could have a lovely chat about the past.'

He blushed and smiled. 'Oh, Miss Hartley. Thank you, that is most kind. It would be a great pleasure.'

The beam stayed on his wizened face all the way back to the Horsemarket.

'These are lovely. I'll just put them in water.' I bore the bunch of daffodils off to the kitchenette, hastily tipped the milk out of its jug back into the bottle, rinsed it out, filled it with water and stuck the flowers into it. Fortunately it didn't look too much unlike a vase. I didn't want to hurt the old boy's feelings.

I came back into the front room and stuck the floral display on the table in the window. The afternoon sun made the yellow trumpets gleam. In the clear light, I saw that they had long orange stamens in their throats, heavily tipped with dusty pollen like miniature cotton buds.

'They're very beautiful,' I said, and this time I meant it. I was quite touched. When was the last time anyone had brought me flowers? Had anyone ever brought me flowers?

He stood up when I returned. '"Fair daffodils which come before the swallow dares and take the winds of March with beauty." They are a lovely flower, and this year they seem earlier than ever. Even in my humble plot, they are in profusion. Not quite "ten thousand at a glance", but a goodly number. My late wife, my Anne, did so love spring flowers.'

'Do sit down, Mr Dyer. That chair there is more comfortable than it looks. And please, can I call you something other than Mr Dyer. In the office it's okay, but here...'

'Of course, Miss, er, Sarah. My parents, God rest their souls, called me Cedric. Although of undoubtedly ancient lineage, it is nowadays thought very old-fashioned and even comical. But Cedric I am, and therefore Cedric I must be.'

'That's fine with me. Now, Cedric, some tea?'

'That would be very acceptable.'

'I'll just put the kettle on. Please, don't get up again. I shan't be a sec. It's Earl Grey, is that all right?'

'My most favourite.'

I breathed a silent sigh of relief. My Sunday tea party was going well.

'More cake? Or there are these chocolate biscuits?'

'The cake is delicious, but I have eaten two slices already. An elegant sufficiency, as my mother used to say. Another cup of tea would be most welcome, however.'

I did the honours and cut myself another slice of cake. I had asked the woman in the shop. 'You can't go wrong with a nice Madeira, that's what I say.' I wasn't much of a cake eater myself, but it seemed to have gone down with his nibs all right. He looked positively beatific, with the evening sun lighting up the fluff of white hairs on either side of his bald pate like a halo. Now he was all relaxed, and I'd got the mechanics of the meal successfully concluded without spilling or breaking anything, or saying anything crass, it was time to get down to brass tacks. In the nicest possible way, he was going to have to sing for his supper.

I put down my cup, and I noticed that my hand shook slightly. 'Cedric, I'm really enjoying those pamphlets you lent me. I'm on the one about the old railway, the Fernsford and Westhampton. It must have taken you ages to research it.'

'I suppose if one totted up the hours I spent delving into that and many other matters, it might produce a very astonishing figure. The history of Fernsford has been my hobby – you could say my passion – for fifty years.

You could say that I'm practically history myself. That's the extraordinary thing, isn't it? The way that we can never fully record anything, because in the time that it takes to record it, yet more events have occurred. It is the dilemma of Tristram Shandy, you may recall. My lifetime, if not my life, has been crowded with incident.'

I could see this was going to be a long haul. Who the hell was Tristram Shandy? 'But what about Chamberlayne's? A lot's happened there, hasn't it? With your interest in history, you could do something really interesting on the firm, couldn't you? Social changes, changes in the law, all the characters who've been clients or partners over the years – it could be really interesting.'

He sighed and took another sip of tea. 'You reflect my own feelings. Some years ago, I did make preliminary moves, collected some material. I thought it might make an attractive handbook. Useful as part of the publicity "package", as I believe the term is, which the modern business, even the solicitor's practice, finds indispensable. I thought that the relative antiquity of the firm might be seen as an advantage – to be seen to be solid and long-established. But regrettably it did not earn the support of Mr ... the partners. Not that I was requesting payment for the actual work – I was intending to do that in the leisure hours which I have in abundance. But I was told that the firm and its clients were interested in the future, not the past. I did not presume to argue with that judgement. Despite the fact that I know that one of the firm's most important clients is a keen student of local history.'

'Trevor Chewton, you mean?'

'Yes. He has shown a keen interest in the work of the Fernsford Museum Trust – of which I have the honour to be a member. Not only that. He has been a handsome benefactor. The local authority makes murmurs of support, but provides little money. A shortsighted view, given the growing importance of tourism.'

I took advantage of his next sip of tea to jump in. 'But you did start to do some work on the history of the firm?'

He hesitated even more than usual before replying. 'As I indicated, the response was not encouraging. It was stated that such investigations might be regarded as impertinent invasions of privacy.'

'So, he told you to keep your nose out? A bit over the top, wasn't it?'

He shrugged. 'Solicitors are keepers of confidences, of secrets. I suppose the feeling was that I might be indiscreet, but that was not my intention. I hope I have by now earned the partners' trust in that respect.'

He had clearly been hurt by the rebuff, particularly as it sounded as if it had been framed in Appleby's special brand of gentle tact.

'Well, I think it's a right shame. I've got dead interested in history since I moved down here. Anyway, it would be a bit like that programme on the TV, *Dynasty*, wouldn't it, being as how the firm was run by the same family for so long?'

'I hardly think so. If there had been such scandalous goings on in the past, then it would hardly add to the firm's reputation. A responsible historian – as I made clear to Mr Appleby – would not in any event interest himself in merely personal matters.'

'So there wasn't anything like that?'

He looked at me narrowly. He might be a bit long-winded, but he wasn't daft. 'It seems to me Sarah that you are confusing gossip with history.'

I took the lofty rebuke cheerfully. 'Well, maybe I'm not unique in that respect. I found what Marion told me about the two Ralphs, father and son, really interesting. You must have known the old man pretty well.'

'I came to, when I had earned his trust. When I joined the firm, in '41, I was fourteen, the most junior of junior clerks. Mr Chamberlayne was one of the prominent men of the town.'

'What was he like?'

'He could seem stern and unbending. He was a man of absolute moral integrity. But there was a lighter side. He loved amateur theatricals. He had a wonderful deep voice. I remember his performance in *The Barretts of Wimpole Street*.'

'Young Ralph was close to his father as a boy?'

'Yes, they were. His mother died in 1949, when Ralph was only seven. He worshipped her. She had never had good health. An irony, considering that she came of such medical stock. She was an Albright, you know.'

'One of Rose's relations?'

'Her aunt. Her father's sister. They were cousins. But Rose is, of course, was, I'm sure she would wish me to emphasize, considerably the younger, her father having married late.'

'Rose never said that she and Ralph were related.'

'She may have seen no need to. Perhaps, like many independent-minded women, she did not wish it to seem that she obtained her place by means other than merit, an unnecessary sensitivity, given her manifest ability.'

'Of course. But eventually Ralph and his father fell out?'

'That is often the way of such things.'

'What did they fall out about?'

'Sarah, why are you asking me these questions?'

'I'm incurably inquisitive, that's all.'

'Mr Appleby finds any discussion of Ralph Chamberlayne upsetting. I'm sure you've gathered that.'

'Well, he's not here, is he? We're in our own time. Come on, Cedric. I'm not asking you as an historian.'

Cedric was not immune to feminine wheedling, I could see that. My skirt had also slipped up my knees a bit and he wasn't immune to that either.

'Very well. But I'm afraid you may be disappointed by my answer. The reasons why the Chamberlaynes had their dispute were never clear. As I said, disputes between fathers and sons are not uncommon. The one may disapprove of the other's choice of livelihood or friends. But that was not the case with them. Ralph was not wild in any sense. He went to Cambridge as his father and his father's father had before him, studied at St Jude's as they had, and joined the family firm under articles to his father. In due course he was admitted to the Roll, and would have joined his father in the partnership.'

'But instead they had a row?'

'A whole series of rows. They culminated in Ralph's resignation from the firm and his departure to London, from where he was posted to Hong Kong. There he stayed until his father's death in 1975.'

'Meanwhile Appleby had taken over the firm?'

'Mr Appleby joined the firm in 1972. By that time, Mr Chamberlayne was finding it harder and harder to cope.'

'So why did he choose Appleby?'

'Mr Appleby was everything the firm needed. Youthful, dynamic, entrepreneurial. In a few years, the firm was transformed. It was an exciting time.'

'He came from London, didn't he? Why did he choose Fernsford? I mean it was a bit of a backwater – legally speaking that is.'

'That I don't know. I am unaware of the circumstances in which Mr Chamberlayne and Mr Appleby first met. He was simply introduced to the firm as Mr Chamberlayne's partner and designated successor.'

'Then Appleby set about changing things? New partners, new clients. Like Trevor Chewton.'

'Yes. Mr Chewton became a client after Mr Appleby joined the firm.'

'That was when he was starting up? He told me Ralph Chamberlayne was acting for the vendor of one of the first big sites he bought at Friars Haven.'

'A not unusual situation. You see the opposite side represented by a firm you consider more competent than those acting for you. Poor Mr Babbage, that was. He was done to death most foully. One of Fernsford's rare, unsolved murders.'

'Old Babbage was done in not long after Ralph's fatal accident, wasn't he?'

This time he gave me a very sharp look indeed. 'That may be the case. I don't recall.'

'Cedric. You're not daft. You saw what I was looking at in the *Packet* offices, didn't you?'

'You told me yourself.'

'I told you a fib. You knew it and I knew you knew it. You're the soul of discretion, aren't you?'

He drank up his tea nervously. 'Miss Hartley, the hour draws on and perhaps it is time...'

'Okay. You don't have lapses of memory. You come from a time when everything was learned off by heart and done in the head. Rose said you didn't need a computer. So you haven't forgotten when old Babbage was killed. You don't forget something like that. Particularly when a property completion involving the dead man is blazed all over the paper and you don't know anything about it.' I was guessing wildly, but even if I were wrong it would provoke a response. I wasn't wrong.

'It was unusual in that Mr Babbage wanted the money in cash. It went straight from Mr Chewton to Mr Babbage. You know these things happen.'

'Yes, of course. But it was more than that. You usually knew about that kind of deal. Appleby would have told you. He didn't have an assistant like me in those days. That time he didn't tell you. Babbage is killed and Appleby says, by the way, Dyer, you remember we completed the sale of his property beforehand. Was that it?'

Suddenly he looked very miserable and very old. 'You don't understand, Sarah. You're young. So very young. I have worked for the firm for my entire working life, apart from service in the Royal Navy in the war. There is such a thing as loyalty.'

'To Appleby? Come off it. And what about Ralph? Didn't you feel any loyalty to him?'

'Mr Ralph was dead. I was employed by the firm. The firm has been good to me. When Anne was dying of cancer, it was the firm who paid for the private nursing which gave some comfort in her final year. It was the firm which paid for the Mediterranean cruise which we took together on the occasion of our ruby wedding. I have been kept on when many firms would have let me go in favour of someone younger and more technically qualified. Besides, I am not accustomed to question the word of a solicitor and my superior.'

I stared at him. 'There was something else. Some other reason you weren't happy with the explanation.'

He sighed. 'Percy Babbage spoke to me on the staircase as he was going out after seeing Mr Ralph, only a day or two before the accident. He was in a rage. He was normally a very taciturn individual. It was in the old offices. They were far more cramped. You bumped into clients far more often. Also they were clients whose families had been with the firm for generations. We used to know one another. Percy said to me, "Mr Dyer, I've told young Mr Ralph I ain't never selling my land to that bastard" – forgive me, that was his word – "Chewton. He's been a devil to good people I've grown up with."'

'Did you mention that to Appleby?'

'No. I've never told anyone.'

'Why did Babbage feel that about Chewton?'

'Mr Chewton had begun buying the houses at Poets Corner, now part of the site of Friars Haven, in the late sixties, mainly from landlords with sitting tenants. They could be purchased for hundreds rather than thousands. By then the area was very run-down. Mr Babbage blamed Mr Chewton

341

for contributing to the decline of the area in which he had always lived and worked. Many of the tenants were elderly. The houses were not all demolished at once. Gradually, though, as the streets were emptied, by death or as they left for homes or places with their children, they were razed. There were rumours.'

'Rumours?'

'Of some of the methods used to persuade the occupants to leave. Of course the law was, in those days, not so heavily weighted in favour of the occupier as it subsequently became. That was one of the reasons why Mr Ralph would not entertain the idea of Chewton as a client. It was the cause of dispute with Mr Appleby.'

'You said it was called Poets' Corner? Weren't there lots of writers there, then?'

He smiled, relieved that we were off more difficult subjects. 'Indeed not. A local in-joke, shall we say? The only poetry of the place was in the names of the streets. Byron Street, Keats Street, Shakespeare Gardens, Shelley Road. I believe Mr Chewton's family lived in the latter.'

'Really? I thought he came from Bradley. Appleby said the Chewtons had a building firm.'

'Yes, indeed. Chewtons had been builders in Fernsford for a hundred years or more. Let me show you. I've got just the thing.' He turned to the PVC shopping bag from which he had produced the flowers and took out a couple of slim pamphlets. 'I brought more of these with me. One of them may interest you in view of your late experiences at Woodcombe. That is, if . . .'

'How very sweet of you. I'd love to read them.'

He was searching through the pages of one of them. I saw that it was entitled 'Fernsford at Work 1815–1914'.

'Here we are.' He passed it to me, his arthritically deformed thumb marking the place. 'The photograph.'

I looked at the grainy black and white image. A group of half a dozen men in workmen's corduroys, waistcoats and broad-brimmed hats, some bearded, some with hands in pockets, others smoking long clay pipes, bearing the slightly foolish grins adopted by those undergoing the new-fangled and bizarre procedure of having their pictures taken, stood around an empty handcart before a terrace of brick houses. Immediately behind them, in the centre of the houses was an arched entrance to what must have been a yard beyond. A board over it read, Chewton & Sons, Builders and Stonemasons. The caption read, 'Labourers at Chewton's Yard, Canal Street, *circa* 1880'.

'It's nice, isn't it? I think the occasion of the photograph was to celebrate the move to the new premises.'

'Canal Street? Not Bradley?'

'No. My understanding is that Mr Chewton was born and brought up in Shelley Road. Not far from Mr Babbage, in fact. He was one of the sons of a factory worker. There were seven children in all. He left Fernsford to do National Service. He did not return to settle in the city until his marriage. I believe he pursued a career in London.'

'I thought you said the Chewtons were old-established builders in Canal Street?'

'I'm sorry, I'm understandably confusing you. Mr Chewton may not wish his family history to be widely known now that he is so successful. But there are no secrets from the historian. It's my hobby to know such things.'

'You're right. I'm confused.'

'It's quite simple. Old Chewton the builder had no one to carry on the family business. He had only daughters. When his eldest daughter Catherine married, he made his new son-in-law his partner and his successor, provided that he changed his name. As fame and the Chewton name are now synonymous, one scarcely hears of his previous incarnation.'

'So what is his real name?'

'It's Denton. He was born William Trevor Denton.'

'Christ Almighty.'

'Miss Hartley, Sarah, my dear, you are most terribly pale. Are you all right? Can I...'

I thought I was going to faint, but I drooped my head, and gradually the humming in my head diminished.

'I'm all right, thanks.' I struggled out a smile. 'It's, you know...'

He went a bit pink. 'Oh, quite, quite. Forgive me for...'

'It's okay. So, our Trevor conceals his humble beginnings.'

'An understandable vanity, perhaps. A characteristic of provincial England. Fernsford is not a melting pot in the manner of London. But life is full of ironies, is it not? The richest man in Fernsford is the son of the housekeeper of the man who previously took that palm.'

'Housekeeper?'

'Why yes. Edna Denton was old Mr Chamberlayne's servant for many years. Strange is it not?'

I nodded.

He took my silence for a hint for departure. He drank up his tea quickly. 'How widely we have ranged. You are a remarkable young lady. I trust, Miss Hartley, that you will respect what I have told you as a confidence. I would not wish the partners to think I had spoken out of turn.'

'You have my undertaking.'

He nodded, relieved. 'You will permit an old man to tender a word of advice? It is simply that old-established firms are privy to many secrets. An untroubled conscience is one that learns to distinguish the matters which are better left undisturbed.'

At the garden gate, he sniffed the air. 'Ah, spring. "In the spring a young man's fancy lightly turns to thoughts of love" – Alas no more. I shall walk back across the park.'

His gait, as he set off down Lochinvar Road, was, for an old man, almost sprightly.

In contrast, I felt about a hundred.

# XXII

'This is an unusual pleasure, Miss Hartley. How can I be of assistance? Let me first of all relieve you of that.'

Giles Matravers took my gold-rimmed bone-china cup and saucer and set it gently down on the silver tray on the mahogany side table by his elbow.

I took a deep breath. 'I have been instructed by Miss Caroline Denton to represent her in the matter of her claim against the estate of the late Mrs Kemble, for whom I understand you act.'

His small eyes behind the square rimless glasses blinked once. Even though his round face displayed no more emotion than if I had asked him for the time, I couldn't imagine that he wasn't pretty amazed. I was still rather stunned myself.

'I see. I don't think I'm acquainted with Miss ... Denton?'

'You are, in fact. You referred to her as the weird girl squatter. She lives at Vale View.'

'Ah, yes. Of course. Now I understand.' The slight tightness in his voice which had accompanied his earlier response disappeared. The guided missile on the horizon was of a known type with which he could deal. 'She was of assistance to you in your, er, little accident. You no doubt feel under some obligation to her. As I told you, my clients have no plans at present to take possession proceedings, but clearly any defence to that action, no matter how eminent the legal representation, is destined to fail. Any permission to occupy the premises clearly ceased on Mrs Kemble's death.'

'You misunderstand me, Mr Matravers. I'm not talking about whether or not she's a squatter. The cause of action will concern her claim to the estate itself.'

He blinked again. The harmless firework had become an Exocet. He smoothly moved to the next stage of counter-measures, to confuse the attack with ridicule. 'With respect, Miss Hartley. If the date had not already passed, I would say that you were having an April Fool joke at my expense.'

I gave him a charming smile. 'No joke, I'm afraid.'

He was beginning to look distinctly less jovial. The moon face, pink and cherubic, was flushed a darker shade. Underneath his bonhomie, friend Matravers had a short fuse, particularly when he thought he was being jerked around by a know-nothing girlie like me. He finally loosed off his own artillery. 'Miss Hartley. I am an extremely busy man. Would you be so kind as to clarify the exact nature of your instructions?'

'The basis of Miss Denton's claim is that she is the granddaughter of Mrs Kemble. Mrs Kemble's son was her father.'

'Son? Mrs Kemble had no children.'

'She had no children by Arthur Kemble. She had a son before that marriage.'

'An illegitimate son? That is entirely preposterous.'

'I never said the son was illegitimate. I have evidence that Mrs Kemble was married before. Miss Denton's father was a child of that marriage.'

He stared at me, weighing my words carefully, probing for the weaknesses. 'That is a most substantial claim. To whom was she married? And when?'

'We're not prepared to reveal that at this stage.'

He laughed. 'Not prepared to reveal? My dear Miss Hartley, that's the worst negotiating position in the book, in your position. You haven't got any evidence. My late client's generosity seems to have gone to Miss Denton's head. I'm only sorry, my dear, that you have become involved. This sort of thing — well, take my advice, it won't do your professional reputation any good, you know. What's more, there's no money. Mrs Kemble's personal estate was minimal. Her husband left her virtually nothing when he died, owing to some unfortunate speculations. Her main source of income was a life interest which, of course, ceased upon her death. She had no other property.'

'Aren't you forgetting Vale View?'

He shot me a swift glance from under his heavy grey eyebrows. 'Vale View was settled land. That was stated in the sale on tender documents which you were intended to read. Do you know what that means? Perhaps they didn't bother to teach it in your law school. Mrs Kemble was only the tenant for life, not the absolute owner. The settlement ended only after her death. The property is distributed to the remaindermen.'

I had a sudden vision of the lecture theatre in the law faculty at the poly, dust motes swirling in the bright shafts of sunlight from the high windows. Blackacre and Whiteacre. The settlor of the trust, S. The tenant for life, T, and the remainderman, R. Colourful characters all. It had seemed at the time like an ancient and fantastic ritual, like beating the bounds or swan-upping.

I said, 'They did teach it, I did bother to learn it, and I did read the documents you prepared. You were bound to disclose the existence of the trust, as any purchaser has to pay the purchase price to the special personal representatives of the deceased tenant for life, not any executors who may be appointed by her will. Of course, the terms of the trust themselves are what they call "behind the curtain". Hidden from the view of any prying eyes. Isn't that the case?'

He nodded, his brow beginning to furrow up in a wary kind of way. Good, I was beginning to get him nervous.

'So, although I don't know what the original terms of the trust were, and you're not obliged to tell me, and won't without your clients' authority, I can still do some guessing.' I wasn't going to reveal the serendipitous inside information I'd picked up from Venetia. 'These things are pretty standard, after all – that's how they manage to teach them in law school, even to people like me. Now, let me see. It's a family trust, on Mrs Kemble's side, the Wootons. I imagine that the original settlor was her father. So he makes a settlement of the Vale View property for his then unmarried daughter – it would help her marriage prospects, no doubt. He had sons, but maybe they were provided for in some other way. So, "To my daughter if she shall attain the age of twenty-one years for her life, then for the lives of such of my other children who shall be living at the time of her death, et cetera", and then? Presumably for their issue absolutely, and if more than one, in equal shares *per stirpes*?'

He sat there without speaking, his chubby face pale, his twinkly eyes gone dull as pebbles.

'But I've missed out a clause, haven't I? Old man Wooton was intending to benefit what he hoped would be Arabella's branch of his dynasty. "To my daughter for her life – and then for her issue absolutely." In other words, if she had had a child, he would have copped the lot – or his child would. It was only if she had no children that the trust went to the rest of the family?'

He gave me the blankest of looks, all pretence of friendliness gone. 'As you say, Miss Hartley, the provisions of the trust are private. I make no comment on your speculations. But, if such were the provisions of the trust – which is not admitted – then your client's claim would rest on her being able to prove that she is the daughter of Mrs Kemble's son. Which she cannot do, as no such person ever existed.'

'Mr Matravers, Giles,' I gushed. 'We are overlooking the person who can resolve the matter.'

'And who, pray, is that?'

'Mrs Kemble.'

He waved a dismissive hand. 'I'm pleased she is not here to listen to this farrago. She would send your client packing.'

'No, she would embrace her. Even from the grave she can speak out. You have her papers. You removed them from Vale View. My client is entitled to examine them, at the very least.'

'She is entitled to no such thing, as you are fully aware, young lady. You're on a fishing expedition. I do not intend to waste a moment longer on this frivolous and vexatious claim. There is, of course, nothing in those papers which would support it.'

'I don't believe you've even looked at them. It would save both sides a great deal of time and trouble if you would agree to my client's reasonable request. I should be very reluctant to have to prevent the sale of the land by registering charges against it, the removal of which might involve your clients in litigation.'

Now I'd really stirred him up. He went quite pink and sweaty. 'Miss Hartley, you go too far. We do not buy off claimants who threaten pointless litigation. Such sharp practices have been, no doubt, honed to perfection in the criminal milieu in which you appear to have been trained. Should you wish to remain in this city to pursue your career, you would be best advised to remember that.'

I gave him a winning smile and spoke very softly indeed. 'Listen to me, you old fart. Listen very carefully. The person who trained me doesn't need any lessons from you in ethics. I'd hoped you were going to meet me on this. Now I'll have to get serious. Remember, I only met Caroline Denton because you accidentally on purpose forgot to mention she was living at Vale View. Just like you forgot to mention the mine shaft I fell down. The mine shaft that made all the difference to the usefulness and value of the site. So let's talk about the Vale View deal. Now there's this silly old condition of the Law Society's Contract that the vendor must disclose to the purchaser all the material facts in his or his solicitors' possession which might materially affect the value of the land. Am I right?'

He was gratifyingly silent, perhaps sensing another missile as yet below the horizon.

'Surveys, for instance. You used a Fernsford firm of surveyors to value the land and send out the documents, not local surveyors who might have had local knowledge. A sale by tender, though? When you invite bids from several parties? You sort of forgot to advertise it very widely. I checked the *Estates Gazette*. No advert. No posters that I saw. No board on the site. Very discreet. Maybe you particularly wanted our client Mr Chewton to bid. He's well known to have deep pockets, even if he's a shrewd payer. I don't do him a disservice if I say he bids first and asks questions afterwards. And in the case of Vale View, it looked risk-free. Firm soil structure, with solid rock underneath. You'd have been at the core-sample stage before the horrible truth sank in. But then, the deal would have been done. No one could have blamed your client or you. You wouldn't have to dust off your firm's indemnity insurance policy. No negligent misrepresentation on your part. A very good deal for your client in the circumstances, even if Chewton hadn't paid top dollar.'

He watched me, pale but composed. The threat was receding. Pogson always said that the best advocates in court didn't go in for rhetorical flourishes in their cross-examinations. When they produced their killer punch, they did it almost imperceptibly, like in those cartoon films when the cat's sliced so cleanly by the circular saw, he thinks he's had a miraculous escape until he falls into two neat halves.

So, I wiped the incipient smile off Matravers's face when I said casually, 'You knew or had constructive knowledge of the stone mine, though, didn't you? No, don't bother with denials. Listen to this.' I fished a battered magazine out of my holdall, thumbed through to the marked page, and read aloud, '"The society had in the last season carried out several explorations in the area, most notably at Woodcombe. The members were astonished at the extent and complexity of the workings. Although much investigation still remains to be done, it is clear that the eighteenth-century miners drove many tunnels and shafts up through the Tarrant cliffs at Woodcombe. It could be said that the hill above is riddled with them. There are very likely to be entrances to the workings in the woods above. Some of the substantial private properties on the clifftop may be built on or near the galleries from which the stone was extracted. In some cases, these may run very close to the surface."' I closed the pamphlet and returned it to my holdall. 'That, by the way, as I'm sure you don't need to be reminded, is an extract from the quarterly report of the North Westerset

Speleological Society in September 1966. There's also a helpful list of the current officers. The Hon. Secretary was one Giles Matravers.'

I wished I'd had a camera to record for posterity the expression on his face.

Now it was time to twist the knife. 'One of the things I learned at law college was that the law functions in this country very much at the sufferance of the people who run it. People expect lawyers to be trustworthy, not to pull fast ones. Now, I daresay that the little passage I've read out could provide the substance for a few days' argument in court. But men of business like our client Mr Chewton don't have time to waste on sophistries. He would take the view, however unreasonably, that you were attempting to sell him a pig in a poke. Once the word got out, then Buckingham's jealously guarded two-hundred-year-old reputation might look a mite tottery. Eh, what?'

He didn't even glance at me, but spoke to the wall as if he didn't want to soil his eyes. 'One of the great virtues of the law is that members of the profession support one another in times of ... difficulty. One day, Miss Hartley, you will inevitably need that support. If you continue to deal with colleagues in the way you have attempted to deal with me, then I can guarantee that that support will not be forthcoming.'

He picked up his gold-handled paper knife and for a moment I thought he was going to chuck it at me.

'Listen to me, carefully. I am not in any way responding to your quite preposterous allegations about this firm's conduct in the sale of Vale View. I never have and never will give way to threats. Frankly, Miss Hartley, I had thought better of you. What little reputation you have so far gained in this city is to your credit. But I am not a vindictive man, and what has passed between us shall go no further. I shall do you the courtesy of treating you as a professional colleague and tell you something which will convince you that your client's claim is entirely without merit. It means I have to reveal matters imparted to me in strictest confidence by a client, the client of whom we have been speaking. As she is dead, the breach is perhaps more allowable, but I do it only because I think it would be in her interests, provided that what I say goes no further than this room. Is that understood?'

'Yes.'

'Some years ago Mrs Kemble visited me in some distress. She said she had something preying on her mind. She told me that in her youth she had been engaged to a young man. They had married secretly in the face of opposition from their parents as he had few prospects. He was killed fighting the Fascists in Spain. She told me that before he left for the Front, they had travelled in Europe. She had become pregnant. She returned to England, to Fernsford, to have the child at the house of the husband's brother.'

I opened my mouth excitedly to speak, but he waved away my interruption.

'Let me finish. As a result perhaps of the trauma, she experienced a difficult labour. But, I regret to say, the child was stillborn.'

'Oh, my God.' I put my head in my hands.

'The reason she came to see me was that she had, understandably, never forgotten this dreadful experience. It had preyed on her mind that as a result of her drugged state – she was very ill and almost died – at the time of the birth, she had never held or even seen the child she had borne. The body had been taken away before she recovered. She never knew, and out of shock and grief had never asked, where the body had been buried. That was why she came to me. She requested me to make discreet enquiries on the subject. Which I did.'

'And what was the result?'

'Inconclusive. The physician who signed the certificate for the Registrar, Dr Albright, was dead long since, and he would have had the business of disposing of the remains. I found no specific records. The practice in those days before the war, when such deaths were all too common, was burial in unmarked graves in plots reserved for the purpose by the hospital. All the relevant records of the Fernsford hospital were lost, presumed destroyed in the Blitz.'

'You told Mrs Kemble that?'

'Yes. She was extremely upset. She said she felt she had never properly grieved her loss. In the course of my researches, I had come across an organization which gives counselling in such situations. I do not know whether she ever went to them.'

We sat in silence for a few endless minutes. I stood up to go. He took my offered hand. 'Thank you.'

I tottered down the narrow twisting staircase of Buckingham's old-fashioned offices, all wood panels and plaster curlicues.

I stood on the pavement, letting the cold air blow through my hair. I hoped the pallor of my cheeks would warm up and my hands would stop trembling before I got back to Chamberlayne's. I had a session with Appleby and I didn't want him to think I was on to something. However, for the first time in my life I actually wished I had had some narcotic to turn to. More than that, I wished I were dead.

Back in the office, I shut my door, having told Penny I was not to be disturbed under any circumstances. I sat down and wrote in longhand two letters.

The first was humiliating, but it wasn't difficult to compose.

STRICTLY PRIVATE AND CONFIDENTIAL. BY HAND.

Dear Mr Matravers,

I wish to apologize unreservedly for my behaviour at our appointment today.

So that no blame attaches to anyone but myself, I wish to make plain that the partners in this firm are entirely unaware of and have no professional liability for the matter which we discussed. The person I purported to represent was also unaware of and bears no responsibility for the action which I took in her name. I freely admit that, whilst I acted in good faith, I was completely mistaken as to the facts.

I accept your generous offer to let the matter rest.

I should add that the facts of the entirely separate matter which we touched upon – and about which I was not mistaken – are not as yet in the public domain, and I see no reason at present why there should be any change in this situation.

Yours sincerely,<br>Sarah Hartley

The second was much more difficult.

Dearest Caro,

I'm writing to you because I can't face telling you in person what a stupid, worthless person I am. I feel so ashamed.

Well, here goes. I didn't drop the business of your being the granddaughter of Arabella Kemble as I promised I would. I found out something that seemed to show that your father couldn't have been the son of Edna and Frederick Denton, despite what it said on the birth certificate.

I marched into Buckingham's, Arabella's solicitors, and made Matravers, the senior partner, give me some confidential information about his client. I can't tell you what he said, but it meant that you couldn't be related to Arabella. It also meant that she hadn't abandoned her child in the way I wrongly and callously made out.

I feel so sorry for having involved you in my foolish behaviour. My only excuse is that I did think I was helping you. I don't know whether you twigged at all – you're so uninterested in that kind of thing – but there was money involved. A lot. But all hope of that has gone. It wasn't just the money, though. I couldn't bear the idea that you might have been cheated as well. I wanted to get back your inheritance to make up for all the rest.

Part of being a lawyer for me was this idea of righting wrongs. I got that from all the movies I watched when I was a kid. Even after my recent experiences, I can't quite shake off the idea. The law has got to be about justice, otherwise we might as well go home.

My misguided meddling has got me into some other pickles you don't know about. The only good thing about Fernsford was meeting you. Now I've messed that up. I'm seriously thinking about leaving, going back to London, perhaps.

I hope you can forgive me.

Love,
Sarah

I addressed the envelope and stuck down the flap. Should I have told her about Billy Denton's new identity? What good would it have done for her to know that the man who had abused her was a pillar of the community? She was hardly likely to find out accidentally. She read no newspapers and watched no TV. One day, perhaps, I could tell her, but not yet. I couldn't risk any more mistakes.

I had thought I had been so clever. When old Dyer told me that Trevor Chewton and Uncle Billy Denton were one and the same man, the odd feeling I had had about Caro's father's birth certificate was justified.

Billy and Thomas Denton were supposed to be brothers. Billy must have been born on or around 10 December 1936. I knew that for certain, as I had attended his fiftieth birthday party on that date last year. Yet Thomas's birth certificate recorded that he had been born on 10 March 1936, exactly nine months previously. Now, I wasn't what you'd call an expert on child birth, but even if that sort of interval between births was technically possible, it hadn't seemed all that likely, even in the days before proper contraceptives. Few women would surely want to have two children one after the other like that. Thomas Denton could well not have been the natural child of Edna Denton.

But now I knew he must have been.

I felt sorry for Arabella. Not only had she lost her husband, she had lost her child. Nor had she had other children. She must have been lonely for so long, as her house decayed around her. Until she found Caroline.

I strolled on automatic pilot along the riverside walk. It was a short cut which led eventually into Fernsbank Park and home. I hadn't come this way for a good while. I rarely left the office before nightfall and it was not a sensible place to wander alone in the dark. On this day, however, I had skipped off after my meeting. I needed somewhere quiet to think.

The walk, after the Jubilee Bridge, becomes little more than a gravel footpath running behind the long overgrown back gardens of the big Victorian houses on the Welscombe Road, with their high crumbling brick and stone walls, in which wooden doors were set.

The river, tidal up to the Brinwell weir, downstream of the Jubilee Bridge, was these days used only by a few pleasure craft ferrying sightseers from the city on river trips to Welscombe Park, or to Fernsmouth and the Tarrant estuary. Cobbled platforms and lines of black rotting stumps on the steeply shelving mud banks, the remains of private wharves and jetties, showed that at one time there had been far more river traffic, for deliveries of coal or other goods to riparian properties. At one of these I stopped, sitting on a low wall, and stared out at the opposite bank.

It was like a bridge to nowhere. As was Fernsford. I picked up a stone and hurled it towards the soupy green water. It fell short and plopped into the soft ooze. It disturbed a party of birds, not gulls but smaller, which had been paddling around on the water's edge. They fluttered around before going back to strutting on their long legs and pecking with their long bills.

The job I'd rashly invested my whole future in was blown. I couldn't go on working for Chewton, knowing what I knew of him. At Vardy's I had worked on the defence of men who had probably murdered or raped – just as I had with Robbie Chewton. That wasn't the same. Chewton's vileness was active, uncontainable, spreading like a great stain. If I stayed, I couldn't avoid being contaminated or compromised.

I remembered Hamlet's vain cry about the world being out of joint. He was dead right.

I turned to find another stone to chuck, and met the face of a man. He had come upon me silently. Now he stood on the edge of the footpath, his hands thrust deep within the pockets of his fawn overcoat, watching me.

It was my father.

He held up his hand, palm outwards. He was close enough for me to see the yellow work callouses at the bases of his fingers.

'Don't say nothing.' His voice was mildly reproachful, like a priest's. 'I know it was you in that car. I recognized the plate. I've been a fool. I hadn't realized till that night that you hated me so much. But you trying to kill me. That was too much. I mean, I know you wouldn't have felt much for a dad who walked out on you, leaving you with a mother like her, in a place like that. You had to do it all for yourself, didn't you? I'm so fucking proud when I see you now, I feel I could burst. That's me in her, I tell myself. But more than that. You've got it all together, haven't you, brains, guts, and a lovely body. I knew you wouldn't take kindly to my coming back, that's why I hung back. But it was more than that, wasn't it? Eh?'

He took a step closer. I'd nowhere to go except the slimy bank and the greasy river. Ahead, the empty unreachable footpath stretched away into infinity.

'The other night I worked it out. I worked out why my clever, beautiful daughter loathes me so much she wanted to run me over. It's because of her, isn't it? Somehow, you know. Some fucking way you fucking know.' His voice was becoming louder and less controlled, and he paced up and down on the footpath, stamping his shiny black brogues into the loose damp shingle.

He gradually calmed down, and stood before me again. 'It is because of her. Because of Josie?'

'Yes.'

'How did you know?'

'I saw you. I came in. You didn't hear me. I saw you. I saw everything.'

'I should have known. I should have felt it. You don't know what I went through. When I realized what I'd done – what the drink, what my ... feelings had made me do. I went through hell. I wanted to kill myself.'

I said nothing.

'You don't fucking believe me, do you? You were only a kid. A bright kid. I had such plans for you. But her, your mother. She tortured me. You surely understand that now. She didn't understand my needs. And Josie. Well she wasn't all there, was she? I mean, she wasn't normal. Not like you and me. She didn't mind what we did. It was only when she said that she was going to tell on me, well, I couldn't have that. But I didn't mean to hit her that hard. I never meant to kill her. I was drunk, I was crazy. She was dead before she went over the balcony. I thought if I made it look like an accident, then everything would be all right. You understand. But I never meant that you should miss out. When Mary Flanagan told me about the school, all you'd gone through...'

I felt the tears bursting from my eyes. So what if he killed me? I couldn't listen to any more. 'All I'd gone through at school? You fucking mad, evil old bastard. I see you murder my sister, and all you're concerned about is whether I got GCSEs. The way you talk of Josie. Not like you and me? No, she wasn't. She was good and kind and I loved her. I loved her and she loved me. You destroyed that love. You destroyed all love. God in heaven, I wish I'd had the guts to kill you that night. You don't deserve to live.' I stood up, and without thinking hurled myself at him.

I jabbed straight for the eyes, just as I had in playground fights, my right hand spread in hard claws, my left grabbing at his hair. He jerked his head back as quickly as a snake and with a similar hiss. As we collided, my hands connected with his neck and tightened around it, my long nails digging into his flesh. For a moment I saw his eyes rolling wide and his mouth drawn open in a gape of pain and anger, then with a roar of pure animal rage, he clamped his arms into the small of my back so hard I thought my spine would crack. He lifted me bodily off the ground and swung me round. I hung on grimly, hearing him start to choke. Then, still holding me, he ran forward and smashed me against the stone wall.

There was a great flash of pain in my head. I let go his throat. He released the bear hug and I fell heavily to the ground.

I lay at his feet, shoulders resting against the base of the wall, dazed and helpless, my legs spread wide, my skirt ridden up to my hips. The power of movement seemed to have left me. Was I paralysed or hypnotized? He stood before me, his face white and his eyes screwed tight, massaging the sides of his neck. There were raw welts where my fingernails had ploughed his flesh.

His chest heaved with the effects of our struggle. He opened his eyes, paler versions of my own. For a second or two they were balefully wide, then the hoods came down.

'I didn't want to hurt you, my darling. You made me. I could have killed you. Don't mess with me, Sarah. Don't ever do that again. Don't you understand? That was, in the end, why I left. I loved you. I wanted you so much. That was why I had to go. I loved you!' His voice was a scream and his hands bunched into fists and rose, it seemed, with their own volition until they smacked into his forehead, once, twice, three times. Then, with that same independence of motion, they descended again and spread into hands once more, the fingers strangely long and even elegant. My eyes and my hands. His blood in my veins. How could I ever forget that? His eyes closed, his body seemed to elongate with the strain within.

Then, suddenly, the fit was over.

'What a fuss we have had, quite unnecessarily. The past, as a famous writer said, is another country. It's time to forget.' His voice was light and whimsical as if we had been involved in a minor dispute which had escalated into confrontation, on, say, the merits of cars or football teams. 'There, now. I was on my way to call at your address, when I came upon you sudden, like. I had come to tell you, that having come into my expectations I would soon be leaving this fair city, and to bestow upon you the parting gift I've so often mentioned.'

I tried to speak but no words came.

'Hush now and listen to what your daddy says. I've finally come into my ... inheritance, so to speak. I had to wait until my old mate Tommy was out, you see. For the beauty of it was, it was in a bank, in a safety deposit box. With two keys. The Bank of the Republic of Cyprus, in Green Lanes, N16, would you believe it! We took it out of one bank and put it right back in another. I've got my share. See my new duds. No more fucking jeans and donkey jackets for Terry Hartley. A week or so, I'll be saying farewell to Friars Haven. I'm in no hurry. It's been a good crib. But I feel like the change. Maybe the Smoke, maybe even the Pool. So, presently, you won't have me around no more. But before that, I had to see you again. Because all them years ago, I said to myself that if ever I came into a little pile, then you'd get half. And here it is. Used notes and quite safe. There's enough to put down on a nice flat – or even a little house with a garden, maybe. The kind of place I couldn't ever provide for you. Whatever – you can do what you like with it. One thing I know is that you'll do better with yours than I shall with mine. I was always easy come easy go with the money. So. Goodbye, Pippi. My love.' He bent down, and to my horror laid his lips against mine.

I tried to withdraw from the violation of his kiss, but I was mute and rigid.

As he stood upright, I felt his hand press into my thighs and I felt something lying in my lap amongst the rucked folds of my clothing. Then I closed my eyes.

When I opened them again, he had gone. I don't know how long I lay there unmoving, watching the bilious tidewater creep up the river bank. Finally I roused myself. I sat up stiffly, my head and neck a fiery agony still. As I got to my feet, using the protruding stones of the rubble wall as handholds, something fell on to the lank turf of the verge.

My father's gift: a thick oblong package wrapped in brown paper and bound with parcel tape.

I picked it up and ripped open one end. There must have been about ten thousand pounds in dirty, creased and crumpled tens and twenties.

I stared at it. More than enough to allow me to stick two fingers up at Chamberlayne's and Fernsford. I could pay off the car loan and the credit card debts, and have my holiday in Italy perhaps, and still have a nice cushion until I found another job. I could get away from the mess I'd made of my life here, the dead-end of my relationship with Paul, and the things I'd imagined I'd uncovered which were none of my business. It was my ticket to freedom.

I hefted the packet in my hand.

The flood tide had by now filled the Fern from shore to shore. It swirled and slopped greasily like washing-up water against the remains of the jetty.

I thought of how this money had come into my hands. My father's skull-like face, grinning as he snatched it from the hands of terrified cashiers or cowed security men, stashing it away as his conscience money. Was this really the price of forgiveness? Of restitution? Was this what Josie's life had been worth?

If I left, would I ever forget what I was leaving behind: Caroline's trusting face, Charmaine's battered body, Ralph Chamberlayne's car smashed to pieces at the bottom of the Tarrant gorge, an old man lying dead in Keats Street?

The money would be soon gone but these bitter reproachful memories would endure.

There had to be a doorway to the secrets of the past. I couldn't absolve myself of my responsibility to find the key which would unlock it.

I raised my arm and flung the packet up and away from me. I watched as it reached the top of its parabola and fell with scarcely a splash into the river. It bobbed in midstream amongst the ripples.

I outpaced it as I strode quickly along the moist gravel of the pathway in the direction of home.

I had no idea whether it would quickly become saturated and sink to the bottom, or if not, where the river's flow, augmented by the ebbing tide, would carry it.

## XXIII

Even though he had his mouth full, Pogson's ebullience reverberated in the earpiece of the telephone.

'They've dropped the case. Just before the hearing. All charges. Insufficient evidence. It helped having Etheredge lined up and that we insisted on a full old-style committal. The girl couldn't cope with that, obviously, in the end. Our friend should even now be bidding farewell to the pleasure of Her Majesty. He's had to spend a devil of a long time on remand, but maybe it's given him time to think about things. A good result, as my friends in the Met express it.'

'Tim. You are, of course, a genius.'

'I know. But I had help. You gave good advice and the client stuck to it. Where would we be without the good old right of silence?'

'I wonder how the girl feels, Tim?'

'That's not my problem, thank goodness. We have played this one absolutely down the line, as we always do. Sarah, why did you ever leave? They can't be paying so much more?'

'You never give up, do you? It was never the money.'

'You ever want to change your mind, call me. Anything, you can have. Within reason. I've been offered some new desks – they're very nice. Anything. You name it.'

'Tim.' I paused, wondering how what I was going to say would sound. 'Tim, I'm flattered but I'm really not coming back. However, as you're in such a generous mood, there was something you could do for me.'

He must have, even over the telephone, detected the uncertainty in my voice because he went cagey. 'What's that?'

'You know when you came to Westhampton to see Chewton in jug that first time a couple of months ago? I saw you off at the station?'

He grunted in assent, and I could hear him take a slurp of coffee – probably from his Charles and Di wedding mug, as he favoured that kind of kitsch – and the rustle of papers as he cleared a space to put it down.

I checked that the office door was closed and lowered my voice. 'You mentioned a case a solicitor called Arthur O'Riordan had once handled.'

'Yes. What of it?'

'Well. If, for the sake of argument, I had an interest in the matter, how would I find this Arthur O'Riordan to talk to him? Is he in London still?'

Pogson started chuckling. 'Oh, he's in London. As for his address, I know that. Not that you'll get much out of him.'

'Come on, Tim. Please.'

'Arthur O'Riordan can be found care of Kensal Green Cemetery.'

'He's dead then.'

'Highly perceptive of you. He drank himself to death. The occupational hazard of the criminal lawyer. Too much work, worry, responsibility.'

Whilst he burbled on, I thought rapidly. 'What happened to his files, Tim? Who took over his practice?'

'Hold on, now. What am I getting into? Is your interest the kind of interest I'm thinking of? A certain person, perhaps?'

'Perhaps. So where are the files, Tim?'

'Even if you located the files – and who's to say they haven't been destroyed by now? – you wouldn't be able to consult them. It would be a gross breach of confidentiality to have access to the file of another solicitor's client. No lawyer would allow you to do that. It's absolutely privileged.'

I ignored this problem. First things first. 'Who took over O'Riordan's practice? You must know. He was a friend of yours.'

'By the time the end came there was no practice. He was bankrupted. His client account was kosher, but the Revenue got him for a few measly hundred. That meant he was struck off. He died of cirrhosis of the liver in the Whittington. He was separated from his wife and kids. There but for the grace of something or other, I thought. It wasn't much to bury him a free man.'

'You're a charitable man, Tim, under that flinty exterior.'

'I'm sorry, Sarah. I can't let you. You know that. The secrets between a lawyer and his client are just that. I owe Arthur that. I don't know what you're doing, and I don't want to know. You should have asked my advice at the beginning. I've given you fair warning, anyway. You've made your bed.'

'But what if it helps nail a bent lawyer?'

A couple of hours later, Julie buzzed me. 'I've got a bloke wants to speak to you. Won't give his name or anything.'

I hesitated a moment. 'Okay. Put him through.' I took a deep breath and said warily, 'Sarah Hartley speaking.'

I needn't have been alarmed. It was Robbie Chewton.

'Hi, Sarah. I'm out.'

'Pogson's just told me. Congrats.'

'I wanted to thank you. For what you did.'

'That's okay. It was Pogson, really.'

361

'He'll get paid. And the barrister bloke with the big hooter, the QC. I bet he doesn't go short.'

'No, there'll be a considerable cost to the Legal Aid fund for leading counsel, though not as much as if it had gone to trial.'

'Little scrubber. I'm going to steer clear of her in the future.'

'That would be advisable.'

'Yeah. Now it's all over, I've got a few things I want to get sorted. It's payback time.'

'Yes?' I said cautiously. I didn't like the sound of this. Being dogged by a grateful Robbie was high on my list of no-nos. I bet he was going to say he fancied me.

'Yeah. And by the way, I really fancy you. I mean we could combine business with pleasure.'

'I'm very flattered, Robbie, but we'll have to stick to business, shall we? It's a real bore but lawyers are like doctors as far as relationships with clients are concerned. It's tough, but those are the rules.'

'Oh, yeah, right, if you say so. You might change your mind, though, eh, when you know me better. Okay, listen up. What I said in that pisspot of a jail. About my father. My fucking father, he's written me off, you know. Fucking x'd me out as if I was dog shit. Never darken my doors, et cetera. It's like fucking Victorian times. I would never have been in there if he'd had words in the right quarters, but he couldn't be fucked. Not even for his own son. Well, I can tell you something about him, make your fucking hair stand on end.'

'Robbie, it's been nice talking to you. I'm sorry you and your father are not getting on at the moment, but there isn't anything I can do about that. He's a client of this firm. As there is a possibility of a conflict of interest, we can no longer represent you as well. So I sugg–'

'Hey, what is this? I don't want legal advice. I want to do you a favour, tell you something for free. You, Sarah Hartley, are in deep shit. It's time you knew. I'll be in the Grounds bar at six.'

'For Christ's sake, Robbie,' I exploded. 'What are you trying to do? Get me fucking well fired? Are you completely stupid? I cannot and will not take sides in your row with your father. Find someone else to moan to. Now piss off!' I slammed the phone down so hard, I broke one of my nails.

I was filing down the jagged edge when James Huxley wandered in with some papers. 'Urgent delivery from the Führer. Action zis day!' He clicked his heels, and gave a Nazi salute. When he became aware of what I was doing, he chuckled. 'Oh, classic, classic! Where's my camera! The ambitious, overworked solicitoress, nails to the grindstone.'

I grabbed the papers. 'Why don't you go and shag the photocopier, James? It's pining for your attention.'

The wittily named Grounds bar was, as you'd expect, on the basement floor of the Coffee House. Its subterranean situation was emphasized by the virtual absence of lights, the most piercingly bright being the green glow of the exit signs. Added to that, the decor was mainly black and dark brown.

Around the outside of the room was a series of American-style booths. After staring blindly around for a minute or two, I made out that one of these contained Robbie Chewton, hunched over a small glass.

'What are you drinking?'

He looked up, unsurprised. The perpetual student of cool. 'Pernod.'

I kept repeating this strange word on my way to the bar so as not to lose it.

I handed him the yellow liquor which smelt like Stewart Spencer's tongue the day he'd squeezed my cunt and french-kissed me outside the Chemi Lab in my first term at Poofters. Aniseed balls. Someone should write a book about tastes and memories.

'Cheers!'

'Robbie. I haven't come for a riotous evening. I shouldn't be here at all. Let's pretend I'm not and you're talking to yourself, like in a play? What's it called? A soliloquy.'

'I knew you couldn't resist it.'

I sighed to myself. The young psychologist. 'Robbie, if this was just an excuse to get me here...'

'Yeah, that too. Hey, no, hang on. Like I said, I wanted to tell you about my dad, the real man behind all the newspaper Midas shit. I mean, you're smart. You should get the fuck out of that firm before the shit sticks. Which it will, because I'm going for broke on this. I'm not keeping quiet any longer. I wanted to warn you because you didn't treat me like a pig's arse, the way that smarmy cunt Appleby does.'

'I'm not here, Robbie. I'm not listening. Just talk, okay?'

'For a start he knocks my mother about. Has for years. She puts up with it. It makes me sick. I used to hear them, when I was a kid. And he has other women. He's been screwing that secretary at your firm, Rose, for years. He knocks her about, too. Even boasted about it to me, when he was pissed. You know, we had what he called a man-to-man talk. About how to treat women. Hypocritical bastard. I've never hit a woman for sex. I don't need to. You should have heard him. "Oh, they may look all prim and proper, but deep down they all want to be mastered. Particularly the upper-class bints. Looking down their toffee-noses. Like a bit of rough-house."'

I couldn't stick any more of this. 'Robbie, believe me. You're not telling me anything I didn't know or guess already. If I wanted an angel for a client I'd have to practise in heaven. So long, then.' I drank up my fizzy apple-juice.

'No, wait! That's not it. Something you don't know. Something you can't know. Do you want to know how he bought Welscombe House? And all the estate? Well it wasn't all fucking plain dealing. Yeah, you're interested now, aren't you? Sit down again. Okay, it was when I was a kid. About ten, maybe eleven, years ago. We were living in Ashton St Michael then. One afternoon in the school holidays, Mum had gone out and he was at home. He told me to fuck off upstairs and watch the cricket because he had a visitor coming. Well, I hung out my window to see who came, some tart or other, even then I knew about that. But it wasn't. It was a fucking Roller, with a chauffeur in a uniform, and he lets this old geezer out, and he says, "Call back in one hour, Simpson." And the driver says, "Very good, my lord." Like in some fucking thing on the telly. So Dad lets in this Lord Snooty and they go into his study. I'm watching from the landing. After they've got started I creep down and put my ear to the keyhole. They're talking about Dad's buying Welscombe.

'Dad's got his pleasant voice on, the one he talks to the punters with. He's saying, "I think you'll find that's a very reasonable offer, my lord, in the circumstances." And then his lordship says something like, get stuffed, you horrible oik. And then I hear Dad's nasty voice, the one he uses when he's beating up Mum. "Listen to me, you old sod. I told you, in the circumstances, it's a good offer. Now you wouldn't have come here at all if you hadn't an inkling of what those circumstances were."

'Then his lordship says all haughty, but with a kind of nerviness, "I don't know what you mean, my man." Then Dad is shouting, "Don't you fucking my man me. You may be a fucking peer of the realm and in the fucking government, but all over the papers it'll be Queer of the Realm. You won't be able to hush up any more what goes on at those tea parties and sports days you have for Welscombe Prep School. You've managed to shut the parents of those boys up so far, but you won't be able to once I get going. So you'd better tell your agents you're accepting, and instruct your solicitors, or I'll be on to Fleet Street. And don't think you'll get away by doing the decent thing and blowing your brains out. I'll go ahead and do it anyway. See how that makes Lady Anglebury feel when it comes out, eh, what?" Then his lordship starts saying things like, "You wouldn't dare", and "This is preposterous." But by the end he's blubbing and begging Dad to go easy on him and that he'll do the deal.'

He stopped, his face flushed and his eyes bright. I wondered again what he was on. Perhaps he was only high on revenge. I knew the seductive power of that drug.

'What do you think?'

'It's a good story.'

'What do you mean, a story. Every fucking word is true as I sit here.'

'From a truly objective witness. I can hear counsel now. He'd tear you into little pieces. Not that you'd get anywhere near a court. You've no corroborating evidence. Lord Anglebury's dead.'

'So, you don't believe me.'

'It doesn't matter what I believe. No one important will. Forget it, Robbie.'

'But do you believe me? If you do, then you should be packing your bags. Sooner or later, my father will get something on you, then you'll never be free.'

'I'll take my chance. I think it's you who should leave Fernsford, Robbie. Forget revenge. It's self-destructive. Do something else with your life.'

'You really don't think anyone would buy the Anglebury story?'

'No. Not without more proof than your hearsay statement. No newspaper would touch it either. It's plainly libellous. Robbie, why are you doing this? You must really hate your father a great deal to want to destroy him.'

'Oh, yes, I hate him. Jesus Christ, I hate him. What if I had something else, something that I could prove?'

'Like what?'

I was startled to see his eyes fill with tears. I put my hand on his. 'It isn't only because of the prison, is it?'

'No, it isn't. But if he'd stuck by me, I might have felt differently. But he treated me like some kind of germ. And he helped to make me what I am. Do you understand what I'm saying? Do you fucking understand?'

'I think so.'

'Well, if I had the guts to stand up in court on that, that wouldn't be no hearsay, would it? It fucking well happened to me. They'd have to believe me, because there's more. He took pictures of us together. Lots of pictures. I know where he keeps them.'

'So what's this about? When you invited yourself, you said you wanted to talk. I do hope it isn't about the men in your life.'

Harriet leaned back in the elegantly striped canvas chair, looking archly over the top of her sunglasses. They were those posh designer ones you see advertised. She'd obviously been wearing them somewhere a bit hotter than Dartmouth Park, too, because she was delicately tanned.

Not that it wasn't extremely pleasant sitting on her stone-flagged terrace drinking coffee after a nice lunch, enjoying the spring sunshine. It had been a bit damp and misty when I started out from Fernsford in the morning, but by the time I was passing Heathrow, the sun was breaking through. The grimy, traffic-choked streets of North London had a bright, holiday air, and I even felt a twinge of nostalgia for the vibrant life of the place, the crowds and the chaos.

Harriet uncrossed her legs, dazzling in white linen trousers, sat up and gave me a poke on the knee. 'Come on, stop day-dreaming and answer my question.'

'Don't worry. It isn't men – at least not in the sense you meant. I'm trying to think where to start. I mean, how do you sell a story to the ace reporter who's heard it all before?'

'You don't um and ah, you start at the beginning and go on to the end.'

'Well, the beginning could be almost anywhere, and there isn't an end. Not yet. Well, here goes.'

She listened, inscrutable behind the dark lenses, occasionally asking me to clarify a point, but otherwise noncommittal.

When I'd finished, she sat silently, her mouth pursed in concentration.

'Harriet, please take off those specs.'

She obliged, and I saw her brown eyes were full of doubt. 'I'm sorry, darling. To me, it doesn't, as the man said, amount to a hill of beans, not even a hillock. But you're the legal expert, you presumably know that.'

'Yes, I do. I also know that if what I've been saying gets back to him, then I'm out of that firm like greased lightning, complete with a placard round my neck saying "Do not employ this woman under any circumstances". And if I give the police an anonymous tip-off, it'll only be something for them to chuckle about over their egg and chips in the canteen. Chewton being Mr Big Cheese and Appleby a mate of the Chief Constable, along with every other tin god in the town.'

'Bit of a problem, then. Why are you telling me? Oh, I see. This is the big story I've been waiting all my life for? You think I'm going to stick out my little neck and use the power of television to badger and bully out of these characters the proof you haven't got? Well, think again, my sweet. We're not looking to be wiped out by a libel settlement the size of China. I'm sorry, Sarah, but what did you expect me to say?'

'I know there's no real evidence of wrongdoing. Nothing to link Charmaine and Appleby except that she said she knew someone of that name in London. I can't prove she was blackmailing anybody, never mind him. I can't prove that Babbage was murdered for his land or that the conveyance was forged, or that the land at Combe Episcopi was sold in breach of trust. The fact that Appleby and Chewton may have known one another in London doesn't in itself indicate a conspiracy. But I'm convinced that those two are up to something, something I don't yet understand. Something to do with those sets of documents for Oak Dean, a development that appears to have no existence. If I came up with more, you would be interested, wouldn't you?'

'Maybe, but I won't hold my breath. Now, let's talk about something pleasant, like how I'm going to entertain you this evening. There's a new restaurant in Hampstead I've been wanting to try. Or what about the theatre? The new Tom Stoppard at the Strand's had rave reviews.'

I coughed apologetically. 'Er, no, I can't do tonight. I've got something else on.'

Her face went sulky. 'You're paying me back for not believing your story. You're meeting some man.'

'In a manner of speaking.'

It felt strange being back in the old offices in Kingsland Road. His desk was, as usual, piled high with paper, the room still lit by one sixty-watt bulb.

'There is absolutely no way I should be doing this. And don't forget, it's useless as evidence. It's absolutely privileged.'

'Tim, please.'

He raised his hands in a gesture of surrender, sighed, then handed over a bulging manila pocket file. 'Go on, take it. I haven't looked at it. I don't know what's in it. You're on your own. Anyone catches you with it, it's nothing to do with me. As far as I'm concerned I've never seen it.'

'Thanks, Tim.' It sounded quite inadequate, seeing I had inveigled him into doing what was probably the only remotely unstraight thing he had ever done.

'I think you'd better go now.'

I picked up the file and stuffed it into the slim zipper document case I'd brought with me for the purpose.

He stood up. 'I'll let you out.'

'Aren't you going home now?'

He shrugged. 'Not for a bit. Now I'm here, I've got a few things to finish. You know how it is.'

I let myself in with the key I had borrowed. She was either still out or had gone to bed. I thought I would be too stressed to sleep but I conked out immediately and entered the deep slumber of the innocent. I woke to the morning sun streaming through the window, the curtains of which I had forgotten to close. It was nine o'clock.

On the table in the cavernous kitchen was a note. 'It would have been cruel to wake you. Help yourself to breakfast. I shall be back for lunch. Love H.' I made myself have toast and coffee, then I cleared the table and stacked the dishwasher.

Finally I put the file on the kitchen table in the full brightness of the day. The thin cardboard was crumpled, dog-eared, stained and decorated with overlapping rings from coffee mugs like so many Olympic Games logos. Covering it was a mass of doodles, scribbled notes and phone numbers. I began to see why O'Riordan and Pogson had got on. They had similar ideas about office organization.

Amongst the clutter, I could just make out the original title: R v. STAPLETON in heavy block capitals, and then after it in brackets, (DECEPTION. T.A. S.15). At presumably a later date the words 'Case not proceeded with' had been added diagonally in red biro.

I took a deep breath and opened it.

In it, there was a bundle of correspondence held together at the top left-hand corner with a treasury tag pushed roughly through the papers without the benefit of a properly punched hole. It was routine stuff about interview and hearing dates. The last letter was from the DPP confirming that the prosecution was not going ahead.

The biggest of the other bundles was a slab of photocopies two inches thick, the documents from the prosecution, sales particulars, contracts, correspondence, together with the notes of the police interviews with victims and witnesses. It was obvious from the dates mentioned that it had been a scam that had gone on for a number of years. A great deal of work had been devoted to nailing Stapleton. I never ceased to marvel at the sheer industry of police officers on a serious case. If diligence could have won through, our friend would not have stood a chance.

But fraud is dead hard to pin on someone. Fraudsters are generally very bright, albeit twisted guys, and even a clever criminal lawyer is hard put to see what goes on. In this case the problem was proving that the transactions with the people who sold their properties through Stapleton were actually shams.

There were references to a number of property companies, but no hard evidence that they were fronts for Stapleton and his presumed associates. Some of the elderly victims had died in the meantime, and judging from the quality of some of the interviews with those still alive, they would have made very poor prosecution witnesses. They said things like what a charming young man Stapleton was, how helpful he was, et cetera, et cetera. There was certainly no fool like an old fool.

The next item looked more interesting: a substantial typed document, its several pages again crudely treasury-tagged together. It began:

Statement of HENRY CHARLES AUDLEY STAPLETON of Flat 3, 25 Grosvenor Square, London W1, who will say:

I was born on 6 March 1934. I am thirty-seven years old. I am a graduate of Oxford University and a fellow of the Royal Institute of Chartered Surveyors. At all material times, I was the principal partner of the firm known as Stapleton & Co., Chartered Surveyors and Estate Agents, whose offices are at Park Lane, London W1.

I shall plead not guilty to the charges laid against me. I wish to state that I consider that I have acted throughout all the transactions referred to in these charges with the highest standards of professional care and conduct, and have received from them only proper and reasonable remuneration for services rendered.

It went on in this tone of injured innocence for pages, in which each of the dodgy deals with which he had been charged was discussed in detail. There were pages of notes of comments on the various police documents, all of the 'I never said that, did that, that has been completely misinterpreted' kind. It was a very thorough piece of work by O'Riordan, a good start to the preparation of the defence. I hoped he'd got a good fee for it, but he didn't sound the sort of fellow who bothered too much with his bills.

I sighed. As for Stapleton, the guy was a louse, that was obvious, but incredibly smooth with it, all that Oxford graduate stuff. He had that armour-plated self-confidence which I had met before in guys of his stamp with three posh forenames to bolster them.

I sat back in the chair and kicked the table leg. What a waste of time and effort. O'Riordan's confidences to Pogson seemed to have come out of thin air. Where in this was Appleby? I felt really sick and deflated. I'd risked a lot to get this, for nothing. I'd been a fool. Why bother anyway? Who cared what Appleby had got up to more than fifteen years ago?

I gathered up the papers and put them back into their original order. I opened up the now limp, greasy-looking wallet to shove them all back in when I saw that there was something else still in there that I had overlooked, something which hadn't formed part of any of the main bundles.

It was a plain cheap manila foolscap envelope which had become wedged in the concertina folds at the bottom of the pocket file. I pulled it out, trembling slightly. I was getting that tense feeling I had when something was about to happen.

On it was written simply Stapleton in biro, in what I'd come to recognize must be O'Riordan's hand. The flap at the end was stuck down. I weighed it in my hand, and took a deep breath, then tore it open.

There were two sheets of paper covered in manuscript, O'Riordan again. And yet another envelope, white this time, also sealed.

I unfolded the paper and read with some difficulty, as the writing, having been done in haste, was hard, at points, to decipher. The first paragraph was less scrawled and had probably been added later to turn the scribbled sentences into a proper note of attendance on a client.

> 15 December 1971. Telecon with Stapleton. He phoned me at home at 10.30 p.m. He sounded distressed, prob. been drinking. Apologized for disturbing me, but said that it was 'absolutely imperative' he spoke to me.

The main part of the note consisted of the mixture of verbatim records of clients' own words and précis with which lawyers try to give shape to the formless rush of words which characterizes telephone conversations.

> I'm v. scared. They think I'm going to talk, do a deal.

> Said his instrns were to pl. NG. Was he going to make a new statement?

> You don't understand. I'm being threatened. Violence. Cd have an accident. Like the old woman in Gibson Sq.

> Asked who?

> Can't tell you their names – but you know who they are. We were in it together. If no one talked, cdn't prove anything. There wasn't any real harm. Not until Gibson Sq. Got greedy there.

> Told him that making it diff. for me to represent and PNG. We cdn't lead any evidence or x-exam to prove NG if he said he was G. Wd have to get another solr.

> I just want you to know not all my fault. I didn't want any of that and if it comes to it, won't take the blame. Got proof. Photos. Send them to you. Use them if anything happens.

The rest of the note appeared more carefully composed, not surprisingly when you considered its contents.

He rang off. He was obviously not in a frame of mind to give full instructions. I am, however, clear that my duty to the court is to refuse, on the basis of this conversation, to allow the client to mount a full defence. I shall advise him to make a clean breast of the matter and PG, or failing that to seek alternative representation.

17 December 1971. An envelope was delivered to the office at 9.30 a.m. by a courier. It contained the photograph and newspaper cutting included herewith. I shall take no further action in this matter until I have seen the client, advised him and taken any new instructions.

A. O'R.

A scrupulous man was our Arthur. I picked up the white envelope. This must be the herewith referred to. I tore it open.

Inside was a small colour snapshot, rather faded with age, and a yellowed, folded cutting from a newspaper.

Heart beating furiously, I stared at it.

It showed the back garden of what looked like one of the tall, thin, stock-brick and stucco early Victorian houses typical of North London districts like Islington and Camden, like the one which had contained my flat in Richmont Row. There was building work in progress: scaffolding reached to roof level, and there were blank holes where some of the tall sash-windows should have been.

It was a sunny day. On the overgrown lawn stood three men. They held glasses in their hands. One of them, his face slightly turned away from the camera, was about to refill them from the dark, squat bottle of champagne which he gripped in his fist. Unlike the other two, his heavy figure was dressed casually in jeans and sweater. It took me a moment or two to realize what, or rather whom, I was seeing. I peered closer, almost sick with the adrenaline surging within me.

Despite the hair, which was still mainly dark, I could recognize clearly the aquiline features of Francis Appleby. And despite the awkward angle there could be no mistaking the square jowls and jutting chin of Trevor Chewton.

What of the third man? A tall, sallow-faced saturnine fellow. I sat back and let the light of the day fall on the small square of coated paper. Then to my absolute amazement I recognized him.

The third man at this little celebration was Ronald Lambert, presently the respected Chief Executive of the FernWest Building Society.

Trembling, I picked up the sliver of newsprint. It crackled drily as I smoothed the deeply indented folds.

Retired Teacher Dies in Fall

Pensioner Marjorie Alexander, 83, was found dead late yesterday at her house in Gibson Square, Islington. Neighbours called the police after becoming alarmed that she had not been seen for some time. Her body was found in the hallway at the foot of the staircase. A post mortem has yet to be carried out. A police spokesman said that her injuries were consistent with falling. Foul play was not suspected but could not be ruled out until further enquiries had been made. The coroner has been informed and an inquest will be opened in due course.

Miss Alexander, who lived alone, was a former English mistress at Camden High School for Girls. She was understood to have no close surviving relatives. A neighbour said today that the dead woman had talked of selling her house and moving to a ground-floor flat in the area, as she was finding the stairs hard to manage.

I felt sick. The message conveyed by the cutting, when read in conjunction with O'Riordan's attendance note was clear. In poor Miss Alexander's case, fraud had turned to murder. Old Babbage had not been the first.

'So, do you still think there's nothing in it?' I sipped at my glass of spritzer.

Harriet was drinking the wine straight, and the pale green bottle was almost empty. She'd come back just before one o'clock loaded with delicatessen goodies.

While I stuffed myself with food and she picked at some pâté and knocked back the wine, I told her about my night in Hoxton, and my discoveries. To my disappointment, she remained unexcited and sceptical. I was irritated at her for playing the intellectual superior.

She reflectively poked the corner of the colour snap with the tip of her index finger.

'More than nothing, but is it something? The photograph shows that Appleby and Chewton and this man Lambert knew each other in London in the early seventies. So, Appleby's claim that he first met Chewton in Fernsford is clearly false, as you'd already surmised. But what does that prove? There could be all kinds of reasons why he didn't want the connection to be known about, none of them sinister. Maybe he wanted it to look as if he'd won Chewton by being a good solicitor, rather than that he was acting for an old mate.'

'But what about the cutting? Stapleton sent it to O'Riordan as an insurance policy. To indicate he didn't approve of what had happened.'

'Whatever that was. It needn't have been murder. It could have been an accident. And nowhere in the file does he name his co-conspirators. It must all have been done on a nudge-and-a-wink basis. That's the way your friend Pogson had it. You went out on a limb to get this, but if you're honest, it's all circumstantial. None of it fits well enough.'

She yawned. 'Let's go out, clear my head. A walk on Hampstead Heath will be good for you, too, before you coop yourself up driving back. All that is old stuff anyway. If they really are villains, what form does their villainy take at present? What exactly are they up to in Fernsford?'

'Yes, let's go out. While we walk, I'll tell you all about my theory on that.'

She groaned. 'I might have known you'd have one.'

We walked up towards Parliament Hill from Highgate Ponds. Around us, the affluent middle-classes of Hampstead and their dogs strolled off their Sunday lunches.

'It's Lambert who's the key to this, I'm convinced,' I said as we sat down on a bench overlooking the haze that was the distant City.

'Why? It's not a crime to be friendly with a building-society manager, even if you're a solicitor, is it?'

'No, of course not. But think of that photo. That wasn't a group of friends. They were celebrating. That house. The building work. Can't you see? Stapleton, behind the camera. He identified the properties and charmed the owners. Appleby was the lawyer. Chewton did the flat conversions – and he would also know his way round the local authority, grease any palms that needed it. And Lambert provided the no-questions-asked finance.'

'Hang on. He wasn't at the FernWest in those days.'

'I bet he was in another outfit. I thought that that was something that we could find out.'

'We? Is that the royal you, meaning me? I told you, I have to be very careful. We have a very limited budget. I'm not at the Beeb now, remember? But what if he was with another building society? Wow, we'll do the exposé of exposés. Old chum in new job scandal. Come on, Sarah, let's talk about something more controversial, like the weather.'

'No, there is more to it than that. I'm sure. A building society has to be an institution of impeccable integrity. Trustee status and all that. Appleby and Chewton were associates of a man who only avoided a fraud charge by the skin of his old school tie. Lambert is in the frame. Integrity, no way. I'll bet the FernWest board weren't aware of his antecedents when they appointed him. You don't knowingly put a drug addict in charge of the pharmacy.'

'You still have no evidence other than gossip. Or maybe he's a reformed character. And how's he done? Is the FernWest bust? I haven't heard that. In fact, come to think of it, I heard only recently that it's been doing rather well. It came near the top of some Building Societies Association efficiency index, I remember. What are their investment rates?'

'I don't know. I don't have any savings to salt away like you. If I had, I wouldn't put them anywhere near it. You haven't heard my theory yet. You've heard of mortgage fraud? You know the principles. A solicitor mortgages the same property umpteen times in umpteen different names to umpteen different lenders. They send you the advance cheques and you pocket them. You do that a few times. You've got a few mill and you piss off to the sun. Eventually the lenders rumble what happens because the loans are never serviced. That's the classic version. There are variations. But they share the same defect.'

'In the end, the fraud comes to light?'

'Precisely. It's unsustainable. There are loads of false mortgages and only one real property. What Appleby and co are doing is the other way round and entirely sustainable. They've got lots of fake properties and only one mortgage on each. They're milking the FernWest by creating mortgages to buy properties that don't exist.'

'What on earth do you mean?'

'I couldn't understand Appleby's barred computer records of an estate that wasn't being built, nor the box of documentation for the same non-development, not until I realized Lambert and the FernWest were involved. Old-style non-registered conveyancing depends a lot on trust. You have these bundles of deeds drawn up by lawyers. You rely on them because solicitors have this reputation for absolute integrity. Astronomical sums of money change hands every week on the basis of lawyers saying that they have the right title deeds. Building societies send out cheques for tens, for hundreds of thousands of pounds on solicitors' undertakings that the funds will be used to acquire a good title to land and that their interest is secured by mortgage. In return, they get a packet of old papers. Solicitors pretend that it's highly organized and secure, but actually it's sloppy as hell. Particularly when you get housing developments. New developments don't even have proper postal addresses. They're Plot X, Rat's-arse Fields. Could be anywhere. Or nowhere. I remember Appleby made a joke about it when I joined. He had great fun with the stupid naff names that Chewton gives his estates.'

'I see what you're getting at. You fake up some deeds for a housing development. The building society hands out the mortgage money, and gets its bits of paper in return. But the houses are never built. It's a mortgage on a practically worthless bit of field.'

'That's right. At the moment, the system is geared up to churn out mortgages left right and centre. Even legitimate lenders are probably not doing the checking they should. When you run the building society, you can fake everything: the surveyors' reports, the applications, the references, the loan-servicing records. An audit check on deeds would reveal nothing amiss. On paper the fake mortgages would look as genuine as the real ones. By creative accounting in an organization that's awash with cash, you can hide any number of frauds. In any mortgage portfolio, there are always a number in arrears. You can juggle things around so that the fake mortgages look as if they pay up occasionally. You can even switch funds out of savers' accounts to cover any discrepancies. It's all computerized. Computers don't ask awkward questions like old-fashioned clerical staff. There's no end to the fiddles you could get up to. People stack money into these set-ups and trust them to look after it. If there's no integrity at the top, no system is completely safe.'

'You really believe that's what's going on? On what kind of scale?'

'I found Oak Dean because it's going into the system at the moment. Fifty plots. Even if the average mortgage is only fifty grand, which is conservative, that's still over a couple of mill. But they've been at it for years. There could be thousands of ghost mortgages by now. In that case, the FernWest isn't just being milked, it's being hollowed out.'

She looked thoughtful. 'It's bizarre. It's ingenious. But again we come back to proof. For instance, how do you actually know for absolute certain that this Oak Dean isn't being developed?'

'I don't. But when I get back to Fernsford, I'm going out there to take a look-see. So, decision time. Are you prepared to do some spade-work for me?'

She made a face. 'I can't promise more than a trowel.'

It was whilst I was driving back that I had another grim thought.

Charmaine's friend had mangled the name, but she'd been trying to tell me that Charmaine's trysting place had been in Combe Episcopi. And what better rendezvous for a murderer than an isolated farmhouse?

# XXIV

First thing on the following Monday morning, I rang Paul at his new offices in the Buttercross. We hadn't seen each other since the afternoon at Friars Haven.

A secretary so green she hadn't even heard of Chamberlayne's, never mind me, answered the phone. I explained that I needed to speak to her boss urgently on a matter concerning his client Trevor Chewton. She'd heard of him, perhaps?

'One moment. I'll enquire as to whether he's available.'

The moment lengthened into a couple of minutes. I was about to slam the instrument down in annoyance, when he came on the line.

When he spoke to me, I wished I had.

'Sarah. This had really better be urgent business. I've come out of a meeting to speak.'

'It is urgent, yes. And it concerns both our businesses. Can you meet me at eleven, in the Grounds Bar of the Coffee House? It's pretty discreet there. Bring a load of files if you want to look official.'

'Look official? So it's not? What the hell are you playing at, Sarah?' He paused as if a thought had occurred to him. 'You're not . . . ?'

'Don't be stupid. Just be there.' I put the phone down in fury. I really resented his suggestion that I would be daft enough to get myself pregnant, and that if I had I would have chosen such a labyrinthine method of communicating it. Deep down, perhaps he really thought of me as his empty-headed mistress. It was a side of him I hadn't seen before.

He kept me waiting through one cup of cappuccino. When he did finally turn up, I could tell he was angry.

'This had better be important. I've had to cancel a meeting with the quantity surveyors.'

'I make a habit of dragging you out on personal whims, do I, Paul? I just had to see your face, darling? I'm like that, am I?'

'No, of course you're not. I'm sorry. Things are very hectic at the moment. The second phase is going out to tender in a few weeks. Trevor's pushing for faster progress on the first. You know what it's like.'

'Friars Haven is very important to you, isn't it, Paul? I mean, to you as an architect.'

He looked at me narrowly. 'You know that. I don't want to be remembered professionally for a public lavatory in Holland Park. That was what my RIBA award was for. What are you saying? Is there some problem with the finance? I thought that was all sewn up.'

'It is as far as I know. The bankers went home to Tokyo rejoicing. No, it isn't the finance.'

Now he was concentrating, he could see the white strain in my face. 'Sarah, you look ghastly. What the hell is the matter?'

'Paul, believe me. I am so sorry to have to tell you this. But you have to know. Please listen to me.'

I spoke as calmly as I could for half an hour. He asked a few questions, but mainly he listened, his face as still and grey as if it were cast in concrete.

'What are you going to do?' he asked finally, although he already knew the answer. Why otherwise would I have told him?

'At first, I thought, it's nothing to do with me. If Appleby's been on the fiddle, if he's on it now, what's that to me? Plenty of businessmen operate pretty near the edge. I thought I could carry on with my job, not get involved in anything crooked, that I'd be all right, as long as I didn't actually know. That's how lawyers operate, after all. A kind of authorized professional hypocrisy. Unless my client says he's guilty, then I can behave as if he is innocent, despite the overwhelming evidence to the contrary. But when Charmaine was killed, that was different. Then I found out about the other deaths. We're not dealing with a bit of financial or fiscal jiggery-pokery here, Paul. This is murder, and conspiracy to murder. No one can keep clean in water that filthy. Trevor Chewton must be damn near a psychopath. You more than anyone must find that believable.'

'I've never heard such nonsense. Chewton's a bastard, but a killer? And Francis Appleby? I thought lawyers had to be more careful than laymen about jumping to conclusions with no evidence. I mean this Charmaine woman – she must have been in plenty of bad company. You can't say that it was definitely Appleby and Chewton. As for poor Ralph. Everyone knows that was an accident.'

'Paul, I've been over and through it a thousand times. It crept up on me like the tide on a beach. One minute there were acres of clear sand and the sea was miles out, the next it was washing round my ankles and threatening to tug me under. I didn't want to find this out. But now I have, I can't walk away from it.'

'So why not talk to Appleby? There's probably some perfectly reasonable explanation.'

'Paul, how can you suggest that? If they're the kind of men I think they are, they won't bother with explanations. They'll find some way of implicating me – or worse.'

'So how long before you go to the authorities?'

'I don't know. Harriet's helping with the research. It depends on what we find out.'

'Have you thought what this means for me? If even a rumour of what you've told me got out, the money-men would skedaddle. The whole project would be sunk. I'd be finished professionally. And Venetia. Chewton will be like Samson and bring the whole sodding temple down on the heads of everyone. Have you thought of that?'

'That's why I've told no one except Harriet. And she won't do anything without more evidence. I know how devastating this will be to the present project. But there will be other backers, other people of vision who may implement your scheme, once this matter is over. Do you think I didn't want to ignore it? For ages, I tried not to see things. I wanted so much for everything to carry on as it was. But I can't absolve myself of it, Paul. Christ, I've tried so hard, but I can't.'

I felt the hot tears forcing themselves from my eyes, and for a few moments I was lost in weeping. He sat on the other side of the table lost in thought. How far apart we seemed suddenly. How quickly all that passion, that emotion, had evaporated as if it had never been. No matter what happened to Friars Haven, we were finished. There was nothing between romance and pornography. I cried for that also.

'Why are you telling me today? You could have left me in blissful ignorance a while longer.'

'I'm going to Oak Dean. This afternoon. I have a set of documents saying it's a prospective building site. I want to be sure it isn't. Also, I think it may be where Charmaine was killed. Paul, I want you to go with me. As a witness, if we find anything. Because you're the only person I trust.'

'Sarah. Is there anything I can say which will stop you from stirring this thing up?'

'No, Paul. I'm very sorry. Believe me. I have to do it.'

'I've no choice, then. Shall we say two thirty?'

'All right. I'll meet you there. At two thirty. I've brought a map to show you where it is.'

'What do you think?'

'It's lovely. Much nicer than that place in the square. No traffic fumes for a start.'

Rose had marched in and insisted we have lunch together, although it was the last thing I'd felt like doing. She was keen to try a new place in the Corn Exchange.

No one exchanged corn in the Corn Exchange any longer. The main trading floor was filled with craft stalls. The rest of the cavernous Victorian building had been let off to various enterprises, of which Salad Days was one. We sat out under a peppermint and white striped awning which filled one of the arches on the St Peter's Piece side. The honey-coloured stone of the cathedral glowed in the sunlight.

I dug my fork into my spinach quiche. I was surprised to find I was hungry. Rose picked at her mushroom pâté.

She was wearing a long-sleeved white silk blouse. As she raised her arm to brush back a strand of blonde hair, the cuff fell back to reveal a dark purple bruise on the underside of her arm. I was quite an expert on bruises. It was the size and shape of a large thumb. In that position, he'd have been grabbing her or forcing her down, perhaps a preliminary to a thrashing of the kind I'd seen the results of in the dress shop a few months back.

She was absorbed in her thoughts and hadn't noticed that I'd seen it. A sensible person would have averted her eyes and commented on the weather. But not me. I couldn't keep my big mouth shut.

'You don't have to put up with that kind of thing, Rose.'

She clicked out of her abstraction. 'I beg your pardon?'

I laid a gentle finger on the bruise. 'That. I mean it's not as if you're married even, is it?'

'I don't know what you're talking about. What's my not being married got to do with my having shut my arm in the car door this morning?'

'You and that car, Rose. You're always having these accidents. Please don't insult my intelligence. You must have known I wasn't fooled in the shop. Let's not pretend now. Tell me to mind my own business if you like, but don't tell me fairy stories.'

'It certainly is none of your business. What right do you have to criticize my private life?'

'None at all. I'm completely out of order. An Englishwoman's bedroom is her castle. If you want to let an evil bastard like Trevor Chewton knock you about, then who am I to worry? Is that what they taught you at your posh school? Grin and bear it? Lie back and think of England? Men are beasts and sex is pain?'

It was as if I'd thumped her in the stomach. She crumpled up at the table, her thin shoulders shaking with her weeping.

'I'm sorry, Rose. But I had to say it. I'm fond of you. I'd better go. This should cover my share.'

I put the note on the table and she covered my hand with hers before I withdrew. 'Please don't go. Please don't leave me like this. I'll go to the loo. Wait for me.'

When she came back, she'd repaired the damage to her make-up but her dark-rimmed eyes were still red.

'How did you know?'

'Hints here and there,' I said vaguely. 'I'm sure no one else in the office knows.'

'You don't understand.'

'Yes, I do. I know if you're locked into that kind of relationship – if you share your life with that kind of man – it's hard to get out. But you're not in that position. You could tell him to piss off any time.'

'Could I? Could I really, Sarah? I won't insult your intelligence by asking who you think pays for my mother's twenty-four-hour nursing care, or who owns the house we live in. Those things have a price.'

'I see. But I thought your family was ... Your father was a doctor and ...'

'My father was a fool. He'd drunk and gambled away what money he'd had before he married my mother. He was massively in debt. His family house, the house his grandfather had bought, was mortgaged to Whiteman's bank. His income from his practice didn't cover a fraction of his expenditure. He married my mother for her money and when that had gone, he killed himself.'

'But Chewton? Couldn't you see what he was like?'

'Trevor is a complex man. He can be very generous. He is a man of vision. Who else in this provincial backwater would have seen the potential of Friars Haven? When I became his mistress, I had no choice. My mother would have died in hospital. This way she has some dignity.'

'And what about you?'

'I have my work. Francis gives me more responsibility than any other solicitor would. He, at least, appreciates my abilities.'

'He exploits you.'

'You can think that if you wish.'

'Ralph would never have treated you as he does. Did he never know you were in love with him?'

By now she was recovering some of her old composure. 'Was it so obvious when I talked about him, darling?' She laughed in her brittle way. 'No, he never did. He never looked at me in that way at all. I was the cousin who came to tea with her parents. I was five years younger. A lot, when you're children. Then Ralph went away to school and I hardly saw him.'

'But he came back to the firm after university and law school?'

'Why do you think I started work there? It wasn't out of love of old Chamberlayne. He was awful to Ralph. I hated to hear him browbeat him. Ralph was not like his father. He was a sensitive man. He left for London. That's where he met Margaret Matravers again. She was at the Royal Academy of Music. They married very quickly. I caught the bouquet. As near as I got to the altar, darling.'

'It must have been difficult for you when Ralph returned to the firm?'

'All things must pass, my dear. By then I was involved with Trevor. Ralph was a one-woman man. Unusual, but there are some. He and Margaret had their differences, but Ralph never looked elsewhere unlike –' She stopped abruptly.

'Unlike? Unlike his father?'

'You're very sharp, aren't you, Sarah? I knew when Francis said that you were ... Well, I knew straight away he was wrong.'

'So old man Chamberlayne was a womanizer?'

'He and my father were friends. Chamberlayne lent him money. He was never repaid. I remember going over to the Firs one evening to fetch my father to attend to an emergency. They would play chess and drink. My father drank a great deal. Even as a girl I knew that. They were having a blazing row. I daren't go in but cowered outside the study door.'

'What was it about?'

'He said, "You're a swine, Ralph. An utter swine. This is the last time. One day you won't have me to feed you penicillin, then your taste for the gutter will send you insane." Chamberlayne got very angry and said my father was the fool, and should remember to whom he was talking. He would have been struck off, or worse, years ago if he, Chamberlayne, hadn't hushed up the business of the woman with arthritis. "You were too drunk to realize you'd administered morphine instead of cortisone."

'Then my father said, "Don't threaten me, Chamberlayne. Soon I'll have no reputation left to speak of. I don't mind if the world does know about the woman you robbed of her child and its birthright. I'll tell the world what a fine lawyer you are."

'It was only later I realized what they were referring to. My father had treated him for venereal disease, and at some time procured an abortion for a woman pregnant with his bastard. Presumably Chamberlayne bullied her into it.'

'Christ. That would have done his image no good.'

'No, indeed. Such things were illegal in those days. And old Ralph Chamberlayne had a reputation for unbending rectitude. It was only those closer to him who saw how that was another way of saying he was callous and ruthless.'

'But your father kept his secret?'

'Of course. He was bound by his oath. Professional men have to learn to keep secrets if they are to flourish. Particularly in a place such as Fernsford was, and still is.'

'Rose, I feel terrible, as if I've made you say things that –'

'I wouldn't tell a living soul. Indeed you have, Sarah, darling. You have that capacity. An unabashed life-force. A sort of pugnacious charm. A power to elicit confession. All of that.' She blew her nose and wiped her eyes. 'Come on, back to the office, or he who must be obeyed will be unappeasable. I'm not the only one who finds you captivating. Mark, poor boy, is completely cow-eyed over you.'

I blushed hotly. 'Mark? What do you mean?'

'You're not the only one who sees things going on, darling.'

Despite its name, Combe Episcopi is not quaint. The original village has long since been swallowed up in a rash of tacky housing estates which stretch almost back to the motorway junction. Why anyone would want to live in a dump like this was beyond me, but lots seemed to. Perhaps they'd been sold on the fresh air and country life bit, but there was precious little of that with the M39 growling day and night and the smell of pig shit wafting over from the factory farm on the Bath road.

Using the estate layout plan from the bundle in Dead Filing, I had identified the location on my OS map and found it without difficulty. There was an old and peeling white-painted sign nailed to a leaning post. Oakdean Farm – Fresh Eggs and Produce For Sale.

I stopped at a muddy lay-by in front of a galvanized tubular-steel five-bar gate, the top rail of which was bound around with corroded barbed wire. On the other side of the gate, there was only a cart track heading downhill and round a corner, two whitish lines worn into the stony clay, with thick wiry tufts of grass sprouting in between.

I sat in the car looking out through the wound-down window. It was bloody obvious even from here that there was no housing development going on. Where the hell was Paul? I checked my watch. I was still a little early so I couldn't have missed him. I'd given him full instructions on how to find the place. He wasn't the sort of dozy bloke who would get lost. I waited another five minutes with increasing impatience, then I got out and locked the car. He would see the Fiesta and know I had gone in.

The gate was secured by a substantial chain and padlock, both rusted and draped with spiders' webs. No one had opened it for some time. On closer examination, however, the rust was superficial. Around the hasp of the lock was the glint of oil.

If Charmaine had come here, as I suspected, then maybe there were traces which a police forensic expert could analyse. I hitched up my skirt and clambered over the barrier, laddering my new tights in the process. I was hardly shod for a country ramble. My pumps had flattish heels, but their thin soles made me wince at the sharp edges of every stone I stepped on.

I hobbled down the track. The entrance was soon lost to sight around the bend. On either side there were high banks, from the top of which trees loomed, the lower slopes of which were overgrown with bushes and thick with dark green, leathery ivy. Down and down I went.

At last the bank on my right fell away and the track levelled out. There was a post and barbed-wire fence, the posts leaning and the wire swollen with terminal rust. The field beyond was covered in tall, brown, unmown grass, interspersed with outcrops of enormously tall thistles. It sloped down towards a wood of stunted trees.

I kept on walking around yet another bend. The lane passed through a gateway with pillars of crudely cemented stones and a broken wooden gate hanging drunkenly open into a substantial yard around which were grouped the buildings of what had once been Oakdean Farm. I didn't rate the chances of buying eggs for breakfast.

Across the coarse concrete, which was smeared with old dried animal dung and fragments of straw, was a stone barn, its central wooden doors crookedly ajar. Within I could see an untidy jumble of bales of hay, apparently damp and rotting, from the sickly sweet smell that drifted over. There were several other buildings, roofless and ruinous, overgrown with nettles, saplings sprouting from their walls. Beyond the barn was a smallish square stone house. Once the frost-crumbled brick herringbone-pattern path must have led to the plank door through the kind of cottage garden you see on TV adverts for wholemeal bread. Now it was a wilderness, with here and there amongst the docks and nettles, a splash of yellow or blue from some surviving flowers.

I reached out to the once black-painted iron doorknob and twisted it. It was locked. I rubbed the grime from the bottom pane and peered in through one of the front windows. It was a small sitting room, with a brown tiled fireplace, the grate littered with cinders and grey ash. A sofa in grubby chintz faced the hearth, and there were two matching easy chairs on either side. In the centre was an orange box turned on its side as an impromptu table. There were a couple of white disposable plastic cups on top of it, and an uncorked dark green bottle with shreds of gold foil round the neck. Tumbled on the bare boards alongside were a couple of similar bottles, and more plastic beakers. Strewn around the room were various food wrappers and small cardboard boxes. Under the window lay an empty dark blue paper carrier bag with 'Thackeray's of Fernsford' printed on it in fancy gilt lettering. I knew Thackeray's. It was the city's most up-market grocer and delicatessen – fifteen different kinds of smoked salmon, that kind of thing.

There had obviously been a party here. Oodles of champagne and the most expensive kinds of nibbles. It was quite a contrast with the dereliction of the surroundings. The house, as was clear when I looked through the other ground floor windows, was completely unlived-in. There was another small, unfurnished room and a kitchen, with a stoneware sink full of grime, and an ancient coal range.

This wasn't the kind of debris left by a bunch of the local yobbos. Take-away and lager would be their scene, not Moët et Chandon and *pâté de foie gras*. The party-givers were Appleby and Chewton. Champagne was their style, as I had seen from the photograph in Stapleton's file. Had they entertained a guest at this gathering? The thought of what might have happened afterwards gave me the creeps. Here was evidence of a sort for the scene-of-crime officer to get stuck into.

I started to walk back across the concrete yard, occasionally glancing back at the blank windows of the house and the silent, ruined farm buildings. As I drew level with the derelict barn, a fleeting gleam of sunlight, escaping through a gap in the dense cloud cover, shone through the gap between the double doors, illuminating the tumbled bales within. There was an answering glint from amongst the mouldering heap.

Curious, I went over to investigate. By the time I crossed the yard, the sun was once again obscured. I peered into the gloom. There was nothing but the sickly warm scent of hay. I pulled my head back into the fresh air. It must have been a trick of the light.

Then I noticed that the gap between the doors was not the result of a casual failure to secure them. Considerable effort had been expended to force the rickety panels closed. The bottom long iron strap hinge, which must have been rusted solid, had ripped out of the jamb when the door had been shoved against the frame. This had happened recently, as the exposed and splintered timber of the jamb from which the fixing screws had dragged was still white and clean. An iron bar lay nearby and shards of rotten wood from the bottom timbers were evidence that someone had tried hard to lever the door shut. Whoever it was had clearly abandoned the attempt as useless.

Why go to all that trouble, recklessly damaging the doors in the process? I stood staring into the gap. Then, my nose wrinkling against the smell, I turned sideways and pushed through into the barn.

I waited until my eyes adjusted. Bales were stacked on either side and at the back up to the great roof beams which straddled the width of the building. Above them, there were glimpses of the white sky where the slates had slipped and shifted on the rafters. The stacks, although old and decaying, were orderly. The bales, like a child's building blocks, formed carefully built walls. It was only immediately in front of the entrance where the neatness had dissipated into a higgledy-piggledy mass, where the binding strings of the bales had snapped, with the straw spilling into loose heaps.

There was something deliberate about the effect of this apparent chaos. On an impulse, I grabbed hold of a pitchfork which leaned against the right hand stack. The wooden handle was worn smooth and warm to the touch. I started to prod it into the disordered pile of straw.

There was a hollow-sounding clang as the tines of the fork hit some other metal object. I probed again, lower down. This time I hit something solid, but springy, like rubber. I dropped the fork and excitedly began to scrabble in the prickly straw like a child in a sandpit. It was like finding a treasure in a fairground bran-tub.

My questing hands found something cold and smooth. It didn't feel agricultural. I threw the straw wildly aside, sweeping it away from the flat metal surface I had encountered. Then, my fingers tingling and my heart pounding with the effort, I stopped to examine my discovery.

It was the roof of a car. It glimmered like a mirror of blood in the light through the crack in the doors. With tension roaring in my ears, I took hold of the pitchfork and stabbed and heaved at the heavy clumps and bundles of stalks. My hands were torn in several places by the stiff stems.

Finally, I wrenched the last obscuring bale aside and stood back to let the waning daylight shine on what I had uncovered.

It was not just any old banger driven into the barn to avoid road tax or insurance. It was a recent model red Vauxhall Cavalier. Even though the rear number-plate had been unscrewed, I knew what I had found. I could see a scratch on the end of the rear bumper where an inexperienced learner driver had scraped it against a wall. I had done that on my second lesson with Charmaine Potter.

I felt suddenly sick with fear as my suspicions turned into embodied certainties.

She must have driven here to pick up the latest instalment of the hush money. They had lulled her with food and drink, then beaten her to death. They'd taken the body to Fernsmouth. Of course, they'd used Chewton's boat. That's how they got the body into the yacht harbour without being observed. They'd put it aboard at the private jetty at Welscombe.

I suddenly felt very afraid. I couldn't go back to the office and pretend any longer. They had killed and they would kill again if they had to. I had never expressed that to myself in full clarity. What had been a piece of intellectual puzzle solving had become a very dangerous game.

I had been so preoccupied that I didn't register the noise outside until its roaring filled my ears. It was the sound of a powerful car engine. There was a squeal of brakes, then the engine stopped. Thank God. Paul had finally got here. I needed all the help I could get. I ran to the aperture between the doors, and was about to yell out a greeting, when I saw that the car which had arrived was not Paul's, but a silver Mercedes.

I stood covertly watching from the shadows as Francis Appleby slid smoothly and unhurriedly out of the driver's seat.

He had driven the big car as close to the entrance as he could. The massive bumpers were hard against the doors. I could have stretched out and touched the shiny chrome three-pointed star. He turned back to look at the bend in the track. Bumping along the rough surface appeared the low, aerodynamic shape of Trevor Chewton's Porsche. It stopped in the gateway to the yard, blocking it. Chewton climbed out and jogged over to Appleby.

I retreated away from the gap in the doors, but not so far as to be out of earshot.

I heard Chewton's harsh voice. 'Where the fuck is she?'

'See for yourself. Straw all over the place. She's been in there. Probably still is. I parked the car tight to stop her running out.'

'She's found the fucking car! This is all your fault, Walter. I fucking told you not to agree to employ anyone. And then you go and get a bitch like that! I knew she would be trouble the first time I saw her.'

'I had no choice, you know that. I was under pressure. It would have done us no good at all if the partnership had folded. I thought she would have her hands full keeping up with the routine work. Her background was –'

'Background! That's all you public-school prats notice. Be thankful that spastic of an architect realized in time which side his bread was buttered on.'

'For Christ's sake, shut up. She's probably listening.'

'Let's get on with it. One out, one in, just like in the old days, Lieutenant Appleby.'

I watched as his thickset form hoisted itself with surprising ease over the bonnet of the car and on to the straw-covered cobbles within. He waited for his eyes to adjust, turning his head from side to side like a radar scanner. I found it hard to convince myself that he couldn't see me. I felt a terrible weary temptation to stand up and shout out, 'Okay, you've got me bang to rights.' Just like on the telly.

I struggled to control my shaking and hunkered further down in my hiding place. My mind had reeled as I heard of my betrayer, but I locked the feeling away. I could not face it at present.

Chewton was a wary bastard. He stood by the doors gazing around, occasionally sticking his massive chin up in his neck-stretching gesture. He looked more bull-like than ever. I almost expected him to snort and paw the ground.

But he yelled out, 'Come on, Sarah. Come out now and we won't have to get nasty. We'll work something out.'

The sound batted around the cobwebbed trusses of the roof, then died away. There was silence in the gloom, and outside, only the soft sighing of the breeze around the eaves.

'Be sensible, Sarah, love. We haven't got all fucking day. We'll make you an offer. We're businessmen, you know.'

I said nothing. Like fuck, they'd make me an offer. The same as they'd made Charmaine.

'You're being stupid. We'll get you out of here. Like we did those fucking EOKA terrorists.' He reached in his pocket and pulled out a cigarette lighter. There was a spurt of flame, it flared for a moment, then died.

'They used to run out screaming, begging us to shoot them. It would have been cruel not to oblige. And we're a long way from the fire station.'

He was bluffing, surely? Trying to panic me into moving. A blaze with my body and Charmaine's car in it would raise too many questions, wouldn't it? Wouldn't it?

He'd been moving as he spoke. He'd climbed up on the low stack of bales alongside the Cavalier, and was using the extra height to see further up the main stacks. Pretty soon, he'd start climbing around. When he found me, I would be trapped. Decisions. If I moved, they might catch me. If I stayed, eventually they would. All they had to do was start pulling down the stacks of straw. Of course, that was it!

I looked down from my position lying on the top of the right-hand stack. My head was slightly below the level of the cross-beams. I peered over the edge. Chewton was still squinting into the upper darkness. He'd moved around to where the front of the Cavalier had been driven into the straw. He was directly underneath the outer wall of the stack on which I was crouching.

Gingerly, I rolled over on to my back, the sharp points of the straw sticking through my thin jacket. A bed of nails, this job. Then I wriggled back under the beam, away from the edge. Then I sat up quickly, turned round and slid my feet forward under the thick trunk. I leaned back and braced my shoulders against it, feeling the roughness where the bark still adhered, centuries after the tree had been cut down. It was thick with dust and bird muck which had billowed into my face as I disturbed it. I screwed up my eyes, desperately trying not to cough and sneeze.

I thrust my feet forward, seeking the hollow place between the layers of bales. I had it. I drew up my knees, thrust my ankles down into the straw and pushed. Nothing. I pushed again. I felt the top bale wobble. I pushed again with all my strength, willing the bale to move.

It moved. I writhed around and flung out my arms to grab hold of the timber, to stop myself from going with it as the front wall of the stack toppled and fell. I heard a yell of pain or fury from below. I looked down. Chewton was nowhere to be seen in the avalanche of straw. I let go my hold of the beam, and half slid, half scrambled down the stack, landing with a jarring thump at the bottom. I felt my ankle bend over and a horrible pain flashed up my leg.

I flattened my lips with the pain. I had started to scramble on to the bonnet of the car blocking the exit when I felt cold steel on the back of my neck. I whirled round to see that Appleby had emerged from the shadows and was holding the pitchfork, one of its wickedly pointed tines only a couple of inches away from my right eye.

'Down,' he commanded.


I woke up with a start. It was pitch dark. I'd been dreaming. At first, it was quite floaty and sexy, drifting along in the sunshine, surrounded by lots of old buildings, my hand trailing in the water, in a kind of boat, a gondola, that was it. But when I turned to give a flirtatious smile to the gondolier, he leered back at me with the hideous mug of Trevor Chewton.

Forget dreams. This was reality. I was blindfolded and gagged, rolled up in an evil-smelling piece of old carpet so I couldn't move a muscle and squashed into the boot of Appleby's Mercedes. I'd lost count of the time I'd been in here. For some of the time at least the car had been moving, but now it was at a standstill. I felt sick and exhausted. What the hell were they going to do to me?

I'd thought that Appleby and Chewton were going to murder me there and then. If looks could kill, I'd have been dead several times over. Appleby had removed his jacket and had gone to the back of the barn to fork the straw back over the Cavalier.

I was left alone with Chewton. His Savile Row charcoal suit was grey with dust and stuck like a pincushion with shards of straw. One eye was closed and puffy, and the side of his face was badly scratched. A bale must have caught him a sidelong blow. Another few inches and it might have knocked his head off.

'You,' he jerked his chin at me, 'no more heroics, or I'll beat you to death here and now.'

I said nothing.

He frogmarched me into the yard and made me lie prone on the filthy concrete. He squatted down beside me and patted my behind. He took my arms and pinioned them behind me, clamping both wrists easily in one hand. I squirmed and he planted his knee in the middle of my back.

'What a silly girl you've been, Sarah. Interfering with the grown-ups like this. You need a good spanking. I've always thought that arse of yours was very spankable. I might just take the opportunity.'

I felt his hand under my skirt, gripping the top of my tights and pants together and dragging them down in one swift movement.

I felt the chill air on my bottom. I screamed out and jerked and kicked as much as I could. I felt a thick finger tracing the division between my buttocks then sliding between my thighs.

I heard Appleby's voice say, 'What the hell do you think you're doing?'

'Having a bit of fun. Perk of the job. It's not every day you see a nicer bum than this, Walter, my old pal. Look at it. Peach-like, isn't it? White and soft. No bikini lines on this one. You've never seen the sun, have you, my beauty?'

'For Christ's sake. Cover her up. We've more important things to do.'

I felt Chewton's hands fumbling with the rucked up underwear at my knees, then he roughly dragged it back over my rear. He let go of my arms and took his knee out of the small of my back.

I twisted round, and was on my feet in a flash, my right fist rocketing towards his face. He wasn't anticipating it and I caught him full in the left eye, the side which hadn't been battered by the falling bale.

He hardly flinched, then, in a gesture so automatic I realized that he was well used to this kind of street fighting, he lashed back with a sweeping blow of his arm which caught me on the side of the head and knocked me back flat and hard on the straw-strewn concrete.

When I attempted to drag myself upright, he put out a black moccasined foot and pushed me down again.

'I don't think you heard me the first time. Any more of that, I'll fucking smash your face through the back of your head.'

'Like Charmaine? I thought at first it was Appleby. He's a smarmy swindling bastard, but you're the expert in beating up women, aren't you? They fucking well missed that out of those newspaper tributes, along with the rest of it.'

He laughed. 'She's got you bang to rights, hasn't she, Walter? "Have you any further instructions, sir?" Well, as it happens, I have. Get the fuck over to the house and see if there's anything in there that we can immobilize our charming colleen with. Not rope. A bump on the head won't matter. Rope burns and people start to take notice.'

'In a moment. I have to get hold of Lambert on the phone. Tell him to activate those accounts I opened in case we had this kind of trouble. I'll do some backdated transfers when I get back to the office. They'll be easy even for the most thickheaded policeman to trace back to her files. You're not the only one who's doing the thinking.'

'Well, that is comforting. Never forget you got us into this mess in the first place. All right, get on with it.' He bent down and grabbed my wrists. 'On your feet, Miss Paddy.'

I was shivering uncontrollably as Chewton towed me at arm's length across the yard to the farmhouse. Appleby stood at the door of the Mercedes talking rapidly into the carphone. Chewton unlocked the door and pushed me through into the narrow hall.

He put me in a half nelson while he looked around. When I kicked at his shins, he casually shoved up my arm till the sinews cracked so much I thought he would really break it. 'You don't fucking listen, do you? Calm down and you'll be all right.'

Appleby came in and Chewton pointed at the stair carpet. 'Just the thing. Rip it up. And a strip of those curtains. Make a good gag. Very Sarah Hartley, very Sanderson.' He laughed heartily then threw me to the floor.

I squirmed feebly in my vile-smelling strait-jacket. I was presumably still alive – even the God of the Pope could make a better fist of the afterlife. My head hurt and I felt sick. While I'd been lying in this pitch dark steel box, I'd worked out what they were going to do.

I was to be discredited so that anything I said would be ignored by the authorities. Appleby must have prepared his fall-back position ages ago. Accounts must have been opened at the FernWest in a number of false names, and these would be supplied with money from the client accounts of files with which I could be shown to have had dealings. Probably some of the ones which Appleby had thrown my way early on, and then taken back again.

Evidence would be produced that the accounts had been opened by me – my handwriting, or perhaps some junior clerk would be leaned on to identify me. Appleby and Lambert, the master fraudsters, could do that kind of thing in their sleep. So, farewell then, my legal career. I'd go to prison. Even as a first offence, judges took fraud on one's employers very seriously. Far more than duffing up one's wife or girlfriend. I'd be struck off. I'd never get another worthwhile job. I'd be in the gutter, from which I had so lately and with such infinite pains succeeded in climbing.

As for Chewton and Appleby and Lambert, they were taking a risk, but not much of one. No one would be minded to believe my story. By the time I was returned to circulation, Charmaine's car would have disappeared and the barn tidied up. The rest of it, I hadn't any proof of. I daresay they would search my place and find O'Riordan's file and destroy it. After a decent interval, they could return to their favourite occupation of ripping off the investors in the FernWest.

A great wave of depression swept over me. I'd never been what you'd call euphoric in my enjoyment of my membership of the legal profession, but that didn't mean I wanted to have it taken away from me in this bastard kind of a way.

I'd have been even more depressed if I'd known what they were really planning.

I woke again from a doze to find that my bladder was bursting. I tried to yell out, but the choking gag prevented more than a feeble mumble from escaping. My mouth was dry, the saliva soaked into the material between my teeth. My whole body was chilled and numb from confinement. And now I was forced to wet myself, like a swaddled infant. I almost cried like a baby from the humiliation of it.

Vaguely from outside my prison, I heard footsteps and voices. Then there was a couple of soft thuds and the car rocked slightly. Doors closing, driver and passenger getting in. I was on the move again. Over the stink of the carpet and the warm moist scent of my urine, I caught the hot acrid petrol whiff of the exhaust. It burbled under my head through the floor of the boot.

I felt the car twist and turn, felt the change in level as it went down hills, heard the squeal of brakes and the deceleration as we stopped at junctions or traffic lights. Then there was the steady vibration of the engine and the whine of the tyres as we drove at speed.

After what I judged was about half an hour, we began to slow, the stops and the braking became more frequent. From the jerks and lurches, I realized that we must be back in town. Appleby's traffic driving technique was unmistakable even from this position. Oh, for a minor traffic offence, a collision, any excuse for someone to look in the boot! But I doubted that I could be heard even from right alongside the car.

After a few minutes, the car was moving much more slowly. Then it rocked on its suspension as it made a sharp turn to the left. The note of the tyres changed from an asphalt hiss to a strange rhythmic rumble. I knew that sound. It was cobblestones. We were at Friars Haven.

The car stopped. Two doors banged. Two sets of feet sounded on the paving. There was a rattle of keys at the front of the boot and it opened upwards with a sigh from the hydraulic supports. I was conscious of no change in the light intensity through the blindfold. It must be dark. I felt a glorious fresh breeze on the thin strips of my face not covered with cloth.

Two pairs of steel hands took hold of my shoulders and ankles through the roll of carpet, and hoisted me into the air. I had an instant's sense of disorientation, then I came to rest again at each end, but sagging painfully in the middle as the unyielding carpet dug into my back. I was being carried on their shoulders.

There was a jolting as they settled the load more comfortably, just like a pair of removal men. Then there was the swaying sense of motion as they began to walk. Occasionally they betrayed their lack of skill at this work as they momentarily lost balance and their leather-shod shoes slipped slightly on the cobblestones.

Where were we going? Instead of stopping to bundle me into another car or van, they carried on, more steadily now as they fell into a rhythm, their feet echoing out the refrain, left, left, left, right, left.

The chill wind grew in intensity and, beyond the anxious pumping of my heart, I could make out the sounds of the nearby city, the roar of traffic on the ring-road flyover, a distant police siren, and overhead the drone of a jet plane. Comforting everyday sounds. And nearer at hand was another sound, a sound which made me realize where we were and what they were going to do: the sound of water lapping against a stone quay.

They set me down not ungently on the cobblestones and turned me over. I must have been in a puddle, because there was a clammy chill as water soaked into the fabric around my head. With all my strength, I lashed out with my bundled legs, but succeeded only in flapping weakly like a landed fish. I felt knees boring hard into the back of my calves and in the middle of my shoulder blades, crushing my head against the hard stone.

Hands were at the bonds at my ankles, knees and shoulders. The carpet was peeled away as if I were a snake being stripped of its skin, leaving me naked and vulnerable. Then the iron band of the blindfold was off my temples, and more fumbling fingers at the nape of my neck released the gag.

For one glorious moment, I was free to scream and kick and struggle in the pitiless grasp of the silent shadowy figures beside me. As I flung back my head to yell out my lungs, I saw the bluish purple sky, shading to amber at its cited rim, and in its zenith the sprinkled constellations of cold bright stars. Then it seemed the cosmos whirled about me as I was hurled into the air by my tormentors. For a dizzy moment I reached out as if to cling desperately to my last view of life, then with a splash I heard but dimly, the stinging cold water of Friars Haven closed over my head.

Five

**THICKER THAN WATER**

## XXV

'Police divers are searching a disused canal basin in Fernsford for the body of local solicitor Sarah Hartley. A note left in the missing woman's car which was found abandoned at the scene is believed to indicate that she intended to take her own life. The BBC have been informed by reliable sources that considerable sums, amounting to thousands of pounds, are missing from the client accounts of Chamberlayne's, her employers. A spokesman for the firm would make no comment on these allegations, but spoke only of his personal grief at the apparent tragedy.'

I leaned forward and switched off the crackling radio of Caroline's ancient Renault. '"Personal grief"! I bet that was fucking Appleby. He was "the reliable source" as well, I shouldn't wonder. The bastard.'

Caroline took her eyes off the road for a second to grin at me. 'So how does it feel to be a master criminal on the run?'

'Better than being dead. But it's a near thing. What I feel worst about though is that I've got you involved as well.'

'It was my own choice.'

'I still feel bad that you're mixed up in this business. I can't quite believe I am. I wonder how long it'll be before they twig that I'm not at the bottom of the Haven marina?'

'Not very long. The police may go on to drag the canal itself. But Chewton and Appleby know where they chucked you in. They must be wondering already why they haven't found your body.'

'Even the police must be suspicious. Faked suicide by fraudster is not unknown.'

'It was pretty clever of them, wasn't it, to have stitched you up like that? They must have been planning this for a while.'

'I know. It works just as well now I'm still alive. They're clever all right. It's me who's been bloody stupid.'

'I don't see how you can blame yourself. You couldn't have known how ruthless they would be. And don't forget it's because you're clever that you spotted what was going on in the first place.'

'The thing is that I didn't find out quickly enough. Now they've got in first and blackened my name, so that nobody will believe anything I say. I've no real evidence. All I've done is ruined my career. I've lost everything I've worked for. I don't know what to do now. If I go to the police, they won't listen to me. They'll keep me banged up on remand. It's the most awful, rotten, stinking mess. I'm not even me any longer.'

I flipped down the visor and sneaked yet another look at myself in the little mirror. As had become my habit, I first screwed up my eyes like a child, afraid of the sight. Then I opened them.

Jesus, it was so awful, I felt like crying all over again. Who was this person staring out at me?

She had short-cropped black hair. Her complexion was deeply tanned. Her eyebrows were thickly pencilled and her eyelashes heavy with mascara. Her mouth still showed signs of the purplish lipstick she applied at intervals throughout the day. Her cheeks were rouged.

I grimaced at her and stuck my tongue out. At least that was still mine, as were the not very even teeth with the crooked front incisor. In their caves of greasepaint, the eyes were green as mine had been, but as hard and bright as emerald.

I turned the visor back and settled into the seat. There was another hour to go, at least. Caroline's eyes were glued to the road, and she was observing the speed limit with meticulous care. We didn't want to be stopped by a traffic cop.

Suicide. That was why they had been so careful to leave no marks of any struggle. That was the reason for all the careful wrapping up. No ordinary plod would have had any reason to suspect a thing. I'd given them the method myself, in the swimming pool, the night of Trevor Chewton's birthday party. I'd told him I couldn't swim. He must have stored it up in his memory: this one I can drown. That was the night when Paul and I . . . I blanked off that part of my memory, as if it were an agonizing tooth abscess I had to avoid disturbing.

I had always feared drowning. I felt a resurgence of panic as I remembered the icy embrace of the water, the churning choking invasiveness of it, the muddy, weedy stink of it.

The shock of that dive into the dark depths will, I think, stay with me for ever. I seemed to go down for an eternity, my clothes suddenly as heavy on me as a suit of armour. Water forced its way into my mouth and up my nostrils. I clamped my lips tight and fought against the temptation to breathe. There was only endless blackness before my bulging eyes. I was sinking. I was really going to drown.

I heard a faint voice inside my head. 'Kick your legs, Sarah. Kick your legs, and sweep the water away with your arms. Kick! Sweep! Kick! Sweep!' I was at Hornsey Road Baths, and Miss Major, the PE teacher at Poofters whom everyone made fun of for her moustache and her clothes and her short back and sides, was trying to teach me, the worst pupil in the class, to swim. 'Come on, you little tart, you can do it!' she roared. But I never did.

Now, desperately, I kicked my legs, and my body at the bottom of its plunge, began to rise. I kicked harder, thrashing the freezing water in a frenzy, flailing my arms.

My head smashed through the surface. I felt the impact of it as if it had been a plate-glass window. I opened my eyes and there were the stars, and on the heaving water lay bars and spangles of orange light. I felt the wind slicing at my numb cheeks and it was wonderful. Then I sank again.

This time, I swallowed what seemed like gallons of water before I forced my mouth closed. My lungs were on fire, my limbs so heavy. A voice within crooned, 'You only have to let yourself go.'

I kicked out savagely with my numb legs, forcing them to move, feeling them respond sluggishly as in a dream. Again I rose to the surface, again I trod water violently and again I felt myself going under.

As I sank, there was a splash of something landing in the water close by. And a voice. Not in my imagination this time, but a real voice.

I kicked my legs with renewed vigour, my arms flat on the surface, dragging and clawing as if it were a solid substance by which to haul myself along, staring around me, with stinging half-open eyes.

A few yards away, an orange lifebelt bobbed in the dark waves.

But not just bobbing. It was moving towards me.

The voice was shouting, 'The ring! Grab the fucking ring! Fucking grab the fucking ring!'

I lunged at it as it came towards me and my frozen fingers brushed one of the rope handles. The touch of the wet cord sent the urge to live surging through me. My body gave a shuddering jerk and my hand clamped tight, drawing the lifesaver towards me. I heaved myself on top. It revolved smoothly and tipped over my head. I clamped my arms tightly on its warm buoyancy.

I felt it move in the water. Someone was towing me back to the quay. Then there was a bump as the far side of the belt collided with something solid. The quay. I raised my head to see above the black mass of the stonework, a figure silhouetted against the orange glow of the sky. It moved and flattened itself and I felt a hand grab the soaking wet cloth of my coat by my right shoulder.

'My hand!'

I reached up my left hand, numb and remote, and it was enclosed by another, hard and scarcely warmer than mine. The grip on my shoulder tightened almost unbearably as I was hauled out of the canal basin. I could feel the water pouring over my skin under my clothes as it made its escape. I kicked and scrabbled with my bare feet against the slippery masonry of the quay, finding a toehold against which I pushed up, swinging my left arm over the shoulder of the man above me in a clumsy embrace.

At last my elbows rested on the lip of the quay and, still gripped by the iron hands, I squirmed and dragged myself up and away from the edge. Then the hands were turning me on my side. I felt a finger at my mouth, opening it wide, then I could hear the laboured breathing of my rescuer as he bent close to me, listening. Hearing the slow rasp of my breathing, he was satisfied and withdrew. He did not speak.

I must have lain for several minutes on the cold hard cobbles of the quay, retching up the water I had swallowed, and gulping in great sucking breaths of air into lungs which wheezed and bubbled as if I had been suddenly afflicted with some chronic, wasting disease.

I writhed myself into a half-sitting position, leaning sideways supported by my arms, my head hanging down, still coughing and spluttering, my nose running with mucus, my saturated hair coalesced into thick ropes, my clothes hanging on me like sheets of ice-cold lead. I was shaking uncontrollably.

When I lifted my head and pulled aside the sodden curtain of hair, I could see no details of the features of the man who had saved me, only a dark figure crouching beside me.

I struggled to my feet, battling against the stiff weight of my clothes and the exhaustion that was clouding my brain. The figure made no move to intervene. He even backed off a foot or two, retreating further into the shadows behind him.

I reached out a hand towards him. 'Thank you, thank you,' I croaked the inadequate words. 'Thank you. You saved my life.'

For a second there was no reply. Then a voice that was scarcely more than a whisper replied, 'Don't thank me, Pippi. I know now why I had to stay. A life was owed.'

I staggered forward, hardly believing what I had heard, but encountered only the empty air. On the cobblestones of the quayside were rapid footsteps echoing in the darkness, crossing the end of the dock then fading into the night.

Then I pelted down the dark canyon between the warehouses. I ran so fast, so unheeding that I almost missed the Fiesta parked outside the Chewton offices.

It was unlocked. On the passenger seat was my handbag. In the dim light of the courtesy lamp, I saw the piece of paper lying on top of the dash by the wheel. I snatched it up.

It looked like my handwriting, though I had never written it.

Dear Francis
I'm sorry for everything. I think it's best if I end it this way. Yours, Sarah.

The car key was in the ignition.

I was about to climb into the driving seat, when I stopped. I had to leave the car as it was. That was the only way they would believe for a while that I was dead. With shaking hands, I took a Phonecard and some small change from my purse. Then I closed the door and ran with the remainder of my fading strength down the straight road between the warehouses, my body jarred as I slipped and slithered in my saturated shoes on the cobbles, through the gate and out into Canal Street.

There was a phone box a little way down Carpenter. I jabbed out the number with frozen fingers, then slumped against the glass wall of the booth while the ringing tone went on and on. I had no idea of the time. She couldn't be out. She never went out. Finally, a voice whose sleepiness was compounded with irritation came on the line. 'Who is it? It's the middle of the night.'

I spoke rapidly. When she spoke again, the sleepiness and the irritation were replaced by wonderful warm concern. 'Stay where you are, I'll come immediately.'

The waiting for her and the journey that followed is a blank. I remember only its end, turning into the rutted drive of Vale View and seeing the dark shape of the great cedar silhouetted against the pale sky, and through the upper windows of the roofless mansion the glitter of countless stars.

I felt the glory of being alive, so alive, as if the immersion at Friars Haven were not a drowning but a baptism.

The car was travelling more slowly. Through the window, I could see the slate rooftops of West London. We were on the elevated section of the M4 at Chiswick.

'We're nearly at Hammersmith. Where I get off.'

'I don't feel happy about leaving you.'

'This is where I belong. My manor. Besides, the best place to hide is in a crowd.'

'What are you going to do? Where will you stay? I wish I had more money to give you, but...'

'Don't worry about me. I'm a survivor. It's better you don't know. I agreed to let you drive me to London, since you insisted. But we also agreed you drove right back home again.'

She pursed her lips. I thought for an awful moment that she was going to go all stubborn again. Then she said, 'You're going to do something crazy.'

I protested vigorously, but she was absolutely right.

A gust of wet, warmish wind assaulted me as I came out of Manor House tube station into the Seven Sisters Road. I looked around me as if I were seeing it for the first time: the traffic roaring and grinding across the traffic lights at Green Lanes, the dreary sodden grass of Finsbury Park across the road, the walls of high rise flats on either side. A film set for Stalingrad.

I couldn't believe I was back like this. I had got out, hadn't I? I'd risen above the grime and the squalor: the vomit in the subway, the alkies slumped up against the piss-stained bricks of the pub on the corner drinking God knows what out of old plastic cider bottles, the old geezer rooting through the overflowing rubbish bin bracketed to the lamp-post. Welcome home, Sarah. Here I was, creeping along in the gloomy afternoon, the conquering heroine, come to reclaim her kingdom on the twelfth floor of Ernest Bevin House.

I knocked on the blue-painted flush-panelled door. I could see her getting painfully to her feet from the easy chair in front of the telly, and shuffling into the hallway. Then she'd stop, remembering that it was only in the old days that you answered a knock on the door with unsuspicious pleasure. Now it could be trouble.

I bent down to the letter box, and pushed back the aluminium flap. 'Mrs Flanagan,' I called through softly, 'it's Sarah. From number 154 on the fifteenth as was. Siobhan and Terry's daughter.'

I heard movement behind the door, then a voice, an old quavering voice. 'Sarah? Is it really you? Haven't I been hearing on that television this day of how you drownded yourself out of remorse for the stealing and all they say you were doing? Praise God you are alive and not in mortal sin.'

'It's not true about the stealing, Mrs F. I swear it by the Blessed Virgin. Please let me in and I'll explain.'

There was silence. Then she said, 'I never ever heard tell that you were a thief, even when the wildness was in you.'

There was the sound of a key turning, the click of a lock and the rattle of a chain. The door opened. She was older, more bent, but the fire still glimmered in her dark eyes. 'God in heaven, Sarah, child! What have you done to yourself? Is that how it is in the world of fashion?'

Half an hour later, I sat drinking Co-op tea and eating white sliced bread and jam in her tiny cold lounge. In the background the television set flickered, the sound turned down.

I'd given her a severely pruned version of what had been going on. 'I feel awful landing on you like this after all these years, but you're the only one I had to turn to.'

'So, you never took the money like they said you did?'

'No. I have to stay free to prove I didn't.'

She shook her head. 'It is hard for me to comprehend. You did so well for yourself, going to college and getting them qualifications. Your mammy, God rest her soul, would have been proud of you. And now to tell me this tale that might be on the television.'

'It's true, cross my heart. Can I stay here, please? Only for a day or so.'

She laid her trembling, swollen-jointed hand on mine. 'Stay for as long as you wish it, my love. And it's welcome you are to do so.'

I went out later and rang Harriet's office from a callbox. 'Hi. It's me. I'm alive. Don't say anything. Just listen. I hate to ask you this, but I need money. A lot. A thousand in cash. Can you get it by tomorrow morning?'

'Yes, I think so, but...'

'Good. Meet me with it in the garden at Leicester Square at half-past ten.'

On the way back, I called in at a supermarket and bought us some groceries. A couple of nice steaks, frozen chips, a chocolate cake and a bottle of Jamesons. Unlike Mrs Flanagan, I couldn't survive on bread and jam. And I had a busy evening ahead.

The mahogany door marked Lounge had a pattern of vine-leaves and grapes cut gem-like into its opaque etched-glass panel. I turned the fat brass knob and entered.

The room beyond was dimly lit, with the hushed and reverent atmosphere of a church. As in a church, the congregation were mainly elderly, and looked up with slightly fearful curiosity as I swung my hips up the aisle between the cast-iron three-legged tables to the bar at the end.

I ordered a gin and tonic, paid the barman, then hitched myself on one of the leather-topped stools. He stood polishing a glass, covertly eyeing me as if he was trying to place me. In congruence with his surroundings, he had the benevolent round face and white halo of hair of an elderly cleric. This was misleading as he had a string of convictions encompassing most of the more serious sections of the Offences Against the Person Act.

'Hello, George, long time no see.'

He put down the glass and leaned over to look at me more closely. 'I says to myself, I know her. But who is she?'

'I've had a make over since we last met at Chelmsford, George.'
'It can't be. Miss Hartley! I heard you'd, well...'
'You shouldn't believe rumours, George. Is Benny around?'
'I could ask.'
'Why don't you do that, George? And in the meantime, I'll have another of these.'

The Royal Standard was in Kingsland Road. Unlike many London pubs, it never broke the licensing laws, did not have brawls at the weekends, and was not an emporium for the sale of drugs or bent gear. It therefore remained tantalizingly immune from raids by the police, despite being well-known as a resort for a number of what the tabloids dignify as 'professional criminals'.

Benny Southgate, known irreverently by Pogson, though not by anyone else, as Benny the Blag, owing to his frequent appearances in the dock of the Old Bailey on robbery indictments, most of which, through the superior quality of his legal representation, failed to convince the jury, was one of the regulars.

Benny had a legitimate business as a supplier and repairer of second-hand office equipment, and I had come across him mostly in this connection in my early days at Vardy's, when menial duties involving machinery fell to me.

This evening, though, I wasn't looking for a good deal on a Xerox.

Benny was, needless to say, hugely amused to find me on his side of the fence, where I suspected he thought I fitted better. He was the sort of criminal who expected his brief to be, if not exactly a toff, a bit more out of the top drawer than I was.

'So you've had your fingers in the till, girl, and done a runner?'
'I've been fitted up, Benny.'

Yes, he had a good laugh at this, as you'd expect. He wiped his eyes with a very clean handkerchief. I drank some more gin and waited for him to get over his bit of theatre.

'Fitted up! Well, ain't that a shame! 'Course when you people say it happens, everybody has to believe it. I mean we couldn't believe that a solicitor's been nicking, could we? That has to be wrong. I mean, we all know that solicitors are the original lily-white boys – and girls, of course.'

'You've never had cause to complain about the way you were treated by Vardy's, Benny. We never applied for Legal Aid and then asked you for money on top. We never bribed or coached witnesses for you. We never –'

'I never said Mr Pogson was bent. But you – Know what I mean?'

If I'd slapped him across his fat red face the way I wanted, our interview might well have been terminated with extreme prejudice, but I managed to control myself. Benny was enjoying himself.

'I always said to myself you were a bit of an odd one to be a brief. I always said you should have been a copper.'

This witticism convulsed him again. I sat stony-faced, waiting for the fit to subside.

'Benny, it's nice talking over old times like this, but I'd like to get down to business. I asked to see you because I need you to do something for me. Not as a favour. I can pay.'

The smile vanished immediately. He swallowed up his vodka and nodded in the direction of the bar. George, who, although out of earshot, was keeping an eye on us, bustled over with another.

When he'd gone, Benny said quietly, 'Do what?'

I took a deep breath and told him.

'Fuck me, you must think I was born yesterday. You've been put up to this, haven't you, you fucking cow? Copper was right. Fucking entrapment is what this is. Now you fuck off right back to whoever sent you.' He stood up from the table. I saw George stop polishing the glass he'd been polishing since I'd come in and go on alert like a guard dog. My bravado was beginning to leak away and suddenly I felt sick with fear.

'Benny, please. It isn't like that. I'm not working for the coppers. I really am in bad trouble. Not just the police. They're the least of my worries. The people who stitched me up. They tried to kill me. It's only a matter of time before they clock me. I need protection. You must believe me. Ask around. You'll know where. You'll hear there's a contract on me, I swear it.'

He stared hard at me for a horribly long time, then he sat down. George started to polish the glass again, and my pulse rate subsided. 'Okay, but you better not be telling me stories. Now, if, theoretically speaking, I was able to get the items, how much are we talking about?'

This was more like it. In half an hour, we'd hammered out a deal. George got me a minicab – 'Don't worry, he won't give you no bother, darling' – and Benny ushered me to the door.

'Tomorrow, then, girl.'

'If I live that long,' I said.

I had the cab drop me by Manor House tube, and I waited till he'd driven off. I wasn't taking any chances. I let myself in with Mrs F's spare key. I felt sick with released tension and woozy with the gin. The tiny flat was dark. She'd gone to bed. I could hear the snores from the hallway. The Jameson's bottle stood on the draining board in the kitchen, empty. In the sink were two blood-streaked, greasy plates.

There was no instant coffee on the single shelf which housed her larder. I made tea and took it through to the sitting room. It had a french window which gave on to a narrow balcony. I opened it and stood with one hand on the steel railing. I didn't look down.

These places were prefabricated in factories, weren't they, like flat-pack furniture? Cheap and easy, just the thing for the people who didn't deserve any better.

On either side loomed high towers from the same do-it-yourself kit, pinpricked with light, like space stations in a science-fiction movie. Overhead, there were red and white flashes from an airliner. From that height, London must appear a carpet of amber light, a city on fire.

I was exhausted, but dared not sleep. I stayed watching until, at long last, the dawn bleached the sky.

I made myself more tea and toast in the kitchenette. She hadn't stirred. The Jamesons had been as good as Nembutal. I left her fifty pounds in tenners under the teapot, all I had left of the money Caroline had given me.

It was going to be a pleasant spring day. The rain and cloud had given way before a fresh breeze, and even the scruffy environs of Leicester Square looked better dappled with sunshine.

Here she was, as punctual as a news bulletin, coming through from the direction of the tube station, wearing a long pale linen skirt, cream shirt and a waist-length buff cotton cardigan, topped with dark glasses and a

Liberty-pattern silk headscarf. Garbo in New York. She paused at the gap in the black iron railings and gazed around.

I walked over to her, waving discreetly.

Her eyes narrowed, then she smiled. 'Darling, you really must tell me where you got it done.'

We embraced warmly. She clung on so fiercely, I had to struggle to breathe. 'I nearly had a heart attack when I saw the item come through the wire in the office. Suicide? I couldn't believe it. What the hell happened? I told you to be careful.'

I gave her the gist. 'I haven't time to go into the details.'

'No, you haven't. There was another flash before I came out. It said the police haven't found your body and are working on the assumption that you're still alive and that you've done a runner.'

'Shit! Have you got the money?'

She opened her milky-coffee-coloured leather shoulder bag and took out a thick envelope. 'Tens and twenties.'

I took it and stuffed it in the front pocket of my jeans.

'Thanks. What about the research? Come up with anything yet?'

She reached in the bag again and produced a spiral bound pad and flipped it open. 'I'll say. Barnsbury Investments, first. It's wholly owned by another company called Parkway, registered in the British Virgin Islands. The basic information it's filed at Companies House is suspect. The registered office is an accountant's firm in Camden Town, who wouldn't, needless to say, discuss the affairs of a client without their instructions. The two directors' and the secretary's names are probably fictitious. They're not listed in the phone book or the electoral register. I had the private addresses recorded checked. They're cheap boarding houses – accommodation addresses, any mail gets picked up for a consideration. It hasn't filed any accounts for years. We've got someone working on the Caribbean end, but once you're into tax havens, things get much less straightforward.

'It's pretty clear that, as you suspected, Barnsbury Investments is simply a cover. No one in the business has ever heard of it doing any developments.

'Next, Redwood's. They did exist back in the seventies and Appleby was a partner. There was "a policy disagreement", and "the partnership was dissolved" – they had a row and kicked him out. Changed the name of the firm. Respectability personified now. The senior man went very quiet when

I mentioned our Francis. They don't even want to wash their dirty linen in private. I suspect Appleby kept the firm going to use as the other side in the sham transactions he did for Chewton, like Babbage. Maybe he had a clerk in an office somewhere to keep up the appearances and answer the phone.'

'What about Lambert? Did you track him down?'

'Yes. He's the odd one out. Dedicated family man. Member of the golf club. Charitable works. Church of England. Successful career. He's a chartered accountant. Born in Hertfordshire. Educated Haberdashers' Aske's. Did National Service. In Cyprus, among other places.'

'Cyprus?' I shuddered. I had a sudden vision of the barn at Oakdean. I heard Chewton's voice. EOKA terrorists. Weren't they in Cyprus?

She looked at me in concern.

I asked her. 'Yes. Maybe they met there. Kindred spirits. Young men on the make.'

'Very likely. Afterwards, he went into articles with a firm in North London and qualified. He's a Fellow of the Institute of Chartered Accountants, no less. He's now fifty-two. He's been the Chief Executive of the FernWest for fourteen years. In his time it's expanded enormously. Industry sources say it's tightly managed, highly profitable. Never been anything suspicious about it. Before the FernWest, he managed a small local London outfit, the Canonbury Building Society. He went there from accountancy. They had one office at Highbury Corner. Very small beer. It was taken over by the Cheltenham and Gloucester a few years ago.'

'No problems, then?'

'Apparently not. If there was a scam there, then maybe he put the books right before he left.'

'What about the other partner from the good old days, friend Stapleton? He seems to have been the weak link. You thought that if he would agree to be interviewed, then we would have the foundation stone of a case. Did you find him?'

'I found him all right. But I should forget him if I were you.'

'Why? Won't he talk?'

She took off her sunglasses and rubbed her eyes. 'You've got me thinking all kinds of silly things now. It's not won't talk. It's can't. He's dead. He was killed in an accident fifteen years ago.'

'Shit! What kind of accident?'

'A very nasty one. He was visiting a building site and he somehow got behind a lorry that was making a delivery. Of concrete. He was crushed against a wall. I read the newspaper report of the coroner's inquest. The driver claimed he shouted a warning. Several witnesses backed up his story. Verdict, accident. Guess who was developing the site.'

'Chewton?'

'I'm afraid so.'

'Any more cheerful news?'

'No, that's as far as we've got. Not bad considering Rupert doesn't know what I'm up to yet. And I'm working on several other projects at the same time.'

'Harriet. I'm very grateful. Be careful, won't you? By the way there is one other thing.'

'What?'

I told her.

'Why do you want that?'

'Old times' sake.'

'A likely story. What are you up to? Why do you need that money?'

'I haven't time to wait for you to build the case. They'll find me eventually, or the police will. The only chance I have is to make something happen.'

'I don't like the sound of that. Sarah, you're awfully –'

'Stupid?'

'I was going to say "impulsive". Please be careful. You know how I feel about...'

I put my hand on hers. 'I do. And I will be. Isn't there a superstition that someone who escapes drowning can't then be drowned?'

'There are lots of other ways of dying.'

'Thanks for that thought.'

'You know the thing that still puzzles me in all this is, why Fernsford?'

'How do you mean?'

She'd put on her dark glasses again. She leaned back against the peeling green-painted wooden slats, pursing her mouth, a slash of dark purple against her pallor. The sunlight flashed on the gold dangling crookedly from her ear lobe.

414

Harriet concluded her silent reflection and sat up straight again. 'We know that their association started here in London. Then, all of them up and leave for Fernsford.'

'Chewton was the Fernsford man. He went, they followed.'

'But why? What was there for them? What was there for him, for that matter?'

'I think that in an odd kind of way he's genuinely interested in creating some kind of monument for himself. And in Fernsford. The town he'd left as a poor boy. I know he gets a kick out of lording it around there. I've seen him doing it. The way he bought out the Earl of Anglebury. It was a sort of aggressive revolutionary act. I can even understand some of that feeling. Of course, as we know, the whole foundation of his empire is corrupt, riddled with criminality. But then probably that applies to many things of that nature. When you look below the surface of the rich and famous, how they made their money, how empires were built, I bet there are all kinds of nasty things there. But that's more your field than mine.'

'You're a philosopher on the quiet, aren't you, Miss Hartley? Chewton, the man who would be king. The businessman whose methods were only slightly more extreme than the norm. Chewton, the Caesar of Fernsford.'

'You've lost me.'

'It was the dynastic title the Roman emperors gave themselves, king being anathema in what started as a republic. You know the legend of Romulus and Remus?'

'Is it likely I would?'

'They were twins, one nice, one nasty. The nasty one, Romulus, killed his brother Remus and founded Rome. Nice guys finish nowhere. There was a tradition amongst some primitive people that a building had to have a human sacrifice buried beneath it. The spilling of blood was the firmest foundation.'

'Fascinating. Chewton's spilt plenty of blood building his Rome.'

'I still think we're missing something. It was a bit pat wasn't it, that Appleby lucks into that firm, and Lambert gets the building society? A bit convenient? Too convenient.'

'Harriet. I have to go.' I'd stopped listening. Time was getting on. I didn't want to be late for my appointment.

415

We got to our feet and hugged. She prolonged the clinch, but I whispered fiercely in her ear, 'Go on, Harriet. I'll be all right.' But I wasn't entirely confident myself.

Hoxton Fields is the crappiest public park in London, possibly the entire universe. Finsbury or Clissold are Buck House's back garden in comparison. The café was burned out and not rebuilt years ago. The children's playground – three swings and a roundabout – has been carted off for scrap metal. The only trees that are still alive, massive planes you'd need an atom bomb to uproot, have their trunks scarified with knife-cut obscenities and their lower limbs ripped off.

The rankly long grass is still intact, but that's because no one has yet found a reason for nicking it. It's mown once in a blue moon by the council and it must be heavy work for the cutting machine, because every square yard is solid with dog shit, curled up like giant worm casts, take-away food cartons, empty cans and bottles and used hypodermics.

The only other thing in this charming oasis which has survived the ravages of time is the sculpture known as the *Spirit of the Blitz*, which, as it is a walk-in re-creation of a wartime bombed-out house, presents, other than a surface for graffiti, little for the vandals' imagination to work on, and besides, it's made, symbolically, from reinforced concrete.

I had been told by Benny to be here at one o'clock. I had been pacing around already for half an hour and no one had shown up.

The park was completely empty. The sculpture is bang in the centre, and you get a good view over the acres of flat turf. I looked at my watch. It was almost one thirty and I was on the point of giving up when I saw a car slotting into a space in the street which bordered the far side. A bloke got out of the car, didn't bother to lock it, and set off on the cracked tarmac path which led in my direction.

He was young, younger than I, in a leather jacket and jeans, with a minimalist haircut. 'Benny sent me. You got the money?'

I nodded.

'Let's have it then.'

I took out the envelope and handed it over. He didn't even look at it, but stuffed it away in his inside pocket. He knew that no one in his right mind would even think of fiddling Benny. He held out a key ring. 'The motor's plates will look kosher, but the rest of it don't bear close examination. I wouldn't get stopped in it if I were you.'

'What about the other item?'

'In the glovebox. It's not what you'd call a lady's model, so I'd watch out with it, eh girl?'

'Oh, I will.'

He set off across the park in the opposite direction, not looking back. Another client satisfied. We try harder.

A wind blew up, rippling the grass like water, turning it silver in the sunlight as I headed towards where he'd parked the battered Cortina.

# XXVI

Quite by chance, just like in the movies, there was a café opposite the building I was watching. I sat there pretending to read the *Evening Standard* and drinking very slowly a cup of incredibly expensive espresso.

It was a smart office block, very hi-tech, a grid of glass squares held together with lines of dark-red metalwork. On one corner a bullet-shaped glass lift slid up and down, packed with young keen-looking types carrying notebook computers in smart shoulder bags. Hoxton could have been on another planet.

I'd stashed the decrepit Ford in a twenty-four-hour multi-storey car park. I couldn't risk leaving it on the street. I hoped it would survive the journey I had in mind for it. Benny's men must have done the owner a real favour when they nicked it.

Then I saw him. He was holding the door for a group of giggling women. I groaned. They weren't all going off to the pub for a Friday night drunk? It seemed not. The gaggle dispersed in various directions. Colin, alone, turned in the direction of his flat, as I'd expected him to do. I drank up my coffee and set off in pursuit.

Harriet had told me that Colin lived in a mansion block a few streets away from his offices on Shaftesbury Avenue, east of Cambridge Circus. Bloomsbury was certainly a step up for him. I'd had a look at the place earlier and seen that the front lobby door was controlled by a key-pad lock and an internal entry phone. I'd have to jump him before he got inside.

He did me a favour by stopping at a local supermarket on the way. I watched him through the window going round with his wire basket, then went on ahead quickly. Past Colin's entrance round the corner of the building, I leaned against the railings waiting for him to reappear. Here he was, swinging his plastic bag of provisions, a pigskin briefcase in the other hand. Hey-ho, hey-ho, its home from work we go.

He put down the groceries to operate the key pad and bent sideways holding the street door half open to pick them up. I trod softly up behind him.

I nipped round him, sticking my foot over the threshold.

'Hi, there.'

His face had shown alarm, then genuine puzzlement as he peered at my face, puckering up in that bemused way I had once found attractive. Then the penny dropped.

'You see it but you don't believe it. It is I. Aren't you going to invite me in?'

I followed him up the carpeted stairs. He was wearing newish Italian loafers, and his grey suit had the deliberately casual hang of some designer label.

He fumbled for his keys.

Inside was a long hallway. The first door was a kitchen. He took the groceries through and dumped them on a marble-topped pine table which was so new I could see the John Lewis tag still hanging from one of the legs.

'I can't believe you're here. What did it say in the paper? Embezzled money. Faked your own suicide. On the run. Unbelievable. Is that why you've gone dark?'

'As you correctly surmise, Sarah Hartley is Innocent OK. Okay?'

'I feel as if I'm dreaming.'

'Why don't you make us some coffee, Colin?'

With his usual, and now painfully irritating, slowness, he assembled mugs, spoons, milk and a jar of instant coffee on the laminate surface. Only then did he remember to put water in the kettle and switch it on.

We waited in silence for it to boil. He handed me a steaming mug, standing facing me across the small room, his back to the worktop.

'Why have you come here?' His voice had, if anything, got worse, even more nasal and querulous.

I drank some coffee. 'I've come to congratulate you on your worldly success. These Kronobyte people obviously pay well.'

He stared at me. He hadn't touched his coffee.

'Seriously, Colin. I'm desperate. It really is a matter of life or death. It'll take too long to go into, but I need help that only you can provide. I know there's no reason why you should care about me. I'm begging you. It's even something that you'll actually enjoy. A nostalgia trip.'

'So what is it?'

'I want you to hack into a database.'

'Oh, yeah. The Pentagon, I suppose?'

'Much simpler. The FernWest Building Society.'

I put the mug of coffee on the desk. 'How's it going?'

'Piece of piss. I'm on the last code now. I'm one of their branches. In Swindon. Fortunately they don't shut the link down out of office hours. There we are. Just look at that.'

The monitor screen display read:

FERNWEST BUILDING SOCIETY

For receipt/payment transactions, enter Account Number, then press Y.
For other services press Return.

He turned away from the machine and took a slurp from his coffee. 'Which service do you require?'

This was Colin in his element. For a moment, I was able to forget the bitterness of our break-up. I was back in the bar of Myddelton Polytechnic listening to a sandy-haired, fresh-faced youth tell me of his delight in games of logic and the higher mathematics, his blue eyes sparkling.

'Press Return,' I said. 'Let's see what's on the menu.'

The computer obligingly supplied a list of options. I scanned it. 'Go for mortgage accounts.'

Up it came, a series of interrogatories.

Account Number?
Customer Name?
Property Name?

He looked at me inquiringly. I took a deep breath and clenched my fingernails into my palms. 'Forty-two Oak Dean,' I said.

The screen blanked out. Christ, what if they'd changed the name of the development? I knew none of the names of the other ghost estates.

But they hadn't. There it was: 42 Oak Dean. Name of mortgagors. Amount of principal advanced. Date of advance. Date of first payment. Dates of subsequent payments. It was all there. All completely invented. Got you, you bastards.

I bent down and hugged his bony shoulders. 'Well done, Col. Can you do a copy?'

The page scrolled out of the whirring laser printer. I grabbed it. 'Now, let's do the other plots.'

I danced around the room waving the sheaf of papers.

Colin stared at me. 'Is that what you were after? I thought you'd want to pinch some money. Now we're in, I could get it to do a TT anywhere you like.'

'Don't tempt me. For Christ's sake get out of there before some security programme clicks in.'

'It probably already has. But they're not usually that sophisticated. I took precautions.' He was about to log off, when I had an idea.

'Perhaps we could leave a calling card?'

He giggled. 'Why not?'

'You were right. That was fun. I'd retired you know. I took the vow, just after I'd hacked into NATO headquarters in Brussels that Christmas. I thought I should quit at my peak. Do you remember?'

'I'll say. For days afterwards we expected to have MI5 come crashing through the door.

'Colin.'

'What?'

'Why did you tell my father where I'd gone?'

'He said he wanted to find you – so I helped him. He seemed a bit crackers, but I was so angry with you then, I didn't care. You'd never mentioned him to me before, anyway. It sounds as if you didn't want to see him.'

'I didn't, but in the end I'm glad you did. Are you still angry with me?'

The Entryphone receiver on the wall buzzed insistently. I looked at Colin. 'Who's that at this time of night, Colin?'

He shrugged. 'One of my neighbours. It happens quite often. They get pissed and can't remember the key-pad combination. They know I'm usually up.'

He picked up the handset. I heard him say, 'Hello' cheerily. Then his tone changed. 'What? Yes, she is. Come on up. Second floor.' He put the receiver down slowly.

I'd got to my feet. My heart was pounding.

He came back to the table. 'That was Harriet. She sounded very anxious. She's on her way up.'

'Harriet? But why...'

The doorbell interrupted me.

He went into the hall. I heard the click of the thumblatch, the squeak of hinges, the scuffling sound of feet on carpet, the door being slammed shut.

Her voice was strangely muffled, tearful, hysterical. 'Colin. Colin. I'm so sorry.'

Then his. 'Hey, what the fuck is this? Who are you? Let her g–'

Then another, the words bursting out through great ragged gasps of breath. 'Back off, cunt! Back off! Where's your fucking girlfriend?' The voice rose in volume, almost to a scream. 'I said where the fuck is she? Tell me. Fucking tell me!'

I threw open the kitchen door.

It was a wild-eyed kid with a crew-cut in a bomber jacket and jeans. He had his left arm around Harriet's shoulders, his right hand grasping a flick knife with the point pricking the soft flesh under her chin.

'Let her go.'

He swung her round to face me, pulled the knife away from her throat and held it in front of my face. She was ashen, her legs buckling as if his arm were a support not a restraint. He was calmer now, but I could see that his hand trembled and his face was pale and sweating, his eyes restless and staring wide. 'You, you're the fucking bitch, then. Come on, we're going on a trip. Fucking one way.'

Out of the corner of my eye, I saw Colin's body bending slowly sideways, his arm moving down, his hand grasping the handle of the briefcase he'd dumped on the floor hours earlier.

There was nothing I could do to stop him. Keep him talking. 'I'm not going anywhere, fucking smackhead.'

I took a step back into the kitchen, tempting him to follow me.

Colin gripped the briefcase, swung it back, then hurled his arm forward.

At the same moment the bloke, in his hyper state, slid his eyes round in Colin's direction. He saw the leather bag just before it smashed into his head. He ducked instinctively to avoid the blow, whirled round and struck Colin, who'd stumbled forward with the momentum of his attack, under the breastbone with the hand that held the knife.

Colin gave a hideous bubbling moan. His eyes bulged.

The junkie's hand stayed pressed against his white shirtfront, the arm as rigid as an iron bar, blood blossoming around the clenched fist. I raised the cast-iron frying pan I'd been grasping behind my back and brought it down with my full strength on the pinkish blond suede of his skull. There was a horrid metallic clunk. He collapsed forwards on to his knees as Colin fell backwards full-length on to the carpet, the black bone handle of the knife protruding from his chest in a great scarlet flower of blood.

The blow had jarred the thin handle of the pan out of my hands. I bent to pick it up, when I felt Harriet grabbing my arm. She sobbed out the words, 'Leave it, leave it, for God's sake. Get an ambulance.'

I dialled 999 on the kitchen phone, as Harriet knelt by Colin's body. She'd grabbed towels from the bathroom to staunch the flow of blood, but had not pulled out the knife. Her bare arms and hands were dabbled red.

After a seeming age the operator answered and I got through to the ambulance service. 'A man's been stabbed by a robber. Flat 203, Duveen House, Museum Street, WC1. Please come quickly.' I hung up, nausea flooding into my throat, the bones of my right hand still singing from the impact.

Harriet looked up at me, her dark eyes like holes pierced in a white ghost mask. Her voice was a whisper. 'I've given him mouth to mouth but I can't get him to breathe.'

'The ambulance is coming. We've got to get out of here.'

'What! We can't just leave him!'

I stood looking down on his pale face, at the blood-soaked towels. More blood. More death. There was no time to think about that.

I pulled her to her feet. 'I know. I fucking know. But we've got to. The ambulance people will get the police. We have to go. Now. Please. For Christ's sake, Harriet!' I shook her savagely. 'Think how it'll look to the cops!'

She stood there, tears pouring down her face.

I left her, ran into the study at the end, grabbed the printouts from the desk and stuffed them into my bag. I felt its weight as I slung it on my shoulder.

As we came out of the apartment, leaving the door open, I could hear the wail of sirens in the distance.

I practically dragged her down the stairs and bundled her out through the street door into the night. I turned and pulled the heavy doormat out of its well to jam the door open. We stood on the top step, clinging to one another. The wailing of the sirens was nearer now, from the direction of Bloomsbury Way. In a few moments they'd be here.

'The car,' she said, her voice regaining a little of its normal dry tone. 'He made me drive it here. I've got the key.'

The Alfa Romeo was parked twenty yards up the road, facing the British Museum end of the street.

Being behind the wheel seemed to restore her a little. She flexed her arm muscles, flipped down the visor, peered at her blood-smeared face in the mirror, grimaced and flipped it up again.

'What now?'

'Wait.'

The sirens were even louder. I turned round in my seat. The ambulance, blue lights flashing, headlamps blazing, careered round the corner from Bloomsbury Way and screeched to a halt in the middle of the road outside

Duveen House. Two paramedics in fluorescent yellow jackets jumped out of the cab. One ran up the steps and into the building carrying a case. The other one went round the back of the van and I could hear the sounds of the rear doors being opened. Where the hell were the police? Then behind the ambulance was another set of revolving blue lights.

'Now. Start up, pull out very slowly. Head for Russell Square.'

There was a throaty rumble from the engine.

We approached the junction with Great Russell Street. Ahead of us, behind tall iron railings, loomed the massive columned portico of the museum, its stonework shining golden in the floodlights.

We were almost on the junction when a police motorbike roared in from our right, screamed across us and stopped in the middle of the road.

He dismounted, and came towards us, holding up his gloved hand, looking like Darth Vader.

'Jesus Christ. He'll want to know whether we've seen anything. For fuck's sake, Harriet, the blood!'

The policeman was tipping up his visor as he approached my side.

'Have you got space to get round past the bike?'

'Just about.'

'Do it, then.'

She revved the engine, the car shot forward and zoomed through the impossibly narrow gap between the back wheel of the bike and the car parked on the corner of the street. She wrenched the wheel and the tyres squealed as we straightened up into Great Russell Street. Behind me I could see that the cop was running for his bike. Then he was lost to sight as we screeched left into Montague Street.

'He'll be radioing his pals. This is going to be a hot car all over London in thirty seconds.' I forced my shocked brain to work. 'A hot car. And why not? I've got an idea. Can you drive it around for a few minutes without getting stopped? Try and shake him off, even, then get back to Soho? I've got a car in the garage in Chinatown.'

Her mouth was a thin dark line. 'I can have a go.'

She hurtled out into Russell Square, ignoring the traffic already circling, floored it round the central garden, and went straight through the lights into Southampton Row on the wrong side of the road, overtaking several cars which had backed up at the junction with Theobalds Road.

'Christ Almighty, Harriet!' I clung on to my seat-belt. Oncoming cars swerved out of the way to a cacophony of hooting.

Fighting hard to stay in my seat, I unhooked her carphone, dialled 999 and asked for police. 'My name is Harriet Weinberg. I want to report that I have been attacked and my car stolen. Yes, it's a white Alfa Romeo, registration number E72 MHT. I saw two men. One was young, white, with a skinhead haircut. The other was short, dark-haired. There may have been a third man also. They made me drive them to a place somewhere near the North Circular, then threw me out of the car. I've been wandering around dazed until I found a phone box. I'm still feeling very ... oooh!' I put the phone down quickly. 'Do you think they'll swallow it?'

She snorted.

Like a bat out of hell we flashed down the dead straight track of Kingsway, ignoring red lights. At the Aldwych end of Waterloo Bridge, she shot the lights again. Over the bridge, she burned rubber round the big roundabout and careened into York Road.

Past the bridge to the Shell Centre, she flicked off the lights, glanced quickly in the mirror, yanked up the handbrake and put the car into a skid which spun it round almost in its own length in the wide carriageway. I was hurled forward, then brought up sharp by the seat-belt. The tyres howled and the car rocked over so far on its suspension I thought we were going to roll. It righted itself, then once more she jammed her foot to the floor, snapping me back against the head-restraint.

We headed back the way we'd come over the bridge. At the other end, she changed lanes at the last possible minute and zoomed down the narrow white-tiled tunnel which led back to Kingsway.

'I think I've lost him. He was with me in Kingsway, but I gained time on the bridge. He wouldn't have seen that rather tricky manoeuvre by the station. He probably thinks I've gone into bandit country south of the river.'

'Jesus, Harriet, I knew you could drive, but not like that!'

'Blame my mis-spent youth in an old banger on Hendon Aerodrome, darling.'

We abandoned the Alfa on a double yellow line in Long Acre, where it would be easily found, and made our way through the late evening crowds in Covent Garden to the car park off Gerrard Street. Harriet had wiped her face and wore an old mac she'd had in the boot of the car to conceal her bloodied arms and clothing.

She waited outside for me to get the car. The parking attendant might have remembered two women more easily than one. She slumped on to the ripped vinyl front passenger seat and I drove us sedately back to Dartmouth Park.

I drew up in the next street to hers, outside a darkened apartment block.

'I don't imagine the police'll be waiting outside your flat. If they are, though, come back here. I'll wait for fifteen minutes. We'll think of something else. Call the police after you've got cleaned up. They'll want to interview you. They'll probably have put your call and your assailant together with the stabbing by now. Stick to the story – after all the main part of it is true. Say you came back on a bus and you can't remember the number or where you got on. That's harder for them to quiz you on than if you say you got the tube or a cab.'

'I'll take the lawyer's advice, of course.' Then she leaned over and clung to me. 'What's happened to us, Sarah? We watch a friend, a lover being murdered before our eyes and yet we're still functioning. It's all my fault. I was terrified when that guy appeared out of the shadows. He said he'd kill me if I didn't tell him where you were. I told him you'd asked me for Colin's address. I had to tell him something. He said he was going to kill me. I had to tell him something.'

'I know. He probably would have. He was high. Anything could have happened. It was my fault. I brought Colin into it.' Hard as I tried to prevent them, the tears poured out.

After a while I struggled upright, and scrabbled in my bag for a handkerchief. 'You'd better go. I'll wait. Then I'll be off.'

'You're going back, aren't you, to Fernsford? You're going to do something desperate. Please, Sarah. Wouldn't it be better to talk to the police?'

'Put those printouts in the post with my note. That may well get something started. I don't know whether they'll be any good in court. They're illegally obtained. And the FernWest could change its records just like that. I have to try to clear myself. Otherwise, I'll be implicated. Chewton and Appleby would be only too pleased if I went down with them. The problem is the authorities are going to be very wary. A society its size going belly up is unprecedented.'

I leaned over and pushed open the passenger door. 'You'd better go now, Harriet. Please. I'll see you again soon, promise.'

I heard her heels tapping along the pavement, saw her cross the quiet street and then she was gone into the night. I waited for a quarter of an hour, but she didn't come back.

# XXVII

I steered the Cortina on to the verge of the narrow lane and thankfully turned off the engine. When the clunking noise it had made all the way from London turned to an ear-destroying whine, and the dashboard warning lights lit up like a Christmas tree, I thought I wasn't going to make it.

I opened the lych-gate, and set off over the still-wet grass of the churchyard.

The Woodlands was hard by the church. I vaulted the iron fence into the adjoining pasture and ran quickly to the briar-girt foot of the wall which surrounded the back of Appleby's rural paradise. It was an easy climb up the loosely laid drystone. I let myself hang full length down the far side and dropped to the soft earth below.

I peered out from the dead heart of the spreading shrub beneath which I lay hidden.

He was up. He was wearing khaki drill slacks and a green Fred Perry tennis shirt, an Englishman on a summer Saturday morning. He was bending down and securing the opened leaves of the conservatory doors with hooks. He stood up, went in and came out a few moments later carrying a laden tray. The smell of coffee drifted over the garden.

I watched him dispose himself and his breakfast. He filled his cup and buttered his toast and spread his marmalade and opened his paper. When he was well and truly occupied with these tasks, I crawled out from under the bush, and ran lightly across the lawn behind him, crouching down behind the cover of the corner of the conservatory, where there was a low screen of rose bushes. This had been the dangerous bit. If he'd seen me, there could have been a problem. But he didn't. He went on munching and sipping and flicking through the colour supplement.

I waited until my rapid breathing subsided and quietly brushed the earth and leaves from my clothing as best I could with my hands. It wouldn't do for the avenging angel to look like she'd slept rough.

Then I fumbled in my handbag and got out the expensive purchase I'd made from Benny Southgate. It hung cold and heavy in my hand.

I walked slowly up behind him. He was oblivious, absorbed in the recipe page. A full frontal spread of some fancy meat and veg on a snow-white plate lay under his hand. The pornography of food.

'Good morning, Francis.'

I saw his shoulders stiffen as he recognized my voice.

'Please turn around very slowly. I have a loaded pistol and it's pointing at your head.'

The way he did it managed to suggest that it was a kind of condescension to an insane person, mixed with a little wry curiosity.

'If that is a real weapon, Sarah, then your fantasy life has entered a new and dangerous phase.'

'This is real. You, this house, your whole life are the fairy story. With an unhappy ending.'

He laughed and took another sip of coffee. 'Sarah, dear Sarah! You're in no position to talk of unhappy endings. To ruin a perfectly adequate career by foolish peculation.'

'You're going to be very sorry about that. To blacken my name, then fake my suicide in Friars Haven. I'm going to make you regret that.'

'I doubt that, dear, common Sarah. You are a lawyer. Not a very good one, I'm bound to say, but some of the basics must have adhered. You must know that the law is not concerned with assertion. It is concerned with proof. And you have none. Blackened your name? No, we have amassed considerable evidence of your criminal activities. Faked your suicide? Nonsense. You threw yourself in. Overcome with the guilt and shame of your embezzlement. Even in that you were unsuccessful.'

'I'm not talking about the law. I'm not a lawyer now. I'm a fugitive from justice, an outlaw. It's what you made me and you'll suffer the consequences.'

'Consequences? What are you talking about?'

'I'm going to kill you.'

He drank some more coffee. There was a very faint tinkle as he replaced the bone-china cup on the saucer. 'Ridiculous. You couldn't kill me. Besides, you'd have nothing to gain by it except a lifetime in prison.'

'I have everything to gain. Let's look at it rationally. I get the very considerable satisfaction of seeing you dead. I make it look like suicide, of course. If it's credible for me to top myself, then it is for you. What's sauce for the gander... And when you're dead, the whole thing falls apart, doesn't it? Eventually, they'll get round to vindicating me. What's laughably called British justice will blunder on the truth. As for my reputation, well, I never had much in the first place. Being a thief and a murderer is as good a CV as any in my manor. Killing you really is the best option.'

I ostentatiously clicked off the safety catch.

'Have you any last requests?'

'You're bluffing. You couldn't do it. You can't use a weapon like that.'

'Want to bet? My father was an armed robber. Brought the tools of his trade home, didn't he? He was so disappointed I wouldn't follow in his footsteps, after all he'd taught me. And me a crack shot, too. Mind you, at this range I couldn't miss.'

I stretched out the pistol and pointed it at the soft nub of flesh where his aquiline nose met his classic forehead. 'Bye, bye, you bastard.'

I eased up the very slight slack of the trigger, my heart pounding.

'We can do a deal.' His gaze did not waver, but his voice suddenly seemed old and strained.

I screamed at him, all my carefully hoarded self-control finally exhausted, 'Fuck off, Appleby, you murdering bastard! No deals! You threw me in that stinking dock to drown. Now I'm going to blow your fucking head right off. It's not just a good idea, I fucking well want to see your blood spattered around. Like this! Now!'

'No, don't. I can put it right. Please!'

I kept the gun on him. 'I'm listening.'

'Sarah, please believe me, I never intended you to drown. That was Trevor's idea. The killings have all been his work. Lambert and I – we got in so deep we couldn't get out. I told him that framing you for the embezzlement was enough. You had no proof. It would stop you interfering with our activities long enough for us to clean up the building society. That side is finished. Friars Haven will make those activities unnecessary. To kill you might cause problems. You had friends. He wouldn't agree. He forced me to help him.'

'I don't believe a fucking word.'

'It's true. I can help you. I'll write a letter to the Chief Constable of Westerset. In it I'll state than an unfortunate series of accounting and computer errors were inadvertently attributed to files of which you had conduct. The result is that no wrongdoing of any description attaches to you. Consequently as you are entirely innocent of any allegations previously made, the firm does not wish to pursue such allegations. I'll copy the letter to the editors of all the national newspapers and to the *Evening Packet*, Fernsford. I'll also write in similar vein to the Secretary-General of the Law Society. I'll write an open testimonial for you in very favourable terms, in which I undertake to supply a confirmatory reference on request. The firm will pay you handsome compensation. You can leave, forget all about Fernsford. That's enough, isn't it?'

'Okay. Get on with it. I'm sure you've got headed notepaper and a word processor hereabouts. You can fax them when you've finished.'

'In my study.'

'Lead the way.'

I kept the pistol pointing at his back as we went through the warm, steamy conservatory into the main house.

Appleby opened a panelled mahogany door into his study. It was on the north side, with a stone-mullioned rectangular bay window looking out over a sweep of lawn towards a tennis court. Standing in the bay, the heavy automatic drooping heavily in my hand, I could see part of the shingle sweep of the entrance drive as it curved round from the main gate to the front of the house. I remembered peering in through those gates not so long before, like a kid eyeballing the guards at Buckingham Palace. I hadn't then envisaged the circumstances in which I would find myself inside.

Appleby was tapping away at the PC on the leather-topped desk. The opulently furnished room was chill, and its furthest corners were thick with shadow.

On the marble mantelpiece of the unused, screened fireplace was a gilt-framed black-and-white photograph. With Appleby absorbed in his typing, while keeping an eye on him, I wandered over to examine it, the one thing in the room which appeared to have some individual quality.

A shortish but very fat man, heavily jowled, bulbous-nosed, wearing a dinner jacket, with a cigar clamped between thick lips was grimly shaking hands with a younger Appleby, his dark wavy hair silvered at the temples. He was the same age as the Appleby I'd seen in the snapshot in O'Riordan's file. Clapping him on the shoulder, champagne glass in the other hand, was a smiling, slim, elegant-looking man, with a high forehead and thinning blond hair. Ralph Chamberlayne junior. I recognized him from the photographs I had seen at Margaret's lunch party.

The fat man must therefore be Ralph Chamberlayne senior. Presumably the photo commemorated Appleby's joining the partnership. Old Ralph certainly didn't seem to be smiling beneficently on his designated successor. Quite the reverse.

There was a whirring sound from the desk. I snapped back to attention and spun around. It was Appleby's laser printer churning out the letters. I picked up the first copy and scanned it, alert for weaselly phrases and lawyerly qualifications. There were none. I absolve you, as the priests said.

I smiled when I read the testimonial: 'diligent'; 'conscientious'; 'a quite excellent grasp of even the most technical aspects of the law'; 'recommend her unreservedly'.

'Good work, Francis. Now you're going to fax them to the recipients. I've made a list of all the numbers here ready whilst you've been typing.'

He slotted the first letter face down into the fax machine. He was about to punch out the numbers to transmit it when I heard the sound of a car engine and the crunching sound of tyres on shingle.

I rushed to the window, but it had already driven round to the front of the house.

I stared at Appleby. A smile was beginning to gather on his face, and his healthy colour to reassert itself. I raised the pistol. 'Don't even think of trying anything.'

The smile never left his face.

We waited in silence. There was the distant thunk of a car door being slammed. I was expecting the sound of a knocker or a buzzer, but instead

I heard the rattle of a key in the lock, the creak as the front door opened, the bang as it was shut and the sound of heels clicking on the chequerboard stone slabs of the hallway. A woman's footsteps. A voice called out, 'Francis, not still in bed? You knew I'd be here by ten! Get up, you lazy boy.' She giggled. 'On second thoughts, stay right where you are!'

I heard the hollow sound as she climbed the staircase, then the creak of the floorboards in one of the upper rooms. The voice called out again, 'Francis, where are you hiding, you naughty man?'

Then she came down the stairs again. I tried to think what to do. All I could do was wait. Then her voice was outside the door of the room. 'You're not working, are you, you terrible man? When you knew I was coming over.' I saw the doorknob revolve, the door opened and in she came.

Appleby swivelled smoothly to face her. 'Come in, my dear. I'm most extraordinarily glad to see you.'

I saw her take in the scene, the broad smile frozen on her face as she saw me, saw the gun in my hand. Her hand flew up to her mouth.

I felt myself struggling to comprehend the arrival of Margaret Chamberlayne.

'Well, if it isn't the grieving widow.'

She sank into one of the wing chairs, staring disbelievingly at me, her face drained. 'What's going on here, Francis?' She spoke in barely more than a whisper.

'Contractual negotiations with a former employee, of a somewhat threatening nature. But of course you've met our Miss Hartley.'

'I'm ashamed to say that I've entertained her in my house.'

'I must say I'm pretty shocked to see you in this one. I thought that if nothing else you had taste. But not in men, clearly.'

'What do you mean?'

I gestured at Appleby with the pistol. 'Him, of course. But then I suppose you know all about him and his criminal activities. I thought I was broad-minded, but even I'd draw the line at sleeping with a murderer.'

I thought she must have known, but she obviously didn't. Not all of it anyway. She got up from her chair and went over to him, taking him by the arm. 'Francis, please tell me what's happening. What is she talking about?'

He put out a soothing hand. 'She has become quite unbalanced, making all kinds of wild, self-evidently untrue allegations. She burst in today, threatening to kill me, unless I wrote letters retracting the charges of embezzlement laid against her. I did so under duress. Fortunately your arrival has prevented the dispatch of these forced retractions.'

He turned to me, the snap of command fully restored.

'I think it's time we stopped all this foolish play-acting. Put the gun down, Sarah. Now. Or are you going to shoot me in front of a witness? Or perhaps you're going to shoot both of us?'

I sighed, thumbed the safety on and laid the automatic carefully on the desk in front of me but well within reach. He'd won, the bastard, the bastard. My bluff was well and truly called. I'd played my only card and lost.

Of course I couldn't shoot him now. I wasn't ever going to shoot him, much as I'd like to have seen him shot. How stupid I'd been to think I could break him so easily. He'd been playing for time.

He picked up the letters and ripped them savagely in half, then threw them in the bin.

Margaret fixed me with a vicious look, then swung back on Appleby. I almost felt sorry for him.

'Is that it? Are you going to let her get away with it? Aren't you going to call the police, Francis? If you're not, then I most certainly am.'

He laid his hand gently on her arm. 'The matter between Sarah and I has been concluded.'

'What do you mean, concluded? You said yourself that she threatened you with a gun. Surely the state of the law in this country has not sunk so far that you can go around waving guns and get away with it?' She shook off his arm. 'If you won't, then I will.' She leaned over and picked up the phone receiver.

'I said no.' He plucked the instrument out of her hand and banged it back on its rest.

'Francis!'

He held both her hands, his face stiff, his mouth a hard line. She stared at him in alarm. She was seeing the side of him that she might not have seen before. The side anyone who worked with him saw all the time. He spoke to her slowly and deliberately as if she were a child. 'Reflect on our position, my dear Margaret.'

I stared at them together, marvelling at the extraordinary permutations of human desire. Margaret Chamberlayne, pillar of her little community, keeper of the flame at the tomb of the saintly Ralph, secretly shagging the most loathsome man, bar one, in Fernsford. No wonder they'd kept it all quiet. It wasn't quite the thing one did in society, was it, darling?

But what had Appleby said? Reflect on our position? Instantly, the penny dropped. Of course, it wasn't the weird misdirections of middle-aged lust that had brought them together. I should have realized that a much more powerful aphrodisiac was at work than Appleby's aquiline features or Margaret's softly rounded rump. Money.

I said, 'That's right, dear Margaret. He doesn't want the police involved for about a million reasons. You've only one. You don't want to be had up for breach of trust and fraud, do you? I mean it wouldn't look good for someone in your position to be caught robbing blind your late husband's trust, would it?'

'That's a monstrous lie. I'm no thief!'

'Oh, yes? Perhaps it doesn't seem like theft to you. Theft is done by men in balaclavas or by old women in supermarkets. All you were doing was getting more of what should have been yours. How mistrustful of dear Ralph to leave you only a life interest in his estate while the capital bloated in the bank for some cousins in Canada nobody knew anything about. I expect when Francis Appleby, your fellow trustee, approached you with a deal for some of the unproductive assets in the trust – old Ralph Chamberlayne's enormous house his son had hated and its rambling garden – you jumped at it. Particularly when he confided that the buyer was a company whose directors were not unknown to him. Sell up, and the proceeds go into the trust. But then after a decent interval the land is sold at its true value. The trustees split the profit. That must have been the beginning of your beautiful friendship.'

Margaret cast an appealing glance in Appleby's direction, but he refused to meet it, gazing stonily out of the window.

'He won't help you. He's far too concerned to protect his own back. After all, helping you fiddle your trust was only a sideshow. When he realized that I had stumbled on his main activity, he tried to drown me in the dock at Friars Haven, framing me for theft at the same time, so it would look like I'd committed suicide out of remorse.'

Appleby turned back from the window. 'What did I tell you, my dear? She's completely off her head.'

I stood up, my hands balled into fists. 'I ought to have shot you.' In my anger, I moved out of reach of the gun on the desk.

It was exactly what he wanted me to do. With vicious speed, he sprang forward and jabbed his arm straight into my stomach. As I doubled up in pain, he grabbed the pistol, reversed it into a club and smashed it into the side of my head.

I heard Margaret's scream and then there was nothing but blinding agony.

I was drifting through a grey, fuzzy world. Somewhere a long way off, I could feel my legs moving. Then they stopped, and I was lying in a soft chair. I could hear a voice. 'Sarah, Sarah!' I remembered the nasty taste of the rubber mouthpiece between my teeth, the dentist saying, 'This won't hurt a bit. Just a little gas.'

'Sarah, Sarah!' My eyes swivelled slowly and painfully open, like a hardly used garage door.

'Nurse?' I tried to struggle upright but it was too much effort.

The woman in the white blouse leaning over screwed up her face in irritation. 'I'm not a nurse. It's Margaret. God, don't you remember?'

I remembered. My head felt as if it had been run over by a bus. More particularly, there was a throbbing, stabbing pain behind my left ear where the pistol butt had struck.

'How long was I out?'

'I don't think you were actually unconscious for more than a few seconds. We walked you up the stairs.'

I looked about from the easy chair. The blinding sun streamed in through a small mullioned window. A double bed. A wardrobe. A chest of drawers.

'Where's your boyfriend?'

'Boyfriend? What vulgar expressions you use. Francis is in the study. On the telephone.'

'I can't believe you. I practically get killed and you try to teach me etiquette.'

'I have no sympathy for you. You burst in and threatened to kill Francis. He had to defend himself.'

'I threatened him because it was the only option he'd left me. He accused me of stealing from the firm. A pack of lies. I had to make him retract. But I wasn't going to kill him. Can't you understand? It's he who's the killer.'

She put her hand to her head. 'I don't know. I've never seen him like that before. You enraged him. He'll calm down, I'm sure.'

'Oh, yes. He'll be very calm when they dump me back in Friars Haven or the Fern or wherever. Don't you see what he's doing? He's making you so implicated in this that you won't be able to go to the police. The trust thing is peanuts. Probably couldn't even prove it. It was a bagatelle to Appleby to get you into his bed. What he's up to now is quite different. Aiding and abetting makes you as guilty as the principal offender. And for murder, the sentence is life. And if you don't go along with it, he'll kill you as well.'

'Sarah, you talk in such hyperbole. I won't listen to such nonsense. Francis is a respectable solicitor. This is rural Westerset, not some ghastly American city.'

'For fuck's sake, Margaret. What do I have to say to you? Okay, then. If everything's normal. Walk out of here. Go home. Forget all about it. Go on.'

'I can't do that.'

'Why not?'

'He locked the door.'

I gave her an old-fashioned look.

'It was to stop you escaping. He told me to stay with you.'

'And you do exactly as you're told, of course. Why do you think he wants to stop me from escaping? He knows that I'll go to the police. I have no other option now. He can't risk that. He wouldn't call the police himself, would he? Can't you understand what kind of man he is? No, you don't. You don't have the least idea. You don't know, for instance, that he killed Ralph?'

'No, I can't believe it. Not Ralph.' I could see doubt spreading like a stain across her face. 'What possible reason was there?'

I told her. 'Even if you don't believe me, let the law decide. Get out of here and get the police. Have you still got your car keys?'

'Yes, they're in my bag right here.'

'Is there a back staircase?'

'Yes, it goes down to the kitchen.'

'Call him up and say that you want to use the loo. The doors out of the conservatory are open.'

She hesitated for a moment, then started to bang on the panelled door of the bedroom.

After a minute or so, his voice answered from the other side. 'What do you want?'

She told him.

There was the sound of a key in the lock. I sank back on to the cushions, and closed my eyes.

'She's still out then? I'll wait here. Be quick.'

I raised my eyelids a minute fraction. He was in the doorway, jiggling impatiently with the keys.

When she didn't return, he started to glance anxiously down the corridor. Then there was the noise of a powerful motor roaring into life and the clatter of small stones flung against metal. He swore furiously, slammed the door, locked it after him. I heard his feet pounding the stairs.

From outside, there was the sound of screeching brakes and more spraying gravel. I jumped up and ran over to the window. I had a good view of the drive below.

Margaret Chamberlayne's green Mercedes had slewed to a halt short of the gates to avoid a collision with another car which had been negotiating the entry.

I saw with despair that it was Trevor Chewton's Porsche.

Below me two struggling figures were joined by a third. Appleby grabbed hold of his erstwhile lady-love and smashed her across the kisser with the back of his hand. Sister, when will we ever learn?

# XXVIII

We were back in the study. Appleby stood staring out of the window at his immaculate garden, perhaps trying to memorize it for when he ended up somewhere without a view. Chewton, his great fists bunched by his sides, had planted himself in front of me where I sat on one of the wing chairs. Margaret was lying on the *chaise longue* at the back of the room, apparently still in shock, moaning softly to herself.

One side of my skull felt it was about to fall off, and over my ear there was a lump of frightening proportions covered with a mat of dried blood and hair. At least I was still alive. Just.

Appleby swung away from the window, and beckoned Chewton over to him. I strained to hear them. I caught only snatches. 'Lambert not at home.' 'Need to get into the offices.' 'Friars Haven.' There were plenty of nods and glances in our direction.

Then Chewton was shouting at Appleby. 'I can't believe we're in this situation. Not only do you get her involved, but the other one, too.'

'For God's sake. There's no point in going over old ground. We have to get hold of Lambert. Where the fuck is he?'

'Enjoying a day out with his wife and kiddies, no doubt. He's the clean-living family man, remember?'

'Wait a minute. You gave him a pass to Welscombe, didn't you? Kids love it there.'

'It's worth trying. I'll have him paged.' He picked up the phone and mashed out a number, then barked a few curt instructions. 'His cousin Walter, got that?' He slammed the phone down. 'Risky, but it is an emergency.'

Appleby went back to staring out of the window. Chewton paced around the room. Every now and again, I caught the waft of his cologne and under it the animal odour of him and I remembered how I had scented it that first time at Friars Haven.

The phone rang. Appleby was on it first. 'Good afternoon, Ronald. Thanks for calling. We're having a party at the marina. You remember Sarah? Well she's dying to meet you again. About an hour? Splendid. Love to the lovely Susan.'

He came over and took me by the arm. 'Let's go. I'm afraid I can't offer you a seat this time either.'

I must have nodded off. It was pitch-dark in the empty warehouse. I had been here for hours, gagged and bound to one of the iron pillars.

The stairs creaked rhythmically. The sound of someone coming in must have wakened me. Now the feet were tramping over the protesting boards, the light of a torch bouncing off walls and ceiling joists.

'On your feet!' Chewton bent over me, his big hands fumbling with the bonds at my ankles, dragging me up. I shuddered at the touch of him but this time he was far too preoccupied to start messing me about.

He marched me down the stairs and dragged me out into the night. He'd looped the rope which had secured me to the pillar round my arms, holding me on a leash like an animal to stop me breaking free. My head ached abominably and I felt weak and shivery as I stumbled after him.

He hauled me to the right, away from the canal basin, and along the front of Brigantine House, Chewton's offices.

There were no lights in the foyer. The lift was waiting. He opened the doors and shoved me in. Third floor.

The big room was thick with cigar smoke. Appleby and Lambert were in shirt-sleeves, kneeling on the thick pile carpet surrounded by pages and pages of computer print-out.

Chewton pressed me down into a chair and took off the gag and untied my hands.

'Hi, boys. Keeping busy?'

I felt the hands on my shoulders move to encircle my neck. They lay there loosely, like the warm coils of a boa constrictor. 'We're not in the mood for jokes.'

I smiled. I knew what was coming.

Appleby got to his feet, dusted off his knees, and stood in front of me. 'Sarah, my dear, you seem determined to cause us even more inconvenience. Ronald is of the opinion that you have something to do with the lock-out of the FernWest computer system. Tell me, is this correct?'

I said nothing.

Lambert snarled at him in the nasal tone I recognized as that of the mysterious phone caller. 'Stop wasting time. She can't put it right. It's an utter disaster. We can't get at the computer files. How the hell are we going to operate on Monday? The spotlight will be on us then, just as we're trying to clear things up.'

Chewton said, 'Don't look at me. This is down to Appleby. He brought this bitch in.'

Appleby's colour had drained from his face. 'Only because of the pressure I was under. You wanted it all, didn't you, Trevor? The legitimate kudos and the illegitimate profits. I warned you at the beginning, Trevor. We should have shut down the operation before Friars Haven came on stream, scrapped Oak Dean.'

'You know the residential division had cash-flow problems. Temporary, but pressing. We needed Oak Dean. But why the fuck are we arguing about this while she sits there smirking? Let's get on with it. Over at the site, there's a fucking hole big enough to bury a cathedral in. We're pouring concrete all next week. They'll never find her in a million years.'

I felt the hands tighten on my neck.

Appleby stood in front of me. I could see the sweat beading his brow. 'We've got to think. Killing her isn't necessarily the answer. When we threw her in the dock, there was logic to it. She'd found the car. We had to prevent her from talking. It would have worked then. She was discredited. She'd committed suicide. But somehow, she got out. We should have waited to make sure. But you were so bloody cocksure she couldn't swim. But now? Everything's changed. She's been in London. We know she talked to the woman in television. She got away from the hoodlum you hired. She hacked the society's system and screwed it up. There are too many things we can't control. She winds up dead, then there are too many questions. The police may not believe she committed suicide. Anything other than that is evidence in her favour.'

Lambert came from behind me. 'I agree with Appleby. You've always been too ready to lead with your fists, Chewton. You know I've never approved of your filthy methods.'

The hands withdrew. Chewton came forward, running his hand through his grizzled wavy hair.

'I don't believe it. After all these years, I find I've been working with a pair of fucking choirboys. Just listen to Lambert here. He believes his own myth. The benevolent and successful leader of the public-spirited FernWest Building Society. "Never approved of my methods." Do me a favour. Where would you be without those methods? Where would any of us be?'

'God, how I wish I'd told you to go to hell right at the beginning, when you came back that time and claimed the old woman in Gibson Square had fallen down the stairs. An accident, you said. Like the other so-called accidents since then. You implicated me in those deaths. I never agreed to them.'

'Of course, you didn't, Ronnie old pal. No more than you deliberately stuck your bayonet in that kid in that dirty little back street in Nicosia. Twelve years old. What a lucky thing that your good mates Trevor and Walter didn't see what you'd done. Without that favour you might have had a very different start in life.'

'You absolute bastard, Chewton. You knew I thought he'd pulled a knife. You've had your pound of flesh a million times over for that favour.' He was twisting his hands so that the knuckles cracked.

'Be quiet, both of you!' Appleby stood between them like a master between two scuffling pupils in some old-fashioned school story. 'We have to start from where we are. Work with the material we've got.'

He turned to me. 'What if we let you go? You'd still be liable to be arrested on the embezzlement charges we laid against you. That would encourage you to stay clear of the police. In compensation we can offer you more money than you've ever dreamed of. You could leave the country. Forget all about Fernsford and Chamberlayne's. Think of it. You wouldn't have to work again. What a prospect for someone with your background. To be securely rich for the rest of your life.'

'Is that what you offered Charmaine? Is what happened to her coming to me one dark night, when things have cooled down a bit? When Chewton's finished Friars Haven and everything's legitimate? Secure? When would I ever stop looking over my shoulder? Poor Charmaine! She would have been happy with a few thousand! I know the kind of money you've swindled out of FernWest. What chance have I got?'

'I would have been happy to pay Charmaine. She didn't have the sense to stick to money. She wanted something I couldn't give her.'

'Oh, yes? And what was that?'

'Me.'

I stared at him in astonishment. There was the beginning of a blush around his smooth cheeks. 'You? What do you mean?'

'She wanted me to marry her. At first she took money. But then she said she wanted a proper life. In the country with someone respectable. When she first told me, it was all I could do to stop myself from being physically sick. Can you think what that would have been like? When I demurred she said she would start to talk about how the three of us had been business partners in London. She knew just enough. We couldn't take the risk. We had to shut her up.'

'It must have been a new experience, Francis. How unnatural to find someone fond of you.'

'You and your women, Appleby. You can't handle them. It was your whore who got her involved.' He jabbed a forefinger the size and colour of a pork sausage in my direction. 'She was even boasting about it at our picnic at Oakdean. "A piece of luck I met that Sarah!" Like fuck it was.'

Appleby had been angrily staring out of the window, apparently engrossed in the distant lights of the city. He swung round, haggard, his eyes burning.

'Never mind all the reminiscence. I made you an offer, Sarah. Yes or no?'

'What did you others do when he killed Charmaine? Stand by and watch? I couldn't live with myself if I let any of you bastards off the hook for that. You won't get away with it now. Whatever you do to me, whatever the law does to me. You see, the process has already started. I took copies of the Oak Dean files when I hacked the FernWest computer. They should be with the Fraud Squad with my notes by the morning. I told my friend Harriet to deliver them. If anything happens to me, she'll go to the police with everything she knows.'

I turned to stare at Chewton. 'So there's no way any of you will get off. Particularly you, Billy Denton.'

I saw his jaw slide forward and his chin stretch in the familiar gesture. The crocodile eyes were wary.

'There are things about your life that even your close associates here don't know about. Oh, they know that Billy Denton, the ex-council official turned jobbing builder, returned home in triumph to his old manor, to marry his old boss's daughter, even change his name as a favour to the old man who'd been disappointed of a son. But they don't know about Caroline Denton. Your brother's child. The child whom you incestuously raped and abused twenty years ago. She knows who you are and where you are. I told her the night I escaped from drowning.'

I saw Appleby and Lambert exchange glances. Chewton's face had the squishy damp whiteness of supermarket bread.

Finally, Chewton said in a flat voice, 'It's a lie. It's her word against mine. After twenty years, to come out with these childhood stories. I never would have credited it. I thought we got on well.'

'But it wasn't only Caroline you abused, was it, Billy? It was Robbie too. You didn't rape him, but you beat him and you tortured him. He told me all about it. Your own son. You won't be able to say that he's lying. He has the photographs you took. They'll make painful viewing for a jury.'

I saw the expression on Lambert's face. Even Appleby seemed stunned.

'You know, Billy, one of the things about an abusive personality like yours – and believe me it's one thing I've learned something about – is that the behaviour is compulsive. You can't help yourself. You can't because you've been made that way. Your father used to beat you as a child, didn't he? Or perhaps he didn't stop at beating? I bet your childhood in that scruffy little terrace in Shelley Road was a living hell. I bet you vowed you'd get out of there, first chance you had. But you never did get out of it, did you? You're still that frightened kid who dreaded Saturday nights, when his dad got in pissed and took it out on you and your mam.'

He sank down on to a chair, his body seeming to shrink inside the silk shirt, the belly no longer bulging so prosperously over the black morocco leather belt of the grey wool suit trousers.

'You think you know it all, don't you? A right fucking amateur psychologist. You know fuck all. Fred Denton wasn't my father. You want to know who was? Mr High and Mighty Ralph Chamberlayne, the uncrowned king of Fernsford was my father. Surprised?'

'Christ Almighty. How do you know that?'

'My mother told me, on her death bed, in 1971. She was proud, actually proud, that she'd been Chamberlayne's whore. "Your real father was a great man, Billy," she said. "Remember that." "Oh, I shall, Mam," I said.

'I went to see him in his office – the old offices in St John's Street. Very dark and dismal they were, real Victorian. "Come in," he says. "What can I do for you, my man?" I'm in overalls, you see, just come off a site. So I said, "You can call me Mr Chewton, for a start, seeing as we're going to be in business together." He sort of starts to go all hoity-toity at that. Then I told him what I knew. That he'd seduced his housekeeper, made her pregnant, and left her to bring up his bastard without acknowledgement from him. You can be sure he went white as a sheet.

'By God, I was determined to make the old sod pay for my childhood. Fred Denton knew, of course, but he couldn't do anything about it. Old Ralph had got him a job at Fernsford Fabrications, and he could get him out of it just as easily. In the war it was a reserved occupation. So he took his resentment out on me. There were seven of us in that miserable poxy little house. No bathroom and a lav at the end of the yard. Two of my half-sisters died of TB in the war. Another was crippled by polio. So there wasn't any way fucking Ralph Chamberlayne wasn't going to pay. In fact, he was so willing to give me what I wanted, I began to think I might have let him off lightly.'

'And what you wanted was to have him appoint your London friends to positions of power and influence, from which you were going to make sure you benefited. Regular partners in crime. That's where the capital to start and sustain your business came from, wasn't it? Mortgage fraud and property swindles.'

Chewton grabbed me by the arm. 'It's time to stop pissing about. By the end of tomorrow you'll be under a thousand tons of concrete.'

'Trevor. Enough is enough. You heard what she said. It's over. Killing her will only make things worse. Let her go. Now.' Appleby held at the end of his outstretched arm the gun I had bought from Benny the Blag.

The pressure of his grip didn't alter, even increased as I struggled. 'Put it down, Francis. You haven't the guts to use it.'

'Let her go, Trevor. Then we can talk about how we arrange this thing.'

'Arrange? I don't like the sound of that. It sounds to me as if Mr Smart Lawyer Appleby is preparing to scrape me off his shoe like dog shit. Well, no dice, friend. We're in this together. All for one and one for all. If you want her so much, then fucking have her!'

With a yank that sent a fiery bolt of pain into my shoulder blade, he pulled me in front of him like a shield and then shoved me across the room straight into Appleby.

I cannoned into him. Thrown off balance, he fell back on to the carpet with me on top of him. But he held on to the pistol. Chewton was charging in and only a matter of feet away when he pointed the gun and squeezed the trigger.

There was no shot, only a click like that of a child's toy.

Chewton's heel slammed down on Appleby's wrist. I heard bones crack and his scream of agony. Chewton deftly kicked the weapon to the far corner of the room, then one hand grasped the neck of my sweater and hauled me to my feet. My left shoulder felt dislocated, a throbbing wave of pain coursing through it.

Appleby sat up nursing his arm. He glared at me venomously.

'Sorry, Francis. There never were any bullets in there. I don't know much about guns. I didn't want it to go off accidentally.'

'Well, gentlemen. Perhaps you'd like to stay here until I return? I shan't be long. Unless, Ronnie, you'd like to come and help? I thought not.'

Lambert had backed away into the far corner. He'd made no move at all to assist Appleby.

Keeping a tight hold on my collar, Chewton pulled the phone off the desk and reduced it to fragments by stamping on it a couple of times. With my good arm in a half nelson, he marched me out of the office door, locking it behind us. The lift doors were open waiting and he bundled me inside forcing my face against the cold mirrored surface. There was a dropping sensation in my stomach, the only sign that the lift was descending.

I heard the lift doors slide open. He swung me round and frogmarched me into the lobby, then through the glass doors into the night.

The wind had risen while we'd been inside. It blew in heavy gusts along the central road between the warehouses, moaning and howling in the darkness.

With my wrist clamped in his huge hand, he jogged over the cobbled way and down the alley opposite in the direction of the construction site. I half ran, half staggered after him, compelled inexorably by the crushing force of his grip. I felt the tears pouring down my face even as I strove to keep them back.

Just before we emerged from the shelter of the buildings, my foot struck a protruding paving stone and I fell full length. For several yards he dragged me along the ground, my jeans ripped and my knees skinned by the rough and broken surface. 'Stop! Please stop and let me get up!'

He did stop. He let go of my arm, and stood, a black shape against the faintly glowing sky. I knelt there, my breath wheezing in my lungs, scorching my battered throat, my body one blaze of agony.

'Get up.'

'Where are you taking me?'

'I told you.'

'Are you going to kill me?'

'You walked into it, darling. Fucking suicide, I call it.'

I got to my feet. I was a head taller than him. 'You fancy me, don't you, Trevor? You did at Oakdean. You do now. You like an edge to your sex. Incest, humiliation, domination, degradation. You can't get much more degraded than fucking someone you're about to murder.'

There was a long silence. Then he said in a voice suffused with desire, 'You mean it, don't you, you mad bitch? You're turned on, you fucking mad bitch. Maybe you're as bad as I am underneath. You seem to know all about me. But one thing you got wrong. There weren't no incest. Caroline was Tom's kid, but Tom weren't no brother of mine.'

'How do you know that?'

'My mother told me when she was dying. Tom wasn't her son. He was another of Ralph's bastards he'd palmed off on her as a baby. According to Mum, she suspected it was some society woman he'd fucked. He didn't let on and she didn't dare ask. She did as she was bid and passed the kid off as her own – had him registered as a Denton. We were almost too close in age but in them days, it weren't so surprising if you had one kid after another.'

'So you never did know who was the mother of the child who was registered as Thomas Denton?'

'No. Nor do I fucking well care. We hated each other. My father never treated him the way he treated me. He weren't no dishonour to him, I suppose, like I was. Now, come here, you filthy bitch.'

He grabbed my arm and shoved me against the blistered woodwork of a loading bay. He pressed hungrily against me. I could feel his hands fumbling at the clasp of his belt, then at the zip of my jeans. With infinite anguish, I raised my wounded arm to run my fingers through his wiry hair. He was panting now, his feverish hands pushing down my jeans, feeling for my pants, pushing them down, lost to everything but his lust. Lost.

I raised my good arm and smashed down on the crown of his skull the jagged lump of cobblestone I'd picked up when I fell. At the same time, I brought my knee hard up into his balls.

It was like hitting a tree. The force of the blow knocked the stone out of my hand and it clattered away on the roadway. For a moment I thought he had withstood the attack, but then the hands had left me, clutching instinctively at his wounded parts, and he slumped away from me. I pushed past him out of the doorway, and ran blindly, crazily, pulling up my jeans as I ran, my fingers slippery with his blood.

Ahead, over half a mile of the scraped and scarified earth of the construction site, was the glare of the halogen-illuminated contractors' compound, a place of safety, as tantalizingly unreachable as the yellow face of the full moon which was rising on the horizon. I ran towards the light, staggering and stumbling over the clods and rubble, my lungs on fire.

I ran and ran, leaping over piles of bricks, scrambling up banks of heaped-up soil, jumping trenches in which water gleamed silver in the moonlight, head down to spot these obstacles, raising it only occasionally to track the beckoning lights.

Then suddenly, I was no longer in the open. On either side there were pale cylinders, concrete columns. Underfoot the ground was harder, and wet. I splashed through sheets of standing water. I looked ahead, but I could no longer see the lights of the compound. I cursed my blind stupidity. In my headlong panic, I had run straight down into the lower level of the development. I was in the great underground car park. Lines of columns marched in front and to the side. Chewton was behind me. I had no choice but to go on.

I turned away from the places where the moonlight fell and where he would see me. I ran to where the darkness was almost complete. The concrete surface at my feet was dry and I sped on unseeing, arm outstretched.

I felt a chill breeze on my face, then something caught at my ankles and pitched me forward. My head connected with something hard and sharp.

I lay there, feeling stunned and sick. As I pushed myself up on to my knees, again I felt a cold wind on my face. I raised my head and above me were the stars.

I had stumbled on a flight of concrete stairs to the upper level. On all fours, I scrambled up.

On the deck, I stood in the clean wind. Ragged clouds flew across the face of the moon like witches on broomsticks. Ahead of me again but no more than a few hundred yards away was the brightly lit compound. I could see the arc-lamps on tall standards like a football stadium. I could make out the spidery filaments of the security barrier enclosing the oblong box shapes of the office cabins. So strong was the light that it shed its gleam even to where I stood, giving a metallic sheen to the smooth cement surface of the deck. With hope renewed I ran towards it, easily with its assistance dodging the gaping holes, the snaking pipes and wires and the steel reinforcing rods which sprouted in bunches through the concrete like tenacious weeds.

And then I stopped, ice-cold as if my blood had turned to water. The proximity of safety was an illusion. Between the compound and the concrete raft atop the car park yawned an enormous pit, the foundation and basement excavations for Paul's domed building, the centrepiece of Friars Haven. I stood on the brink and looked down. The sides were sheer, clad with rust-streaked steel shuttering. At the bottom, the concrete, slick with water, reflected the moon like an enormous well. There was no way across. And no way round, either. The decking to the side was uncompleted. Work was still in progress. Girders lay in stacks, waiting to be lifted into place. A forest of isolated columns sprouted in the dark gulf before the start of solid ground.

I should have to go back. But as I turned away from the abyss, I heard a cry of triumph from behind. Chewton emerged from the stairway, and jogged unhurriedly towards me. He knew I was trapped.

I stared wildly around. He was near enough for me to make out the blood streaks on his face, black in the moonlight. There was only one final desperate way, not an escape, but a refuge, a redoubt.

When he saw my intention, he tried to head me off. He was too late. Ignoring the searing pain from my dislocated shoulder, I reached the structure of yellow-painted steel lattice. I scrambled recklessly up the access ladder of the tower crane which hung over the deck like a giant wire coat-hanger.

I was halfway up before he reached the base. I halted and risked a quick look down. He raised his battered face to mine, holding a riveted strut in one hand, as if uncertain how to proceed. This wasn't in his plan. Then, as if realizing that he had no choice, he hoisted himself on to the first rung and came after me.

As I climbed higher, the buffeting of the wind strengthened, tearing at my matted hair, tugging at my clothes, almost playfully threatening to pry me loose like an autumn leaf and set me whirling into the void. I clung close to the ladder and let the gust flow over me like a wave of the sea. Above, the contractor's neon sign glowed in the middle of the jib. Through the web of steel in front of me I could see the flaring lights of the compound then, beyond them, the amber pinpoints of lamp-posts which illuminated the new Friars Haven roundabout on Free Trade Way. Beyond that, cushioned on the night's black velvet, were scattered jewels, shining from the houses on the low hills to the north of Fernsford, where ordinary men and women prepared for sleep in the confident expectation of the morrow.

The ladder trembled under my hands as Chewton climbed steadily. He was only a matter of twenty feet below.

My hands grasped the last rung. I reached up to grasp the railing to haul myself on to the platform. I stood on the cold diamond-pattern metal plate with my back to the rotation mechanism at the base of the cab. The wind hummed in the rigging, and the whole structure groaned as the jib swung gently from side to side. The moon was behind the flying clouds, leaving only a ghost of its presence like a headlamp seen through fog.

Above the sound of the wind I heard the metallic bonging of Chewton's feet on the ladder. I braced myself, grasping the railings on either side, waiting for him. Top of the world now, Ma!

Just below the platform he stopped. I heard his laboured breathing, heavier than it ought to have been from the mere climb.

'Come on down, Sarah, love. It's a dangerous spot, if you're not used to it. If you've no head for it.' I was surprised at the nervousness in his voice. And the surprise gave me heart more than anything that had happened since the terrible chase had begun. Hadn't got a head for it? Speak for yourself, Chewton, you bastard.

I didn't reply immediately. There was a squeak of leather on steel as he shifted position. The wind was stronger now, setting up a deep thrumming in the hawsers. Above the jib swayed and the gearwheel at my side creaked as it began to turn.

'We're ever so high, aren't we, Trevor, you and me? Do you think we're the tallest people in Fernsford? Just look down and see how high we are. Look down, Trevor.'

'Come down, Sarah. I can't wait all night. Otherwise I'll have to throw you down.'

'I'm all right, Trevor. I love it up here. It's fresh and clean.'

The tower shuddered under the impact of a strong gust and the jib screamed as it revolved.

'Feel that wind, Trevor. Look down. See what's happening below? Eventually, someone will see us. In the dawn, they'll see us. You'd better make your move, Trevor. What are you waiting for? Are you scared? Do you feel dizzy? Do you feel you're going to fall? Are your hands shaking? Look down and see how high we are.'

I heard him shift on the ladder, felt the vibration through the soles of my feet. I was ready for him.

He sprang up into the gap at the top of the ladder. I saw his face white in the moonlight. He had one foot on the platform and was hauling himself upright.

Gripping the railings on either side, I revolved my body back, then swung both feet forward with all my weight behind them. I connected with his legs, knocking them from under him. He fell heavily face down on to the deck. His hands scrabbled at the metal plates, but found no grip. His heavy body slipped with gathering speed over the edge of the platform. With a terrible scream which cut through the sighing of the wind, he disappeared into the void.

I crouched on the edge of the platform, peering into the darkness below.

Some residual instinct of self-preservation had caused him in his hurtling descent to grab a handhold on one of the corner struts of the tower about ten feet down. He clung there, one arm flung up, the great fist clenched bone-white. The other arm hung useless, broken in the fall.

His face twisted with agony. 'Help me! Help me!'

I climbed down the ladder until I was parallel with him. The moonlight gleamed on the crust of dark blood which surmounted his skull like a tonsure.

The wind was even stronger. It tore at my clothes and roared in my ears. Above us, the jib swung wildly, the cables squeaking a protest as it rotated so far that the illuminated sign no longer shed its light upon us. The tower, massive though it was, seemed to flex under my fingers.

'Help me!' He was screaming, like a child, the power of the adult dissolved in elemental fear.

'Why the fuck should I?'

'I don't want to die.'

'Promise me something and I'll help you.'

'Anything, I'll do anything.'

'Promise me, whatever happens to you, you won't use what you've got on Paul and Venetia.'

'Why do you want that? He was the one who –'

'Do you promise?'

'Yes. Yes. Now, for God's sake help me.'

The hand which grasped the steel strut was covered in blood. The sharp metal had sliced into his palm. His left foot was jammed into the angle of one of the braces triangulating the box of girders. His right leg was curled up, with a precarious kneehold at the side of the tower.

The vertigo which he had desperately tried to master in his pursuit of me had overwhelmed him. His body was rigid in its desperate intent to hang on.

I yelled in his ear, above the noise of the gale. 'Straighten your right leg. Bring it down a foot or so. You'll connect with a strut.'

'I can't move.' I saw the glint of tears in his eyes. 'I can't move. I'm going to fall again.'

'You'll have to fucking well stay here, then. Do it! Move your leg down! Now!'

He remained frozen.

I moved down a rung, swung my legs sideways on to a strut and, letting go of one hand for a brief but terrifying moment, reached out and grabbed Chewton's rigid leg and forced it down to the foothold. Then I scrambled back to the ladder.

'Now swing your left leg across to the ladder!'

He stared down, his eyes wild with terror. 'No!'

'Come on, Trevor, you can do it. Just do a sort of shuffle. A couple of feet, that's all.'

'I won't fall? Please don't let me fall. Promise you won't.'

'Cross my heart.'

Sobbing, he moved his leg stiffly as if it were no longer part of him.

I gently took hold of the shiny black heel and lodged it on to the rung in front of me.

After that he loosened up. He slid the other foot across so that eventually, with my help, and screaming in agony, he could hook the upper part of his broken left arm over one of the rungs, giving him sufficient confidence at last to move his rigidly clamped right hand along the strut to the ladder.

We both hung there, exhausted after these manoeuvres had been completed. It was only when I roused us to make the final, painful descent together that I heard over the drowning clamour of the wind, the distant familiar hee-haw of police sirens.

From my eyrie I saw figures running through the compound to throw open the tall gates, and then the sirens were deafening, and pouring through the gap were dozens of revolving blue lights.

Summoned by some means of which I had no knowledge, a little after the nick of time, the cavalry had arrived.

# XXIX

I found out later that it was Harriet's earring, would you believe, which brought in the police.

When they went round to her flat to interview her, a sharp-eyed WPC noticed that one was missing, and recalled that a similar piece of extravagance had been found near poor Colin's body. Harriet was given the third degree at the station and eventually confessed all.

The coppers at Bow Street were puzzling over the situation, and being besieged by calls from everyone whom Harriet knew in the media, when the smackhead I'd coshed with the frying pan woke up in the Middlesex, started screaming for a fix, and coughed his whole life story in order to get one.

By Sunday evening, things really started jumping. They raided the FernWest and Chamberlayne's offices, and the houses of the principal players. It was after they burst into the Woodlands and found Margaret trussed up in a cupboard that they finally moved in force on Friars Haven, just in time to help me get a very shaky Trevor Chewton down the last few rungs of the tallest tower crane in Western Europe and release Appleby and Lambert from captivity.

I was in hospital for a couple of days, then they allowed me to go home. Caroline stayed to look after me.

There was a letter waiting for me on the mat. Delivered by hand, and dated a few days previously. It had, I thought, a Welsh lilt about it. Penny, bless her.

Dear Sarah,
   We don't know where you are or what is going on — no one tells us anything here and we wouldn't credit it if they did — but what we wanted you to know is that we don't believe ONE WORD about what's been said about you in the media. If you're a thief, the Pope is a Protestant.
   We'll stand up in Court to say it too.
   We hope we'll see you again very soon.

   It was signed by everyone in the firm except the partners. It made me cry more than anything that had happened to me my whole time in Fernsford.

Scrawled at the bottom in his awful handwriting was a message from Mark: *You're a bitch but I miss you.*

It was only when I'd more or less recovered from my injuries that I realized the implications of what I'd learned from Rose Albright and Trevor

Chewton. You've probably worked it out already. I had been right all the time, though wrong about the details.

Thomas Denton, Caroline's father, was indeed the son of Arabella Kemble and Edward Chamberlayne. Arabella took refuge in her brother-in-law's house when her baby was due. She was attended by old Ralph's personal physician and crony, Dr Albright. It was a difficult labour and birth. While Arabella was unconscious, Ralph Chamberlayne took the baby away. He told her it had been stillborn. He made Albright sign the necessary certificate for the registrar. Meanwhile he persuaded his mistress and housekeeper, Edna Denton, to take the child and register it as her own.

Ralph persuaded Arabella to hush up the whole business, to forget it had ever happened.

It's hard to believe that a man could be so diabolically, callously cruel. And all because of the money. Edward and Ralph's father was still alive. If Ralph Chamberlayne's brother Edward had died without issue, then all the Chamberlayne fortune would eventually go to Ralph's side. If Edward had had a child, he would have got his father's share. *Per stirpes*, as lawyers say.

When Trevor Chewton blackmailed Ralph Chamberlayne, Ralph was terrified about what else would come out if his affairs were exposed to public scrutiny. He was only too glad to give Chewton what he wanted. He probably thought he was a chip off the old block.

Caroline is now established with title to Vale View, as well as to half the remaining Chamberlayne estate. She's using the money to restore and develop Vale View as a centre for young artists and craftspeople and it has been the most enormous success. Her own work has changed too. It's less tormented, and more sensuous. She says that art has become so brain-oriented. She wants to put the body back in there. I wonder where she got that idea from.

Harriet adores having her own current affairs programme, as you'd imagine. *Viewpoint* has started winning awards. She still has the flat in Dartmouth Park. We sit in her lovely garden sometimes, and talk and talk. For all her success, she's lonely still and casts wistful eyes in my direction. I'm glad, though, that we can be friends.

I never saw my father after he pulled me out of Friars Haven. A month or so back, I read a small paragraph in the *Guardian* that the body of a man had been found on a railway track near Lime Street station in Liverpool. He had been hit by a train. He had been sleeping rough and had almost certainly been drunk. The only identification on the body was a colour snapshot of a red-haired schoolgirl.

There'll probably be books about the trial of what inevitably became known as the Fernsford Three, but I shan't be writing one. I'd uncovered only a fraction of what was going on. It'll take years to sort out. That's the kind of problem lawyers like.

Writing this was hard enough. It was Mark's idea, not mine. Yes, Mark is around. Quite a bit, actually. After all, we don't work in the same office any more. When Chamberlayne's collapsed under the weight of litigation against it, he went back to the City – to his old firm Dansom and Randall Bond. Dense and Round the Bend as they're known in the trade.

He's changed. Or maybe I can see more clearly what he always was. A decent, unpretentious man, who for some reason persists in thinking that I'm the one for him. Perhaps I am. Perhaps I will be. But not yet.

I went back to London too. I refused Giles Matravers's offer of a job and the prospect of a partnership. I couldn't stay in Fernsford. Tim Pogson welcomed me back with open arms. I can't quite believe it, but I've recently been put in charge of Vardy, Leadbetter's first branch office.

I'm doing all the things I set out to get away from: crime, domestic violence, divorce and child custody. I've also added immigration appeals and personal injury litigation. All of it keeps me busy. I shan't get rich, but I've seen enough to cure me of any longing for wealth.

We've got a titchy office in Doughty Street. I was really tickled to discover it's just near where Charles Dickens used to live. Good old Charles. I'm not reading him at the moment. I've discovered George Eliot, who, I was really pleased to find out, was a woman, though why she didn't use her own given name I've no idea. Anyway, she's brilliant. I'm halfway through *Middlemarch*. That book is so modern in many ways – certainly it is if you've spent time in Fernsford.

Am I content? I suppose I am, as much as anyone can be. As much as I deserve to be. As much as a red-haired cockney-Irish scrubber with no education ever dreamed of being.

From my flat near South End Green, I can walk to the top of Parliament

Hill. There, on a clear Sunday afternoon, I often look out over the whole of London. I know now that this is where I belong.

I walk past men playing with their kites, watched by their small sons and daughters. It makes me think of Paul and that other afternoon centuries ago when I blundered into his life. I never saw either of them again after that morning in the Coffee House. He and Venetia sold up and moved away. I don't know where.

The Friars Haven scheme he worked so hard for was never built. The Chewton group went bust and the bankers pulled out. Most of it is still a wasteland, apart from the marina and the converted warehouses, which are apparently a big success. The latest scheme is for a retail park – huge sheds in red corrugated metal. Not Paul's thing at all.

I don't hate Paul for his betrayal. I don't think he realized what Chewton was capable of.

Sometimes, I sit in my bay window in the evening and watch the setting sun. I might put on my tape of the incomparable Felicity Lott singing like a wounded angel the old English folk song *O Waly, Waly*.

> O love is handsome and love is fine,
> And love's a jewel while it is new.
> But when it is old, it groweth cold,
> And fades away like morning dew.

But the tears don't last for long.